I, MATILDA

My Life with William the Conqueror

Jane Cox

ISBN: 978-1-5272-9964-1

Edited by Anna Connolly

Cover photo: Shutterstock/Guryanov Andrey

Designed, printed and bound by Witley Press Ltd
www.witleypress.co.uk

Royalties will go to Dorothy House Hospice who looked after Jane's late husband Tom for four years.

Previous publications

The Norman Conquest of Box, Wiltshire (2016)

ACKNOWLEDGEMENTS

To Anna Connolly, for her highly professional editing and advice and the support of my family and friends to finish this book.

CONTENTS

Dukes of Normandy, Kings of France, Kings of England, 9th-12th C

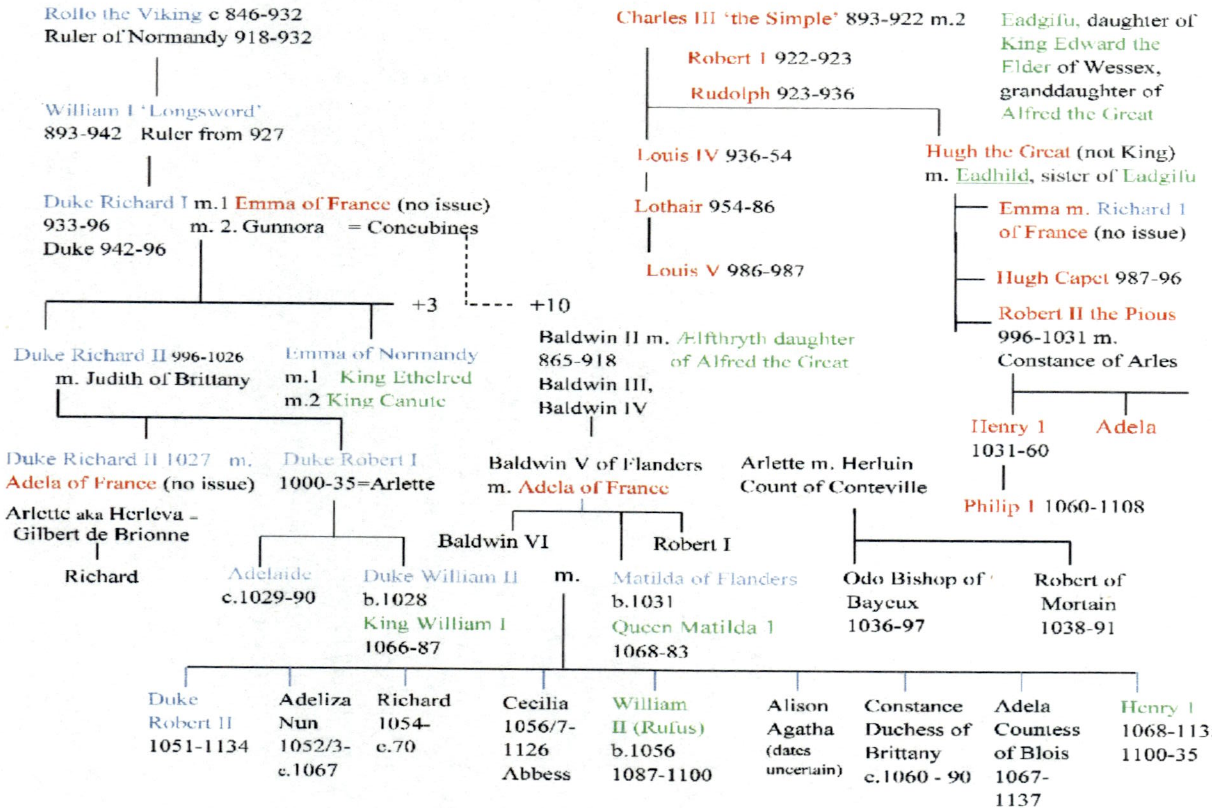

CHAPTER 1

THE DISGRACE

Lille Palace, Flanders, February 1049

I am in disgrace. After what happened yesterday, I am completely confused about everything in my life. I am trying to understand it all, but first I must explain some things. I am Matilda, seventeen-year-old daughter of Count Baldwin V, Ruler of Flanders, and Countess Adela of the Frankish Royal Family. We are presently at Lille to celebrate the Feast Day of Saint Amandus as we do every year at this time. The actual Feast Day was last week when we made the eight-mile pilgrimage from Lille Castle to pray around his tomb at the Monastery he founded at Elnone.

You could say that yesterday's shocking incident explains why I became disgraced. When you read what happened, you may or may not agree with me. So, this is it.

After Mass I was walking along the old stone-flagged path from our chapel to the castle. The sky was overcast and it had been raining which is typical for February. I was with my parents although 'with' is not exactly true because they were walking some distance ahead of me, their backs stiff with disapproval. As I said, I was in disgrace. My ladies were following further behind, reluctant to approach me in my ill-tempered mood. I had thought it would be a relief to get out from the castle and see people apart from my family. I wore my blue dress to Mass; the colour I believe was the clothing of Mother Mary as I especially wanted to pray to her in her sacred house. My cream light wool cloak would protect me from gentle wind or rain and my laced-up hide boots would keep my feet dry.

Yet, going to Mass turned out to be a disastrous idea. We were plodding along the moss-covered stones when a pounding noise ahead signalled a horseman approaching at speed. Everyone stopped to watch, uncertain of his path. I saw him pass my parents rather too close and without acknowledgment of their presence. He slowed up and made straight for me. Dismounting, he slung the reins of his horse round a tree branch in one unfettered action. I could see my parents peering back to see what was going on. Behind them, in the distance, our castle servants were running after him, no doubt fearful of my father's wrath having failed to intercept this intruder to our domain.

The rider stood towering above me, his face somehow familiar. I stood my ground and stared up at him. He leant down to look at me closely, then reared up to his full height and shook his head like a horse tossing its mane. The next thing I knew was a sharp pain in my head for he had seized my braided hair and was now dragging me along the path to where my parents stood like statues, their faces frozen with disbelief. I had to run beside him to lessen the pain in my head, my feet skittering along the stones.

'So, I'm not good enough for you? We'll see about that.' He pushed me face down on the rough ground beside the path, sour mud smearing my nose and lips and dead grass stalks prickling my face. I heard him lift his crop with a swish of air and then I felt it whip my buttocks so it stung, although lightly.

'And that's for the insult.' Flick. 'And that's for your foolishness with that milksop English Lord Brihtric.' Flick. 'He was never the man for you.' Flick. 'Unlike me.' Flick. I could not cry out for I was absorbed by a sensation in the core of my body which travelled up my back, into my neck and chest and then all through me like nothing I had ever felt before.

'Leave her alone you brute,' shouted my brother Baldwin trying to push him away, but he was brushed aside like an annoying insect. *His* voice was just above me, deep and rasping, 'Arrogant and obstinate, Lady Matilda, just like me. We suit each other well and when we marry we will become the most powerful couple in history. When we triumph, we will praise God together and when we sin, we will do penance together seeking absolution from Mother Mary. You'll see.' I felt him leave me, heard him mount his horse, felt the earth beneath me shudder from his horse's hooves and I hear him shout, 'I'll be back.'

I heard him gallop away. Of course, it's Prince William of Normandy. Who else? I lifted my head to spit out grass and mud, my tongue a gritty intrusion in my mouth. I half-turned over and tried to prop myself up on my elbow, but fell back, unable to move my jelly-like legs. I managed to roll onto my back and saw against the sky a gallery of faces, the horrified expressions of my parents and other onlookers, gasping with outrage and concern. They were twittering like birds. I stared at their opening and shutting mouths and burst out laughing which made them gasp even more.

'She's lost her mind!'

'Get help, get a physician!'

'Get a cover to keep her warm.'

'Typical Viking behaviour!'

'That Prince William ought to know better.' My ladies helped me get up, slowly.

I brushed myself down a bit and while struggling to regain my dignity and composure, remarked, 'We shall not be late for Dinner.'

Hearing the commotion, the priest came out and after a quick word to my father, drew me aside.

'Are you all right?'

'I am.'

'I think it is what you needed. Bless you my child.' *Needed?* What *is* he talking about? My parents stood by helplessly leaving my ladies to assist me into the castle. I was put to bed and the physician came and decided my pride might be hurt, but I was all right and I should have rest, quiet and light food.

I cannot take it in. I keep going over and over it, reliving every part. It is life-changing and I need to think carefully. How am I going to handle it? What will become of me? Is this *really* me, Matilda, that confident golden girl? Well, maybe I was in the past, but certainly not any more. Now is the start of another life. In my old life nothing on earth would have persuaded me to contemplate marriage with Prince William of Normandy who I considered to be a big rough sort of a man typical of his uncouth Viking ancestors. I still think this if I'm honest, especially now, yet something has changed because his explosive language, even when flicking me with his whip, was compelling and well expressed. Yet, I never had respect for his position as Duke-in-waiting and certainly no respect for the Dukedom of Normandy, a wild God-forsaken place intent on continued anarchic existence outside the rest of the Frankish Kingdom. And he is a bastard, no other word for it, born to Arlette, low-born concubine of Duke Robert of Normandy. I know that's no fault of Prince William's and he must suffer for it, but the fact remains; his birth makes him an unsuitable husband for me.

I am of royal blood, granddaughter of Robert the Pious, King of the Franks and descended from the Kings of England. The present King of the Franks is my Uncle Henry who did once mention Prince William as a possible suitor for me. I was shocked at the time for how could he even consider such a union knowing that my birth and background place me at a far superior level to that of Prince William? What possessed him to allow any thought to our marriage? Thinking this over I did wonder if the subject had come up when he was with Prince William two years ago in the Battle of Val-ès-Dunes. Off the battle field, they could have discussed Prince William's need of a wife and heir and maybe my name came up. Of course, marrying me would also forge a valuable alliance with Flanders. Prince William and King Henry famously won this battle against the much bigger army of rebel barons desperate to seize the Princedom of Normandy from the one they still call 'Guillaume le bâtard'.

While I continued to protest I would never marry Prince William, I conveniently ignored the fact that when the leader of a country, like King Henry or my father Count Baldwin, decrees a marriage it is immediately a Betrothal, a legal contract. No-one can gainsay it including the couple named. Surely my Uncle who has always had a soft spot for me would never force me to marry against my will. Nor did I think my father would consider Prince William as a suitor because of his own past history with his father, Duke Robert of Normandy. After he married my mother, my father sought to be Count of Flanders himself and drove out his ageing father to exile in Normandy. There the old Count was supported by Duke Robert who presumably did not think much of Father's failure to honour his own father, thus breaking one of the Ten Commandments. He brought forces against Father who had to submit although Grandfather generously allowed him to reign jointly. I think they were alike in character, easily persuaded into action and when faced with opposition, ready to concede. Surprisingly, I learnt it was Mother who persuaded Father to insist on becoming a count before his due time which shows she was not always as virtuous as she appears now. My father and grandfather became reconciled, but Duke Robert and his men would remember the Battle. Men always remember every detail of every battle which they relate over and over again and with increasing embellishment as they consume more ale.

My father certainly knows Prince William because last year he was with him witnessing a Charter at my Uncle's court at Senlis. After this meeting, Father may now favour Prince William's suit and insist on our betrothal, leaving me little chance to oppose his wishes, but after witnessing what happened right in front of him this morning, how could he favour this man who beat, muddied and humiliated his daughter in public? Earlier this year a Norman envoy arrived at our palace at Bruges with a marriage offer from Prince William who said he has seen me in the Frankish court and I was the only woman he would consider. My father was pleased with his offer, but I was neither flattered nor impressed. I declined the offer, gracefully of course. And now this man says he loves me and is determined to marry me. I do not know what to think because surely what he did this morning is an extraordinary way to impress the bride of his choice.

I have to say more about myself otherwise none of this can be understood. I was an unusually welcome female baby because my father's heir was already in place, my elder brother Baldwin. As I said before, Father is Count Baldwin V of Flanders and Mother is Adela, born a princess of the Frankish Royal Family. My younger brother Robert is a reserve heir should anything happen to Baldwin, God forbid.

As I grew up, I was constantly told what a gorgeous baby I had been and then such a delightful child with my golden hair and perfect tiny form, explaining my family nick-name of 'Poupette', the little doll. Everyone praised my sweet nature not discerning that under this surface lurked a strong will. I expressed my wishes with such charm that few could resist. I grew up in a warm glow of self-confidence in my protected, privileged world.

I accepted as normal our home and wider domain being a natural refuge for a train of exiles from England and Normandy. As a young child, I remember my parents welcoming Emma who had been Queen of England and who was also Prince William's aunt. Two years later her son Harthacnut arrived, exiled by his older half-brother, the Saxon Harald Harefoot, now crowned King of England. In the same year came Richard and Baldwin, sons of Gilbert de Brionne who was murdered like most of the guardians of the young Prince William. Yes, I do realise Prince William's name crops up repeatedly as I tell my story. Exiles are here at the moment, Swein, the eldest son of Godwin, Earl of Wessex and other Viking enemies of King Edward. Now I am older I privately question my parents' wisdom in taking sides in these foreign political battles. King Edward must surely bear a grudge against Father and may take action against him one day.

When I reached the age of twelve years, I gave no thought to it being the legal age of marriage. Why should I be concerned with suitors continually at my side? People would have observed me as the perfect young noblewoman: beautiful, pious and dutiful, my leisure time taken up with playing musical instruments, embroidery and lively conversation; a desirable bride for any high-ranking nobleman. Few knew that I was also a serious scholar. My passionate interest in religion was shared by my father's half-sister, Judith of Flanders. She is about my age and not just a relation, but also a real friend who enjoys deep discussions. An elderly monk inadvertently furthered my education by coming to teach my brothers the classics, languages and religious studies, but as they were hardly ever present, I was invariably the only pupil. My mother arranged this tutoring for us children because she herself had been similarly educated and saw her duty as ensuring we had the same experience. She and I used to discuss what I had learnt and this was a happy time for us both and I felt close to her. We are alike in both being of small stature, but I am fair-haired and she has brown hair. We also share our strong religious beliefs and interest in artistic and intellectual pursuits. To be truthful, I don't find her a warm person and have to be careful what I say to her. I once told Judith this and was immediately repentant; I was not honouring my mother as I should. Judith asked if I knew that Mother was placed in the Flemish Court as a tiny child and although she would have been well looked after, that is not the same as having the special love of her own mother. Poor Mother, how hard that must have been, although I suppose she knew no different life.

Father is a different character; straightforward and you always know where you are with him. He is popular with everyone because of his friendly manner. His passion is the Chase, but his time is almost wholly taken up with the duties of ruling his beloved Flanders, ever seeking the best for his people. He confides in me about matters of the state so I know what is happening or about to happen. He is always in some conflict, invariably defending his land or claiming more territory. From him I learnt politics, military action and economic matters, a wide range of subjects. My parents advised keeping this learning and knowledge a secret myself because a future suitor of noble class might think studying ill befits a lady. It is true that such a man would most likely be illiterate having spent his youth like my brothers on outdoor pursuits like fighting and hunting rather than indoor study. So in public, I hid this part of myself and engaged in enjoyable light-hearted banter with men, with marriage a vague event of some future date. I never felt any strong desire for a man. Not in that way. Well, sort of I suppose.

And then there was Brihtric. I feel hot waves of shame when I recall my wilful action concerning him. Brihtric, Duke of Gloucester in England, was King Edward's ambassador to Flanders. He was a wealthy man of some standing, although not comparable to my social position. He was tall, fair-haired, well-dressed and considered handsome. I dismissed him as a possible suitor because he was not of high enough status. This was a relief because I didn't find his slight body and limbs appealing in the physical sense; my preference being for more stalwart men like the Englishman who was in our court at the same time. His name was Hereward and I was disappointed to be told that his family was of obscure Danish and Anglo-Saxon descent, thus out of question to be my suitor. I do have to say I still remember the dream I had about him that night.

Returning to Brihtric, he was often at Bruges, paying me the attention I had come to expect from male guests. I liked him from the start because he was not flowery in his speech. Nor did he write me poems and songs and insist on reading or singing them to me. He brushed away small talk by introducing matters of culture: Art, Music and Theatre. I enjoyed these discussions which were a change from the trivial gossip of the royal courts. He was some years older than me and I was impressed by his knowledge and grasp of affairs and the respect he showed me by inviting my opinions. He was the first man I'd met who did not continually mention my beauty and that was refreshing. I'd heard it all before. I was still ignorant in many areas and somehow Brihtric sensed this without asking directly. He brought me beautiful books with illuminated scripts. We would discuss the words and ideas and whatever I said, he praised me. We had small competitions to see who could best copy the scripts which I usually won. When he left Flanders this last spring to return to England, I really missed his companionship.

That accursed saying, 'Absence makes the heart grow fonder', took hold of me as I started to build him into a demigod in my imagination. I was convinced that I had fallen in love with him and he was constantly in my thoughts as I tried to block my ears to the clamour of discussion between my parents and their advisors about who I was to marry. This went on continuously while I, sitting nearby in earshot, was ignored. I was desperate to escape my parents and the restrictive nature of my life and for the first time began to realise that marriage was the obvious answer. Prince William of Normandy's name came up from time to time which caused them to lower their voices knowing my extreme opposition to his suit. Brihtric's name never came up, at least not in my hearing, because my parents could not have known of our special relationship and probably just viewed him as a minor English nobleman with little to offer to Flanders or to me.

One day, fed up with them all, I stormed up to my boudoir and sat at my writing desk, quill poised. How dare they talk about my marriage and not consult me! It was my business and I made plans to send a messenger to England with a note asking Brihtric to consider making me a marriage offer. It was meant to be a light-hearted suggestion rather than a deeply serious matter. He would be flattered and of course, he would jump at this chance. I knew he loved me and I would escape to England. At least that's what I told myself as I waited anxiously for what seemed like an eternity for his response. I told no-one because I knew how people would react, especially my parents, but to think I could keep such a thing secret was fanciful. I was the confident girl who could do what she liked with no rebuke and nasty consequence. How wrong I was! The messenger returned eventually with a short note, 'The Lord Brihtric is honoured to receive an offer of marriage from the Lady Mathilda, but regretfully, he must decline.' I could not believe it at first and then was mortified and only too soon the word got round.

My parents said at least my chastity was not compromised and our story must be that what I'd meant as a jest in girlish foolishness had been misunderstood. Yet, I knew what I had done and immediately, in self-pitying delusion, told myself Brihtric really loved me and no doubt was pressured by people in high places to refuse me. Of course, I didn't believe this deep down and soon a heavy resentment started to grow in me. He had gone out of his way to make me feel special so how dare he reject me?

'Or *was* your chastity compromised?' persisted my mother in the sort of rage I had never encountered in her before. When we next go to the Monastery of Elnone she would see me swear before the bones of Saint Amandus that I was still a maiden, threatening to get some sort of proof if I was reluctant to be honest with her. That's what I had to do last week. I could feel her stare at my body as I made my oath as if she could get a glimpse of my sullied maidenhood.

'I will certainly have a physician test me if you wish it, Mother.' I knew she would not carry this through as news of any test would never remain a secret and would prolong the gossip. She took another tack. 'You have disgraced our family name for ever. Do you not know that my family is Frankish and English Royalty and your father's ancestor was Baldwin, the first Count of Flanders, Peer of the Holy Roman Empire? You are the first and only person in either family to behave so rashly.'

Defensive now under attack, I retaliated, 'Oh yes, wasn't that the Count Baldwin who eloped with Princess Judith, without the permission of her father King Charles the Bald?'

'Trust you to bring that up. Ungrateful girl!' She stormed off at this point leaving me alone. I asked our priest Father Paulus to come round and hear my confession. He was surprisingly kind and understanding and blessed me telling me that Mary Magdalene was forgiven by Jesus Christ and to say my prayers and ask Mother Mary to guide me.

After this, life was quiet and more boring than ever, the silence of disapproval from my parents stifling every part of me. All I did was go to Mass every day and then to my boudoir where I ate alone, said my prayers and read my books, but after what happened on the way back from Mass yesterday, everything has changed and nothing will be the same again.

We got home to Lille two days ago after a silent journey from Elnone, every tedious wheel turn of the carriage shaking my startled body. Since our return, I've stayed in my boudoir seeing only my maid Megina who wants me to eat and to wash, but I have not the strength to do either and just take sips of weak ale. Now my parents wish to speak to me. A servant brings this message. I am still in bed, tired and in some discomfort and realise I definitely need Megina's attention before I do anything. The rank smell of my unwashed body is apparent even to me and I am ashamed. I send a message that I am not well enough to come to see them yet.

There's a knock on the door and Mother comes in. 'I know you are still not recovered, but it's time for you to come and speak to your father. Here is a shawl to put round you and I will help you along.' She gets me out of bed and the effort makes me realise it is not just my physical strength that is lacking. Mother is kind and gentle and so unusually understanding that I gradually begin to relax and we go down to their stateroom where I am directed to the pink velvet chair in front of them like a prisoner in the dock. Father addresses me. 'Please sit, Matilda. You know you have failed to meet the high standards we have always expected of you and have now been through a difficult experience which was caused entirely by your own rash behaviour. Now please understand that we want the best for you. It is clearly time for you to marry a suitable man of our choice. You do not wish to marry Prince William of Normandy and we respect that opinion having just witnessed his true character. We have names of suitors to put to you, albeit very few.' They look at me apprehensively, but they are resolute, their expressions expectant of a strong response.

'With respect, a list of suitors is not needed as there is only one man I wish to marry.' They are alert with anticipation. 'The man I will consent to marry is Prince William of Normandy.' Their faces are pictures of disbelief. Father sits bolt upright. 'I will not allow you to marry that man!' 'What are you thinking of?' Mother gets up and circles about in bewilderment, wringing her hands. 'How can you forgive what he has done to you? How do you know he won't beat you again? That savage Viking!' I put up my hand to stop this barrage.

'I find it as hard as you to understand, but at last here is a man who is not only pious, but also strong like me. Our marriage will be tempestuous at times, but I do not want to be a noble lady having to pretend she is not educated or interested in matters of state. You have seen to it that I have an education and opinions on many matters and for that I am grateful. I have the same strong will as William of Normandy who wants to marry me knowing my faults, and that is what matters to me.' Father looks at me sternly. 'Oh yes, your strong will! It was your strong will that got you into the recent regrettable situations which have caused us much distress. Firstly, your proposal of marriage to Brihtric, Duke of Gloucester, was a headstrong defiance of our religious and familial customs and disrespectful to your mother and me. Duke Brihtric's refusal of your offer has further disgraced our family and will persuade any suitable nobleman that marriage to you is out of the question. Secondly, the retribution taken by Prince William of

Normandy after you refused his offers of marriage was understandable, but carried out in public in such a manner it will be the talk of the royal courts for years. We can be sure the detail will be further exaggerated to further damage your reputation. You will learn from these bitter experiences to temper your will with discretion and think hard before you act. We are proud of your accomplishments and would not want you to have to hide these in any marriage. Are you sure Prince William knows your true character?'

'He does and in detail. I need hide nothing from him.'

My mother moves into the fray. 'What of your disdain for his family and background which does not match our Royal heritage?'

'I have thought about it again and I think I have been mistaken in my views. Mother, I do not want to be disrespectful to you, but you were betrothed to Prince William's Uncle, Prince Richard III of Normandy. If he was considered suitable for you, a Royal Princess, Prince William must be good enough for me. I will be following your example.'

'What of his mother, that low born daughter of a common tanner?' presses Mother.

'Mother, it may have slipped your mind that you and Father approved Arlette, Countess of Conteville as one of my guardians.' Mother shakes her head and mutters something. I have not finished.

'I am sure you will agree with me that the Countess of Conteville is now a noble lady who commands much respect as do members of her family.'

'You are right of course.' What else can she say? After some minutes, Father gives his judgement.

'Before we asked you to come and see us, your mother and I decided that following what happened on Sunday, you are unlikely to have any suitors to offer you marriage. We made a list, but it is not promising. After your words, the position is much clearer. Prince William has offered marriage and you wish to accept. Your reasons for acceptance must be more than you have told us for this whole business is incomprehensible. There is no doubt that Prince William is well-qualified to be your husband and his extraordinary treatment of you was more like that of a wronged husband than suitor. We shall assent to the marriage and ask the same of your Uncle Henry.'

Mother looks at me closely, 'Are you surprised Matilda?'

'I am, but also happy. Thank you and I'm truly sorry about everything.' Father gives me a small kiss on the cheek; Mother is occupied blowing her nose.

'I shall speak to the King and then I will inform Prince William himself.'

A horseman is sent immediately with a message to Uncle Henry and we all go to bed. I lie awake worrying and going over all that has happened. I cry and pray and get hot and uncomfortable and gradually start remembering Prince William himself, his words and his strength and then suddenly his skin, his hair and his thighs. His *thighs*? What *is* the matter with me? I get out of bed again and kneel to pray for guidance. I am calmed and reassured that all will be well. Perhaps Uncle Henry will reply in the morning, but this is only a matter of etiquette because now my father has decreed the marriage, it is settled. I kneel to pray that he will agree.

The next morning Megina brings me a hot drink and food and rubs some potion into my head which is still tingling. My hair is greasy and dirty and there's caked blood in it.

'That's not blood,' she says, 'it's mud!' She promises to bring warmed rain water to clean it when I am ready. Megina says she cannot mend my blue dress and it will have to be rags. My cloak is also ruined and my boots have been sent to the cobbler. She puts out my second-best dress which is of cream woven Flanders wool with lace round the neckline and the new fashion of gathering under the bust. I tell her I should be wearing black and she asks if I am in mourning. Am *I* in mourning? No, certainly not! I am over the Brihtric business, but I shall not forget it. I'm back in my parents' approval so I laugh and tell her I hope to be rejoicing soon. She looks puzzled, but has the sense not to question me further. She knows she will be told soon. I cannot dress yet or even touch my dress for my hands are still grazed and my nails black with dirt. After a while Megina reappears with warm water and she sponges me and combs my hair in the water. She dries me like a child and helps me dress and immediately, I feel better. I am given a cup of hot milk and bread with honey from our bees. It revives me like the Holy food of Mass.

'Your mother wants to see you when you are ready', she tells me. I feel cleansed and strong enough to face Mother who I do love and want to please even if I no longer want to live with her. She is in her Morning Room although it is past mid-day. She beckons me to sit beside her and puts her hand round my shoulders,

'What a time you've had my poor girl, but I think you must be feeling better as you are looking lovely again. We are expecting a messenger this afternoon from my brother Henry who never wastes time in replying.'

'Is Uncle Henry at Rheims?'

'He is, so his horseman should soon be here. Will you join us for Dinner?'

'I've had a hot drink and eaten as Megina has been looking after me. I don't think I can manage Dinner, but I will come and sit with you later this afternoon. Thank you, Mother.' She kisses me and I return to my room to lie down and wake to hear a gentle tap on the door. It's Mother again.

'Well you've had a few hours' sleep which I prayed would happen and we've just had a message delivered from Henry to say he observes the fact you are now formally betrothed to Prince William of Normandy. He adds, "I just hope they are not related!"'

'We are certainly connected, but definitely *not* related! So, Uncle Henry agrees?'

'He does, although we don't need Henry's approval because your father's confirmation is enough, but we thought asking him was a good idea, a matter of courtesy if you like. Don't forget that Prince William was my brother's ward for a few years after his father died. They know each other very well.' I did not know about that; most illuminating. What else is to come? Mother continues, impatient with my reverie.

'Now the Betrothal is established I want to tell you something I've known for some time.' This is interesting as Mother usually says what she thinks immediately, but I must ask her something else first.

'Has Father sent a message to Prince William and do you know where he is at the moment?'

'Yes, a messenger has gone to Eu where Prince William is staying.'

'He's at *Eu?*' I begin, but she cuts me off.

'You will hear from him soon I know, but as I was saying.'

'I'm sorry, Mother, please tell me.'

'Do you remember Queen Emma of England who came to Bruges when you were about six years old?'

'I do, she was kind and spent time playing with me and I know the people of Bruges loved her and still talk about her.'

'All quite true and this is what she said to me when she had been visiting us at the palace. She asked if I minded her being outspoken and I said I would tell her if I wished her to change the subject. She said that she had noticed what an intelligent child you were and how determined, knowing exactly what you wanted and getting it with charming manners. Of course, she said, it helped you being such an attractive little girl. You reminded her of her great-nephew William aged nine years who had the same strong character under a persuasive front. He had a difficult life being born outside wedlock and becoming Prince of Normandy at such a young age. He missed his mother who had remarried and was not at Falaise Castle. Effectively an orphan, he suffered the murder of one guardian after another, especially the bloody murder of his Steward, Osbern de Crépon, who was guarding him by actually sleeping in his bedroom. As a ten-year-old, William witnessed the death of this man who was more than a relation, more than his Steward, the one he looked on as a father.

William would be Prince of Normandy at twenty-one years, a soldier and leader of men and learn to be loyal and considerate to his friends, but would have to be tough and uncompromising with his enemies. This young boy had enemies plotting against him since his birth, especially after his father died, and Queen Emma thought his life would always be in danger from those seeking to seize the Dukedom of Normandy. The other similarity between the two of you was your piety and readiness to do penance for your sins. Queen Emma predicted your marriage all those years ago and now she is proved right.' I am amazed, but pleased to hear this and am about to talk further with Mother, when there is a knock at the door.

The servant announces a visitor.

'William, Prince of Normandy.'

He's here in this room. Prince William. Mother and I stand to receive him. He is so tall. And big! He fills the room with a powerful presence. He places a package on a chair and bows to Mother.

'Countess Adela, it is gracious of you to receive me.' He bows to me.

'Lady Matilda.' Our eyes meet and we stare at each other. It is probably only a few seconds, but it seems like an age. Mesmerising! He's got thick reddish hair. Clean shaven. Such big shoulders! He is huge! Mother watches us carefully and then takes control.

'Since you are now officially Betrothed, it is right that you sit down and talk to each other calmly. Prince William, you will show proper respect to my daughter and Matilda, you will show proper respect to Prince William. I will be in the next room.' She leaves, closing the heavy door. William is down on one knee in front of me, almost face-to-face. His face is eager. 'Lady Matilda, I love you. Will you marry me?'

'I have said I will marry you.'

'I know, but I want to know what you feel. Am I forgiven?'

'You are not!'

'What must I do to earn your forgiveness?'

'I'll have to think about that.' He looks so sad, crestfallen. I can't have that.

'Of course, I want to marry you. Get up and put your arms around me.' He stands and then bends to cradle me in his arms and this exactly what I have been wanting for a long time. He has such wide shoulders and big arms like a bear. He lifts me so we are face-to-face, looks at me with the piercing blue eyes of a Viking and then sits down and puts me gently on his knee. I lay my head on his shoulder and feel our hearts thumping together. I lift my face to feel the skin of his cheek, his light stubble apparent, quite arousing if I'm honest.

'What if Mother comes in?' I am a bit nervous, but he laughs, a sort of male honking sound, deep and joyous. In the depth of my body my passage contracts violently. Oh William! Concentrate Matilda! William looks at me, a half-smile fleeting across his face.

'Your mother will want us to be happy as does my mother. Mother is very cross with me and has told me to treat you gently and behave properly and not let her down again.'

'Your mother said that? When was that?'

'After I left you on the ground on Sunday I rode straight back to Eu, galloping as hard as Rollo, that's my horse, could take and she was there waiting for me.'

'Your mother was at Eu Castle? I thought she lived at Conteville.'

'She does live at Conteville, but when she heard what happened at Lille, she went straight to Eu to await my return. She's staying with her younger sister, my Aunt Beatrice, married to my cousin, Count Robert of Eu. And no, Mother's not at Eu Castle because it has been commandeered by Robert's younger brother William Busac who refuses to move. He may be my cousin, but he's someone I need to sort out because he's a troublemaker and no friend of mine. I intend to get him out of the castle and give Robert and Beatrice their rightful ownership. As it is, I stayed with them on my way to Lille, a perfect stop on the journey from Rouen. Oh, I should tell you that Rouen is where I work, but my home is Fécamp Palace, on the coast of the Narrow Sea. Robert and Beatrice have always supported me unlike other members of the Eu family who are not to be trusted. Anyway, back to your question. When Mother heard what I did to you at Lille, she was furious and despite her failing health set off immediately for Eu. It was not pleasant being told off like a naughty little boy, but I deserved it.'

'Did she give you any advice?'

'She asked me what I thought I should do next, and I said I must replace your garments which had been spoilt. She said no, first I must beg your forgiveness. I told her of course I would, that goes without saying. She then returned to the subject of your garments because she loves to discuss such matters. I'm sure you know she was a seamstress in her youth.' He puts me off his knee on to the seat and gets up.

'This is for you.' He picks up the package from the chair and gives it me.

'Please open it. I'll help you if you like.' Of course, he must open it because men always want to open packages with some knife or other they invariably have on their person. I pull the wrapping paper apart and oh my! It is the most exquisite blue fine lawn dress embroidered with tiny cornflowers, the fashion now. Quite perfect! He looks at my face to see my reaction and begins to smile.

'I think you like it?' Oh, I like it all right, in fact I love it and I give him a hug which lasts longer than it should I suppose, but why not as he is my Betrothed.

'It is beautiful! Thank you so much and please tell your mother I am delighted with it. How did she know my size and what I like?'

'Mother knows everything about ladies' clothes and always manages to get exactly what she wants. I think she said your dress came from Paris, but how she organised that so quickly I really don't know. You'll have to ask her when you see her. There are some more things for you, but they are taking a bit longer to organise. Matilda, I need to talk to you about my mother.'

'Of course, the Countess of Conteville.'

'Do you look down on her?'

'I admit I did once through ignorance, but what I know now is that she is a

much-respected and loved noble lady.'

'She is indeed, but I should tell you some of her story because if I do not, then others will be seeking to do so. Do you remember Richard, son of Gilbert of Brionne, who came to seek refuge with your family in Bruges?'

'I do. He came with his brother Baldwin, the same name as my father.'

'He's my brother.'

'Your *brother*?'

'Yes, Mother's eldest son, born out of wedlock when she was about fifteen years old. It was hard for her at the time because her beauty attracted the attention of many noble lords and she found it difficult to resist their advances. Mother had no-one to give her proper advice and like any young girl, flattered by the attention she got, was seduced by

Gilbert de Brionne. My grandmother Doda died after giving birth to her. My grandfather Fulbert was on his own struggling to keep his tannery going and at the same time take care of his children, my Uncle Walter and Mother. Of course, he later became a successful local business man, but at this time he knows he did not fulfil his duties to his daughter as he should. However, Mother told me that her father did make sure that Gilbert de Brionne gave her financial support, but it was clear he would never marry her. The money did make Mother more independent, but she chose to continue her work at the laundry and people still talk about her beauty and grace.

Mother had many suitors and when she realised that the young man who kept watching her was Duke Robert himself, she decided to approach him. My parents were the same age and very much attracted to each other. The fact she had a child was no obstacle to Duke Robert's wooing. Mother realised her fortunes would change completely if she was with Duke Robert, but she insisted that she must become the First Lady of Normandy and not just his concubine. He agreed and she entered Falaise Castle in fine style on a white horse. I know my parents loved each other, but their relationship was ever tainted by the undeniable fact that her humble birth ruled out their marriage. I have been told, unkindly you might say, that Father planned to marry Mother to one of his counts and find himself a lady of noble birth. Father chose one of his oldest friends, Herluin, Count of Conteville, for Mother, but before he could marry anyone, let alone a lady of high-class, he died returning from a Pilgrimage to Jerusalem. None of these plans happened except Mother's marriage to Count Herluin. Of course, if Father had married and a legitimate heir was born, he would now be Prince of Normandy, not I.

After Father's death, Mother moved into Conteville Castle with her new husband and took my sister Adelaide with her. I was left in Falaise Castle at the age of seven years in the care of guardians. And I'm sure you know what happened to them. Nearly all murdered. I still have nightmares about Osbern's death in my chamber, blood everywhere. It was a terrible thing for a child to see. I loved Osbern who was our cousin and our Steward. His son Gilbert de Brionne, who fathered my brother

Richard and was now my tutor, was also murdered in the forest. The one guardian who survived and saved my life more than once was my Uncle Walter, Mother's elder brother. In those years, he and my grandfather Fulbert held positions in my household. In fact, Mother's relations have always been more loyal to me than Father's family, probably because they have no plans to get rid of me, my safety being in their best interests. Anyway, I like them a lot more which is also important. Sadly Uncle Walter died when I was ten years old but I still had my guardians. By 1040, my enemies had killed all my guardians. I was on my own, but I did have a companion, my oldest friend, William FitzOsbern. At twelve years-old, I was very strong for my age so I decided to fend for myself and was soon riding to battle accompanied by Fitzo. I've still got the same enemies, but I won't let them get me, I can assure you.

I did miss Mother and my sister Adelaide when I was growing up but now, I am very glad that Mother and my step-father Count Herluin have a good marriage with two sons and some little girls, who are more of my brothers and sisters.'

Before I can comment on this intriguing family history there is a perfunctory tap on the door. It's Mother who exclaims with delight when she sees my new dress.

'That's a fine dress Prince William! I believe your mother had something to do with it. Time for Supper, you two,' she says crisply and sweeps out. How did she know about his mother having anything to do with my dress?

'Are you staying tonight?' I ask him.

'I am and after Supper your father and I are to have a talk about the future.' He pulls me to him and we kiss on the lips gently and chastely. I know everything will be all right. We have so much to talk about and so much to look forward to. All the time I am with him there is an underlying atmosphere of suppressed passion between us which thrills me. I know he feels it too. I cannot remember being so happy.

After Supper, I sit with Mother and do my embroidery, but it is hard to concentrate as my thoughts are whirling round in my head. After an hour or so, Father and William come in and Father invites him to sit, while he himself remains standing.

'Prince William has something important to say.' He sits while William gets up to speak.

'I have sought Count Baldwin's agreement that Lady Matilda comes to live with me in Normandy because we are betrothed and will formally marry as soon as possible. I do not want to live without Lady Matilda at my side. I need her support with all I have to do, especially with planning the official ceremony of becoming Duke of Normandy later this year. I have not yet spoken to Lady Matilda about this.'

'This is all rather sudden. What do you say, Baldwin?' asks Mother.

'Matilda needs a change of scene after her recent troubles and her place is indeed with Prince William. Is this what you want too Matilda?'

'Yes, it is what I want.'

Mother looks at me anxiously, 'What happens if you have a child?'

I prepare to speak, but William answers for me, 'Betrothal is official like Marriage and the baby would be legitimised as soon as we marry.' I see Father is about to speak. 'That does happen quite often and I don't see it as a problem myself.' Did Father really say that? I cannot believe how well things are going. William smiles.

'I will look after her you know. What I did at Lille is unforgivable, but I felt such passion and yes, I plead guilty to the Crime of Passion. I think Lady Matilda has nearly forgiven me, but I will have to keep making it up to her for a long time I'm sure.' He looks at me with a particular expression with lifted eyebrows. Does he really mean *that*? He obviously does and we both try not to laugh. This has escaped Mother, who is fidgeting, obviously with something on her mind.

'We should discuss something my brother Henry mentioned about you possibly being related. Like all noble families, both of our families have complicated interwoven connections and anyone against your union may well be examining this fact.'

William looks serious. 'I have many enemies who know that I am an ambitious man and in forming this connection with Flanders with you Count Baldwin, we can expect opposition even from King Henry himself. I am sorry to have to say this, especially after he came to my aid in the Battle of Val-ès-Dunes, but this Betrothal is a threat to his position because he would like both Normandy and Flanders within his

Frankish Kingdom, not making an alliance on his border.' Father looks anxious.

'You think King Henry will look for reasons to oppose the Betrothal?'

'I hope not, but we need to be vigilant.'

Father nods in agreement, 'We do and I have enemies myself, particularly Henry, King of Germany and Holy Roman Emperor, who may also see our alliance as a threat and oppose the marriage.' Emperor Henry has good reason to see Father as his enemy. Father and Count Godefrio of Upper Lorraine burnt down the German Royal Palace three years ago and then attacked the town of Verdun. And that's not all, for Father also joined a rebellion against him as soon as he became Holy Roman Emperor. If there is anyone who will make trouble for us, it will be him.

'And there's the Church, our new Pope Leo and his counsellors have started to impose stricter rules for the clergy and are encouraging marriage for nobility…' Father breaks off and looks at me, 'Matilda, here we are talking about problems which may be non-existent and this should be such a happy time for you. Do you want to say something?'

'Yes, I do. Prince William, I know that if I come with you now as your Betrothed, we may be blessed with a child who will soon be legitimised by our marriage, but what happens if you were killed in battle before our marriage takes place?'

'I have thought about this and have a suggestion. You know that the circumstances of my own birth are a continuing sorrow to my mother and to me. Although you will never be in the same position as my mother who had no prospect of either betrothal or marriage to my father, I will not allow any child of ours to be shamed by his birth. Lady Matilda, we are already betrothed by your father's decree, but I think we should back it up now by Formal Betrothal carried out by your priest here in Bruges Palace Chapel. I know this is not the same as Marriage, although some declare it is, but it will give our Betrothal a secure and sacred foundation. Traditionally, marriage follows in forty days and I suggest we arrange a State Marriage later this year.'

Well, this is a surprise and my parents look at each other, trying to gauge each other's response. They have some sort of coded communication between them and Father responds, 'We'll ask Father Henryk to call tomorrow and arrange the Formal Betrothal in our chapel and now we should have a drink to celebrate.' So, that's that. Father bangs the gong and the manservant is tasked to bring wine, which is kept in the castle and brought into Bruges on our tidal inlet. Sadly, this may not continue as the inlet is becoming silted up. We have a small glass each and I see William does not quaff it down like most men and I wonder if he's hiding a liking for alcohol from my parents. He proposes a toast.

'Let us ask God's blessing on our Betrothal and give thanks for his loving care of us all. Gezonheid!' William lifts our spirits with his Flemish salute and we smile, but we are all tired and after a short time and a brief embrace between us all, we go to our chambers.

Father Henryk attends us after Mass and we are to have a Formal Betrothal tomorrow. That being settled, Father takes William on the Chase, just the two of them with the castle grooms to assist. They will be gone all day which will be just what they need and Mother and I can get on with planning my journey and new life in Normandy. We are to take my carriage and we already have a posse of William's men who will escort us. They always accompany him as he travels and others have been summoned from Rouen and Fécamp to bring another carriage and extra horses. I'm taking my grey mare Galathea and plan to ride some of the way. We are going on Tuesday. So soon! We will travel to our castle at Lille to spend the first night. Megina is coming with us. I am not really nervous about it all because I feel safe with William, but he is such a huge man compared to me. I am quite small and worry just a little that I could be a bit squashed under him, but so far he has been so gentle with me. He has a relaxed face and readily smiles. I know he has a reputation for being hard and brutal, but that's battle and as he's the leader and has so many enemies trying to kill him, he's got to be like that at times.

I am to take clothes, books, musical instruments and all my sewing equipment. From Lille we are to travel to Eu and stay with William's relations, Count Robert and Countess Beatrice of Eu. William's mother, the Countess of Conteville, will also be waiting for us. Of course, she will! William will leave Megina and me with his family for a few days while he goes back to Fécamp to organise smartening up his palace before my arrival. I can imagine its state having been a bachelor pad and sometimes the lodging of soldiers. He will then return to accompany us on the journey to what will be our home.

When will we have our first night together? Tomorrow? If I ask him to come to my chamber he might think I am being unladylike so I should really leave it to him. And would Mother be spying on us? Would Father accept us being together or would this undue haste put me in disgrace again? What will it be like? Will it hurt even if he is gentle? Stop it, Matilda. Get on with laying out your clothes and possessions. Megina has come to help me. I ask her if she minds leaving her family and she says she is pleased to have the opportunity to travel and go to Normandy. She says it's her place with me and it will be reassuring to have her familiar presence in my new life.

The men are back and the message comes that they have had an excellent day's Chase. Megina tells me the servants have filled the water tub nearly to the top so William can wash his whole body. I'm not surprised to hear this as one of the first things I noticed about him was that he has a clean smell which pleases me. I have always been acutely aware of noxious body odours and sometimes it's hard to be in the same room as some people let alone near them.

Father and William killed two hart today and we have venison for Supper with Father's best red wine. Everyone is in good humour except my brothers Baldwin and Robert who were not invited to the Chase. The men describe in great detail how each beast was stalked and then dispatched adding to my brothers' mounting discontent. Given a breathing space, they launch into boasting about their sword skills to the point they are about to attack each other as they cannot agree who is best. William invites them to visit Falaise Castle one day to take part in jousting with his knights. This is a welcome pause in their arguing and a generous offer, but they take little notice and continue to snarl at each other. They ought to know better, especially Baldwin who at eighteen is three years older than Robert. Robert is already taller than Baldwin and still growing which probably explains Baldwin's need to have the competitive edge in all sports. Father has had enough of them and orders them out of the room.

As they open the door to leave, a servant enters to say that the priest is back and he'd like to see us about tomorrow's Mass. I hope nothing's gone wrong and we look expectantly at Father Henryk. His kindly face and understanding of the failings of his flock gives me reassurance that he will look after us.

'Forgive me troubling you at this late hour, but I want to put a plan to you. It is entirely your choice as to whether we go ahead with it. You have asked me to officiate at the Formal Betrothal of Prince William and Lady Matilda. This is an exchange of vows where the man says "I will take you for my wife" and the woman says "I will take you for my husband"'. The only difference in the later Marriage Service is that the word "will" is left out. So the man says "I take you for my wife", and the woman says "I take you for my husband". Having been consulted by Count Baldwin about the particular concerns each of you has expressed in this short period since Betrothal, I suggest tomorrow's service is Marriage.' He pauses while he briefly measures our reactions and then carries on, 'The only witnesses will be the four of you, my cleric and me. Should a child arrive before your State Marriage or if for any reason that marriage is delayed or does not happen, God forbid, I can swear the child was born in wedlock. There is no reason why your marriage vows cannot be repeated at a state occasion at a later date.' I knew Father Henryk was a theological scholar, but had not anticipated such practical and compassionate understanding of the Sacrament of Marriage.

'Sounds like an excellent idea to me,' says Father. I look at William who looks at me, raises his eyebrows and we nod agreement. I suddenly remember that Baldwin and Robert are not in the room, having been sent out after squabbling at the table.

'What about my brothers. Shouldn't they be told?' Father sets his jaw as he always does when making a firm statement, 'No, the fewer who know the better. I shall send them on an errand on horseback first thing and say they are excused Mass for once.'

'They will not be troubled by that,' says Mother exchanging a knowing glance with Father Henryk who continues his efforts to change my brothers' indifference to the Faith, his only success being the retention of their respect. Mother wants more information, 'Father Henryk, do you know of any other noble couples who have chosen marriage over Formal Betrothal?'

'Not personally, but what I do know is that traditionally, a marriage ceremony has been of less importance to dynastic families like yours than the confirmation that children can be conceived. It follows that physical consummation is accepted, even encouraged in betrothed couples, but I agree with Count Baldwin that things are changing under our new Pope. His single-minded elevation of the status of Marriage supports what has been decided, the only risk being that if no child is born, decisions about inheritance are more complicated.'

'Would there be any trouble if anyone found out we'd done this secretly?' I ask.

'Certainly not,' states Father robustly, 'your Betrothal and Marriage are my decision and Marriage tomorrow is the perfect answer. Having said that, we will pledge to keep this to ourselves. Thank you Father. We'll see you tomorrow.'

'My blessing on you all. Good night.' Father Henryk takes his leave.

CHAPTER 2

OUR SECRET MARRIAGE

Lille, March 1049

The Sabbath, our Wedding Day! William and I are actually married. It is a joyous occasion, sanctified by God's blessing, conducted by Father Henryk and his cleric. We take our vows standing outside the open chapel doors, William on the right and I on the left, as is the custom. My parents, who are witnesses as well as the clerics, join us inside for Nuptial Mass. As we go into the chapel, I feel especially close to Mother Mary because this blessed lady is the one I always confide in, comforted and inspired by her eternal forgiveness and understanding. This cannot be expected of an earthly being, and of course, I'm thinking of Mother whose usually cold and distant manner has been a sorrow to me and maybe to her as well. I feel sure this is a sad legacy from her lack of contact with her own mother and close family from early childhood. Now I am about to leave Mother for the first time in my life, my guilty feeling of disloyalty is suddenly overtaken by a realisation that we must have a stronger bond than I thought. Oh, Mother Mary, thank you for so blessing me, an undeserving sinner, with a renewed warm feeling towards Mother and for the union to this man beside me, my husband, Prince William of Normandy.

We never eat before Mass and today, we forgo our usual light refreshments afterwards, for we are to have special dinner at one o'clock. Mother has organised our favourite Flemish dishes of Potjeveleesch terrine, Waterzooi made with local fish and finally,

Rijstpap made of rice-pudding and saffron. My brothers are most enthusiastic about the food and, being kept in the dark about our secret marriage, assume this sumptuous feast is put on in honour of our guest, Prince William of Normandy. I observe my husband has a hearty appetite, exclaiming these delicious dishes are new to him. At the same time, I notice he keeps to ale, avoiding strong drinks. Afterwards we all sit together in the Hall, digesting the food and just chatting about nothing in particular. I discern some tension in the room as though none of us knows what to say or do which ends when William stands up.

'Lady Matilda and I will go for a ride this afternoon. I have ordered the horses to be ready for us.' We all express enthusiasm, but I am careful not to show what I really feel. I know what William is thinking from the way he is looking at me. What a relief to get away on our own! I respond hoping not show too much pleasure, 'I'll get ready and meet you in the yard.' Megina helps me into my riding clothes; stout over hose to prevent chafing, full riding dress, boots and a head cover. She escorts me to the yard to find the grooms have done their job and there is William with his horse Rollo tethered nearby. Galathea whinnies when I greet her and stands still while the groom helps me mount from the block. I always ride astride because I feel more secure, probably because I am small and light. William comes over on Rollo, bends to give me a little pat and then winks at me which makes me smile. I see he has panniers on either side behind his saddle and wonder what he is carrying. We wave good-bye to Megina who appears to be holding hands with a young man, presumably William's groom. I start to ask William, but he has other things on his mind.

'Come on, let's get going.' He leads the way as we trot out of the castle gates and then through the city gates into the countryside towards the forest. We canter along a path which is reasonably clear of growth so it was probably where Father and William came yesterday for the Chase. After what seems like a long way, he slows and turns to wait for me. 'We'll go down here and hitch up the horses.' He leads us down a winding path with the branches of bushes and trees brushing against us. We get to a clearing and hitch the horses to a tree trunk. He takes a roll from one of his panniers.

'Guess what this is!'

'It looks like a sleeping bag.'

'Yes, quite right and my wife and I are going to get into it, but sleep is not my intention.' He smiles reassuringly and puts his arm around me.

'You aren't scared, are you Matilda?'

'No, but you won't squash me will you?

'I'll try not to.' He lays a waterproof mat on the mossy grass and pulls out the bag which seems exceptionally big and puts it on the ground.

'Right, I'm getting in first and I'll hold it open for you. He gets in and lies down on his back and beckons me to lie on top of him. He pulls the back of the bag over my back so we are snug inside. We kiss and I feel him beneath me. His hands move down my back to my legs. He plucks at them.

'What's this you are wearing?'

'Ah, my over hose, stout and functional.'

'So that's what you think of your new husband!'

'Of course.' I can hardly move as I am laughing so much.

'Pull the cover back and I'll try and wriggle out of my hose.' As he helps me to pull off the awkward garment we giggle like children, his honking laugh a joy to hear. At last, it is off and our inexperience makes no difference to our urgent need to couple. I lie on top of him and he is in me. A brief pain registers the end of my maidenhood followed by a surging all-absorbing movement I can't explain. So calm afterwards. I had not expected this. Thank you Holy Mother, for you blessed this wondrous thing we do together. Bless our child who may be planted deep inside me.

We gather ourselves together and ride back companionably, the rhythm of the horses' movement echoing the satisfaction of our day.

'Did you plan this?' I ask.

'If a stout functional husband can also be your lover.'

'No doubt about that. Race you back!'

Back at the castle, things are peaceful as they should be on the Sabbath. We spend the evening discussing our plans, and the best way to keep in touch with my parents when William and I have left. As ever, carrier pigeons are the answer as long as there is some forward planning and a basket of Lille homing-pigeons will come with us on Tuesday. My brothers are unusually subdued, no doubt ashamed of their behaviour of yesterday. I notice they are deferential to William, probably worried he has changed his mind about inviting them to joust with his Norman knights. I think they will miss me as I have often acted as negotiator between them, uniquely aware of the different family traits that make them so competitive. No doubt, Father will be arranging marriage for Baldwin soon. William joins me in my boudoir and it is all good and no, he doesn't squash me.

'Are you sad to be leaving home?' he asks.

'In some ways, yes, but it's also the right time to do this, especially with you.'

'Are you worrying about anything else?'

'Not *worrying* exactly, but I do realise that you have Normandy to command and battles to fight so much of my time will be spent alone. I don't know if I'll have anyone except Megina to talk to. And I like to keep studying and to know what is happening both at home and from now on in Normandy. I don't know anyone in Normandy or who may be there when you are away.'

'Of course, leave it to me.' He sleeps well, but sometimes I am awake with concerns about my new life. Then the warmth of his big body against mine comforts me back to sleep. It will be all right. William has said so. The next morning after waking early and coupling, we lie comfortably together, I ask William about Beatrice being his aunt because I thought his mother only had a brother, his Uncle Walter. He explains that his grandfather Fulbert remarried and Beatrice was born, a generation younger than her step-sister and William's mother, Arlette, Countess of Conteville.

CHAPTER 3

EU, NORMANDY

May 1049

I am still living in Count Robert's household at Eu as the improvements at Fécamp are taking longer than expected. William is able to supervise the work as during Lent, military operations are put on hold. It has been a change for me coming from the luxury of Bruges Palace to this modest home, but it is delightful and I'm happy here since Robert and Beatrice are so kind to me. As I expected, they were both here to greet us as well as William's mother, obviously anxious to make sure I am good enough for her son. She invited me to address her as 'Countess Arlette' and she addressed me as 'Lady Matilda.' This formality is fitting, but so different from my hosts who immediately said to call them 'Robert' and 'Beatrice' and they would call me 'Matilda.'

The Countess is most affable to me and clearly pleased with our Betrothal. She tells me that to see William content is her great joy, but at the same time I sense her watching me for any sign of condescension. Perhaps it's her humble background that has fashioned her particularly formal manner and resulted in a lady who expects due deference. She appears quite frail and looks older than her age of about forty-five, but it's obvious she was a real beauty in her youth. She has a fine bone structure and large expressive eyes. I don't know what ails her and feel it's not my place to ask. I am careful about what I say to her as the aspects of her life that I know about have been challenging to say the least. I think it's unlikely she had much if any education or the chance to study music or art and I do not wish to embarrass her.

Safe subjects for conversation are fabrics and stitch craft about which she has knowledge and expertise. She is naturally pleased that the blue dress she chose for me is such a success. So, we discuss clothes, fashion and furnishings and apart from daily household matters, she gives me some information about her family members and makes many enquiries about my family. She is obviously impressed with our connection to the Frankish and English royal families, this ancestry being her greatest focus. She herself benefits from her son's Betrothal to me.

I don't know how long she plans to stay here. She must surely have plenty of servants at home because the maids here have to help her quite a lot. She also relies on Beatrice who does far more than a younger sister could be expected to do by being her companion and friend. At least Beatrice shares the same background and understands what her sister has been through except that she herself was not in the humiliating position of being considered of too common stock to marry a Duke. Her subsequent marriage to the Count of Conteville should have helped to repair the hurt she suffered. I am puzzled that the Countess chooses to be called 'Arlette' rather than 'Herlève', her birth name, 'Arlette' being derived from the word 'harlot.'

I also wonder why she chooses to be away from her husband and why the subject of her return does not arise. Beatrice tells me she has a tiring time at home with boys of twelve and ten years and three little girls. She certainly deserves a rest and I am pleased to offer her continued hospitality for she must feel the effects of giving birth in her forties to five more children. Perhaps they are all too much for her so that she's in no hurry to return to Conteville.

I am much more relaxed with Beatrice and Robert, who are the same age of twenty-six, six years older than William and nine years older than me. The fact that Beatrice is at least a generation younger than Countess Arlette and in contrast very friendly and informal could well reflect an easier passage through life. There's no sign of a baby on the way though. Perhaps there are difficulties over this.

Considering the subject of family, I realise I've hardly thought about my own family back in Flanders since coming here. I miss discussing national matters with Father although my recent circumstances meant that in my final few weeks at home I was not consulted as I used to be. Perhaps his former trust in me and our intimacy are lost forever. I am relieved to be away from Mother as her disappointment in me could well smoulder as a backdrop to our relationship. I think about my brothers. Baldwin, the elder of the two, is a good-natured young man like Father, but his inheritance of my mother's short stature makes him jealous of Robert, already much taller. I remember their quarrel and bad behaviour when William came to supper so I must remind him of his invitation to Falaise Castle. Perhaps he could plan a joust which Baldwin would win to boost his confidence. I must also send my parents a message soon.

Megina helps in the household as she has little to do for me now as I lead a quiet life compared to the comings and goings of the Flanders court. I have not worn my best dresses yet as Beatrice dresses simply from what seems a limited supply. Ralf, William's groom who I saw holding hands with Megina, has been left to look after Galathea and accompanies me on a ride about three times a week. Megina is delighted he is here because she and Ralf have become close. Inability to speak each other's language has not put them off forming a strong relationship so immediately. I hope this is permanent because it means that Megina is more likely to stay with me. She is keen to learn to talk to Ralf properly and I encourage her to speak Frankish to me. From my experience, it is usually the woman who makes the effort to learn the language of the beloved. I am ever grateful for my education and converse not only in Flemish, but also Frankish, English and German. It's just as well I do speak Frankish as William has no knowledge of another tongue.

William comes here to be with me as often as he can. Privacy is an issue in this modest dwelling so being together is more difficult than at Bruges. He is here now and we acknowledge the New Year and celebrate Easter in fine style. He takes me to the forest to repeat the afternoon of our wedding day. We agree to go 'riding' again soon. We also have time to talk privately so I ask him to tell me more about his family.

'What about your sister Adelaide? You don't talk about her much.'

'That's true. I haven't seen her for some time. We got on well as young children, but I saw little of her after my father died when I was seven. When Mother left Falaise Castle to live with her new husband, Herluin, Adelaide was five and went with her. I missed her very much.'

'Well, I suppose she would go with her mother.'

'Exactly, although some people say she was not her real mother.'

'She may be Duke Robert's daughter by another lady then?'

'So they say, but I don't believe that's true.'

'Is your sister married?'

'She is, to Count Enguerrand of Ponthieu. I arranged their marriage to make myself a powerful ally in Upper Normandy. I gave Adelaide the dower of Aumale; she is known as the Countess of Aumale. Of course, we met again at that time and we got on really well as though all those years had not passed. We must make an effort to go and see her. I know you'd like her.'

'I'm sure I would. What a good idea.'

'It is. Matilda, all these questions are fine, but I think there's something you are not telling me.'

'What do you mean?'

'I saw Megina when I arrived today. When I greeted her, asking her how she was, she replied "Well, thank you Monseigneur. And Lady Matilda, she is *particularly* well, is she not?" So, what was she saying to me?'

'I'll be having words with Megina, but yes, as she said, I am particularly well and I was waiting to tell you why until I was sure…'

'You mean…?'

'Yes William, I think it's our baby who we started in Bruges Forest.' William has tears in his eyes. He hugs me and can hardly speak.

'Are you sure?' he gasps looking at me with amazement.

'Both Megina and Beatrice know I am having some sickness in the mornings. I just feel different which is hard to explain. The signs are there, but it is early days and we should wait to tell our parents and other people for at least two months.'

'Does it matter coupling like we did just now, with such vigour?'

'I asked Beatrice about that and she said carry on right up to the birth. In fact, when it gets to the time and the baby seems to be late arriving, coupling encourages him to get a move on. He will stick fast until the last minute when he is ready. William, I want to ask you something and you must be honest. Will you be disappointed if the baby is a girl?'

'Immediately yes, because a son and heir means the Dukedom of Normandy continues through me, but not disappointed for long because if we can start a baby so easily a boy will turn up soon enough and if it's a girl just like you I can't wait to meet her.'

'That's a relief. Thank you. We'll welcome whoever it is. And William, I am so glad we are married.'

'So am I and don't worry, I fully intend to be around to greet our first child. Don't you think we should tell our parents now because Mother is soon going to find out you are pregnant, especially as she's in the house? I don't want her to start worrying that our child will be born out of wedlock like me. Unlike your parents, Mother doesn't know we are married and we should tell her about that if only to reassure her, but say it is to be kept between ourselves. On that subject, Matilda, why does our marriage have to be kept between ourselves?'

'I want to be prepared in case there is any opposition to it. Our family and friends will soon know about the baby and if they ask, we can say we will be having a State Marriage in Normandy later this year which is the truth. No need to spread the news too widely. I just want to keep quiet about the baby for another month or so just to be sure everything is all right.'

'Why shouldn't it be all right?'

'No reason at all, but it's usual to wait about three months into the pregnancy to tell people.' He looks concerned and obviously wants to shout the news from the roof tops. He is about to speak then decides to leave the subject alone.

'We'll be going to Fécamp soon. Everything is nearly ready, but don't expect anything on the scale of Bruges Palace. I will build you a grand palace as soon as I can.'

'I know you will. And William, I don't want to be difficult about telling the family about the baby. Beatrice already knows which probably means Robert does too. Let's tell our parents as soon as possible.' William nods and is about to answer when he is called to see a visitor.

The relief of knowing it's not long before we go to Fécamp is mixed with regret as I shall miss this household, Beatrice in particular, and the old fears of being on my own return. I've hardly had time to think about how I used to spend my time back in Flanders although I have kept up the familiar task of embroidery in the evenings. Beatrice and Robert continue to say we should all be in Eu Castle which has its own chapel, but we are not in it because of the awkward brother. This house does not have its own chapel, so we walk a short distance to a small monastery and say Mass with the holy brothers. I go every day as is my custom and find the routine comforting. Megina and Beatrice come with me as do Robert and William when either or both are here. William tells me that his palace at Fécamp is in the grounds of an Abbey which has two chapels. His Uncle William and Aunt Matilda were both at Fécamp in Holy Orders, but today there are no nuns. I suspect his family is just as complicated as my own, its members interrelated and deeply involved with the Church. The big difference of course, is that through his mother, the peasant class is also woven into his family but then reflect on the fact that most of my ancestors were roving land-hungry Vikings, hardly refined nobility.

I am anxious to get to Fécamp and start finding out what goes on in Normandy so that I can support William as he reaches his majority in a few weeks' time. Eu is a beautiful place with its forests and the River Ou running through. It is so near West Frankia that I wonder if it is more Frankish than Norman, not that I know what being 'Norman' really means. I have always thought Normandy an uncivilised place and hope that Eu is typical and not exceptional in its charm. William, Beatrice and Robert are now so close and dear to me that I am somewhat reassured about the nature of the Normans. However, I remain fearful about William having enemies who want to oust him from being the Prince and even kill him. The Franks call the people here the 'Eudois', but I don't suppose this makes them different from the rest of Normandy.

I asked William how Normandy is ruled when he is away and he told me his Steward, Count William FitzOsbern, is in charge. 'FitzO', as William calls him, is usually at Rouen, but sometimes at Falaise Castle where William was born and spent his childhood. Count William's father Osbern was Steward to Duke Robert and after his death, Osbern became like a father to seven-year-old Prince William, who was now left without family at Falaise Castle. William's life was in constant danger and his guardians would often sleep in his bedroom to protect him. Three years later Osbern, guarding young William, was murdered before his very eyes. Fortunately, Osbern's son, also called William, stepped up to become his companion, like an elder brother and has been his closest friend from that time. Count William is also his cousin through his great-grandmother Gunnora and betrothed to a young lady called Adeliza de Toeny.

Count Herluin has arrived to take his wife home to Conteville. William asks for me to come and meet him. I don't suppose the Countess is particularly pleased to see him as she seemed set to stay here. The Count is a delightful man and courteous in expressing his pleasure in the news of his step-son's betrothal to me. He is the sort of person who makes others feel comfortable and appreciated because he actually listens and doesn't dominate the conversation with his own opinions and stories. Now that we are all here except my parents, William and I agree it is time to tell his parents and Beatrice and Robert about our marriage and the baby. Unfortunately, the number who knows will grow in a few minutes time.

There they are: the Count and Countess of Conteville, the Count and Countess of Eu and Prince William of Normandy and me. I realise I am a princess at present and will be a duchess later this year.

'I'm sure you will want hear our good news that Lady Matilda and I are expecting a child in the spring of next year.'

All except Beatrice express surprise and begin to congratulate us, but Countess Arlette is agitated. She stands up, a bit unsteadily.

'When is your marriage arranged?' she asks abruptly. What *is* the matter with her? Is she beginning to worry about her clothing for the occasion? There's clearly something bothering her. When I realise what it is, I'm ashamed of thinking it was something trivial. She watches William with her mouth open.

'At the moment our plan is a State Marriage around Christmas just after I reach my majority.'

'Far too late William! You know your life is in such danger that you could be dead by then and your son and heir, *my grandson*, would be born out of wedlock. You *promised* me that would not happen.' She is flushed and visibly upset. William puts his hand on her shoulder.

'Now Mother, do sit down. You do not need to worry. We have already taken steps to avoid that by having a private marriage ceremony in the chapel at Bruges Palace.'

'You are *married*? What do you *mean*? Why didn't you tell me?' She is crying, dabbing her eyes with a lace handkerchief and Beatrice comes over to look after her. The men look away, embarrassed at this display of emotion.

William takes charge. 'We were advised by the priest to have a simple marriage ceremony rather than a formal betrothal so that if anything happened to me, any child of ours would be born in wedlock.' The Countess has more to say. 'Why did it have to be a secret? Why have I been kept in the dark when Lady Matilda's parents knew all about it?'

I'm not having that, 'Please understand what a difficult time my parents had in coping with the circumstances leading up to our betrothal. When William suggested a Formal Betrothal…' She interrupts. 'Naturally, I was the first to be consulted about William's idea for a Formal Betrothal, but no-one said anything about marriage.' She looks accusingly at both of us and William intervenes. 'I didn't even consider marriage as an alternative at the time we spoke and I was surprised when the priest suggested it. It was a good idea and we agreed to it. We were at Bruges Palace which is why Lady Matilda's parents were involved. It all happened so quickly that we didn't think of everything. Of course, I planned to tell you and Count Herluin but the subject of our marriage went to the back of my mind when I found out about the baby. You, my close family, are first to know about our baby. We want to keep this knowledge to ourselves for another month or so before we tell people, just be quite sure everything is all right. We do ask you to keep the knowledge of our marriage strictly between ourselves and of course, Lady Matilda's parents. Eight people. Ten if you count the priest and his cleric, no-one else.'

Count Herluin is the conciliator, 'Prince William, considering the continuing threats to your life and the enemies who want to make trouble for you, it is wise to be careful about who knows what. I'm sure my wife respects your decision as much as I do.' However, Countess Arlette is not appeased and now addresses me. 'Lady Matilda we have been together here for some days when you could have told me about your marriage, especially as your parents already knew about it.'

'Countess Arlette, I am truly sorry. I knew William would want to tell you himself, but I hadn't even told him about the baby at the time you and I were talking together so I kept quiet. My parents will not be pleased to find out they are the last to be told about the baby. I shall get into trouble for not sending a message immediately.' William gives me one of his quizzical looks and I turn away so no-one can see my expression. That look of his makes me want to giggle. Countess Arlette spends time folding her handkerchief and putting it into her pochette. She appears mollified.

Count Herluin then tells me about his sons Odo and Robert, William's brothers. They are twelve and ten years old, a few years younger than my brothers. He says they send greetings to me; I suspect this is not true, but duly respond and say I hope to meet them soon. I added that if they like practising sword skills like my brothers, I expect William will set up some jousting for them all at Falaise Castle.

Megina comes to help me before I retire and I ask her to keep quiet about anything she has observed recently which could become gossip. She agrees to ask me if and when she can mention certain facts. What a treasure she is! I ask her how her relationship with Ralf is progressing. Very well, she tells me, they love each other and Ralf would like to ask William if they may be together when we get to Fécamp and would I consent to this? Of course, I would and told her I was sure William would agree too.

Then William comes to my chamber and he is more exciting than ever and I love every bit of him. Our coupling has an even greater urgency and the relief so comforting. When he is lovely and talks with tears in his eyes about the baby, I cannot believe that he could ever be cruel or capable of the brutal acts attributed to him. When I asked Beatrice about this, she said that William can get angry. It's all to do with his bastard status. Although he is known throughout Normandy and beyond as 'William the Bastard', it is dangerous to mention it in his hearing. Nor does he allow anyone to insult his mother which I suspected when I saw how he watched my reaction when he asked my opinion of her. Beatrice also said that he suffered nightmares for many years having witnessed Osbern's bloody murder. His knowledge of being in permanent mortal danger means he must always be watchful and prepared to meet any threat to his dukedom or himself. Known opposition must be dealt with immediately with however much force is needed. I understand that, but pray that he is able to act reasonably. For instance, if the enemy surrenders, I pray he does not order further mutilation and killing of those merely obeying orders.

We sleep soundly all night in my bed and in the morning, couple again, as is our custom. After Mass, we gather in the Hall before we depart for Fécamp and William looks round at us all.

'So here we are, all about to leave this house.' What does William mean? Surely, we are not *all* leaving today? Robert is first to respond.

'I'm pleased you enjoyed our company, but do you really need us to escort you to Fécamp as well as the considerable force I see in the yard?' We laugh, but rather uncertainly. William laughs, 'I'll put you out of your misery! You're right, we shall not need you to escort us, but you are leaving this house because I've just ousted your brother William Busac from Eu Castle!' He throws a large bunch of heavy keys on to the table in front of Robert and Beatrice who look at them in astonishment.

'We haven't heard anything about this. When did it happen?' asks Robert.

'Two days ago, after a week of siege, which would not have been apparent outside the castle walls. We shored up the gates and kept watch on the lower walls, preventing all entry and exit. He had to submit when the water and food ran out.'

'Didn't he send messages to bring help?'

'He tried that, but my archers dispatched the few birds flying out and if one did get through, none of his rebel cronies turned up. If they had we'd have dispatched them as quickly as the pigeons.' William is in his fierce mood and I can't imagine anyone wanting to challenge him.

'Where is your brother now?'

'My spies tell me he has gone to exile in the court of King Henry of West Francia.' William sees my expression, 'Taken in by your Uncle Henry.' I nod so William knows I realise that Uncle Henry's harbouring of one of William's main enemies is a provocative move, showing what side he favours. And it is not ours. Right!

We start to discuss the poor character and disloyal behaviour of William Busac, but William cuts us short, steering the conversation to the happier outcome of his action as he asks Robert and Beatrice about their plans for Eu Castle. They talk excitedly about the prospect so that's all fine for them, but I see the storm clouds gathering as we approach William's majority and our marriage. How could Uncle Henry do that? It's an outright insult not just to William, but also to me. I shall discuss the matter with my parents.

As we sit talking, a message marked 'Urgent' arrives for me. It's from Father saying that Flanders is under attack by King Henry of Germany, Holy Roman Emperor and his old enemy. What did he expect? He is being backed by Pope Leo IX and Geoffrey Martel, Count of Anjou. They are advancing and he cannot escape to sea as King Edward of England has placed a naval blockade round the coast, backed up by my Uncle Henry and King Sweyn of Denmark. How dare Uncle Henry join in attacking Father and Mother? Bad news and I fear for my parents, but I am not remotely surprised considering Father's provocative actions in the past. I tell William that I have some important news, but too sensitive to relay to our present company.

'My parents send greetings,' I tell our guests, 'family news to be read later at leisure.'

They laugh fondly, quite unaware of the situation. Back in our chamber I show William the message and he agrees this action is not surprising. Do I expect him to support my father? I say 'no' because I don't think direct action like sending a force to repel the assailants will help anyone. It's not actually our business and we have enough enemies without making more. Father must deal with this himself having provoked both parties and I think in the end he will be forced to capitulate. While suggesting we take a neutral military role, I think we should make sure that essential supplies continue to get through at our Flemish border. William is relieved that my approach is the same as his and we get on with final arrangements for our departure.

Before we leave, I send a message to my parents with commiserations about their position and advice to keep themselves secure in the palace. We shall pray for them. I tell them about the baby and our travel plans. We will send a Fécamp basket of pigeons as soon as possible as we are anxious to keep up with what is happening in Flanders. I remember to make sure our Bruges pigeon basket is put on the baggage cart. We say fond farewells to Beatrice and Robert and also, though more formally, to Countess Arlette and Count Herluin who are departing for Conteville. William tells them all that we expect them at Fécamp before long. Just let us get settled.

CHAPTER 4

FRIENDS AND ENEMIES

Fécamp Palace, June 1049

We travelled here easily, the journey being shorter than from Lille to Eu a month ago. Fécamp is in a beautiful setting on the coast of the Narrow Sea. It is framed by impressive white cliffs and is a port like Bruges. I was told by Brihtric, whose name is damned forever in my heart, that England has the same white cliffs on the opposite shore of the Narrow Sea. Our palace is in the extensive grounds of Fécamp Abbey and I am amazed at the scale of this site stretching as far as the eye can see. It is similar to the present home of Robert and Beatrice, but on a much grander scale. William told me his father built the present stone dwelling on the site of the original wooden one built by his great-grandfather Duke Richard I. He pointed out two chapels, one adjacent to our palace for our family and guests and another for the servants. There is a smaller palace-like building for William's senior courtiers like his Steward William FitzOsbern, as well as accommodation for important guests. In the abbey grounds there are also many outbuildings, stables, wash houses, courtyards, barns and a farm. I can hardly take it all in.

I'm going to feel at home here because in many ways it is like Bruges, being a port, but it has much more land around it, beautiful countryside which I look forward to exploring on horseback. William and I have adjacent chambers so our servants can attend us separately: and both have large beds so we can sleep in either. The Hall is a good size with a large oak dining table at one end and rush-seated chairs. The wall-hung tapestries are brightly coloured and cabinets house books and a collection of musical instruments.

'Do you play one of these?' I enquire of William.

'No, but you do,' he replies watching my reaction which makes me realise he has got these for me. I am touched by his thoughtfulness.

The kitchen and servers' quarters adjoin the Hall and William has rooms where he conducts his business. His Steward has an office to himself. I have grown up in the household of the Counts of Flanders so I know something about national affairs from Father, but do not know if or how the rule of Normandy differs from the rule of Flanders.

Shortly after our arrival, Abbot John of Fécamp bustles in to welcome us. He is a small man, barely taller than me, with a warm manner combined with a powerful spirituality. He says Father Henryk has told him that I am well informed and enjoy debate with an enquiring mind. He is looking forward to many hours of discussion of religious matters with me. I am overwhelmed and can only stutter my thanks and say how blessed I am to meet him. This acquaintance is promising beyond anything I ever expected. He leaves saying he'll see us at Mass tomorrow and just as I'm taking all this in, there's more news.

A message from Bruges Palace has arrived from Mother and Father who are clearly delighted with the news of our baby. They hope to visit us soon. My brothers have been told that they are to become uncles and have taken bets on which of their names will be given to our son. Nothing changes there! I will reply that the baby might be called Constance or Arlette so neither would win the bet. They also say the attack and blockade of Flanders is over. No other information, so I suppose Father has had to submit. Will my parents be able to leave Flanders and visit us? I do hope so because I miss them more than I expected.

Our first Supper is suckling pig washed down with ale, followed by candied ginger, local cheese and warm fresh bread. I am pleased to have the ginger as it is the best thing for nausea. The servants have made a great effort and I get the feeling that our daily fare will be much plainer than I am used to. William and I eat together at the big table.

'I see our baby enjoyed that meal?' he says slyly.

'He certainly did, an appetite like his father's!' William's honking laughter echoes round the walls.

'I will introduce you to the household tomorrow,' he says, 'Count William will help you all he can. Megina will attend to your needs as you wish, but she is also happy to work with the other servants. What an effort she has made to speak our language and no doubt Ralf being her sweetheart has spurred her on. She puts me to shame as I speak few foreign words. We've got a few days together here to settle down and then I go to Falaise Castle where my loyal barons and knights will assemble to celebrate my majority. After that we engage in military action from our base at Falaise to remove some of our defences in the South to other regions which need urgent reinforcement. My three closest friends will be with me and I have invited them and their wives to come and stay here the following week. I want you to meet them as soon as possible.'

I gulp back my immediate and horrified reaction to this news and manage, 'I'm looking forward to meeting them. I will talk to the servants about the arrangements when I see them tomorrow. Working together to make the visit a success will help me get to know them more quickly.'

'I knew you would want to get involved immediately, my dearest wife!'

'Your dearest betrothed you mean.' He laughs.

'Your oldest friend Count William FitzOsbern must be one these guests, but he's here already, isn't he?'

'He's in Rouen today and coming here to meet you tomorrow. He will accompany me to Falaise and after we've achieved our objectives there, he's going home to fetch Adeliza his betrothed and bring her back with him.'

'I'm certainly looking forward to meeting her. How old is she?'

'About your age I think.'

'Perfect! Who else is coming?'

'Two counts, both called Roger. One is Count Roger de Montgomery and his wife Mabel and the other, Count Roger de Beaumont and his wife Adeline. And since you like to know such things, these ladies are older than you by varying years.'

'Any children?'

'Count William hasn't, but the others certainly have. I don't take in the details of what children people have. You'll have to ask the ladies who will love to discuss all that.'

'That's reassuring, thank you.'

William looks relieved. He has business to do so I go to my chambers to find Megina unpacking my baggage. She is pleased with her quarters which she is to share with another servant, whose sweetheart is one of William's grooms like her Ralf. Megina seems happy so I don't need to worry about her. I am concerned, however, about fitting in with William's friends because it obviously matters so much to him that I do. I pray silently. 'Gratia Plena, grant me a true friend among these ladies whose husbands are so close to William.'

Megina is looking at me, 'Are you praying Madame?'

'I am because Prince William's best friends and their wives are coming to stay next week and I want them to like me.'

'Why wouldn't they like you? Everyone likes you!'

'Megina, you know that's not true, most women actively dislike me from the start!'

'Jealous of your beauty and position, but once they get to know you...'

'You are a kind sweet girl, but all I ask of Mother Mary is one good friend.'

'I'll pray for you Madame.'

My boudoir is feminine with a coverlet of blue and gold woven fabric. The sheets and head cushion covers are soft cream cotton. The mattress is deep and quite firm although soft to feel. There is a pretty writing table with its own delicate wooden chair with a blue silk cushion for comfortable sitting. Rugs cover the wooden floor and are patterned with the red and gold Coats of Arms of the Dukes of Normandy. What effort William has put into this! No wonder it has all taken longer than expected to finish. William has tried to give me some of the luxury of Bruges Palace and I am so grateful.

Yet, this pleasure is overshadowed by the impending visit of William's close friends, especially the ladies. The men are not the problem because they will they probably be out all day at the Chase and anyway I've never found it difficult to get on with men. Ladies are a different matter. How am I to entertain these guests all day? Such a short time remains to make any plans in this new place where I have no connections or knowledge. William returns and sits me down beside him on the bed. He puts his arms round me and is about to pull me down to lie with him, but feeling some resistance, pulls back and gives me a straight look.

'Now I can see you are worrying. Is it about the ladies coming to stay?'

'I don't what there is for us to do around Fécamp.' William smiles, looking rather pleased with himself.

'You will have the use of the big carriage and any of the smaller ones. A journey to Rouen is always enjoyable and you could ask the servants to take chairs and a table and pack food to eat somewhere with a good view. Another day, you could ride out from here along the paths beside the sea. I suppose it's all right for you to ride at this stage?'

'Yes, it's fine for a while. Galathea is steady.'

'I have also instructed musicians to attend us tomorrow. If their music is to your taste, invite them to stay in the guest quarters and perform for us in the evenings. Maybe you and the ladies would like to join in. We have instruments here.'

'You have thought of everything! Thank you.'

'One more thing to say Matilda and it's important. A group of bodyguards will attend you ladies on every outing as well as grooms if you are riding. They will be there to help and protect you if needed. They have orders from me, but will also take orders from you while keeping a discreet distance when you are not travelling.'

'I expected no less as that was Father's practice when we went out in Flanders. I quite understand.'

'I'm not sure you do because without wishing to frighten you, the situation here is much more dangerous than Flanders simply because there are those who will stop at nothing to seize the Dukedom of Normandy. You will be a target, the prime hostage to get what they want from me. You will have to keep your wits about you all the time just as

I do. I knew from the start that you are a strong independent woman who I can trust to be careful for both our sakes and for our baby's sake.'

'You can trust me, William.' He gives me one of his bear hugs and lifts me up so we are face-to-face as he did on our first time together, again strengthening our bond. We retire to my chamber.

After Mass the next morning, we have bread and cheese to stay our hunger and then go to the Hall. I am introduced to a rather serious looking gentleman, Count William FitzOsbern. He bows to me.

'Lady Matilda, it is an honour to meet you at last. Please sit down at the table so we can talk.'

As William makes for the door, he looks pleased with events. 'I'll leave you two together as you have much to discuss. I'm going to the yard to look at my horse that's picked up a stone in his hoof.' Count William FitzOsbern looks at me kindly. 'I am at your service at all times. You can ask me anything you like from household to national matters and tell me any worries you have. What you say to me is confidential and I'll tell you if I think Prince William should be told.' 'Thank you, that is reassuring.'

First, how would you like me to address you?'

'Prince William calls me FitzO!'

'I'd be more comfortable with Count William.'

'Settled. So, is there anything particular on your mind?'

'William says he has enemies who want to get rid of him and I am to be careful and only go out with bodyguards. Who are these enemies?'

'You remember the Battle of Val-ès-Dunes two years ago?' I nod. 'The ringleader of the rebel barons was Guy of Burgundy, also called Guy of Brionne, Prince William's first cousin. He insists he has a stronger claim to the Dukedom of Normandy than Prince William.'

'His first cousin, how shocking! Was this Guy killed in the Battle?'

'No, he escaped to his heavily fortified castle at Brionne where he's still plotting no doubt.'

'Can't William do anything about him?'

'He could in a concerted campaign which is certainly on the present list of urgent matters to resolve.'

'Is there still a threat from any of the other rebel baron leaders?'

'Not a substantial one for they were either killed in the battle or dispossessed leaving them lacking any power. However, Prince William does not rule over every part of Normandy and in consolidating his Dukedom, he must challenge other barons who will resist.'

'Any other claims to the Dukedom from William's relations?'

'You are astute and yes, one of the most determined is Prince William's Uncle, Archbishop Mauger of Rouen. He thinks his younger brother William, Count of Talou, also called Count of Arques, has a better claim.'

'Legitimacy again?'

'Yes, but not entirely. It's a delicate subject. You take my meaning I assume?'

'I'm afraid I do, but surely the Archbishop didn't fight in the battle?'

'He did not, but his son Haimon Dentatus was one of the leading rebels and was killed in the event.'

'Did William of Talou fight?'

'He appeared half-heartedly in Prince William's rear guard, but was never seen in in engagement. What we do know is that he and the Archbishop conspired in the background to support the rebels. The two of them are a real threat.'

'Anyone else?'

'Yes, after the Battle, Prince William repaid King Henry for his rescue mission by joining him in repelling the hostile advances of Geoffrey Martel, Count of Anjou. In doing so, Domfront and Alençon were returned to Norman hands, but these fortresses remain at risk of further capture. Geoffrey is now William's enemy too.'

'I'm beginning to see what William is up against. I suppose this is one of the other urgent matters?'

'It is and I applaud your quick understanding. I know we shall work well together. I was told that you have experience in these things having been a confidant of your father, Count Baldwin.'

'I was and I would welcome that role again in Normandy so that I can support William.'

'Indeed, and he has asked me to keep you well informed, but for now I think we must address the impending arrival of the Counts

Montgomery and Beaumont and their wives and servants as well as Adeliza and me.' So sensible and diplomatic. William obviously trusts him so if we are to work together, I must speak my mind.

'I'm not worried about you and Adeliza or the counts, but I am nervous about their wives' reaction to me. Is there anything I should know, any subject I should avoid?'

'Countess Adeline de Beaumont is a delightful lady in her thirties and already has a family. Her first husband died so this is her second marriage which took place last year. I'm sure you will like her. Now, Dame Mabel de Bellême, as she styles herself, holds strong opinions which she has no hesitation in expressing. I don't advise arguing with her until you have been with her on several occasions and got the measure of her. We all have to remember her husband is a close friend and a strong ally of Prince William so we all need to bite our tongues! She will no doubt mention her grand marriage last year, naturally far superior to that of Countess Adeline.'

'Has she asked for any special treatment for her visit?'

'You must be clairvoyant! In a word, yes. Dame Mabel is ever mindful of her status as sole heiress to her father's lands and considerable fortune. Her Ladyship requests accommodation for fifty bodyguards which she declares a small number as she usually travels everywhere with a hundred-armed men.'

'What is our answer?'

'Four and of course, she will bring her maid, man servant, groom and probably others who she will arrange to be sneaked in at night.'

'Do we know her response to only having four bodyguards?'

'I asked Seigneur Roger and he said "unrepeatable" and roared with laughter. He lets her get her own way when it suits him, but he puts his foot down when it doesn't.' We laugh about this conspiratorially and despite my first impressions I see he has a sense of humour.

As Lady of the House, I am in overall charge of domestic arrangements, but in fact the planning is done by Count William as Steward and the servants under him have their particular responsibilities. I learn that Dinner in this household, indeed in all Prince William's households, is mid-day. I am also informed that Prince William obliges everyone on site to attend Mass daily. Since our personal servants must be available at all times and an armed force always on guard, there are two morning Masses in the Servants' Chapel to allow this cover. Count William suggests a meeting this evening before Supper to introduce me to the more senior staff: the Chamberlain, Master of Wardrobes, Pantler, Cook and Butler.

Count William joins us to eat and the meal is delicious, country pork sausages on trenchers, the meat grown on our farm and served with a light mustard sauce. Fresh bread, cheeses and dates follow. I ask Count William to convey my praise to his staff.

William eats robustly as always, but he seems distracted and I sense he has something on his mind. 'Business.' he says when I ask and he departs. I go to my boudoir to refresh myself.

That evening the servants are waiting for me. I speak to the cook who tells me his name is Antoine, a man of generous figure probably from sampling his dishes. He is cheerful and apparently placid, not common among cooks in my experience. He is obviously pleased when I praise the food we've had since our arrival and then I ask him to compile a list of meals during our guests' stay. He bristles a bit at this request and says that he does not make forward plans. Each day he rises early, chooses the meals for that day and collects fresh produce from the palace farm and local market at sunrise. He only consults the Steward if he has a question, but of course, he could change this procedure and consult me instead. I say no need to change anything as the results are so good. This reassures him, his pride intact.

How difficult it is for those without the basic skill of writing a list of meals! How tactless of me to ask Antoine to do this because I know of no servant who reads or writes and these skills are rare in the nobility too. Forgive me for this sin of disrespect to Antoine. I had forgotten how fortunate I am to have had the opportunity to read and write and will make sure our children have the same. William FitzOsbern is clearly educated, but I wonder about the other two Counts, Beaumont and Montgomery, and even more about their wives.

Thinking yet again about us ladies, Adeline and Mabel were married last year, Adeliza is betrothed and I am Formally Betrothed, but in fact, already married. I must be careful to keep my story consistent. I'm sure I will get on with Adeliza since she is about my age and Count William has told me she has had the same sort of education as me. He also says I will certainly like Adeline. The problem guest is obviously Dame Mabel, a malign force to be reckoned with by all accounts. Can she really be as dreadful as described? I have been advised not to rise to her spiteful remarks so, am I apprehensive? Certainly not! In fact, I find myself looking forward to dealing with her! I shall do some homework on her family in preparation. Abbot John knows what's going on so I shall go and see him tomorrow. I shall be a worthy adversary of the Dame!

William is tired and taciturn when he returns so I tell him he has sired a warrior who is beginning to flutter in me, preparing no doubt for the joust. I don't think it is the baby, probably wind at this early stage, but the mere idea cheers him up and he puts his big hands on my belly to feel the flutter himself. Delighted, he cradles me in his arms while touching my skin reverently. He's sorry he's been grouchy, but he's had a lot to do regarding the plans for the celebration of his Majority and military operations at Falaise. He has to go away tomorrow and he'll be leaving me on my own. I tell him I'm well looked after here and a strong woman who understands his job. I remind him I am used to my father being away on military operations. I tell him I'm thankful I did not marry a milksop even if I once thought it a good idea. He looks at me sideways and we both burst out laughing. He whispers that a milksop would gravely disappoint me in bed and he doesn't want that. He is relaxed now and we couple quietly and peacefully, not driven by heated passion, but gently fired with knowledge of each other's body acquired in the short time we've been together.

William left this morning after Mass led by Abbot John himself. With William FitzOsbern at his side and a considerable escort, he's gone to Falaise Castle to meet his other close friends and the barons and knights willing to swear allegiance to him. I pray for them all at Mass and will continue to do so while getting to know this palace and all who work here. I'm also planning a gentle daily ride on Galathea accompanied by

Ralf and Jean, Marie-Clair's sweetheart, plus a posse of soldiers of course. The day of the Visit gets ever closer.

The pigeon keeper brings two messages. Beatrice is missing me and would I like her to come and stay for few days as Robert has gone to Falaise on a military operation. The second message from Countess Arlette is identical apart from it being Count Herluin who is going to Falaise. So, William is mustering his forces. I send quick replies to explain what is happening here and that I will be in touch again soon to invite them to stay. Countess Arlette also suggests that her two sons come and stay with us under the supervision of their older brother. I promise to pass on her request to William when I next see him, but I doubt he will have the time or inclination to take on yet another responsibility.

CHAPTER 5

THE VISIT

July 1049

Today is the day. I wake after a disturbed night without William in my bed to turn to for comfort. He is in his own chamber, retiring straight after supper, exhausted from whatever he's been doing. I lie here, light penetrating the drapes, thinking about our guests and then call Megina to help me if we are not to be late for Mass. As we go to chapel, William comes hurrying along to join us and I notice that he is especially prayerful as if needing absolution. His powerful presence beside me gives me strength. I am calmer having been with Our Lady because I know she will look after me. Back in the Hall, we have delicious bread and honey and would eat far more if we were not to be hosting a special Dinner for our guests, due to arrive at eleven o'clock. As we are finishing, William FitzOsbern comes in accompanied by a young lady noticeably younger than him who must be Adeliza.

She smiles warmly when introduced and looks me straight in the eye as if she knows exactly what I am feeling.

'Is everything ready for the guests?' she asks in a mischievous tone suggesting that Count William has already told her about Dame Mabel's demands and our response.

'I think we're as ready as we could be, but there may well be something we need to address when they inspect their accommodation. Have you met Dame Mabel and Countess Adeline?' At this point the men depart to check the stables and I indicate that Adeliza should sit with me.

'Oh yes, and I believe William has given you some background.'

'Indeed, he has. Countess Adeline sounds a lovely lady, but is Dame Mabel really as difficult as he suggests?'

'Worse and when she's challenged, she takes on a sort of joking manner before delivering more poisonous comments!'

'Count William advised caution in responding to her provocation so as not to upset our husbands' close friendship. What's your advice?'

'I feel it's not my place to advise you Lady Matilda.'

'Please call me Matilda and it is absolutely your place to advise me. I can't begin to tell you how pleased I am to meet you at last. I thought we would get on well and now we've met I know we will. So, how you think I should cope with Dame Mabel?'

'Please call me Adeliza. William described you to me and I also knew we would get on. My advice is to stand up to her because the bond between Prince William and her husband is far too strong to be upset by Dame Mabel being put in her place now and then. They both know her only too well. If you allow her to get away with her spiteful remarks, she will make all sorts of trouble for you.'

'She is heiress to Bellême our southern border to Brittany and the castles of Alençon and Domfront belong to her father. Her enmity to me could affect our future defences.'

'You *have* been doing your homework! And you are right of course, but Prince William is Ruler of Normandy and her father William de Bellême, not a count you notice, is his subject just as she will be when she inherits from him. Yes, she is wealthy and well-connected, but you are placed well above her in a number of ways including being betrothed to Prince William. You can expect her little pinpricks of malice trying to persuade you otherwise. She will goad you by insinuating that the Dukes of Normandy have a common background compared to the longer-established Montgomery family.'

'Don't worry, I have done my homework and will be quite able to hold my own on William's background.'

'Well, Dame Mabel had better look out! I'm rather looking forward to this meeting!' The men return and seeing us talking and laughing look at each other and nod, knowing we are getting on well. There are two hours to wait so we retire to our chambers to prepare. Luckily, some of my dresses are loose enough to wear, but at the rate my belly is growing it won't be long before I need them altered. Megina helps me put on my best blue dress that Countess Arlette chose for me and brushes my hair. She tells me I look beautiful. She always says that! I look at her more closely and realise that she is looking rather the same shape as me. She sees my gaze drop to her belly and she gives me big smile. I can't believe I didn't notice before.

'Why didn't you tell me?'

'I don't know Madame, but Ralf and I are pleased. I hope it will not alter my position.'

'Of course not, but when is your baby due?'

'Probably the same day as yours, Madame?'

'Megina! How can you know that?'

'Well, that day when you and Prince William went off to the forest, Ralf and I went back into the stables. He had to muck out and I helped by sweeping up. I watched him put down clean straw and he smiled at me with his eyebrows up, questioning. We hugged each other and started kissing and just lay down on it. We couldn't help it, Madame. I'd never done that before. Nor had he.'

'I think we share quite a lot Megina and I am delighted with your news. It could also work out well for us both when our babies are born. You'll see!'

My head buzzing with Megina's news, I go down in good time to meet Adeliza in the Hall. She looks lovely in a pink dress which suits her dark colouring. The two Williams come in to say they are going out to the gate to greet our guests. We look out and see the castle servants gathering in the yards ready to do what is required of them. There is distant noise of our horses whinnying, the sure sign of the first arrival. Here comes a grand carriage with, oh my goodness, gold adornment, surely fit for a King! It is drawn by four grey palfreys in immaculate harness.

'Guess who this is!' whispers Adeliza. Stifling our giggles, we go out, with me expecting to greet a grand lady of noble demeanour, but here is this tiny, thin person with a face I can only describe as "rat-like".' She is being handed out of the carriage by William, who bows to her.

'Dame Mabel,' his penetrating voice booming out around the yard. She inclines her head in his direction and then stands up straight completely ignoring him as she takes in her surroundings, her pointed nose turning in each direction, her face set in lines of habitual disdain. I doubt William notices her discourtesy as a loud 'Bonjour mon ami!' resounds from a most cheerful looking gentleman who descends from the carriage and now embraces him in the men's fashion of serial back-slapping. Roger de Montgomery of course! How can he look so jolly when he has this sour-faced rat woman to put up with? I approach and William introduces first Dame Mabel and then Count Roger.

'Lady Matilda', she says appraising me with her narrowed eyes pointing straight at me as we are of similar height.

'Dame Mabel, we are honoured to have your company.' I look her firmly in the eye until she drops her gaze.

'Will you come to the Hall for refreshment?'

'Thank you, but I wish to be shown my quarters immediately so that I can check everything is in place and direct my servants to put my belongings where I want them.'

'Of course, I'll call the Chamberlain. Please let him know if there's anything you need. Dinner is served at twelve o'clock.' The Chamberlain appears and escorts her to her rooms. I wonder how long it will be before she finds fault!

Adeliza, who must have heard this exchange, gives me a look and now points towards the gates where I see another carriage drawn up. Apparently, no passenger has emerged because the scrum of servants unloading the Montgomery carriage and the baggage piled up at the sides prevent any forward movement.

I find William and we battle through the assembly to find a carriage of more modest size and appearance than the previous arrival. The Beaumonts are emerging, their man-servant in attendance. First out is Count Roger, a large man with a bushy beard which makes him stand out among the clean-shaven Normans. He bows to me, his military bearing consistent with his position as one of William's top marshals. I then see Countess Adeline as she descends, handed by her husband to a warm greeting by William who I know is fond of her. She is a comfortable-looking lady who beams at me and I think she must be more my mother's age than mine. She seems to be in the late stages of pregnancy. I foresee an easy relationship with her as she accepts the invitation to gather for refreshments in the Hall with grace and alacrity.

The company, apart from Lady Mabel who I imagine is still bossing everyone about and complaining elsewhere, gathers in the Hall. The conversation is lively and the men excitedly start planning a half-day Chase after Dinner. I knew they would. They just can't resist it! We three ladies sit together and Adeliza begins talking about Countess Adeline's wedding, saying how lovely she looked and what an occasion it was. Countess Adeline is clearly delighted with Adeliza's comments and I imagine she and I are both thinking what a generous spirit in this girl despite being betrothed to a much older man. They ask me how I am settling here in Normandy and I tell them I like it very much and having two new friends will make me even happier. Adeliza says surely I have three new friends and we all look at each other and dissolve into helpless laughter. William, seemingly disapproving of this levity, comes over to say he's called the servants to show our guests to their chambers. Dinner is put back to one-thirty, later than planned because everything has taken longer than anticipated. Back in our quarters, William asks if I am all right and I say I am particularly pleased to have met two ladies with whom I can become friends. So, a third friendship among our guests looks unlikely he comments, and I say only if one of his male friends is prepared to be my friend too. He laughs and tells me not to take Dame Mabel too seriously and he's quite sure I will not put up with being bullied by her. Good, I've got his clearance so that's all right. I'm almost looking forward to the fray.

Dinner is not what was planned, instead a quick meal ordered by William only today so that the Chase can be started as soon as possible. With the present light evenings, the men will not be back until seven o'clock and the more substantial meal of today will be Supper at eight o'clock. I am annoyed with William for keeping this change of plan from me. I should have been consulted, but I'm beginning to understand that the Chase takes precedence over all other activity. Perhaps battle takes first place when it has to, and I think our coupling is probably an equal rival just now. As we grow older and more babies take their toll on my body, our coupling will not give quite the same thrill as in the early days whereas the excitement of the Chase will never diminish. I snap back to the present and wonder at Antoine's ability to change his menu at the last minute to present us with this quick but appetizing meal of today's catch of white fish in a subtle saffron sauce. His custom of taking each day as it comes is ideal.

Dame Mabel is the perfect guest, the most gracious of noble ladies, as she praises everything in the castle, her chambers, the view, the staff and this delicious food. She has only tasted the like in the best restaurants of Paris. She would like to steal our chef to be on her staff at Beaumont-le-Roger Castle. She sits at William's right hand, simpering as she heaps him with compliments which bewilder a man uncomfortable with extravagant words. He is uncharacteristically quiet. The men wolf up their food and gulp down their ale and are off with alacrity to the stable yard.

Here we sit, we four ladies, three of us on tenterhooks to see if Dame Mabel changes her tone. We do not have to wait long.

'Lady Matilda, I do compliment you on all aspects of your palace, especially as it must be such a change for you after the splendour of Bruges.'

'Thank you, Dame Mabel. I'm gratified to hear you find so much to your liking. As for a change, I assure you that I am delighted with Fécamp which is similar to Bruges, being also a port in beautiful surroundings.'

'Bruges Palace is very much larger is it not?'

'Indeed it is, but by the time Duke William and I are at my parents' stage of life, we expect to be living in a palace quite as large Bruges.'

'Oh, your parents yes! What a distinguished ancestry you have within the English and Frankish royal families! And your mother, a royal princess, a sister to Henry, King of the Franks! I expect Prince William has told you that the Montgomery family also traces its ancestry a long way back just like the Frankish royal family and your family too of course.'

'No, he has not told me about the Montgomery family's royal connections and I find what you say most interesting! I shall enjoy hearing every detail from you. Be assured I do know about Count Roger's Viking ancestor, Gomeric, who established the Montgomery family among the earliest nobility in Normandy. I believe there may have been a Roman connection too. That is *most* impressive.'

'Impressive, indeed! You are quite right, Lady Matilda and as you are respected as a scholar, people listen to what you say. After this talk, I know I can rely on you to remind Prince William of our family's heritage and, at last, persuade him to honour our family appropriately. We have always known that the Montgomery dynasty was in place centuries before that vagabond, Rollo the Viking, appeared and established the Dukedom of Normandy. That was a recent event in comparison to the Montgomery family's long history.'

'Indeed, quite recent, and I'm sure we all lament the lack of fortune that resulted in your husband's ancestor Gomeric, roaming the Normandy shores like Rollo, but sadly failing to secure any treaty with the Kings of West Frankia. In comparison, our fortunes were established for ever by William's ancestor, the Viking chieftain, Rollo Thurstan le Goz Brico Bigod. His negotiation with King Charles the Simple in 911, made him ruler of Normandy. His grandson Richard I, Duke William's great-grandfather, became the first duke and Duke William, his direct descendant, is the present duke. We must agree that both our noble families are distinguished, yours by being by far the longest established and ours by being the hereditary dukes of Normandy.' Is she is going to start up again as she is breathing hard and fast, her face a shade of mauve? She opens her mouth, but I get in first.

'And I want to say this, Ladies. You know how much Duke William values the loyalty and friendship of his closest friends, your husbands and yourselves. We are confident that he can rely on this support, especially now he has reached his Majority.'

There is a deadly hush as Dame Mabel makes an effort to compose herself. Adeline and Adeliza look stunned having witnessed this power struggle. Dame Mabel rises.

'I beg to take leave of you now to rest in my chamber. It was a long journey today and I am fatigued. What hour would you like me to return to the Hall?'

I ignore the appealing faces of the other ladies and reply, 'I have ordered the carriage to take us to a charming place by the seashore and thought we could take a stroll in the sunshine and feel revived by the sea breezes. We would be pleased to have your company Dame Mabel, but we do understand if you feel you must rest.'

'Thank you, but I will rest. I wish you a pleasant afternoon.' I call after her, 'Please inform the servants if there is anything you need. I suggest we meet in the Hall at seven o'clock, where we will take refreshment and wait for the men to return. Supper will be at eight o'clock.' There is overwhelming relief that Dame Mabel is not joining us later.

Our outing is most enjoyable. With bodyguards behind and in front of our carriage we travel to the white cliffs. We walk along the coastal path, the salty air refreshing us and rhythmic pounding of the waves below settling our nerves. Countess Adeline is feeling the heat and our pace is slow. We admire the view and do not walk far as the ladies want to stop and go over and over the exchanges with Dame Mabel. They are delighted with how I'd dealt with her poisonous remarks. Both declare I have well and truly won this bout, but Countess Adeline warns that she will now seek every opportunity to get back at me. She's a dangerous woman she says. Oh dear, what have I done? She's probably cursing me as we speak. Countess Adeline is a bit quiet and the saying 'two's company, three's none' probably explains it. Or perhaps she is just tired. We drive back and as we go through the castle door, there's Dame Mabel apparently waiting for us and scowling. She does not greet us, but launches into a tirade, aimed at all of us.

'I suppose *you* all know what Duke William's present military operation involves? *I* was not told and now I get this message from my father.' It's my time to take charge.

I go up to her and face her squarely, 'I do not know what the military operation involves and Duke William will tell me if and when he sees fit.' Adeline and Adeliza are mumbling that they don't know either and appear nervous which is not surprising since she is almost snarling like a dog ready to bite an intruder to its domain. I take her by the arm and try to guide her to the entrance of the Hall.

'Dame Mabel, I will not tolerate this unacceptable behaviour. May I suggest we go into the Hall, at least away from the yard where everyone can hear our conversation?'

As we begin to move, it's like trying to hold a child having a tantrum. She jumps up and down and shrieks, like a banshee, 'It's my father's castle of Bellême and his other strongholds Alençon and Domfront. They have *all* have been seized by Prince, I mean Duke, William!' She is puffing now, standing there, rigid with rage, and about to start again, so I take her very firmly by the arm and propel her into the Hall to a chair where I push her down to sit. Quite hard. Adeline and Adeliza hover behind me. I stand in front of Dame Mabel. 'Is your father all right?'

'Of course, he's all right, but he should have been warned and now there are garrisons of soldiers all over the place and it looks as if they are going to stay.' I need to calm her.

'I think your father will be most willing to co-operate with this operation and put the defence and safety of Normandy before his own comfort. I am sure we all applaud him as a loyal subject and I'm sure Duke William does too.' She is red with anger, aching to say her bit, 'He's not *a subject*, he's Seigneur William de Talvas de Bellême, a top-ranking nobleman, his status enhanced by my marriage to Count Montgomery, Duke William's right-hand man.'

'Then you should know that Count Montgomery has been at Duke William's side leading this operation, together with these ladies' husbands, Counts FitzOsbern and Beaumont.' This news clearly shakes the treacherous self-made victim.

'*My husband*? Are you sure? Why didn't he tell me? I'm made to look foolish.' She brings out a lace handkerchief and dabs her eyes, but

I see her squinting at me at the same time. I am not taken in by this charade.

'You are not alone, none of us was told because if vital information is passed on, even to a wife, it can leak out and the element of surprise in the mission is lost.' Off she goes again.

'My father would have co-operated. There was no need to invade his castles and treat him like an enemy.'

'Dame Mabel, this conversation ends here and now. You may choose to address your concern to your husband on his return, but not in public in our home. We ladies are called to preserve a dignified and amiable presence in the face of adversity. This I ask of you now and through this evening, but if you are too distressed to do this, you must plead fatigue or a headache and retire to your quarters.'

'I am *never* distressed; I am far too strong for female weakness. You ladies will see that I take a jocular manner in reprimanding the men on their return.' I remind the ladies that we will meet at seven o'clock.' Dame Mabel stomps off giving everyone the evil eye. My mind is all over the place. What on earth could have happened?

As we leave to go to our chambers, a servant appears to tell me that the Countess of Conteville has arrived. She can't have got my message. This is not good timing. I hurry to the Hall. 'Countess Arlette, what a pleasant surprise!'

'I got your message, but I knew you would like some company as the men are still in Falaise.'

'The men are not in Falaise, they are back here although out at the Chase at present. Are your sons with you?'

'No, Odo and Robert remain at Falaise Castle with their father, still involved with the military operations. Oh, and their elder brother Raoul is not coming as well for the same reason.'

'*Raoul?* I don't think I know about him.'

'Raoul's Count Herluin's son by his first wife, Frégonde.' Oh, so it was not their elder brother William who was expected to keep an eye of them, but Raoul. I didn't know he existed; he must be quite old. As if reading my mind, the Countess explains. 'I did say Raoul would be coming to supervise his brothers, but of course, everything's changed now. I'm sorry if my visit is inconvenient, but as Count Herluin is still in Falaise I assumed Duke William and his other senior counsellors would still be there too.' I see I must put her mind at rest and be gentle with her, 'Quite understandable and I'm so pleased to see you. I'll call the Chamberlain to arrange your quarters although I'm afraid the best ones are already occupied by the FitzOsberns, Beaumonts and Montgomeries. You have just missed the ladies who have retired to their chambers until we meet in the Hall at seven o'clock. Meanwhile let me order some refreshment for you.'

'Thank you and I'll retire myself as soon as the chamber is settled. I'd be most obliged to have a rest and a little light refreshment. I have brought my maid Agnês with me.' I send a servant to inform the Chamberlain of the Countess's requirements. She looks at me closely.

'How are you?'

'Quite well thank you. Your grandson is beginning to be active.'

'That is good news and I'm sure William is delighted. I thought you might like me to find you some suitable dresses for the next few months?'

'That would be so kind and you know what I like. I shall wear my favourite blue dress this evening as it still just fits.'

'I look forward to it. And how are you coping with Dame de Bellême, known throughout Normandy as "Mabel, The Poisoner"?'

'Well, I've having quite a time with her as you can imagine! You will be pleased to hear that I have not let her get away with her spiteful remarks, but the ladies warn me that she is now my sworn enemy! Something has happened in her father's domain and she is distressed and on the war path. She thinks she's the only who was kept in the dark regarding details of the present Battle. I told her that is not true and thankfully, she has retired to her chamber. I've given the kitchen instructions that neither she nor any of her servants are to go anywhere near food or drink being prepared as she probably has plans to poison me!'

'I'd expect nothing less of you! Well done, and I am looking forward to seeing what she's like this evening. Oh, and I've also come to wish William a happy birth time of year!' I daren't admit that until William mentioned his Majority was last week, I've been ignorant of his birth time as we both take little notice of these events. I see this does matter, especially for nobility, because reaching a Majority brings significant change, like Prince William becoming Duke William. Most people we know can say the year they were born and possibly the time of year, but very rarely the exact date. If anyone is entitled to know something of William's birth time, it's his mother so she is welcome to this little victory. I just smile and bid her well as the Chamberlain arrives to escort her to her chamber. The Countess seems in good form and looks better than when I last saw her. I wonder how long she is planning to stay. She has made me think about my own birth time of year which is November and as I go to my chamber to rest, being exhausted, I hear the men are back. I hope they bathe before Supper.

I go down at the appointed time and we ladies convene in the Hall, but Countess Arlette has not yet arrived. Dame Mabel appears composed as if nothing has happened. She is worryingly silent and I wonder how soon she will allude to Alençon. I do hope she does not and if she does start addressing the men in a jocular manner as she promised, this would infuriate the men this evening. Platters of nuts and raisins are laid out and our butler is on hand to serve us a good variety of drinks. I recommend the ladies try our light and delicious Perry from last year's pear crop. Dame Mabel requests Mead and I only have to look at Adeliza's expression to know that we are both thinking that no amount of Mead would sweeten that woman. Dame Mabel is uncharacteristically still, seemingly lost in her own thoughts and not joining in with the conversation. She sits with her back to the entrance whereas the rest of us ladies are positioned to see who is coming in. Suddenly, her head comes up, her thin face screwed up as if she is in severe pain. She sighs audibly amid a deathly hush.

'I do pity poor Duke William having to suffer such unkind words from so many people.' Silence.

'And pray, what unkind words are those?' The voice comes from the doorway behind her. Dame Mabel, turning to look at the speaker, stands up and begins to move forward in small hesitant steps.

'Oh, Countess, I didn't see you come in.'

'Clearly, and since you appear to know who I am and I am not aware we are acquainted, perhaps Lady Matilda would introduce me.' I go over to where the two protagonists face each other.

'Countess Arlette, may I present Dame Mabel of Bellême.' The Countess nods to her stiffly, 'Well, Dame Mabel, I will sit down and await your answer to my question.'

Dame Mabel stutters, her body twitching, 'Well, I did hear that some people think being Duke of Normandy is too hard a task for a person of such a young age and of such forceful character.' What a liar!

'And is that your opinion?'

'No of course not, I just meant...I expect it was a joke.' She is babbling and gesticulating. The men are outside, about to make their usual boisterous entrance. And, here they are, their loud conversation ceasing as they take in the tense atmosphere of the Hall.

'Mother, I wasn't expecting you!' William appears, straight to the point as ever. He looks round, the other counts now beside him and sees the ladies watching Countess Arlette and Dame Mabel who face each other like cockerels ready to fight. William takes charge.

'What's going on here? Mother?' 'According to Dame Mabel, many people say you are too young and forceful to take on the full job of Duke of Normandy.' 'They can say that to my face, and I will deal with them robustly. Repeating such words is the spread of rebellious slander, do you not agree Dame Mabel?' Dame Mabel nods vigorously, but Countess Arlette is still on the warpath. 'Let us pray that Dame Mabel does not follow in her father's footsteps. I will never forget the day when her father, William Talvas de Bellême came to Falaise Castle just after your birth, William. He cursed you, an infant in your crib, saying you would destroy the House of Bellême.'

William is now in full control, everyone hanging on his next words. He looks round the room, focusing on each person in turn, everyone watching him. 'What good fortune it is that we have fortified the castles of William Talvas de Bellême, with his full support, and now have the confidence to reduce our garrisons to just a few men. Let us go to the table and put an end to this subject. No more of it!' I see Count Roger de Montgomery pull his wife aside and what he says to her is not amicable, judging by his angry expression which stands in strong contrast to his usual jolly demeanour.

Despite an excellent Supper of suckling pig and accoutrements, just like William and my first meal here, this is not a relaxed or enjoyable occasion. It is obvious that the men wish to eat heartily and quickly and depart as soon as possible to William's conference room to drink, discuss today's Chase and plan the next Chase on Monday. I know they must be exhausted, especially after the recent events, but I am not prepared to put up with this. It is their duty to show consideration for us ladies and respect the traditions of courtly etiquette. As I announce the musical entertainment for the evening, I see the men's faces, eager with anticipation of detailed discussion of today's Chase, now contort with disappointment. William shows signs of thunderous rage, forgetting it was he who organised musicians to come and visit me. Now seeing my expression, he smiles broadly, putting out his hands, palms up in a gesture of resignation. I smile at him as I bang the gong for the servants to clear the table.

Monks from St George's Abbey Boscherville enter the Hall and prepare to play for us. The men shudder at the discordant squeaks of their tuning up, but the ladies appear delighted at the prospect of music or in fact anything in place of another bout of female point-scoring. I note Dame Mabel looks even more miserable than the men. The music is lively and the men tap their fingers to the rhythm. Although I am enjoying it, I feel my eyes beginning to flicker and realise I am tired. Today has been a challenge. After half an hour or so, William goes to speak to the musicians and they prepare to play their final piece of the evening. The holy brothers play softly now and sing a Gregorian chant, manna to the soul, which should put us all in a positive mood for tomorrow, the Sabbath.

William is particularly loving to me as we lie together in my bed. Between kisses, he whispers, 'Do you know what a wonderful wife you are?'

'Shush, if you keep calling me that, you'll say it in front of the others!'

'Of course, I won't. How's our baby?'

'He needs to sleep now and so do I.'

'See you both in the morning then.' He is asleep immediately and I hear the gentle rasp of his snoring, which reassures me he is alive, but not loud enough to keep me from falling asleep too.

After Mass, we have a quiet day being the Sabbath. A riding party goes out in the afternoon and the Countesses Arlette and Adeline stay behind, saying they prefer to do a little walking after Dinner. It's clear that they know each other well, Conteville and Beaumont-le-Roger being only thirty miles apart. Adeliza and I enjoy a gentle ride accompanied by the grooms while the men challenge each other to races, all the while betting on the outcomes. Most unholy behaviour on the Sabbath! Dame Mabel is determined to gallop with the men and she is certainly strong considering her slight frame. As you would expect she is ferociously determined to keep up while the men strive to leave her behind.

We all attend the abbey's chapel in the early evening where we are soothed by the holy brothers singing Vespers. After a light Supper, the men depart to their own devices. Dame Mabel pleads fatigue and retires to her chamber and we ladies do our embroidery and talk quietly about ourselves. Countess Arlette talks about her expected grandson as if she is carrying him herself. She tells them that he is already moving strongly. The other ladies smile at me sympathetically. We hear about Countess Adeline's sons by her first husband William Mauduit, who are now ten and eight years old. Their younger brothers are three and two years. So, she married after these last two births as did Dame Mabel after bearing three children. Adeliza is yet to marry and give birth.

William and I have more energy tonight and our coupling is exciting like our first time. He is in a good mood considering everything and teases me about being fat. We sleep well and wake, feeling ready to cope with another day of guests in the palace. William tells me that he and the other men have business to discuss this morning. After Dinner, they will go to the Chase and return on Saturday, about seven o'clock. He asks what are we ladies doing? I tell him I have ordered the big carriage to take us to Abbey of Jumièges at Rouen where a monk called William will receive us and provide simple refreshment. He asks if I know this man and I say I do not, but Abbot John has arranged this hospitality. William asks if the Abbot refers to him as 'William of Jumièges' and when I say yes, he tells me is a much-respected person of great learning. He asks what I have done to have I done to have received this rare invitation? I tell him I do not know and will report back this evening. He says to note we will be served Dinner at three o'clock in the priory so we should break our fast more substantially than usual.

Dame Mabel declines the outing as she has had an urgent request to return home where her two young sons have a fever. She will travel in her carriage, her bodyguards ensuring her safe passage. One of her castle servants from Saint-Germaine-de-Montgomery left at daybreak to bring Count Roger's horse for him to ride home when he's ready. I am concerned,

'I do hope you find your children recovered when you get back.'

'Oh, they're strong, but only five and seven years old, and they are calling for their mother. Their elder sister seems all right.'

'Of course, you must go. I quite understand. Please let us know how they are.' So off she goes and the whole palace seems to relax in her absence. Are her children really ill? Count Roger does not appear to be worried and is his jolly self as he contemplates a few days without his rat-wife. The day looks brighter already.

We remaining four ladies travel to Jumièges. The Countesses Arlette and Adeline sit on one banquette and Adeliza and I on the other. I feel there is something bothering Adeliza and perhaps she will confide in me when we are on our own. Now that Dame Mabel has gone, the ladies tell me lurid stories about her family. She is her father's sole heiress because her elder brother Arnoul is dead, strangled in his bed. Was she responsible, the ladies wonder? At this titbit, Adeliza becomes visibly upset. What is the matter? I'll find out later.

We find William of Jumièges to be a wonderful host and a great gossip. Word of Dame Mabel's spat with me has no doubt reached him already. He declares that the Talvas family has a reputation of cunning and cruelty and that the worst of the four brothers in the elder generation is Dame Mabel's father, William, who had his first wife murdered on her way to church. Must be inherited, I think privately. Our Dinner is vegetable soup, bread, cheese and fruit, all from the abbey kitchen garden. William tells me that Robert, one of the first abbots, was a close companion of King Edward of England who spent his formative years exiled in Normandy. No doubt he knows that my father continues to host King Edward's enemies so I manage to divert him from this awkward topic. He says he would be pleased to visit me at Fécamp to which I agree with decorous enthusiasm. However, he should not expect me to give him inside knowledge of state affairs. I shall be careful what I say. Yet, he may well relate news of advantage to us. He is also good company. As we leave, he asks me if I know that three years ago Count William founded Lyre Abbey in the department of Eure. I tell him I did not know that and I shall be asking the Count to tell me about it when I next see him. I see this exchange pleases Adeliza who looks more cheerful.

After a tour of the peaceful chapel and gardens, we travel back to find Count Herluin and his sons, Odo and Robert have arrived at Fécamp. William has unexpectedly invited to them to join Countess Arlette and stay for two nights because he has some importance business to attend to which requires their presence. How mysterious! William and his loyal counts turn up on time and have had the best Chase they can remember, putting them all in a very good temper. Supper is a relaxed occasion with a sumptuous range of dishes before us. The Chase has been productive with hare, pigeon and rabbit in the bag although not the elusive hart they really wanted. The Beaumonts are leaving tomorrow and after making a detour to escort his wife home, Count Roger will go on to Rouen because it seems that the new military operations are to be managed from there rather than from Falaise. Roger de Montgomery is to stay here and then go with William to Rouen. I consider what may be the next military operation and decide because of the comparative proximity to Rouen that the next target is Brionne and ousting of that dreadful Guy of Burgundy.

Adeliza is also to stay for a few more days while Count William is busy here with state affairs. William's young brothers are to help out on the Estate in the morning and join the Chase in the afternoon. Odo, a serious boy of thirteen years, asks to go to the abbey to help the monks.

Robert, younger by two years, asks if he could work in the stables. William agrees to their requests. Both look a bit like William, but as neither has the big stature gene of Rollo the Viking, they will not grow as tall and wide as their elder brother.

Who will our baby resemble? William is so big and I so small so will he be middle-sized, red or fair hair? I am not showing much yet so perhaps he is small like me. Or, he's a girl. God knows, but I pray for a son and heir.

It's all bustle this morning after Mass as some of our guests prepare to depart. Before they go, we have light refreshments in the Hall. Countess Arlette fusses over William and makes sure everyone knows it's his birth time of year. William, restless with embarrassment, remembers he has asked his groom to look at Rollo's hooves this morning and departs rapidly. His mother is undaunted. *She* has a son of twenty-one years! Can we believe it? No, it can't be true, we chorus dutifully. She tells me she will visit again soon. She wants to make quite sure I am well and looking after myself. Anything to get away from a household of young children, I think. We wave good-bye to our departing guests, noting there's quite a party setting off with all the servants and bodyguards. Countess Arlette retires to her chamber, saying she will have a quiet day in bed.

Adeliza and I have the day to ourselves and plan a gentle ride this afternoon. Meanwhile, we sit outside, protected from the hot sun by the shade of an apple tree. The servants bring us some cool drinks and we chat comfortably. I waste no time in asking her why she was so particularly upset when the subject of Dame Mabel's elder brother being strangled in his bed; a horrible subject of course. Adeliza pauses and takes a deep breath.

'It reminded me how William has never got over the dreadful death of his father, Osbern, murdered in his bed. Of course, you know all about this because Osbern was your William's steward and guardian. My William didn't witness it first-hand like your William, but he still won't discuss how he feels about it. In fact, he finds it hard to talk about what he feels about anything.'

'It's distressing to see someone you love suffering and frustrating when they won't let you help.'

'It certainly is. You seem to understand.'

'I certainly do, and I can tell you that my William is also still traumatised by this same event. He did tell me about it, but then started to get angry, which I find hard to deal with.'

'My William doesn't show anger; he just gets silent and miserable.'

'Don't you think men are brought up to be strong and not show what they feel like, and we ladies have to work on them a little bit?' She laughs which briefly lightens her mood, but then she suddenly bursts out, 'I see how you and your William look at each other and I don't think that's ever going to happen to me.' She looks at me beseechingly, her eyes filling with tears.

'Your William is incredibly proud of you. When he talks about you, I can tell he loves you very much.'

'Why doesn't he tell me that?'

'Some people just can't I suppose. They are not used to talking like that, especially men.'

'Do you think he ever will?'

'Well, one thing I can tell you is that when he finds out he is to be a father, he will begin to change.'

'Is that what happened to you?'

'Yes, as soon as William knew about our baby, he began to show a much softer side. It will happen to you, so don't you worry.' This is a white lie as he was gentle and loving to me before he knew about the baby; Mother Mary, forgive me, but the poor girl needs my support.

'I just hope I'm blessed soon. Pray for me won't you. And please pray for my William too because he doesn't seem to be interested in anything but battles and land. You do understand what I am saying don't you?'

'I do and I will pray for both of you. Is there anything else on your mind?'

'Well, since we are talking frankly, there's another matter connected with the murder of his father Osbern.'

'Go on.'

‘Well, the murderer was Roger de Montgomery’s elder brother William! I thought you should know.’

‘I didn’t expect *that*. So, what happened to him?’

‘He’s dead now, murdered by someone else, but the whole matter is not forgotten and lurks in the background which must be embarrassing for Count Roger. Sorry to bring up such a depressing subject. Shall we take a walk?’

As Adeliza and I take our parasols and venture into the sunshine, I am wondering what other scandalous history is going to emerge. Surely the murder of a person in his own bed is a rare occurrence yet it has happened twice within our close circle. The two victims were William FitzOsbern’s father and Dame Mabel’s brother. One murderer was Roger de Montgomery’s brother and the other murder was likely to have been organised by Dame Mabel herself. I don’t want to believe that the Montgomery family has the same wicked streak as the Talvas family. I’ll keep these thoughts to myself.

We bid fond farewells to the FitzOsberns the next morning. They are going home to Breteuil which is a day’s journey from Rouen so Count William can help to oversee operations from there. I shall pray that Adeliza will somehow get her man to be more interested in coupling to improve her chances of bearing a child. She must be so sad and lonely. Talking of that, I’ve got William to myself at last, but for how long I don’t know! His brothers, Odo and Robert, are still with us, but I haven’t seen them since William asked them to come and introduce themselves to our remaining guests. They only eat with us if invited so I have asked them to Supper tonight. What has given me much pleasurable anticipation is the arrival of Beatrice who is coming to stay next week.

William seems quite relaxed at Dinner and we plan to go riding this afternoon. I tell him it had better be a good one as I don’t see myself on the forest floor in a bag when autumn comes and I will be rounder than ever. He says he’s sure he will manage his son perched on his belly and it will show him, down there in the womb, how to be an active husband when he grows up. We laugh and he honks with glee. I see that the way to keep him relaxed and happy is to be continually with child. Our outing is everything I could want. I’m surprised at the passion I feel in my present state. We agree our son approves his active parents. We laugh a lot and tease each other and couple again before falling asleep only to wake when an owl calls. We are reminded of approaching evening and Supper when we not only have Count Herluin and Countess Arlette still with us, but also William's brothers who are waiting to hear what William has got to say to them. William tells me that Abbot John will also join us. He does not say why and I am pleased he is coming because he makes things so easy. We pack up in a hurry and canter home at a pace. On return, we find Raoul has turned up since most of the military have left Falaise for a break after the recent military operation. He would like to stay if convenient and escort Robert to Falaise when he leaves us. We find him a well-mannered, thoughtful young man, very much like Count Herluin, and consider he is a good influence on his teen-age step-brothers.

CHAPTER 6

NEW APPOINTMENTS

Fécamp Palace, August 1049

When we go to the Hall before Supper, Abbot John is waiting for us and is as delightful as ever. He greets Raoul, asking him about himself and listening to what he has to say. Count Herluin and Countess Arlette are gracious, obviously anticipating good news from William. Odo and Robert greet him dutifully and look suitably reverent as he says Grace before we eat. They are on their best behaviour at Supper. Both resemble William in character being fond of the Chase and are presently absorbed in the details of battle strategy. They are proud to have been invited to William's July gathering of barons and knights to celebrate their brother reaching his majority. They relate their knowledge of the military operations at Domfront and Alençon castles. Yes, they did meet William de Talvas and his daughter Dame Mabel de Bellême who came to inspect the new and unwelcome garrisons at their castles. It's clear that Dame Mabel's plans were never to go home to tend to her sickly children, but to go straight from here to her father's domain. The boys seem to have found her rather overpowering. Did she know who they were? Oh yes, she knew exactly who they were, and she used all sorts of persuasive tactics to get them to reveal details of Duke William's next military operations. They deflected her questions to the senior marshals as ordered.

William tells his brothers he is satisfied with their military progress and sensible conduct. He has plans for their future which he will announce shortly. They are obviously flattered, but like so many young men of their age, unable to manage anything beyond a muffled grunt towards appreciation. I find Robert an easier personality than his elder brother Odo who, like my brother Robert, shows a highly competitive streak. At only thirteen years of age, Odo already has a doubtful reputation here at Fécamp. Megina caught him pinning a young servant girl against the wall, about to molest her. I also hear he drinks too much ale although not in front of William who strongly disapproves of such excess. So, what is his reason for choosing to spend all his time here in the abbey? Is it because monks at all levels are founts of local, national and even international information and share a love of gossip? Does ambitious Odo see them as useful to him in the sort of position he would like to hold in William's Dukedom? It's a mature reasoning for a young man of thirteen years and I wonder what's behind it. I am startled out of these thoughts when William stands and invites us to the Hall to hear the important news. The Count and Countess, Raoul and I settle in four seats facing the high back wall decorated with red and gold Arms of Normandy. Forward on our right stand William and Abbot John and, facing them, forward left, Odo and Robert stand side-by-side. A large bible is placed on a table.

The scene is set, the drama about to unfold. Abbot John, wearing a pectoral cross with a heavy silver chain, holds a large bible. William asks Odo to stand and move forward to face him.

'Odo of Conteville, my brother, I appoint you to the Holy Order of Bishop of Bayeux, as witnessed by all present.' Abbot John puts his hands on Odo's head and blesses him with the words *typos tou Patros*: 'he is like the living image of God the Father'.' William continues. 'Abbot John will oversee your induction as a cleric of the Holy Mother Church here in Fécamp Abbey.' It is a moving occasion and Odo is uncharacteristically humble and grateful for this honour. I wonder how much is genuine. Can this lustful youth change his ways?

It's Robert's turn now and he stands before William.

'Robert of Conteville, my brother, I appoint you Count of Mortain, as witnessed by all present.' Abbot John picks up the bible.

‘Robert, I bid you kneel before Duke William. Duke William, I bid you repeat after me, “Robert of Conteville, I appoint you Count of Mortain”.’ William steps forward. ‘Robert of Conteville, I appoint you Count of Mortain.’ Abbot John continues, ‘Robert of Conteville, I bid you stand and repeat after me, ‘“I become your man”.’ Robert complies. Abbot John hands the bible to Robert. ‘Take this bible, put your hand upon it and repeat after me, “I promise to remain faithful to you for the rest of my life”.’ Robert complies, ‘I promise to remain faithful to you for the rest of my life.’ Abbot John steps back and William addresses Robert. ‘From now, you will live at Falaise Castle with the support of Count Roger de Montgomery who lives a half-day ride from Falaise.’ It’s hard to tell whether Robert is more pleased about becoming a count or by his new life in the Montgomery household.

This done, the boys are established in high-ranking positions in William’s Dukedom. We are all delighted and sit together talking happily about these new and exciting circumstances within the family. I watch Raoul while all this is going on and if he feels left out or envious of his brothers, he does not show it, instead congratulating them with the usual male slap on the back. The next morning, Abbot John says prayers for them at Mass and after light refreshments, we bid the Contevilles a fond farewell. After collecting their belongings, Odo is to return and go straight into the abbey and Robert will come with him and stay with us for a few days’ holiday. He is delighted Raoul will still be here and they make plans to go riding before returning to Falaise together. There is no respite from continual visitors as now Beatrice arrives. I am pleased to see her and relax in her company. William is back and forth to Rouen where he is making plans to stamp his authority on his new Dukedom. He will sort out the resistant barons whatever it takes.

Our visitors leave and I decide it’s time to have a serious talk with William. I ask for a formal appointment in his office after Mass tomorrow. He tells me I don’t need to do that; we can just have a chat any time. I say, no, it is to be formal, a business discussion. No time like the present he says. In his office I start the proceedings.

‘Who do you rate as your closest ally and most loyal subject?’

'William FitzOsbern', he says without hesitation, 'followed closely by the two Rogers.'

'Are you not forgetting someone?' He looks puzzled.

'Who?'

'Me!'

'You?'

'Yes, me. Think about it. I have no other agenda except to support you. No other family takes my energies. I am well qualified in matters of state, economic, military and political, having been my father's confidant and adviser for many years. Apart from being Duchess of Normandy, I have no formal involvement in state matters so I can observe, gather information and give objective as well as personal advice which could be of help to you. Being a woman, men confide things to me that they should not because they perceive me as either too ignorant to know their significance or too uninterested to pass them on.'

'I would welcome your involvement, but you have so much to do already that I feel it's not fair to worry you with the challenges facing me. However, it is clear that you are strong, not like a woman at all, which I saw in your practical approach regarding the blockade of Flanders. And as for your handling of Dame Mabel and all our guests, that was a lesson in diplomacy!'

'Thank you and never forget, your problems are my problems and we should share them and work together with your senior councillors to solve them. First, is your present military operation the siege of Brionne Castle to oust your cousin Guy?'

'It is and proving a challenge because it is so heavily fortified with its surrounding stone keep and deep moat.'

'What is your plan?'

'Build a number of siege castles to encircle it and prevent supplies getting in, but this will take time and a large work force to accomplish. It is our present military operation.'

'I do hope the Abbey of Bec is far enough away from these siege towers and inevitable warfare?'

'It is and Abbot Herluin, another of my relations, not to be confused with Herluin of Conteville, continues to make it one of our most respected abbeys, largely because of its famous school run by Prior Lanfranc. Have you heard of him? He is an authority on religion and my spiritual advisor when I have time to see him.'

'I am pleased to hear that and that Bec Abbey is not in danger. What a relief! Now another matter, you know that Pope Leo is attending Uncle Henry's Great Council in Rheims as we speak?'

'I do and I know that there has been competition between the two of them about whose meeting it is. The Pope has ordered the bishops to attend with the threat of excommunication if they do not. King Henry has ordered his barons to attend. Each has a different agenda. They won't be able to get all these people into the same hall at once. It will be chaos!'

'Do you think either agenda includes any reference to you?'

'When I heard about this meeting, I thought there would be discussion about the implications of my new status as Duke of Normandy. My name would also be connected with the recent blockade of Flanders because of my betrothal to you, Count Baldwin's daughter. I have made sure that my Norman bishops attend the meeting. I have sent Prior Lanfranc as well as a contingent of bishops from here to report back to me.'

'You are so wise in doing this because news of your magnificent celebrations with your barons will be spread abroad. King Henry of the Franks and Emperor Henry of Germany will expect you to take an increasingly forceful role as Duke of Normandy. This will not only involve consolidating your Norman territory by challenging rebellious barons to submit to you, but also you will seek new alliances and look to take land beyond your borders.'

'You really do know what's going on so what else do you know about this council?'

'Pope Leo is a wealthy and well-connected German lord, eager to be generous after what it took to be appointed Pope by Henry, Emperor of Germany. Forgive me Mother Mary for my disrespect to the Holy Father by declaring him to be a man so grateful for this honour that he will now do whatever the Emperor asks of him. We must pray that Pope Leo seeks spiritual guidance in considering secular decisions. This papacy will demand resilience and scholarship of its new incumbent which may bring welcome change in established religious practice or cause conflict through his ignorance of this practice. I really feel for him!

Going back to the Emperor, consider his issues with you. He attacked Flanders in revenge for my father's past attacks on his domain, but he also seeks to prevent you and my father making a treaty giving you access not only to the coast of Flanders, but also his own borders. Pope Leo will soon find out you have just appointed your brother Odo as Bishop of Bayeux and that it was Abbot John who officiated and not Archbishop Mauger of Rouen, head of our diocese, your cousin and enemy. Uncle Henry will also see you as a threat, acting like a King in appointing your brother Robert as Count of Mortain. And of course, in doing that you dismissed William Werlenc, another of your cousins to add to the list of hostile relations. Your enemies have gathered at this council and will be seeking any opportunity to get rid of you by fair means or foul and at least weaken your power.'

'Of course, you are right. I feel we can at least rely on Abbot John's support and seek the advice of Prior Lanfranc when he returns.'

'I don't know about Prior Lanfranc, but I do think we need to be careful about Abbot John because when he was Abbot of Saint Bénigne in Burgundy, he was close to Emperor Henry and his wife. Your cousin Guy comes from Burgundy too and we do not know where Abbot John's true loyalties lie. Although we are fond of him, we should remember he lives here beside us and be aware he could be passing on information which would not help our cause.'

'Please consider yourself my closest ally and most loyal subject as well as my beloved wife.' He pulls me to him and gives me a hug. We are all right. As the days pass, I grow bigger, but not obviously pregnant, which is odd considering my small size. Perhaps the baby is small. Oh no! Mother Mary, please grant me a son.

After our guests departed last week, I was hoping to have some time to myself, but William is eager for me to accompany him to Falaise so that I can see his place of birth and childhood home. He says we should go now before I become too uncomfortable to travel. He slips in the fact that a large number of his barons are gathering at Falaise to continue celebrating his Majority. While they are there, he wants to plan the next phase of military strategy. Clearly, I am not invited to take part, his recent enthusiasm for my involvement forgotten or shelved. I will ignore it this time and, trying not to put on a martyred face, say how much I welcome the opportunity of meeting his barons. These men are wealthy landowners and William's loyal companions, but not close friends like Count William and the two Count Rogers. Will I really be needed hanging about round this male conclave of some importance? Surely it's the wrong time to plan all this and go away when we need to know what has happened at the Great Council meeting. Oh well, I suppose we will get news at Falaise just as easily as at Fécamp. I am really quite tired, but it is my duty to accompany my husband.

CHAPTER 7

THE BAN

September 1049

It is about a hundred miles from Fécamp to Falaise and although the road is better than some in Normandy, the carriage ride is bumpy at times. I ride Galathea for some of the way as I find a gentle trot or canter more relaxing than being jolted along in the carriage. Megina accompanies me and probably a good thing she does not ride as she is so big at this stage, looking as if she is to have her baby at any time. If she were not so strong, she would be struggling with the journey. William rides all the way alongside our grooms and a posse of Fécamp soldiers.

'There it is!' William cries out, his joy making me realise what it means to him that I've come here at last! It's easy to be enthusiastic about Falaise Castle, imposingly built on a rocky crag, its stones reflecting the late afternoon sunlight. It is much smaller than I expected, but in the surrounding fields below the rocks there is a large yard and many outbuildings which serve its current main function of being the head-quarters of William's defence forces in the South. William takes great delight in showing me round and telling me stories of what he did here and what happened there. I dare not tell him what I really think of the inside which bears witness to it being a garrison. It is not dirty, but shabby and uncared for which is understandable considering the number of soldiers who sleep and eat here. I do think William might have made more effort to get some cleaning done and provide a few refinements to make life more bearable for its occupants. Even our quarters, the best chambers, are basic and the beds and furnishings, although bearing the red and gold of the Arms of Normandy, are faded relics of this once superior ancestral home of the Dukes of Normandy. William tells me his mother has never returned since she married Count Herluin which is just as well as she would be dismayed to see it like this.

We have a simple supper brought by men clearly used to feeding an army rather than attending the table of nobility. There is no butler or proper service, but they do their best to please. We eat the stodgy food, but I cannot manage much as the portions are a fighting soldier's size. William is sorry he will not be able to show me round tomorrow as he has a summons from Bellême to sort out another grievance by Dame Mabel. That ghastly woman is probably making it up, but as her domain is vulnerable to attack, I suppose he has to go. Nor is this going to be a relaxing evening as he is defensive about the castle, now seeing it through my eyes. As I take out my embroidery to calm myself, he rushes out saying he has to send an urgent message. When he returns, he is much happier, especially when I tell him his son is excited by the idea of being a soldier. He knows he's in his ancestral home by kicking me hard and when William puts his hand down to feel the kicks, he laughs which clears the tense atmosphere between us. We both sleep surprisingly well after a good coupling spurred on by frequent kicks from our son. William got a particularly good prod which gave him great joy. He declared the baby has big feet, which means he will be tall like his father.

When I wake, he is already gone and Megina is here with my breakfast. She says we can go to Mass later. At least Falaise Castle has a chapel. I ask her to accompany me on a walk round the castle grounds about ten o'clock as I have nothing to do and no-one else to talk to. She says a walk at about eleven o'clock would suit her well. Being used to her dropping everything to put me first, I am about to speak, but looking at her resolute expression, decide to say nothing. What *is* going on?

Just before eleven, there is a gentle knock on my door and Megina, smiling broadly, tells me I have visitors in the Hall. And it's Adeliza! What a relief! She has brought her maid, who she introduces as Berthildis. I can't wait to find out why she has suddenly come here!

Leaving our maids to get to know each other, we ladies relax in the Hall and the servants bring us refreshment. Adeliza tells me she received William's urgent message last night, asking her to come and rescue me from his shabby castle full of soldiers. This is excellent news and thoughtful of William although it also solves a problem for him as he cannot spend time with me due to his big celebration tonight and his military commitments. I'm clearly in the way so Adeliza and I will go back to Fécamp. Our home-bound party will travel after Mass the day after tomorrow. Count William will return with us with our servants and bodyguards both from home and Breteuil. I just hope that suits both the FitzOsberns.

I return to my chamber to rest while Adeliza settles in giving me time to contemplate the next phase of our lives. I think about William and me and realise the great differences between us are unimportant in our relationship. He is illiterate and although a duke, is more like a basic soldier, unrefined in many ways. He has leadership and organisational skills, ambition and ruthless determination whereas my learning, knowledge and skills are in quite different fields. Others will value one more than the other, some will question how we are suited, but what matters is that William and I respect each other. I appreciate William's skills and knowledge in his field and recognise I am married to a powerful man. His strength of body and character continue to attract me despite that extraordinary assault on my person at Lille. Of course, this attraction was so strong I decided to marry him, not that I had much choice of suitors at the time. I must have been out of my mind! Yet, what could have been a disaster turned out to be anything but and I could have never foreseen how perfect a match he would be for me. As soon as he came to see me at Bruges Palace, I saw the thoughtful, sensitive side of him. I found him humble, gentle and kind, belying his reputation as a brute.

Since then, I have had no cause to think differently, but accept that that retaining and extending his dukedom may require tough, even brutal action. I refuse to dwell on this and instead reflect on how much I enjoy his companionship and the fact we can laugh together. I've never had a true friend before William and we are passionate about each other. I shall miss him sorely in my bed these next days or even weeks, although the time will pass quickly and pleasantly in Adeliza's company. Yet, whatever I say or think, I know that hovering over everything in our lives is the impending birth of our child. I keep saying it's a boy, but I know I should not be raising William's hopes. Mother Mary, hear my prayers.

William is back and I was right. Dame Mabel had nothing of consequence to report, her real motive being to persuade William that her father's co-operation over the defences of his castles deserved promotion to rank of Count. He endured her simpering and ingratiating manner for long enough before thanking her for her hospitality and leaving promptly.

Adeliza and I try to go walking, but as men are pouring into the castle, our excursions are limited. The barons gather for the Celebration and their knights and foot soldiers muster for some military practice outside. We are served both Dinner and Supper in our chambers which is thoughtful as the servants have so much to do for all these men. We hear the festivities start in the Hall with speeches, loud cheering, roaring, stamping and, no doubt, drinking of much ale. William will be encouraged by their enthusiastic support. There will be no chance for me to meet any of these men before we leave and that's just as well as they will not be fit to see us in the morning. I doubt if William has overindulged but he does not come to my chamber, retiring at a late hour I expect.

The next day, Adeliza and I go for a carriage ride round the countryside and then prepare to return to Fécamp tomorrow. In the evening William comes to find me in my chamber. Something has happened. He looks awful, his face white and tense. Bad news has come from Rheims. Pope Leo has banned our marriage, citing consanguinity. I am speechless but suddenly realise we should have expected this.

'*Are* we related, the same blood in our veins?' asks William, misery etching his face.

'No, we are not related and we do not have the same blood in our veins, but we are connected. Your great-grandfather, Duke Richard I, married my great-aunt, Emma of Francia. As there were no children of the marriage, there is no consanguinity in our blood from them. My mother was betrothed as a young child to your uncle, Duke Richard III of Normandy, but as he died before any marriage or consummation took place, no children were born so any consanguinity in our blood is impossible. My father is the son of Count Baldwin IV and his first wife Ogive. When she died, he married your Aunt Eleanor of Normandy and they had one child, my Aunt and dear friend Judith of Flanders. No consanguinity in our blood from them.'

'No other they can drum up?'

'Not that I can find and I did quite a lot of work on the subject when Uncle Henry made that remark on hearing of our Betrothal.'

'It seems that everyone is my enemy, even the Pope.'

'That is not so! Look at all the loyal barons who are here now celebrating your coming-of-age. Their number far exceeds his Great Council, filled by those who, threatened by your position, seek every opportunity to diminish your increasing status and power. Pope Leo knows nothing of our background, rather followed the advice of his patron Emperor Henry of Germany and your arch-enemy, your Uncle Mauger, Archbishop of Rouen. Nor was it in Uncle Henry's interest to do anything to stop them. If they swore in God's name that consanguinity is in our family, Pope Leo had no option but to ban our marriage.'

'Is this still about my right to be Duke of Normandy as a bastard?'

'Never question your right to be Duke of Normandy! Your father, Duke Robert, swore an oath to name you his heir before going on that fateful crusade. You are Duke of Normandy by birth right and by legal decree and it is now your duty to rule Normandy and seek every advantage for your people by settling your barons, and establishing your borders.'

'How do we respond to the Ban?'

'We acknowledge the Ban to our marriage by his Holiness Pope Leo IX and we pray for grace to accept it with humility. We would be grateful to know exactly where consanguinity took place within our families so no future members may make marriage decisions in ignorance of the will of the Mother Church.'

'That *is* diplomatic!'

'I also think that you and I should pray for the Pope's enlightenment and do penance to satisfy everyone including ourselves that we respect the laws of our land and the Church.'

'What would I do without you?'

'Well, fortunately you don't have to because we are in this together.'

'Listen Matilda, we have a problem. The Pope has banned our marriage!'

'Indeed, but the timing of this ban makes me wonder if the knowledge of our secret marriage in Bruges has somehow got through to your main opponents with influence on the Pope. If it has, they will realise their plans to get rid of you are seriously compromised because your alliance with Flanders is already established. To retrieve the upper hand, they would hope this ban will not only negate our secret marriage, but also prevent a formal state marriage. Most people don't mean to tell a secret, but sometimes it only takes a glance or a pause to hint at the truth. And it may not be just your opponents. Those who know your mother see her being completely happy about our expected child and the obvious reason comes into their minds! So, what do we do about our proposed State Marriage next month?'

'We shall have a State Marriage, but not next month. We will wait for the right time. Now we will take the news of this ban quietly and submissively, but send envoys to the Pope with the details you have outlined above to try and change his mind. Anyway, in a few months it will probably be less of a major issue.'

'Pretty diplomatic yourself, aren't you?'

'Just learning from the best diplomat I know!' We retire and are comforted by our coupling and thoughts of our baby before falling heavily asleep. However, this doesn't last as we are both restless in the night, our brains overburdened with recent events. I've got to keep William positive as I worry that he will become downcast without me.

He is up early, off to see how the military operations are going. After Mass, as I am preparing to leave, he comes rushing back to say his men have been on the march since dawn. They are on their way to Rouen where they will be based for the siege of Brionne. So, this was the military operation being planned at Falaise. I should have guessed. It was a clever move as Guy of Burgundy would have heard if they had been assembling at Rouen and made extra fortifications to his castle. Count Roger de Montgomery has already left, leading the force to secure the outskirts of Brionne and oversee the building of the siege towers. William himself, riding Rollo, is about to leave with the mounted troops. I give thanks to Mother Mary because this campaign means he will be close to home and able to bed with me. He takes a few moments to update Count William FitzOsbern who is leading our party. He then bid us a safe journey and says I am not to worry if he does not come home tonight.

On the journey back, I have no energy to ride Galathea so Adeliza and I sit bumping along in the carriage, our conversation almost entirely about the Pope's ban on our marriage. Of course, Adeliza does not know we are already married and I wonder if we should now tell her and Count William the truth.

CHAPTER 8

AFTER THE BAN

October 1049

It's such a relief to be home! I'd been looking forward to some peace and quiet, but as soon as we enter the palace, I am handed a bundle of messages, all marked 'Urgent'. What has happened now? Mother Mary, protect us from more bad news. I should have guessed the senders. The first is from my parents giving support about the Ban and expressing dismay and confusion about consanguinity being the given reason. We are to keep them informed of any developments. They end by saying how relieved they are about our ceremony at the chapel at Bruges. The second, almost identical in its wording, is from William's mother. Countess Arlette also says she has sent me some dresses which should be arriving at the palace now. At the end of her message, like an unimportant afterthought, is the news that the Pope has also banned the marriage of William's sister Adelaide and Count Enguerrand of Ponthieu and the Count has been excommunicated. Whatever next? The third is from William of Jumièges, who wants to visit as soon as possible. He cannot bear to be left out of anything which is true to his character and I will respond later.

Now I see Abbot John scuttling across the yard, his usual cheerful face set in anxious lines. As the servant answers the door, Abbot John rushes forward.

'Your Grace, please, I must speak to you.' Oh, of course, this is how I am now addressed.

'Abbot John, I need to rest now. If you would like to come and see me for a short time after Supper at about half past eight, that would be fine. I don't think anything is going to change in the next hour or two.'

'I'm so sorry. I shouldn't have presumed. I would be honoured to see you at the time suggested.' Adeliza and I settle down to a quiet evening. We get a message to say our men will stay in Rouen tonight on military business, but will come back here tomorrow evening. Abbot John arrives promptly after Supper and Adeliza tactfully withdraws.

'Abbot John, please come and sit down. May I offer you a drink?'

'No thank you. Your Grace, I've come to say how sorry I am that you and Duke William suffer this Papal Ban to your marriage. It must be so distressing considering all.'

'Thank you for your concern. It would be more distressing if there *were* any consanguinity in our family. You know me well enough now to understand that I have thoroughly examined the facts and conclude there is none.'

'Then can you not arrange for these facts to be presented to His Holiness?'

'We are doing that, and we are also responding to the Ban with respect and acceptance, realising there may be other issues prompting the Pope's edict.'

'All right, I'll come to the real reason why I wanted to see you. I expect you know that in my youth I was in the household of Emperor Henry, King of Germany?'

'I do.' What can it be? I see he's shaking.

'As we both know, the Pope was not in holy orders before Emperor Henry appointed him to the highest position in the Church. This was not unusual, but we did not expect this wealthy lord to take up his ministry with such eagerness. His Holiness, like others who give up one life to take another, is zealous in promoting the strictest tenets of the Mother Church. At first, we clergy gave thanks to God for finding one whose hidden calling emerged through an unpromising, but not unknown channel. Now some of our clerical brothers are dismayed because he is suggesting radical change, for example insisting on celibacy for bishops and dismissal of those who bought their offices. Bishops who failed to attend his recent gathering at Rheims have been excommunicated. He brooks no questioning of his reforms and Emperor Henry is content to stay out of battles on the religious front as long as he gets the Pope's support for his own objectives. Put simply, Emperor Henry does not want Duke William to have rights in Flanders through marriage to the daughter of his old enemy. He wants to keep control over Flanders as we have seen in his last military campaign. He also sees Duke William's increasing power as a threat to his own domain.'

'William and I have come to the same conclusion and feel that whatever evidence we present, the Pope will continue to insist that consanguinity is present and be implacable on the subject of our marriage.'

'Ah, your marriage. I'm now getting to the root of the reason for wanting to see you because I have to tell you that I know you are already married.'

'I am not surprised and I'm afraid we did suspect that it was you who relayed this information to Emperor Henry prompting this sudden and unexpected ban.'

'It was not me and I am sorry you thought that, but I can see why. I can assure you I have said absolutely nothing about it nor given any form of a hint to any person.'

'It is only known to our close family, sworn to keep it secret. So, who told you?'

'One of your close family who stayed here this summer.'

'Ah, I should have guessed!'

'The Countess of Conteville could not resist telling me and we both know why she is so pleased, given your blessed situation for which I give thanks to Mother Mary. Wonderful news!'

'Thank you and don't worry, she will not know you have told me. And I do hope we can rely on your total and continued support because Duke William is faced with a heavy task in uniting Normandy. His enemies are determined to make things difficult for him and would kill him at any opportunity.'

'Indeed. I gather the present military operation from Rouen is to oust Count Guy of Burgundy from his castle by siege?'

'Correct and it could take months if not years. He is firmly ensconced behind high fortress walls and can only be assailed from a high position. Siege towers are being constructed as we speak. Sometimes it seems that William has few really loyal friends beyond his immediate group of Counts FitzOsbern, Montgomery and Beaumont.'

'If it would help and if the Duke agrees, I could arrange for some more of his loyal barons to come here and meet you.'

'That would be excellent. I'll ask William when he returns tomorrow. Now, changing the subject, how is Odo getting on with his induction into Holy Orders as the new Bishop of Bayeux?'

'Odo has a lot to learn about the deportment of a bishop. He is a worldly young man much like many of our present bishops who are reluctant to forgo carnal pleasures like having concubines. I hear he is not impressed with the new Pope's views and must be wondering what he has got himself into!'

'I think ambition drives him and he will play the game. Let us pray that the high moral standards set by his parents and Duke William are a good influence on his future deportment. One more thing before you go and it's concerning the Ban; Duke William looks to Prior Lanfranc of Bec as a spiritual adviser, but is he the person we should ask to support our cause?'

'Lanfranc went to Rheims and is still there I hear. He is energised by the reformist zeal of Pope Leo and is said to be against your 'non-canonical' marriage. This could be the impediment of consanguinity or, if he knows you are already married, he may think the sacrament was not conducted properly within the Catholic Church.'

'Father Henryk will testify he conducted it properly in our chapel at Bruges Palace. We did this so that there was no possibility of a bastard child.'

'Forgive me asking, but why did you not take the path of celibacy followed by marriage?'

'We had both been through difficult times. I don't know how much you know about it. Our first encounter was unconventional to say the least, but through it we fell in love. Our ranks were entirely compatible and my father agreed to our Betrothal. We both had reasons for wanting to be together as soon as possible for mutual support. Duke William has suffered relentless challenge all his life, especially from his father's family and approaching his majority, we feared it would worsen. He needed a wife and help-meet and after my troubles, I needed a husband and protector. Due to Duke William's sensitivity about his bastard status, living together betrothed risked bearing a bastard child should Duke William be killed before we married. When Father Henryk suggested marriage, it was the perfect solution. Although the only people present at our marriage were the priests and my parents, it was the same sacrament as in the big state marriage we plan to have before long.'

'Perhaps by keeping it secret, some would think you had something to hide.'

'I see that, but we did not want to provoke inevitable political opposition until Duke William could secure more support among his barons. Now the news of our marriage has reached Emperor Henry and the Pope, their opposition is expected, but giving consanguinity as the reason for the Ban is a shock. Who will believe me when I say it's unsubstantiated?'

'Well bless you, my child. Thank you for being so open to me. One day Normandy will truly appreciate your strength and loyalty, all backed by your deep faith. I bid you good night and will call again any time you like. Just send a message.' Off he goes, such a good man and I thank Mother Mary he is on our side.

William returns and I tell him about my conversation with Abbot John. He is relieved to hear he is loyal to us, but disappointed that Prior Lanfranc is against our marriage. He will summon him tomorrow. While William approves Abbot John's suggestion that I should be introduced to some of his loyal barons, he says curtly that the arrangement should be the business of Count William FitzOsbern, not Abbot John. He's not in a good mood and I should have guessed why because I know that expression! We go straight to our chambers. We couple with great passion and again, both of us hungry for each other. I cannot begin to describe the pleasure of his great body and my light but fast-growing frame fastened with his, feels weightless and thrilling. William, feeling the baby's heels and fists against his skin, declares he's a good soldier already. As he says this, I ask Mother Mary to forgive me for going along with William's firm conviction that our child will be a boy. I know I should challenge him, but I hate upsetting my beloved husband when he is so happy. I speak silently to our baby, who may be a little girl fluttering inside me, and tell her I shall love her with all my heart. This reminds me, I must make arrangements for the local midwives to call on me to make sure they are prepared for the birth which is only a few weeks from now.

William summons Prior Lanfranc after Mass and reports an unsatisfactory response. The Prior refused to listen, insisting he must follow the Pope's edict and declare our marriage 'uncanonical'. So, he knew about our marriage? Oh yes and no-one is saying our ceremony in Bruges failed to conform to Catholic religious practice. He has taken his stance because he trusts His Holiness to know for certain that we're both descended from Rollo the Viking. Asked for the detail, the Prior was evasive, claiming that most of the top-ranking noble families can trace their antecedents to Rollo the Viking. So, what next? William looks at me, his face set with that determination I know so well; he tells me Lanfranc has until Noon tomorrow to provide the information that proves our marriage 'uncanonical'. If he does not, he is exiled forthwith.

I tell William he has done the right thing. I doubt we get a result in our favour for I suspect neither the Prior nor the Emperor has any knowledge of the complicated details of our respective family trees or any motivation to reverse the Ban. Pope Leo has no option but to believe what he is told. His papal agenda of religious reform compels him to act when told that the marital status of the Duke of Normandy fails one of its tenets. It's not a promising situation, but I do have an idea to put to William if Lanfranc is exiled and the status quo of the Ban is unaltered.

William goes back to Rouen, but Count William is still here and tells me he has a visitor for me after Dinner. Adeliza did not accompany me to Mass this morning pleading a headache. On return, I sit in the Hall to have a hot milky drink with bread and honey. Adeliza comes in looking pale. She doesn't feel well. I wonder! I hand her some bread and honey, but no butter and suggest she nibbles it. I give her a drink of light ale, little sips I tell her. I watch her colour returning. She would like another piece of bread. I say wait a little while. I ask her a few questions and she looks amazed. Mother Mary, let it be true that my dear friend is with child, blessed at last.

We discuss it all the morning and from what she tells me, there seems little doubt, but she needs to wait a week or two before telling the Count. Do I mind if she tells me a secret? Only if you're sure and it will go no further from me, I say. She smiles and confides that she decided to encourage her William by creeping into his chamber at night and slipping into his bed, telling him she was lonely without him and could he hold her. He seemed pleased, but was sleepy so she just slept beside him. Yet, when he woke, he was keen to couple, and this still happens every morning. Things are quite different now, she explains. It was just change of routine. What a relief! My prayers have been answered.

After Dinner which I eat on my own, Count William invites me to his office to introduce one of William's most trusted barons, Wigod of St Denis-le-Gast. He is quite old with white hair and twinkling eyes and I take to him immediately because he is warm and friendly without being obsequious or over-familiar. He is reassuringly loyal to William, praising him for his direct and fair approach to his Norman barons. The support for him at his Majority celebrations was strong and encouraging. He has no time for rebels who must be dealt with firmly. He has made the long journey to Rouen from his domain in the South to support, rather than take an active part in the present campaign. He asks me if I know about the Battle of Val-ès-Dunes two years ago.

'A famous victory indeed,' I say.

'And was it not your Uncle Henry, King of the Franks, who came to help him?' This Wigod may be old, but he is perceptive.

'Yes and his support much needed, but since then things have changed.' He nods and I see he knows what I mean.

'I mention that Battle because I continue to feel betrayed by my liege lords Hamon Dentatus and Grimault du Plessis, two of the leading rebels.'

'At least their betrayal was punished by death in the Battle!'

‘So, Your Grace, the rumours of your extensive knowledge of Norman affairs are true!’

‘I have a lot to learn, but thank you.’ I bid him farewell and off he goes, a good old boy. We need more like him.

I go for a rest and fall asleep, waking when I feel someone familiar stroking me gently and William slides in beside me. We kiss and hug each other each other, but I am dozy and about to fall asleep again when he puts me on my side so we lie face-to-face.

‘Lanfranc refuses to change his mind about the Ban so two of my men are escorting him to the border and into exile.’

‘Quite right, well done. Presumably, he’ll go straight to Emperor Henry’s court.’

‘I expect so. Matilda, what can we do about this?’

‘We wait. Soon, Lanfranc will tire of Pope Leo’s reforms and Emperor Henry’s political agenda. Neither man has the scholarship to engage in learned debate which is Lanfranc’s life-blood. Their plotting and conspiracies are far removed from his chosen academic and religious life. His students, his library and his research are all at Bec and he will become desperate to return to his peaceful priory.’

‘What do I say if he asks to return?’

‘Be firm. He is exiled until he agrees to examine the facts about consanguinity in our families. If you wish, I will put these facts before him and he will find no reason to reject them. He must swear on the Holy Bible to be loyal to you and promise to use his new knowledge to persuade the Pope to lift the Ban.’

‘If he refuses?’

‘He remains in Exile.’

‘Do you trust him?’

‘I do, he is a holy man.’

Poor William. He is so tired and so am I. We ask the Chamberlain to instruct Antoine to make us a simple Supper and serve it in our chambers and then we can have an early night. So that’s what we do.

The days pass peacefully, the last warmth and bright flowers of summer fading into the mellow days of autumn, with the satisfying feeling of all being safely gathered in. Adeliza and I doze in our chairs and take small walks. We both try on the beautiful dresses sent by Countess Arlette; one a pale pink faintly striped cotton with delicate lace insets round the bosom which suits Adeliza so much better than me. I don't like pink clothes or anything pink if I'm honest, but dare not risk upsetting the Countess by giving Adeliza the dress.

The day I have been dreading, the lying-in, cooped up in that horrid little room next to my chamber where I keep my clothes and do my toilet, is creeping nearer. The window will be closed and it is supposed to be quiet and peaceful like a womb. William is not supposed to see me let along 'fornicate' with me during this time. The Church forbids 'fornication' during a woman's bloodshed. It is impure, a sin. Since I shall not be in Menses, I do not believe we will be committing any sin by coupling, but we will have to be careful so that no servant sneaks on us to the clergy. Officially, only women can come to see me. Thank goodness Adeliza is still here for a while and Megina too. There's no lying-in for Megina for women of her class work until the birth. She will be back with me quickly. That's another thing. I have to wait, cooped up for about four weeks after the birth before I can be churched. I get the news that Countess Adeline has given birth to a daughter, named Aubreye which is a beautiful, unusual name. I send my love and say I hope she will visit me before too long. I suppose it all depends on how her confinement after the birth fits in with my own. I wish it was all over!

Now here's a surprise, Megina has had her baby in the night, a boy called Stefan! It dawns on me that our baby may not have been conceived on our wedding day in the forest as we liked to imagine. William and I often refer to the event with great joy, embedding the time of conception in our minds as a fact rather than a possibility. I do not discuss this thought with William.

CHAPTER 9

BEFORE THE BIRTH

Fécamp, November 1049

William is either back here or at least nearby all the time now, awaiting the birth. I have another week before entering the prison of the birthing-chamber. He will sleep in his chamber because he is not supposed to be with me at all and certainly not to couple. Only one week more of Mass. I say my prayers morning and evening and through the day, all of them for a son. I know that's unkind and if our daughter is born, I worry that she might feel unwanted. I thank Mother Mary that Adeliza is here to talk to. The men have gone to Rouen today, coming back this afternoon. As they left, William and I saw Count William give Adeliza a hug and more than a peck-like kiss as he said good-bye. William looked at me and lifted his eyebrows asking silently what that was about. Such a gesture is an unaccustomed behaviour in this gentleman whose courtesy to his Betrothed has always been so proper! I gave William a brief nod and I think he understood. So she's told him! Already!

Yes, she couldn't wait and he is delighted with her news. She's never seen him so joyful. We laugh when we realise that our conversations with the prospective fathers of our babies have been so similar. Both expect a son, but both say they will welcome a daughter, though her William said this through clenched teeth, remarks Adeliza with a chuckle. I am so pleased to have her company. We have much in common besides our age and circumstances for she is well educated and likes to discuss Art and Literature. It does not matter that History and

Politics are of no interest to her as my other regular visitor, Abbot John, engages in animated discussions about these. As he expands on the latest political topic, I find I know enough of the background to store knowledge and make connections which I do not always choose to share with him. I don't mean to be critical of Adeliza in making this comparison because she and I have further interests like playing music together, she on the harp and I the viol. The best thing is that I feel comfortable with her here. She's no effort.

The Second Steward comes into the Hall to say the midwives are here and is it convenient for them to see me. I agree and ask Adeliza to be present. Maria is the midwife in charge who William recently employed because she has experience of delivering the children of nobility. She exudes calm and is reassuringly stout, but not over stout with strong-looking forearms capable of work. Maria has two young women with her, Ava and Colette, who have helped deliver babies in their own families. I have seen them around and know that they live on our estate where their parents are employed. I invite Maria to sit down, but she says she prefers to stand. She asks about my health and I think she is the sort of person in whom I can have confidence, although I don't warm to her. She does not smile. She asks me who I have chosen to be the wet nurse waiting to take over the baby at birth and I tell her I haven't thought about this yet. Although this is not true. I have already decided I want to feed the baby myself, for a short time at least. I just do not wish to tell Maria yet. She must be reading my mind for her expression shows she does not approve. She says quarters have been arranged for her and her helpers to be nearby and when my labour starts, they will come to me.

A new message arrives from William of Jumièges who is visiting Abbot John today for a brief discussion of a clerical matter. He knows my time is limited, but he would be pleased to speak to me if convenient and is sending a man to the Palace to seek an answer. The servant tells me the messenger is here already. I suspect William of Jumièges has accompanied him and is keeping out of sight in the abbey.

I tell the messenger that I shall be pleased to see William of Jumièges for Dinner at one o'clock. Countess Adeliza FitzOsbern will be joining us. Our visitor is prompt and courteous and entertaining as ever. We're served Waterzooi, my favourite Flemish fish and vegetable dish that Antoine has prepared as a surprise. Adeliza and I are delighted and when it's followed by Rijstpap, it's even more of a treat. William of Jumièges, to whom these dishes are new and a change from his usual fare, calls Antoine 'a treasure.' I send a servant to summon Antoine so we can thank him. He is obviously pleased and says he met a Flemish sailor at the dock who told him about Flemish food. He goes off with a distinct spring in his step. We discuss food and music and just about everything with our visitor except the elephant in the room which is surely why he has come to see me. Adeliza excuses herself, leaving us alone.

'Brother William, I assumed your visit today was prompted by the news of the Pope's Ban on our marriage.'

'What Ban?'

'You mean you don't know about it?'

'I do know about it, but I choose to ignore it.'

'It's hard for *us* to ignore. Do you think we should?'

'Certainly, just carry on and hold a marriage ceremony as if nothing had happened.'

'We could be excommunicated!'

'I think that's highly unlikely. Pope Leo insists on the sacrament of marriage for noble couples in his programme of reforms. I have taken the liberty of sending a message to Prior Lanfranc insisting there is no consanguinity in your case. It's you who says there is not and can prove it, it's you who will be believed as your reputation for scholarship is increasingly respected abroad. Also, Lanfranc himself is strongly motivated to agree to the terms for ending his exile and he will be diplomatic in persuading the Pope to do nothing at all rather than lifting the Ban too soon. I'm sure you appreciate the Pope will not want to lose face or upset Emperor Henry so he may take time to formally remove it, but mark my words, he will.'

'So, you think Prior Lanfranc will change his mind?'

'I do.'

'Is there anything you don't know?'

‘Only God knows everything and I pray that I can support my friends in His name. I’ve come today is to say you and Duke William are in my prayers and if there is anything I can do to help you, let me know.’

‘As your abbey is near Rouen, from what you see and hear of Archbishop Mauger, do you think he remains a serious threat to Duke William?’

‘His continued support of his brother’s claim to the Dukedom of Normandy still makes him a threat. You might think that because he supports the Pope’s opposition to your marriage, he would be in the Pope’s favour. Well, I can tell you he’s not because according to those that know, Mauger is excessively addicted to the lusts of the flesh and distractions of the world. His position is shaky, but while he holds it, he remains an enemy with some power on your doorstep. I humbly advise you and Duke William to increase your vigilance regarding the Archbishop’s activities.’

I thank him and bid him farewell before retiring, having ordered a light supper to be served in my chamber.

The next morning, we are taking refreshment after Mass when a servant arrives with more messages, sent when we were in Falaise and now recovered from some safe place in the palace. Our parents and siblings are coming to stay next week in order to be present to witness the birth of our child. I was not expecting them so soon and for so long? It could be weeks, forgive me Mother Mary. I tell Adeliza I did not realise this is the custom.

‘It will be exhausting, but at least you’ll be here if I get fed up with them all!’

‘No, I’m sorry Matilda, but William and I are going home in few days’ time.’

I had assumed Adeliza would be staying for the birth, but alas, no. As is the custom of royal and superior nobility, families insist on presence at the birth to ensure they witness no swapping or stealing of the newborn. I am relieved that William’s siblings will only include Odo, who is already in the abbey, and Robert who is on his way from Falaise. The family already numbers eight, but I see another message which must have dropped on the floor. Robert and Beatrice are coming too. So that's ten to stay. What a relief that Beatrice will be here! I must go and talk to the staff about arrangements.

We are sorry to see the FitzOsberns leave, but they assure us they will be back when our relations have gone. I shall miss Adeliza, but at least Beatrice will be here. Our waiting days fall into a pattern. We all need things to do because it is all quite tedious. The men, apart from Father, have Normandy affairs to discuss and go to the office, in fact anywhere, to escape the ladies. Baldwin and the two Roberts help round the Estate in the morning and ride out in the afternoon, usually with the men, but not too far in case they are called back. The older ladies seem happy to talk and go for little carriage rides while Beatrice remains available to prop me up just like Adeliza. Mother is well and it is good to see her again. Now I am settled, she is much more respectful of me, treating me like an adult rather than a foolish young girl. She is pleased I am capable of managing this household and coping with marriage to the Duke of Normandy with all that his position demands. She tells me what gives her the most satisfaction is that I'm obviously happy with William which she was not confident would be the case. I give her a hug and say I was not totally confident of that myself despite my assurances that we would be well suited. Now we are sure and the anticipation of the imminent birth of our baby is a joy to us both and I suddenly feel much closer to Mother.

Countess Arlette is delighted to see me wearing a particularly enchanting loose dress she sent in my favourite blue and quite like the first one she sent after my dress was ruined by her son throwing me into the mud. This one is of soft wool suitable for colder days, not the fine lawn of summer. It is so comfortable and pretty that I feel good in it despite the bloating and exhaustion of late pregnancy. The ladies agree that blue is a suitable colour to cover the heir of Normandy. They are certain it's going to be a boy although they do remark that I am not of the sort of size they have ever seen in a late pregnancy. They discuss the huge 'bumps' experienced by ladies they have known, an endless history since noble families like ours tend to have large families. Spare heirs are needed in this life of continual battles and even murders. How *will* I cope if we have a daughter?

When I do manage to avoid them, I find Father who seems lost away from his beloved Flanders. We rekindle our old relationship for he appears to have put the Brihtric business behind him and he wants to know what challenges lies ahead now William is Duke of Normandy. What is William doing to keep his enemies at bay? Who are his allies and what are his plans? I love discussions with Father, but I am careful what I say to him, like the churchmen who visit me. Who knows where a confidence is repeated and what could result from an unwise remark? As usual, Father has his own troubles, saying he is not popular with Uncle Henry, Emperor Henry, Pope Leo or King Edward of England. Of course, he's not! I do miss our talks and look forward to getting back to learning more about the rule of Normandy.

Mother and Countess Arlette appear to have interviewed Maria without consulting me and ascertained my ambivalent attitude towards breast-feeding my baby. They would like 'a little talk' with me and it's obvious what it's about. Beatrice comes to support me and we endure a barrage of advice. They say how important it is to become pregnant again as soon as possible because I must continue producing heirs and spares. While breast-feeding, I cannot become pregnant. I must have a wet nurse ready. Ignoring their obvious distaste for mentioning such matters, Beatrice intervenes, saying quietly that coupling will not take place until after I am churched so it's impossible to become pregnant then. Surely breast-feeding during these first few weeks establishes a precious bond between mother and baby and then a wet nurse could be considered. Bless Beatrice! What a good friend! The two matriarchs see they have met their match and nod their heads in grudging acceptance.

Today starts my lying-in and we have a special Mass and take Communion. I kneel beside William and pray for strength to cope with the whole process. I don't pray about holy things, but beseech Mother Mary to forgive me for wanting him to be with me. After Mass, I embrace everyone and Maria comes to take me away to my cloister.

It is tedious in the birthing-chamber, the days passing slowly. Under Maria's instructions, the midwives insist on putting up bunches of aromatic herbs which become overpowering in this confined space. She tells them to rub lotions on my belly. I wish they'd stop fussing and leave me alone. Their conversation is limited to matters surrounding the birth, to 'focus my mind.' Of course, I like to discuss the birth of my child, but not all the time and I do not want to know all the things that could go wrong. I am a healthy young woman and there's no reason at all why I shouldn't push our baby out with no problem. After all, its passage has had vigorous use since I first coupled with William. My muscles are strong. Worse than all this birth talk is the absence of discussion of interesting topics like Art, Music or national affairs. To be fair, I don't suppose these women know anything about them. If they did, Maria would shut them up quickly. They watch my every move, every mouthful and every action until I could scream with frustration. Dear Adeliza travels quite a distance to pay me an unexpected visit and tells me that my Aunt Judith has married Tostig Godwinson! Well, that's a surprise, although we agree he is rather a dashing Viking type. King Edward of England will be even more displeased with my family.

Thankfully, Megina is back now. She brings Stefan, a placid baby who sleeps most of the time in his baby basket. I thought young babies cry all night but when Stefan is just outside my door, he is obviously too well-fed to make even a little squeak.

Visits by Megina and Beatrice are most welcome and visits by Mother and Countess Arlette to be endured. They asked to be present during the birth, but I have said there is not enough room and only Beatrice will be present, her younger legs being better able to cope with all the standing about. They say they are disappointed, but actually I think they're quite relieved. Now Maria is getting on my nerves as she is bossy and rude to those she considers beneath her. She wouldn't dare speak to me or my noble relations as she speaks to Megina and her two young helpers, Ava and Colette. I have mentioned this, but she still does it. I'm beginning to dislike her. However, it is becoming less of an issue regarding Megina as her visits become less frequent. This is understandable as she probably wants to avoid Maria, and of course, she's got baby Stefan to feed and care for. I hope she's all right.

Day and night, there's a palace guard at the foot of the stairs to our quarters. The only noise he can hear from above is the opening and shutting of William's door. Maria sleeps in the palace in a servant's room and the others go home. William is in his chamber, I in that smelly prison, but on most nights, we sneak out to my chamber to be together, returning in the early morning to our approved beds. Megina knows about this, but tactfully, makes no comment or shows any expression of judgement. She is the only person allowed in my chamber, going in daily to ensure no clue of our illicit habitation. I return to the birthing-chamber well before the female sentries appear. All through the endless day, the women watch me, wishing I'd get on with it. I want to get on with it too. We wait. And we wait. And we wait. Christmas comes and goes in a flash. Tonight, as I lie in the increasingly stuffy birthing-chamber, William creeps in.

'Remember what Beatrice said about coupling at this stage?'

'I do, it could be awkward though!' We creep into my chamber. Our coupling is a bit difficult, but after much giggling, we manage it and it's intense in a different way. As we lie together afterwards, I feel a trickle coming from me, but not the usual one. My waters have broken! Oh, so he's ready to be born! Or her! And Megina's not here. We need to tidy the bed!

'Grab the sheet and smooth it over and throw those cushions on it,' I say to William. I creep to the birthing-chamber and begin to call out loudly. William calls the guard. The midwives are summoned, Maria to the fore. She must have been sleeping in her uniform. I hear the family come up the stairs and settle in my chamber. Abbot John arrives as an independent witness to no family trickery. Another palace guard passes his comrade on the stairs to keep watch on the door to William's chamber. So, it starts.

CHAPTER 10

THE BIRTH

Fécamp, 1051

He's here. *He* is here! Blessed, *blessed* are you among women for answering my prayers. A boy! Baby Robert, named after William's father, is small, but a healthy weight I'm assured. He is absolutely perfect. The placenta is born and the covered bucket containing it is handed through the door to a trusted female member of our household. She will be accompanied, under escort, to dispose of it to ensure that no midwife or other person steals any part for use in witchcraft or other unchristian practices. William creeps in, although I don't think he is supposed to, and holds his son, tears pouring down his face and unable to say anything. He hands him to the midwife and gently kisses me, my face becoming wet too. My precious man! Now we have our precious son. He leaves and after Robert's had a bit of a clean-up and a cuddle from me, the mid-wife carries him to my chamber so William can introduce him to the family. The door is firmly closed so my privacy and continued seclusion is decently maintained, but I can hear everything going on. I hear Father saying 'Goed, goed', over and over again, clearly pleased, but not really knowing what is expected of him. I hear Mother, in her somewhat insensitive manner, declaring, 'He's a real Fleming, exactly like his mother at birth.' She's right. He certainly is small and fair like me. Countess Arlette, who cannot pretend that the baby looks anything like his father, calls out, 'Hail Mary, it's a boy, a son and heir to the Dukedom of Normandy!'

The rest of the party, who have witnessed the passage of my labour through the wall of my chamber and kept watch to ensure no fraud, now crowd round William to see the baby. I hear the two grandmothers say how gorgeous he is, how perfect he is, one in Flemish and the other in Frankish. They sound like a couple of pigeons, their comments echoing those said about me as a baby as I was repeatedly told over the years. The men say 'Bravo' and clap William on the shoulders, lightly of course, since he's holding the baby. I hear my brother Baldwin and the two Roberts grunt some sort of benevolence followed by the noise of their footsteps descending the stairs at speed. I smile to myself as Odo, the new bishop, gives a theatrical blessing, his resonant voice reflecting his self-imposed important role in the proceedings. I doubt if anyone present shares the admiration of his gushing devoted mother.

Maria goes out to fetch Robert and take him to the nursery as the midwives have things to do for the child. Now the ladies come in to see me. The two grandmothers dutifully kiss me and make all the right comments, their maternal point-scoring suspended by delight and relief in the news of a son and heir. Yet, it's Beatrice who puts her arms round me and gives me a kiss and says, 'Well done!' I love Beatrice. She promises to return tomorrow. The midwives return to attend to me so the ladies depart, to relay the good news and wet the baby's head.

Eventually the rules allow me to go to my proper chamber to sleep, leaving Robert in the nursery with a midwife who will bring him to me when he cries. I lie there exhausted and say my prayers to Mother Mary. I treasure the image of William's face as he held little Robert in his huge forearms and feel the love that flowed from him. This will keep me going in the next lonely weeks. All I want is to be with William and the baby, but I know that he and I have to be apart until my flow stops and I am churched. I sleep between the baby's feeds which cannot satisfy him yet as this breast-feeding takes time to get used to. This all goes on the next day too and I'm desperate to go outside. Despite having just given birth, I feel quite well and in need of fresh air. It will be cold out there, but anything rather than being cooped up all the time. At least my chamber is better than that birthing-chamber. Beatrice is a great comfort, but she will be going soon and I am trying not to think about the long days without her. Just when I'm feeling sorry for myself, Megina turns up with Stefan who has lots of black hair and is much bigger than Robert. He looks placid whereas Robert is quite lively even at a few days old. We discuss feeding which she seems to find easier than me. She puts Stefan down on rug and starts tidying my room. I tell her to rest and not start working and she stops, looking at me seriously, 'I know noble ladies do not usually feed their babies so if you would like me to be Prince Robert's wet-nurse, I'd be pleased to do that.' I stare at her, speechless. She hurriedly starts again. 'That was presumptuous of me. I expect you have a lady of noble birth ready to feed your baby instead of someone in a lower position like me…?'

Oh, *why* didn't I think of asking her before? It is obvious.

'Megina, it's a perfect idea, who could be better than you? Are you sure you can manage the two to feed?' 'Of course! I might have had twins! Don't forget I come from a big family myself and I'm used to babies and young children.'

'That is wonderful and I will make arrangements for you, Ralf and Stefan to have your own quarters nearby. Please ask Ralf to speak to Duke William about it and he can instruct the Chamberlain to organise it all. However, I would like to feed Robert until I am churched and then we'll be all set up for you to take over.'

I have now been confined for three weeks and three days and as everything is returning back to normal, I am to be churched on Sunday. I have been feeding Robert, ignoring Maria's disapproval when she made dutiful visits to see how I was getting on. Thank goodness she stopped being here full time the day after the birth and the two young nurses left to help me are much more supportive. I love feeding Robert and he is such a good baby. In fact, he is adorable and I'm sure he smiled at me today. I told him it was my birth time in November and his mother is now eighteen years old. His Baptism took place last week in our palace chapel. By this time, our families had departed and the FitzOsberns, Montgomeries and Beaumonts had arrived to stay as Count William and the two Count Rogers were asked to be godparents. When Adeliza told me this, I sent William a message to say I'd like Adeliza to be his godmother. I was rather upset that William did not consult me about godparents. Perhaps he assumed I'd realise his three close friends were the obvious choices or maybe he was trying to avoid the subject as I, being 'impure', could not go to the Baptism. As expected, it was lovely to see Adeliza and Adeline and predictably dreadful when Dame Mabel appeared. She is expecting her fourth child, but that does not soften her character in the least.

'What a tiny baby!' she exclaimed, 'nothing like his father. The Duke must be disappointed!' Ignoring her, I began to discuss with the other ladies what I should wear for my Churching. Yet, Dame Mabel wouldn't let it go and interrupted our conversation in her hissing sly manner, 'Yet, this baby is a pretty little thing who looks just like you, being fair and small. You'd think it was a girl. It must have been an easy birth, but wait until you have a huge baby with shoulders like Duke William. I've had two girls and one boy, so I know what I'm talking about although my husband is nothing like the size of Duke William. Oh, you poor thing, just thinking about that painful experience makes me feel quite faint. Most women would not survive that.'

I imagined her babies being born, hairless like new born rats, their snouts peeking out of her. I started laughing helplessly, but could not say why, even if she deserved it, so when she left in a huff, it was a great relief. I did not tell the other ladies what I was thinking as that would be going too far, tempting though it was. I did confess it later to Adeliza who hooted with laughter. I ask her if she knows how Count Roger de Montgomery came to marry Mabel, the rat woman. Adeliza said Mabel's father, William de Talvas, had been cast out by his family and was charitably taken in by the Montgomery family. Finding out that William de Talvas was Lord of Bellême with Domfront and Alençon, Count Roger offered marriage to his daughter Mabel, heiress to these possessions, sacrificing his personal happiness in support of Prince William and the future of Normandy. We agree that was some sacrifice!

Now our visitors have gone and my Churching is to be on Sunday in our chapel with Abbot John. Megina tells me she is also to be churched on Sunday, but not in the servants' chapel because William has invited her and Ralf to join us in the palace chapel. I must look worried as she now looks at me nervously. I hope she doesn't think I would not want her in the palace chapel. It's nothing like that, but concern for Churching is only for women who have been baptised and married in the Catholic Church.

'Megina, forgive me, but I didn't know you had married?'

'I am so sorry; I should have told you. Abbot John suggested we should marry when he noticed my condition. He does look after us all.'

'That's a relief and of course, it means a lot to us both if you and Ralf are with us.' She looks happy now and as William has told me they can expect some good news tomorrow, she will no doubt be even happier. I expect a nursery and rooms have been organised for them.

We take Communion at the Churching according to *Rituale Romanum*. I stand in front on one side of the chapel with Megina a few paces behind me. William and Ralf do the same on the other side of the church as they may not be near us until we are purified. Bishop Odo, oh such a holy young man, now stands beside Abbot John, but takes no part. Thanksgiving prayers are said for each of us for our survival and safe delivery of our children and that's that over.

On return to the palace, William invites Megina and Ralf for refreshments, telling them he has an announcement to make. He appoints Ralf his Gentleman of the Bedchamber and Megina my Lady of the Bedchamber. They are stunned and so am I as I realise he continues to act independently of me in family and household matters. I intend to work on that, but in this case, I am truly delighted for Megina and Ralf. What more loyal servants could we have? I am not surprised by their elevation of rank as I have come to know that William respects peoples' qualities above their birth status and he values loyalty above all. Afterwards, William suggests we go to my chamber. He has something to tell me. Of course, he wants to begin coupling again, and so do I, but I am worried I might still be a bit tender for too much energetic thrusting.

'You're worried aren't you?'

'Just a little bit.'

'If it's about coupling, we can do it like our first time in the woods and then you can control it. And you know I'll wait for you to be ready.'

'I'm always ready and I'm looking forward to it. What were you going to tell me?'

'You and I are going on a holiday.'

'A *holiday*? When and where?'

'In a few days' time, to a special place, Château de Bonneville-sur-Touques.''I've heard about it. People say it's beautiful, but private. No-one they know has been inside. Who owns it?' William's face lights up with his huge smile.

'You might know the owner, a stout functional sort of man.' That makes me laugh, 'I just might know the one. How exciting! It's good timing because Megina is about to start feeding Robert which means I need to be out of the way to let him get used to her.'

'It was Megina who suggested the holiday.'

'Ah, I see! Will we go on our own?' 'No, we never go on our own. We shall have palace guards doubling as grooms, a priest, a cook, my man servant and those two young girls you liked who assisted with Robert's birth.' 'Perfect. I shall miss my baby, but he will be in good hands.'

'He will, but now I've got to be away for a couple of days to up the pressure of this siege and get rid of cousin Guy once and for all.'

'Any other pressing business?'

'Domfront and Alençon seem quiet at present so I'm planning to reduce the garrisons quite soon. If there's any trouble it will be from Geoffrey Martel of Anjou who has already seized pockets of Frankish land in Maine and no doubt plans to add Normandy lands to his domain. On a happier note, we've got our official marriage to plan.'

'Despite the Ban?' 'Despite the Ban. However, we don't want to attract too much attention and provoke the Pope, so I suggest we don't make it a big occasion, but marry quietly at the Château of Eu. Robert and Beatrice will be delighted, and it is an easy journey for your family.'

'Good choice and well away from Archbishop Mauger.'

'Quite! If it's all right by you I'll get my things together and leave for Rouen, keeping well away from Mauger.'

'You're not staying tonight?'

'No, I think you need another few days and at Bonneville, we can relax and take our time. You can enjoy thinking about it while I'm away.'

William's so considerate. People would be amazed if they knew what he is really like. I shall be thinking about it. A lot! Off he goes having given me a bear hug and a kiss, whispering, 'Just wait, I'll be back and on my back before you know it!' Now I must stop giggling to myself and talk to Megina about getting help with the two babies as well as the regular tasks she does for me.

Megina suggests two young women and possibly their mothers too, all living here. I say I hope she approves of my asking Colette to come as my maid on the holiday since she is otherwise engaged. She laughs generously and she does approve, and asks how long we'll be away. I tell her I'm not sure but we always send a daily pigeon message back to Fécamp from wherever we are. Megina says Ralf knows the Pigeon Fancier so if she or Ralf want to send us a message, Ralf will speak to him. I pack my things, but not my riding clothes as I'll wait a bit before being in the saddle and also the ground is quite wet and icy at this time. No doubt William will want to go to Saint-Gatien Forest for a day's Chase, but I don't see him going on his own just with the grooms, so who will go with him?

William is back in a black mood because the siege is a hopeless cause. There's no sign of movement even from the top of the siege towers so supplies must be getting get in at night. I am not going to say it to him, but it's obvious the night guards are pretty useless. I make a suggestion.

'Why don't you pardon him?'

'*Pardon* him? You must be mad! He is the worst of the rebels!'

'It's a ploy to get rid of him. It shows him that you are powerful enough to discount him as a threat. His status is reduced to a biting fly, so insignificant that his freedom is irrelevant.'

'He'll just stay in the castle and carry on plotting right on our doorstep.'

'We remove the siege towers and ignore him. Soon enough he'll be lulled into thinking he's safe and after nearly three years of being cooped up, he'll be desperate to leave the castle. Who will he go to for refuge?'

'Straight to his Uncle Geoffrey Martel, Count of Anjou, our enemy on the southern border. William of Jumièges calls him "a treacherous man in every respect".'

'Can he get through Maine to Anjou without hindrance?'

'He can because Hugh of Maine is an ally of Geoffrey Martel.'

'Well, you could put a watch on that route and as soon as Guy is seen, have an escort to make sure he leaves Normandy, naturally for his own safety.'

'Good analysis. You're right. I will consider it.' William looks thoughtful, but in a definitely better mood so that's more promising for our holiday. We pack up and say good-bye to Robert and go. It was hard to leave him behind. I was full of milk and he was crying, so Megina picked him up and cuddled him.

'He's hungry,' she said, 'he'll soon take to me. Don't worry.'

We've arrived at last and it is such a beautiful place. Breath-taking! We settle in and go to sit by the big log fire the men have built in the Hall. Our holiday cook Abram puts out platters of food for us to help ourselves to. Everything is quiet and calm. I feel relaxed already. We go to our chamber and couple as we did the first time. I need not have been nervous and when William says 'Woah, I'm not your horse,' we start laughing uproariously and it is as good as ever. Hail Mary, you have blessed me in abundance.

This holiday is just what we both need, away from the palace and respite from William's problems for a while. Of course, we discuss them as we walk in the grounds or sit by the fire because it's what absorbs us. I value my increasing part in Normandy's affairs, just as I did with Father in Flanders. What is your ambition, I ask William and he says to be King, not just a duke. So that's it! King of where I ask and as I say it, it's obvious. We smile at each other, no need to say more. William asks me my ambition. I tell him I want to continue as a respected confidant of his plans, to provide male heirs to his dukedom and then his kingdom and provide daughters who we may marry to our advantage. Our children will enrich our lives with their companionship and loyalty. I want them to be respectful of us, well-educated, firm in the Catholic faith and enjoy musical and sporting pursuits. That reminds me.

'Are you planning a Chase in Saint-Gatien while we're here?' He's a bit uncomfortable, 'Only if you don't mind.'

'Of course, I don't mind. I was expecting you to go so who's joining you?'

'Well, FitzO is coming tomorrow and he *is* bringing Adeliza.' He's planned it all along! 'Good news! I'm so pleased!' He smiles broadly, pleased with me of course.

Tomorrow is here, and soon enough, the FitzOsberns appear. Adeliza looks well and I give her stomach a little pat as we hug each other. The men are off at once, the Chase never failing to lift their spirits. Adeliza and I settle down for a good chat. She is in excellent health with no nausea at this half-way stage of her pregnancy. Does Count William enjoy feeling the baby flutter I ask and could bite my tongue as her faces crumples and tears start welling. Oh no! He thinks it's wrong to couple in case the baby is harmed, and she should keep to her own chamber because he might forget if he half wakes up and she's in his bed. His son is his most important concern. I say I'm sure everything will be back to normal after she's churched; he's probably trying to be considerate and I hear that a lot of men think as he does. Forgive me Mother Mary, that's not true, but I say it to reassure my dear friend. She asks me about feeding Robert and is interested in what I say. She will have to make some plans too.

The days go by, the men at the Chase and Adeliza and I mainly resting, but also taking turns round the abbey grounds for fresh air and exercise, though limited by only a few paths being cleared of undergrowth and a chilly wind. William has been discussing the Guy of Brionne situation with Count William and just after All Saints Day, the siege towers will come down and we'll see what happens. I bid a fond farewell to Adeliza and tell her that next time we meet will probably be at Eu for our official marriage. Adeliza gives me one of her looks and just nods her head which makes me think she knows that we are already married.

Back at Fécamp, William and I sit in the Hall after Mass with Robert asleep in his crib beside us. William brings a small packet from his pocket and hands it to me.

'This is for you my dearest wife. I must be the luckiest man in the world.' He's giving me a present and I have nothing for him. It is a gold cross with tiny sapphires and pearls on a chain. I am speechless with joy at its beauty and William's thoughtfulness and generosity. We sit peacefully together and could not be happier. We look at Robert and wonder at his perfect little face as he sleeps, no doubt well nourished by Megina. Life goes on and the siege towers round Castle of Brionne Castle will come down this week. A messenger has delivered William's sealed parchment with Notice of Pardon to the gatekeeper at the castle.

Life is peaceful and at present uneventful. Our routine is settled, mainly because of Megina's tender care of Robert and her attention to me as Lady of the Bedchamber. Ralf is equally supportive of William although his duties are to his horse as well as his person. On the milder days I ride Galathea with two grooms as my escort, but do not venture far. It's so good to ride again and as I canter gently along the paths lined with the bare branches of winter, I wonder if we have another baby on the way. After the rapid conception of Robert, whenever it was, Chase on most days and his companions this time are Roger de Montgomery and William's brothers. Odo is enjoying some leisure time from his ecclesiastical duties and Robert, who is staying with the Montgomeries over the holiday period, is on leave from his military training at Falaise. Robert is a nice boy who tells me he is now twelve years old.

He likes staying with the Montgomeries because Count Roger treats him like a son and his friend is Matilda, Count Roger's eldest daughter who is a year younger than him. Apparently, Dame Mabel is rarely at Montgomery-le-Roger as she spends most of her time at Bellême with her father, keeping an eye on the garrison no doubt. The Montgomeries have Supper with us while Odo goes back to his abbey to join the monks. Count Roger, satisfied with the progress of removing the Brionne Castle siege towers, returns to Montgomery-le-Roger, taking Robert with him.

We celebrate Epiphany with 'Galletes des Rois', each decorated to represent gold, frankincense and myrrh. It's not obvious which is which, but Antoine's biscuits are so delicious it doesn't matter. All seems quiet and we send a message to Robert and Beatrice saying we would like to be married in the chapel of their Chateau of Eu. We suggest a date in April or May when the wild flowers are out.

Good news! Count Roger de Beaumont's men have intercepted Guy de Brionne as he fled his castle. William says just as he predicted. In fact, it was I who predicted that, but I kept my mouth shut and agreed with him, which makes for a harmonious relationship. Count Roger knew exactly which route he'd take down through Normandy, passing near Beaumont-le-Roger to refuge with Geoffrey Martel in Anjou. Scouts picked him up just north of Alençon and accompanied him under guard to the border. The small band of horsemen who were supposed to be protecting Guy scattered quickly as soon as they appeared. So that's got rid of him from here, but a closer watch will be needed on the border now he will be teamed up with Geoffrey Martel, both men hostile to William. Orders are given to seize the castle of Brionne now before its occupants get a message from Guy that his new status as a free man commands little respect.

Having looked forward so much to Robert's arrival, I have to admit that I don't find babies good company. I'm not a maternal person, my interests being in political and military affairs and not the nursery. Of course, Robert is adorable and precious to us, but I am thankful not to have the boring job of looking after him. Ladies of my class do not look after their own children so it's just as well I don't want to, but when Robert begins to talk, things should improve. William and I enjoy seeing him in the early evening when he's brought down to the Hall because it's only a short visit and we like it when he smiles. William is much more physical with him than me and likes to hug him. Robert's tiny size is brought into sharp relief as he is cradled in William's huge arms. Megina says he is putting on weight as he should, but it's hard to believe.

A more compelling subject is our forthcoming marriage. William suggests we order special clothes for the occasion and ask Countess Arlette's advice. What about guests? We start with my parents and brothers and William's mother and step-father and his brothers Odo and Robert. William says his little sisters are too young to attend. Although

I've never met them and William rarely sees them, we are to invite his elder brother Richard FitzGilbert de Clare and his wife Rohese Giffard. His younger sister Adelaide will be invited, but since her marriage is now annulled, we will not invite her ex-husband Count Enguerrand de Ponthieu. Another invitation will go to one of William's most loyal knights, Walter Giffard, father of Rohese and now a widower. Obviously, Bridget and Robert will be there as hosts and we must invite William's liege lord, my Uncle Henry, King of the Franks and his new wife, Anne of Kiev. Our closest friends, the FitzOsberns, Beaumonts and Montgomeries will be invited as a matter of course. William looks at me quizzically and says the most important consideration in deciding the date is when Dame Mabel is to be confined before and after the birth of her next baby. He is *wicked!* So is she, he says. Abbot John is to marry us with Bridget and Robert's priest in attendance. If our marriage were not banned by the Pope, it would be a much bigger occasion with a host of bishops and dignitaries, but at least these circumstances spare us from having to ask Uncle Mauger, Archbishop of Rouen, or any other of William's scheming relations. The replies arrive and we have two non-acceptances. One is William's sister Adelaide who will be confined, a sad situation, given the circumstances of her marriage. The other is Uncle Henry and his wife which is disappointing, but hardly unexpected since we have doubts about his relationship with William. No reason is given.

After Mass the next morning, Abbot John calls us aside for a word. He's heard on the clerical grape-vine that Prior Lanfranc has declared he now considers consanguinity to be absent from our union and has put this view to the Pope who says he will consider the situation. William is delighted and invites Abbot John to take a message to Prior Lanfranc in person, renouncing his Exile and inviting him back to the Priory of Bec. He tells Abbot John of our desire that he should be the Officiant at our marriage in Eu which is received with grace and humility.

We are to be married on the second Sunday of May, when our countryside is abundant with wild flowers, the trees bursting into new leaf and Dame Mabel unable to attend. I have increased our vigilance over any future visit by Dame Mabel by instructing the palace servants to ensure she is accompanied at all times, including a guard on her chamber door at night. It's for her own protection, knowing her insistence on proper observance of this protocol. Nor is she to be left alone with Robert under any circumstance. As soon as we send the invitations, a message arrives from Countless Arlette who wishes to visit as soon as possible to discuss our ideas for our wedding clothes, which means she will tell us what to do and note our measurements. She comes quickly and stays a few days and enjoys her mission all the while becoming increasingly animated. She is planning gold for our clothing which sounds rather ostentatious, but exciting too! William and I agree she is looking much frailer than the last time we saw her, thin and her skin almost transparent. Agnês, her maid, says no-one seems to know the cause of her decline. We think that the prospect of our official marriage is keeping her going although she is clearly disappointed it will not be the big grand occasion she had anticipated.

The first anniversary of our wedding in Bruges is Ash Wednesday this year, the beginning of Lent. Because of this we had a special Dinner yesterday, Shrove Tuesday, with Suckling Pig from the farm and pancakes of course. Megina and Ralf joined us for the first time and it was most enjoyable. The babies were brought up to see us and we thought they were trying to communicate with each other with a series of gurgles. Stefan seems to have grown considerably, while Robert is still quite small. I note that Stefan looks far more like William than his own son and I don't mean anything by saying that. It's more about size than their features.

William continues to ride, but there's no Chase now until after Easter. His men continue military practice, but no tournaments are held. Talking of abstinence, some clergy proclaim no coupling during Lent, but we consider the bond of marriage and the procreation of children above this rule. Nor has Pope Leo gone this far and is instead concentrating on zero tolerance of all wilful sexual activity among clerics. Some might say William and I pick and choose our religious observances, and that's true, but we do show due penitence for these sins as our faith asks of us. Thinking about this, I wonder if William has quite the same depth of faith as me as he does not pray down on his knees before getting into bed and he likes to make sure people witness his holy observances. Forgive me Mother Mary for these critical and disloyal thoughts about my husband for I am a sinner myself.

William is so proud of Robert that he grants the tithes of church lands in Guernsey to the Abbot of St Martin at Tours, 'with approval and assent of his wife, Meheldis, and his son Robert', followed by other nobles and clergy present. I'm not sure if Robert's gurgle counts as assent, but what a precious document! It is dated c.1048, evidence that dates are not of the greatest importance.

CHAPTER 11

OFFICIAL MARRIAGE

Eu, Normandy 1051

The Annunciation to the Blessed Virgin Mary is today, the twenty-fifth of March, which we also observe as New Year's Day, the start of 1051. Tomorrow is Easter Sunday, so we seem to be at Mass nearly all the time.

After Easter, everything is back to normal and the next few weeks are spent on our marriage plans. We have tried on the gold wedding garments sent with a messenger from Conteville. They fit well and are grand and expensive, but they are worth it. Beatrice has organised the Wedding Feast in the Chateau of Eu and I'm beginning to look forward to the occasion. Robert will stay here with Megina in the nursery, but I'm not going to pretend that he does not exist and remind William and myself that if anyone makes an awkward remark concerning his new legitimate status, we pass it off lightly. However, I have doubts about Countess Arlette managing self-containment. Mother Mary, grant that no remark regarding Prince Robert's legitimacy is made in the hearing of Duke William's mother at our wedding. Perhaps we need not be so secretive about our first marriage after this more public occasion. Colette will come to Eu as my maid as Megina is still feeding Robert. Ralf is to be in charge of Fécamp Palace in our absence which helpfully disguises the fact that we would not have been able to include these dear friends as guests being neither family nor nobility. Most of the guests are to stay at the Chateau of Eu and others at the former home of Beatrice and Robert which the family has kept for this purpose.

The great day arrives and our party assembles at the door of the chapel of Chateau of Eu. Count William stands behind me in the classic role of best man and my protector. We joked with him saying we could trust him not to abduct me like villains of storytelling, but he was not really amused since he takes his position seriously. After our vows and the Blessing of the Dowry and Blessing of The Trinity by William placing the ring on my thumb, fore and middle fingers before the wedding finger, Abbot John leads us to the High Altar for Mass. A veil is put over our heads and he blesses us again. All is done quietly and simply and I am thankful to now be able to wear my ring on my wedding finger and not hidden on a chain around my neck and then only when my bosom was covered.

We go back to the Chateau and to our chambers where our servants remove our outer garments and help us prepare for the festivities to follow. Magnificently adorned in our golden garments, William says I look like an angel so would I like to fly away with him now instead of joining the party. He makes his funny face while I stifle my giggles as we approach the Hall where we are served pink champagne. I actually prefer our own Perry because I like the bubbles, but expensive imported wines from Champagne are expected on special occasions like this. The decorations are magnificent with bowers of flowers and banners with our various Coats of Arms. Our Master of Ceremonies is young Bishop Odo and while unconvinced of his commitment to the religious life, I admit that his loud theatrical voice and pomposity make him perfectly suited to this task. He announces our names as we take our places, succeeding in getting titles sufficiently right to avoid giving serious offence. Even Countess Arlette smiles as she sits in place of honour at William's right side, but she looks so pale that I feel she may not last the day let alone have the energy to be discontented. Next to her is Count Herluin with the Beaumonts and Count Roger de Montgomery.

I look round the table from William's left side. Beside me is Father, then Mother next to Count William and then Adeliza, in blooming health, her bump almost inconspicuous in the silken drapes of her burgundy-coloured dress. She wears pink roses in her hair and looks quite stunning. Father is in good form and wants to know how his grandson is progressing. Mother looks across and asks if they may come to stay with us after the wedding to catch up and see Robert. I am starting to say yes when William, overhearing this exchange, says he has made plans for the two of us to have a holiday which is news to me. It is a lovely treat, so I suggest to Mother and Father we arrange their visit in a few weeks' time. Mother seems disappointed and I know I have not done my duty as a daughter lately so I must make an effort to sit with her after the meal. Servants bring in platters of food which they place on a table. A butler is assigned to one lady and one gentleman for taking orders for food and serving it and it seems the choice is almost anything we could ask for. My family is most appreciative of the inclusion of our favourite Flemish dishes. I order Waterzooi to start with followed by the Norman favourite roast meats, a slice each of game bird, venison and pork with crackling with vegetables and bread. The butlers are quick and efficient and soon we are all eating. William's platter is twice as big as mine, but as he is at least twice as big as me, that's understandable! Glancing up the table, I see that Countess Arlette is toying with her food and hardly has the strength to eat. William helps her by cutting her food into small pieces which she can then spear with her dainty gold-handled knife.

After abundant sweetmeats which include saffron-flavoured Rijstpap, William stands to make a speech. He praises me and says how happy I have made him, especially in giving him a son and heir to the Dukedom of Normandy. He thanks Robert and Beatrice for hosting our wedding and then addresses each person present with a word of thanks for their particular support and friendship. He notes that this is a modest number gathered here, but this is just how he likes it. Now a toast! À votre santé! Gezonheid! Bring in the Minstrels! These players are popular and we are having a jolly evening.

I move to sit with Mother who appears content with the occasion although she must be disappointed not to have been able to organise a more splendid occasion at Bruges for the wedding of her only daughter. She is more relaxed and easy-going than I remember and perhaps it's a relief it was not at Bruges after the recent trouble with Uncle Henry and Henry, King of Germany. Father's continual skirmishes must be exhausting to live with. She praises my hair, complexion and golden dress. She establishes, tactfully for her, that I am not pregnant and says Mother Mary will bless me again before long. She asks if I know that Father has just signed William's Charter giving rights of jurisdiction to the Abbot of St-Pierre-de-Préaux? I did not and what rights are these? Jurisdiction over Arson and Rape, she says. My goodness, William will be relieved to be rid of these and I realise yet again that there is so much about my husband that I do not know. I must ask him as I expect to be told everything concerning his ducal duties. Sharing these responsibilities does not come easy for him, but I am working on it.

Mother tells me that Father continues to seek a bride for my brother Baldwin, one whose dowry has to include land bordering Flanders. I restrain myself from remarking that a suitable bride is more important than more land and agree it must be a challenge. I suggest that I go to Bruges Palace to stay for few days in the summer, bringing Robert to see his grandparents and also Megina and Stefan, along with other servants. Mother is delighted and I think I have re-kindled our good relationship. I leave her now and make my way round to talk to our other guests.

Everyone is generous in praise considering this one evening of entertainment is a parsimonious offering compared to the usual wedding celebrations of people of our rank. These usually go on for several days with jousting tournaments, the Chase, outings, feasts, music and dancing. I hope that all our guests understand that we do not wish to provoke the Pope with ostentatious festivity. News of our wedding will get round, but not as it would have had we entertained the usual great host of the nobility and dignitaries of Normandy, Flanders and West Frankia. To make up this omission to the men, William is to hold a jousting tournament at Falaise Castle over several days in the summer so his knights have that occasion to anticipate. Also, those of his men who share William's disdain for dancing, will be thankful to escape that ordeal. At the tournament, they can relax in male company, saved from having to watch their deportment in front of the ladies.

We retire to the modest but immaculate chambers of Eu Castle and I sit on the bed in my gold dress, exhausted. Today was quite an effort from beginning to end although it's a relief we are now officially married, despite the Pope. Colette helps me change and rapidly disappears. What now? There's nothing special to look forward to and then realise I have so much and should not feel sorry for myself. I kneel to ask Mother Mary to forgive me when William comes bounding in. Hearing the words 'Mother Mary', he raises his arms heavenwards and bellows 'Mother Mary, praise to you for my dearest wife', then he picks me up, lays me on the bed and leaps on the bed himself which amazingly does not break. He pulls me down with him and seizes me in a great hug.

'Guess where we're going tomorrow?'

'Home?'

'Yes briefly, to see Robert and pack what we need for our honeymoon.'

'Honeymoon? Where?'

'Guess!'

'Oh, you don't mean …Bonneville?'

'Of course, I do!'

'That is wonderful news. Shouldn't we take Robert?'

'I thought about that and decided he is perfectly all right left with Megina and we should have some time on our own. Also, I am planning some outings and there will be no Chase!'

'Well, a Chase of some sort I hope!'

'Of course, let's start now!' Despite our initial enthusiasm, we are not our usual energetic selves, but any sort of coupling is a comfort, bonding us even closer to face the inevitable challenges ahead.

After Mass the next morning, we go home and have a lovely time with Robert before we go to Bonneville. Our baby does seem to have grown a bit and is now sitting up firmly by himself, rolling over and even showing signs of crawling. He smiles at us and when William picks him up and throws him up and catches him, he laughs, little bursts of joy like his father does! Of course, he is the most advanced baby in the world and undoubtedly clever in all sorts of ways. Stefan could not be more different, far bigger and rather serious, gazing at us steadfastly with an owl-like expression. He sits stolidly, but is quite happy not to move much as if he is waiting for more important matters like walking. There is definite interaction between the babies and when Robert rolls over and pushes into Stefan, his face relaxes into a tolerant grin of acceptance. Megina laughs too and tries to teach Robert to wave bye-bye, but he just smiles. He is getting much more interesting and we look forward to the next stage.

Off we go to Bonneville and it's the start of a truly wonderful honeymoon. Everything I could ask for. Peaceful, relaxed, but also passionate when we can't stop coupling as another surging wave sweeps us together as if to the sky, birds tossed by the wind. William has planned our days out and we take the carriage to Caen and wander about admiring the old buildings about which he has considerable knowledge. He plans to build a large chateau for us and also move his present base of administration from Rouen. Caen would be an excellent choice, but why not Rouen, seat of his forbears back to Rollo the Viking? William explains he feels the ghosts of his ancestors watching him, anxious he should remain in Normandy like them and ready to thwart his ambitions to be a King. They will not haunt his new base built to meet the needs of his present position and ambition for the future. His enjoyment of Rouen is further marred by the malign presence of his cousin, Archbishop Mauger. Mauger is a wicked man, he says darkly.

When we get back to Bonneville, I ask him about his Charter to the Prior of Préaux Abbey. He is disappointed that I know already because he had been looking forward to telling me about this charter himself. It is a benefaction in thanksgiving in the year of our marriage, he explains. I tell him that Mother told me and I'd like to know the details. He says the abbey was re-founded on an ancient abbey site by Humphrey de Vieilles, who this year made a second foundation, the Abbey of Saint-Léger for women. And this Humphrey is Roger de Beaumont's father! We agree that the de Beaumont family provides an exceptional standard of benefaction and duty. He discusses the Charter which relates to the jurisdiction of Arson which is straightforward compared to Rape which is not. Many noblemen insist that the crime of Rape is only committed by the peasant classes and consider the ravishment of a woman by a nobleman as something quite different, 'Le Droit de Seigneur', they assert. William declares all Rape is an abomination and if such an offender comes before him, he feels 'le feu rouge' welling up inside him affecting proper judgement. He is relieved to hand over this duty to the equable, but firm Prior of Préaux who will be pleased to add his fee to the treasury of Préaux Abbey.

This is the first time that William has mentioned 'le feu rouge' and in this case I suspect it results from his feelings about his mother's deflowering by the much older and powerful Count Gilbert de Brionne. A nobleman who uses his power and position to seduce a woman of lower class against her will is as guilty of Rape as a common man who uses base brute force. I am pleased that William has the self-knowledge and humility to hand over the duty to the Prior. There is a knock on the door and our manservant comes in.

'Monseigneur and Madame, the Count and Countess of Beaumont are here.'

'Show them in', says William going out to greet them. I follow behind. This is an extraordinary coincidence as we've just been talking about their family. What are they doing here? Something serious must have happened to interrupt our honeymoon. When I get to the door, the men have disappeared. Adeline tells me that Roger's father, Humphrey de Vieilles, has died suddenly and Roger is distraught. She has never seen him cry before. She could not comfort him, and he brushed her off. The person he must see is William so here they are and she's really embarrassed about disturbing our honeymoon. Roger insisted on riding all the way accompanied by his groom, but she thought he was in no state go without her, so she ordered her carriage and followed.

'How did he know we'd be at Bonneville?'

'William's three close companions are always told where he is, regardless of his honeymoon, Even if they were not told they would guess it was Bonneville because you both love it here. I can see why!'

'Where are the men now?'

'William took him into his chambers and said I should come in to see you.'

'My dearest Adeline you did the right thing. You must be exhausted. Perry?'

'Yes please!'

'I'll get your chambers prepared. Are your servants with you?'

'Four grooms, but of course, I have no maid.'

'I've got Colette and another young girl from Fécamp called Pleasance so I'll ask her to help you.' We sit quietly and she tells me about her father-in-law. Humphrey was a lovely man. His wife Aubreye de La Haye died five years ago and it was always her wish to endow a nunnery. When Humphrey thought his days were numbered, he founded the Abbey of Saint-Léger in her memory. Just in time, says Adeline. I call Abram to tell him we have guests for Supper who will be staying here for a while. The men return, Roger looking drawn and tired.

'Oh Roger, I am so sorry. Call for some ale, William.'

'Always my dear wife's solace', says William. Teasing? Probably not!

'A little in moderation, my dear husband. Now how about this for an idea? Adeline and I shall visit Caen tomorrow so I can show her its beauty. I'm sure you two could find something to do like a visit to Saint-Gatien Forest.' Both men look as happy as could be expected in the circumstances. The Chase is a restorative in all situations it appears. During Supper, I hear that Adeliza is now confined and I will increase my prayers for my dear friend's health and safe delivery of a son. The man servant comes in again looking sombre.

'What is it?' asks William rather irritably.

'Counts FitzOsbern and Montgomery are here.' What *has* happened now?

'Show them in.' William gets up to greet them. The two friends go over to Roger de Beaumont and each puts a hand on his shoulder in acknowledgement of his bereavement.

'What is it?'

'Geoffrey Martel and Guy de Brionne have seized Domfront and Alençon and are heavily fortifying the defences. Both our garrisons destroyed and our soldiers slaughtered. Another force is marching north and is well into Normandy.'

'Bellême?'

'Not so far. Mabel sent news of all this.'

'Matilda, I have to go to Rouen immediately.'

'Of course, Adeline and I will return to Fécamp tomorrow.'

'Do not leave until extra guards arrive to escort you home. They will stay at Fécamp until further notice. Do not venture out of the Abbey grounds until I say so. I will send guards to Fécamp with instructions that the nursemaid does not take Robert out of the castle under any circumstances. When you return, you will manage security in my absence. Even inside the grounds, you and Robert must always have an armed escort.' As our husbands leave, Count William tells me Adeliza is near her time and sends her love. They go, these four men in charge of Normandy and facing heavy responsibilities. Adeline and I talk about the implications and it's all serious of course, but not totally unexpected. Should we have anticipated these enemies' invasion during our honeymoon? It was the perfect timing, and it only takes one traitor hanging around the tavern to pass on idle talk of our movements.

We leave Bonneville in our separate carriages, both accompanied by a posse of armed men. Adeline is going straight to Beaumont-le-Roger to support her husband. I travel in the company of the two young girls from our Fécamp estate, Colette and Plesance. My mood is sombre, but I am determined to be strong with a proper perspective on the situation. I count my blessings and say prayers for William and his men in the challenging tasks of retaking these enemy occupied castles and fighting off the invasion force. I give thanks to Mother Mary for the precious time William and I had together before all this blew up. The young girls look at me nervously having seen my eyes closed and my lips moving, so I tell them what is happening and ask for their prayers. Their responses are mature and sensible, and they ask what they can do to help. How nice they are!

Colette is a tall gawky girl in her mid-teens with strong features, which while not immediately attractive in repose, take on an engaging visage when she smiles. I found her work satisfactory at Eu over the period of our wedding, but she would be better suited to run round after lively Robert than a lady's maid. Plesance, with her pretty face and plump figure, is best described as 'a natural-born mother'. Although only thirteen, she already exudes an air of quiet confidence and will make a trustworthy and competent lady's maid. She also cares for young children in her own family so she will be very welcome in out household. I am pleased with both girls' attention to Countess Adeline and myself at Bonneville. I plan to talk to Megina about giving them permanent positions.

I go to see Robert and rejoice in his robust health and cheerful character. I wonder what his life will be like as heir to the Dukedom of Normandy. I invite Megina and Ralf to Supper as I do not want to eat alone. Megina has organised the nursery and is ready to do the lady's maid bedtime duties for me, a time when we can have good talk. I can say almost anything to Megina, but am careful not to give away any military information beyond the bare facts. Nor do I talk to her about my relationship with William or to anyone in fact. Marriage is private matter and I talk to Mother Mary if I need to say anything.

Megina says she would be very pleased to train Plesance in the duties of a lady's maid, but says she needs to be a few years older before taking on this job full-time. We agree she will not need any training to help with the children. However, I remind Megina that she must tell Plesance that looking after the children of a duke brings the extra responsibility of having to consider their safety at all times. She may have to go into some detail and determine if Plesance is mature enough to understand the implications. Megina understands this perfectly and I know I can trust her to do all that is needed. She laughs when we discuss Robert's energy and antics and agrees Colette is the perfect nursemaid for him. She is sure he is going to be crawling soon and pulling himself up in the next few weeks and before we know, he will be walking and climbing into everything. Megina suggests that a young male could be found to play boisterous games with him in the few years before he goes to military training. After Megina departs, I'm reminded of my determination to educate my male children so that they do not have the disadvantage of illiteracy like their father. This will require much thought and tactful planning so that Robert is properly educated and William is not embarrassed.

I retire, but sleep fitfully, worrying about William. Mass is a comfort this morning and Abbot John says he will look in later. I invite him to Dinner and look forward to his company. Of course, he knows about Domfront and Alençon because it seems that the monks always get the news before anyone else. I sit in the Hall with refreshments and a visitor is announced; Prior Lanfranc to give us his blessing. Has the Pope said anything about our marriage? He has not and the Prior thinks he is persuaded that consanguinity between us is a myth, but will take his time to remove the Ban. I think the Pope will not want to lose face, but I don't say this to the Prior and instead thank him for his participation in the matter. Prior Lanfranc knows about William ousting Guy of Brionne after his Pardon and his flight to Anjou, but does not know the present developments. I tell him the overall situation which does not surprise him as Guy has always been hostile to William. He then tells me about his latest work which examines the arguments of St Paul the Apostle in the light of the Rules of Logic. I am fascinated as his presence diverts me from my worries, making the time pass quickly. Abbot John arrives and we three dine together and continue the same subject about which Abbot John also has opinions. All most stimulating and I realise I have been missing this level of conversation. Prior Lanfranc promises to visit regularly as he particularly wants to see William too.

CHAPTER 12

THE DOMFRONT CAMPAIGN

1051

William returns, dejected. They have seen off the invasion force with some loss of our men, but it looks as if sieges of Domfront and Alençon will be just as ineffective as the siege of Brionne. His generals are summoned to Rouen to discuss strategy. We have a quiet Supper and I try to comfort him, but he is really tired and out of spirits. We retire to bed quite early and find great comfort in each other.

Prior Lanfranc joins us for Mass and Abbot John says prayers for William's well-being and strength and for the unity of Normandy. Back at the palace, William and the Prior retire to the office and refreshments are taken into them. A servant brings a message from Count William to tell us that he and Adeliza have a son! What blessed news! I send their pigeon back immediately with our love and good wishes. What is his name? I shall have to wait as Breteuil is over a hundred miles away. William seems more positive having talked with the Prior who is obviously going to be of great support. What a relief he is back with us and all that trouble following the Ban apparently over. William is delighted to hear about the FitzOsberns' son and heir and predicts he'll be called 'William'. Won't that be muddling deciding who is being addressed, father or son? Why not 'Osbern' like his grandfather?

Just before Supper, our pigeon returns with a single word: "William". Of course! Did William know that beforehand? Maybe, he says. The next days pass slowly and despite my pleasure in Robert's progress, I would be bored without the stimulating conversation of Abbot John and Prior Lanfranc during their regular, but infrequent visits. On the last occasion, we were told that the Prior has been accused of heresy by Berenger of Tours. This Archbishop and Christian theologian has written to him accusing him of supporting the belief that the bread and wine of Mass contains 'The Real Presence', the actual body and blood of Christ. Berenger does not support this crucial tenet of our Catholic faith, but instead believes in 'Transubstantiation' by which God instils the spiritual essence of Christ's body and blood into the Eucharistic bread and wine. Surely, this is *heresy* against what we all believe! Christ told us the bread and wine of Mass contains his actual body and blood. Of course, it's true so who dares support Berenger? The Prior tells us that Berenger's fiercely loyal supporter is Count Geoffrey Martel of Anjou. Who else? That man is everywhere, fighting my husband and now interfering with our faith. What next? The Prior is taking Berenger's letter to the King's Council; to your Uncle's court he says, looking at me intently. Indeed. We shall be most interested to see what happens. I greatly enjoy this theological discussion, but I would rather be at William's table discussing Norman military policy.

This difficult time means we are not able to visit my parents as I planned with Mother. William is too busy and nearly always away and has forbidden me to leave the abbey grounds. Nor can Robert travel and it looks as though he will have his first birthday before they see him. I send my parents a message explaining what is happening, but no doubt Father knows the situation already. William and I are now godparents of the new baby, William FitzOsbern, but sadly we could not go to his christening. Just as I'm thinking about this and praying for baby William, Adeliza asks if she can visit, bringing baby William, her maid, her wet-nurse and a posse of bodyguards. I reply immediately saying please come! What good news!

Prior Lanfranc visits again and tells me he sent Berenger's letter to Pope Leo IX which resulted in Berenger being condemned as a heretic without being heard, by a synod at Rome and another at Vercelli. His enemies in France cast him into prison, but the Bishop of Angers and other powerful friends had sufficient influence to procure his release. I don't agree with Berenger's views, but I defend his right to speak out in theological circles if he is trying prayerfully to understand his faith. However, as his main supporter is Geoffrey Martel, I would not expect to have anything in common with that man and would prefer he was the one in prison where he could think about his alliances.

A sizeable force arrives, bodyguards for Adeliza and her entourage and in the throng, there is Count William and there's my William too so now we have three Williams in the palace! Baby FitzOsbern has his father's prominent nose, but of course, I do not mention it while saying what a handsome child he is, just like his father! Count William is clearly delighted with his son, but too nervous to pick him up and when placed in his arms, he holds him firmly to his chest as if afraid he will drop him! Relieved of his child, he gazes at him with adoration. Adeliza looks well and she is pleased with her wet-nurse, wife of one of Count William's knights and mother of a baby daughter. I'll find out how things really are when she and I are alone.

The men go off and I take Adeliza and baby William to the nursery where her wet-nurse and maid are being welcomed by Megina. Robert approaches, crawling at speed, and pulls himself up using a chair and makes noises of welcome and excitement, 'bé-bé-bé.' Is he trying to say 'baby?' He certainly is! Holding on to a chair, he jumps up and down, waving his arms, a bundle of energy. He will be walking any minute now. Stefan still sits resolutely still, his big dark eyes wide open, taking it all in, but uninterested in making any effort to join in. It's as if he wants to ignore baby things like crawling and is waiting for serious stuff of being a big boy. Megina is totally relaxed, saying he is a happy child who is determined to do exactly what he wants so he will crawl precisely when he chooses which may mean never.

The next day, our men go to Rouen where Counts Beaumont and Montgomery will join them with other top generals including Walter Giffard and William's brother, Robert de Mortain, step-father Herluin of Conteville and Uncle Robert d'Eu. Quite a family gathering! Sadly, old Wigod of St Denis has recently died. Adeliza and I are left on our own and we walk round the abbey grounds, with bodyguards at a discreet distance. It's getting cold now and it must be near the time of

Robert's first birth. Adeliza says that things are back to normal now and she creeps into William's bed every morning again. In fact, he has become so much more interested in coupling that he visits her chamber at other times too. She thinks that the birth of his son and heir has made him come alive and she is not objecting to this at all! We laugh together and count our blessings. Looking at her, I get the feeling she's pregnant again, but tactful enough not to tell me as she knows I am not. Why not? I hope this is not going to be a problem. Apparently, Dame Mabel has given birth to a daughter named Aimeria. Poor wretched baby! I'll pray for her. The days pass and Adeliza is still here. She is a loving friend and good company and it's not her fault that she cannot enter the theological debate which I need to sustain me. I also wish I could be part of the team planning military strategy on our southern border. I pray that these wishes may be granted, at the same time asking forgiveness for my poor appreciation of my privileged life. Mother Mary, hear my prayers.

Mother Mary has answered! Already! A message comes early with Megina, arriving to help me rise and dress for Mass. The Williams, Count Herluin and the two Count Rogers will be here today for Dinner at one o'clock. Tomorrow, all our guests will go home. This afternoon, William and his generals wish to discuss their military plans with me. I can't believe it! With *me*? Apparently, my participation in Father's 'Flanders' Policy' is known and respected, but I doubt if they know how often I had to restrain Father from unwise courses of action. Since I left home, I have disapproved of some of his actions and would have tried to stop him on several occasions. Well, this is a great opportunity for me and I must be careful how I respond to their plans. Also, I must be careful not to convey my pleasure and excitement at this request to Adeliza in case she thinks I'm pleased she is to leave.

When we return from Mass, the palace is buzzing with activity and I hear Antoine giving instructions in an unusually strong tone of voice. The boy is being sent back to the fish market as Antoine is not satisfied with the amount he has returned with. He has to feed the Duke and his most important generals who have good appetites. Doesn't the stupid boy understand instructions? There's a loud bang in the kitchen and I shut my door.

I sense disappointment in Adeliza's voice when she tells me she is going home tomorrow.

'I shall miss you so much, it's been lovely staying here.'

'I shall miss you too. Have you any close friends at home?'

'Not like you. I do know some people, but I would not call any of them "close".'

'What about the lady who is wet-nursing William?'

'She's nice, but so quiet and all she does is embroidery, which is beautiful but she is not really interested in other art forms or music and does not play an instrument.'

'Why not ask Countess Adeline if she knows any ladies of your age who live nearby? Or I could ask William's Aunt Beatrice at Eu?'

'Good idea and I could go and see either happily, but both are a generation older than me which does make a difference.'

'I believe you said you had no sisters. What about your brothers and their wives?'

'Oh dear! Since we're on the subject of the male members of my family, did you know that my father Roger de Toeny was one of William's cousins who objected to him becoming Duke of Normandy because of his bastard birth?'

'I did know that and none of us can be responsible for our parents' actions.'

'Father was Ancestral Standard Bearer for the Duchy of Normandy and it upsets me to think he was so disloyal.'

'He's passed on now, I believe, as are your elder brothers. I understand your brother Ralf is now Ancestral Standard Bearer and loyal to William?'

'You seem to know everything! Yes, that's right. He's twenty-one, but not yet betrothed or married and my brother Robert is only eleven.'

'I give up! You'll just have to come and stay here more often!' Off she goes to prepare for her departure tomorrow, a little happier by the look of her. It must be awful to feel so lonely. Mother Mary, bless my dear friend Adeliza and give her the opportunity and will to make more close friends. Our Dinner is a superb tribute to Antoine's culinary magic. We start with lobster and scallops, with his delicate homemade sauces and our abbey's baked bread. Then a haunch of venison and little portions of tender rabbit and more meats, but I cannot eat a lot because of my anticipation of this meeting this afternoon. Such a lot of food, rapidly disappearing. Are these men going to be sensible after eating so heartily at this feast? I'm pleased to see that wine is not served and the men keep to their usual ale, quite weak at William's request. I am enjoying the food, but desperate to get on to the real business of the day, discussing what to do about the seizure of Domfront and Alençon by Geoffrey Martel and his allies. Will they present their ideas and expect me to agree? Will my opinion be respected? Matilda, this is ridiculous, they have invited you so of course, you will have a part to play. Guide me I pray. We finish the meal and William, his three close friends and Count Herluin sit with me at a table in the Hall. William starts the proceedings.

'We are here to discuss our response to Count Geoffrey Martel's invasion of Normandy and seizure of Domfront and Alençon castles. Duchess Matilda, we would value your response to the situation given your experience in advising your father and me.' Somehow, I didn't expect my new formal form of address to be used by our friends, but I'm pleased because it reinforces the formality of this business meeting. They await my response.

'Thank you, gentlemen. I think we all agree the underlying motivation for this recent attack is the campaign by Duke William's enemies to replace him with their preferred claimant to the Dukedom of Normandy.

The present situation is that Geoffrey Martell, supported by Guy of Brionne, has invaded and seized Domfront and Alençon castles and our land between Domfront and the Maine border. We successfully engaged Martel's forces when they invaded further north into Normandy and drove them back to Domfront Castle and beyond. We have set up a four-tower siege of Domfront Castle. We have placed a defence unit at a distance north of the castle, backed by soldiers checking routes to repel further invasion of Normandy.

So, our aims are to drive Geoffrey Martel out of Normandy and back to Maine, protect our borders against future invasion and re-take our castles at Domfront and Alençon. Timing is crucial and I suggest we act immediately, because we'll catch the enemy unprepared and while we also have the support of King Henry of West Frankia. On that subject, although King Henry is still William's avowed "Liege Lord", there are indications that he is becoming threatened by William's increasing power base and may withdraw his support at any time. We are nearing Christmas followed by Lent and Easter when we do not fight. If we don't act now, the enemy has four months to become further entrenched. What do you all think about timing?'

Count Roger de Montgomery, the strategist, is first to speak, 'I agree, we should act immediately. Our army is in good shape following military training at Falaise during the summer. What do you think Duke William?'

'I agree and the timing is auspicious, November being when my ancestor Rollo became leader of Normandy and also very near the birth time of my son and heir.'

The other men nod. William smiles at me, 'Please continue, Duchess Matilda.'

'Thank you. I have made a map as I am not familiar with the places we are talking about.

Driving Martel back to Maine *is* our main aim, but using subterfuge we can fool Martel into believing our main focus is on regaining both castles, with the most emphasis on Domfront. We should give the impression that the present siege of Domfront Castle is being escalated although we know as well as he does that it is unlikely to succeed, especially in the short-term. If we get this right, he will be complacent about our direction of attack.

Our objectives: muster three armies, two at Falaise to head towards Domfront and one at Rouen to head towards Alençon to further convince Martel of our intentions. This is a bluff because our real intention is to set the armies to form a pincer movement from the East and West of Domfront to defeat the enemy now occupying our ground between Domfront and the Maine border.

The reason for two armies going from Falaise is again subterfuge. Army One marches straight towards Domfront and joins our defence unit to the castle's North so Martel's scouts report a large force assembled to attack. A wagon of tar barrels will go too. Army Two from Falaise follows at an interval and musters behind Army One, impressing on the enemy an ever-increasing number and threat. Army Three marches to Bellême Castle and camps on its West side so Martel's scouts report that Alençon Castle is also a target, whereas the actual target is the enemy-occupied land South of Domfront. Before Army Three sets off from Rouen, King Henry's agreement is needed to take a direct route across West Frankian land towards Alençon rather than the longer northern route through Norman territory. Army Three will ignore Alençon and head straight along the Maine border to the East of Domfront Castle to be joined by half of Army Two. Army One and the other half of Army Two march West of Domfront Castle. When armies One and Two are well on their way the tar barrels are set alight to the North of Domfront Castle to make a pall of smoke alerting the enemy that the attack is coming from the North.

Timing should include an element of surprise, so these manoeuvres need to take place at night. At an agreed time, both armies go into battle to regain the land between the castle and the border by attacking Martel's army from each side. Domfront Castle is ignored as the land between Domfront and the border is regained leaving its inhabitants, Martel's soldiers and any Norman traitors, marooned. Gentlemen, you are the experts in warfare, and I hope these plans might be of help.'

The generals look at me and then at each other. William eventually speaks.

'I'm glad it's Saturday. Do we all agree we'll have the Sabbath to pray and to rest and start our campaign on Monday at dawn?' The men look rather dazed but nod kindly at me and while I'd like appreciation, I also revel in the fact they are treating me as an equal, not as a contributor of inferior status.

'We do,' they say in unison. I leave them to talk and go to see Robert who is now walking. He is his usual exuberant form. I'm pleased to see that Adeliza and everyone else in the nursery is taking delight in the children's progress. Everything has gone well today so why do I feel unreasonably miserable? Back in my chamber, I sit on my bed feeling deflated and sorry for myself when in rushes William who gathers me up and lies me gently down and lies beside me, holding me tight.

'We *will* go to Bonneville to finish our honeymoon, Matilda, but we'll have to wait until we get this campaign over.'

'I know, don't worry.'

'The other thing is that Count Herluin tells me that Mother is ill. I really need to go and see her, but unfortunately the timing is difficult at present.'

'Of course, you must go. Now before it's too late. You'd never forgive yourself if she died before you said goodbye. Why don't you and Count Herluin go this afternoon so you can spend time with your mother and then set off for Rouen on Sunday so you will be ready in good time for everyone to arrive to discuss the details of your campaign?'

'You really are a most amazing woman, a first-class military strategist, mother of my son and heir and my dearest wife who may care to join her husband now in some practice for our postponed honeymoon?' Oh yes, I much care to join him and of course, now realise why I was feeling so miserable! Our pent-up passion gives renewed energy and excitement to our coupling and the memory of such joys will sustain me when he goes away. Perhaps he has just planted a baby, but I know that pregnancy does not depend on the quality of coupling, however pleasurable. On many occasions, I have listened to a pregnant servant girl who tells me how she was cruelly forced resulting in a baby. She loves her baby despite its savage planting and she knows that her previous poor but regular circumstances will change to much harder work and poverty. Also, there's no doubt that while we noble ladies accept it is our duty to bear children and we delight in them, some are used by their noble husbands in a brutish manner, in other words rape. Praise Mother Mary I am not in that situation.

William and Count Herluin leave for Conteville and the rest of our guests make plans for tomorrow. The two Count Rogers and Count William are going straight to Rouen as going via their homes would make too long a journeys. Adeliza and her entourage will travel with a substantial force to protect them on their way to Breteuil. I wonder how much the generals will tell Dame Mabel about their strategy, if anything.

She's still at Bellême where she appears to live rather than at St-Germain-de-Montgommery and when she sees the troops approaching, she may well think they are about to further reinforce her father's domain. Much as I distrust her, I don't think even she would dare to act against her husband Count Roger, William's Chief General who did tell me that baskets of pigeons had been exchanged between Bellême Castle and Rouen. I think we can be reassured about Dame Mabel's loyalty if her husband is prepared to rely on her. Despite Dame Mabel, that will probably be our safest passage of communication.

After Mass today, the rest of our guests leave. Last night we had a simple supper and retired early to our chambers. I shall make preparations for Christmas and will be at home to my usual visitors, Abbot John, Prior Lanfranc and William of Jumièges. I always enjoy their company and may get some information which could be helpful to our campaign. This is a difficult time waiting for news so I must keep busy. Megina comes to help me before I retire and says she knows it must be a major campaign because Ralf has gone with William's spare horses. Now she looks at me intently as if she has something more to say.

'Megina, what is on your mind?'

'I have just received my first message ever, addressed to "Madame Megina, Lady of the Bedchamber to Duchess Matilda of Normandy".'

'Who sent it and what was it about?'

'Agnês, Lady of the Bedchamber to Countess Arlette. She says to tell you her mistress is dying and she is asking for you. Could you please come immediately?'

'Of course, I will. Please tell my bird keeper to send the Conteville pigeon back as soon as possible saying I will leave after Mass tomorrow.' I sleep fitfully, full of foreboding for this campaign and thinking about Countess Arlette and her extraordinary life and how this lady of humble origin is the ancestor of generations of Norman nobility.

After Mass, Abbot John asks if I would accept his company on the journey to Conteville, along with the large force of bodyguards left in charge by William. He would enjoy the chance of talking to me and he would also seek to give words of comfort and blessing to Countess

Arlette in her last hours. When she was here, he found her to be a deeply religious lady, which is an aspect of her I had not formerly appreciated. Of course, his presence would be comforting to me too and I know William will be pleased to hear his opinion of his mother and his offer to accompany me. We arrive just before Dinner and are ushered by a servant into the Hall where two ladies are sitting taking refreshment. Seeing us, they rise to greet us. Bridget! We embrace warmly and I turn to the other lady who looks somehow familiar. Beatrice introduces us, 'Adelaide, Countess of Aumale.' I see a tall well-built lady of about my age whose resemblance to William strikes me immediately. She towers above me.

'Your Grace.'

We shake hands gently and smile tentatively, appraising each other's response as we know we have much to say to each other. I ask her to call me 'Matilda' and she responds accordingly with the invitation to call her 'Adelaide'. She smiles and tells me she and Bridget have been in to see Countess Arlette, but found her asleep. Bridget suggests I go in now as she is near her end and this afternoon may be too late. I sit by her bed and look at her thin pale face turned to the side on the pillow. I don't know if she can hear me, but I tell her how proud William is of her and how much his position in life has been moulded by her. At the same time, I'm thinking it's likely she had very little influence on his life having had to leave him at such a young age. Mother Mary, forgive me for these thoughts and guide me in saying what will make her last moments happy. I tell her that her deportment as First Lady of Normandy and then as Countess of Conteville has won her great respect. Noble ladies seek to follow her example. She turns her head just slightly in my direction as I say how much I love William and that I will look after him, baby Robert and the other children we will have one day. I tell her how much we love her and with her eyes still closed, she makes a tiny movement of her hand towards me. I put my hand on hers. I tell her how much Count Herluin and her children love her as her breathing becomes rasping and laboured. I call downstairs. I hear Agnês call again. Bridget and Adelaide come in followed by Abbot John and I beckon Agnês to come in too. Abbot John takes one look at her and begins to administer the Viaticum. As the Countess cannot physically take the sacramental bread and wine, he brings out a small phial of holy oil and makes a sign of the cross on her forehead. He says the holy words and reads aloud the twenty-third psalm, 'The Lord is my Shepherd' and we say 'Amen.' Abbot John suggests we say good-bye and leave her in the tender care of Agnês and Mother Mary, but I stay as William and Count Herluin would expect me to do. Abbot John and I continue to pray, now joined again by Bridget, Adelaide and Agnês. We see the Countess pass gently away.

We are now well into the afternoon and Bridget is in charge. She calls Count Herluin's Steward and asks him to see to the arrangements for wrapping the body in preparation for burial. The funeral will have to be postponed until Count Herluin returns, but due dignity and respect must be shown in the necessary interim measures. We ladies sit together and talk a little about Countess Arlette. We agree that as she has been ailing for a while, the arrangements for care of the younger children will be in place at least until Count Herluin returns. Odo is settled at Fécamp Abbey learning how to be a bishop and Robert is no doubt involved in the present military campaign under the supervision of Count Roger de Montgomery. Having ascertained I can be of no further help to Bridget just now, I retire to my chamber.

When I go down to the Hall before Supper, I sit with Adelaide and tell her how sorry I was to hear that the Pope excommunicated her ex-husband, Count Enguerrand, and hope that this was not the cause of the annulment of their marriage. Adelaide says it did not help and she noted that the same reason of consanguinity had prompted the Pope to ban our marriage too. The real trouble was that her husband's sister married William of Talou who claims he should be Duke of Normandy in place of William, her brother and my husband. She's sorry to say that Count Enguerrand supports his claim. Oh dear! She says that the Terms of the Annulment are being negotiated and she hopes William will find her a handsome lord who is loyal to him! We laugh at this and I promise to relay her message to William.

She is pleased that he and I seem so happy which is generous of her considering the sad end of her marriage. She has a baby daughter

Adeliza, a first cousin for Robert. We agree she must come and see us and bring Adeliza to really get to know each other. I'd genuinely like to keep in touch with her. She is so like William to look at but I don't know her character. Bridget comes in, looking tired as she is having a lot to do concerning her sister's death. Raoul has gone on the campaign with Count Herluin. Thinking about all our men and boys, I can only suppose of all of us present, it is only Count Enguerrand who is fighting with Geoffrey Martel and he doesn't count having abandoned poor Adelaide.

Next morning after Mass, Abbot John and I bump back to Fécamp in the carriage, and he is particularly understanding about my present concerns. No, he has not had any news and would not expect it. Sending pigeons during a campaign is unwise as the enemy can intercept information which could obstruct the sender's military plans. We discuss theological issues of interest to us both including details of the Viaticum which he has just delivered to Countess Arlette. As we drive into the palace courtyard, I see another carriage and recognise it immediately. My parents are here! Oh no! Not what I need just now. I'd been looking forward to some peace and quiet and a chance to prepare myself for the outcome of the campaign. Mother Mary, forgive my selfish wish to ask them to go away. Of course, they should be here, and I had promised them with Robert until Martel's invasion put everything on hold. Forgive me for being thankful that Martel's invasion broke my promise to visit them. The truth is, I can't face the journey to Flanders or prospect of days in my parent's company away from William. Now I have twice disobeyed the Holy Commandment to honour my parents. I make a quick confession to Abbot John who absolves me of these sins, blesses me and off he goes.

Servants come out to greet me and tell me Count Baldwin and Countess Adela are in the nursery. Naturally, they are! I peep round the door and see Robert walking confidently round the room, laughing happily and Father and Mother gazing at him adoringly. They take a brief moment to respond to my greeting as they are absorbed in watching their first grandson. Both embrace me, but I feel them tense with longing to return to the object of their present interest who plays up wonderfully, enjoying the attention. I have to say he is an engaging child with his blonde curls and friendly happy manner. Megina looks in and I think she is probably pregnant again which reminds me that I've had no flow for a while. She looks well and I ask after Stefan who she has obviously removed allowing Robert to enjoy his grandparents' full attention. It is time for Robert to go to bed so Megina takes him now. Father and Mother have already been given their chambers and say they will now retire and hope to see me in the Hall before Supper. I go to my chamber and lie on my bed thinking about everything going on. Mother Mary, protect William and bring him home soon. Pray for us who support his campaign and grant that it is successful with little loss of life in the process. Oh, and Holy Mother Mary, grant that a new baby is growing within me, preferably a second son for William and if a daughter, she would make us happy too.

I sit with Mother and Father and we ladies are served Perry and Father has the best ale. They have news for me. Did I know that Hermann of Mons has died? I did not, but suspect his death is significant to our family. Mons is the capital of Hainaut, land adjacent to Flanders. Father says his widow Richilde is now Countess of Hainaut and I'm beginning to see where this is going. Of course, a desirable bride with some inheritance! I'm right; my parents announce that my brother Baldwin is formally betrothed to Richilde. I express my congratulations and wonder if I shall ever hear how Father managed this. Father looks at me.

'Thank you, Matilda, but knowing you as I do, what is on your mind?'

'Well, as Hainaut is in West Frankia, Baldwin will become Count of Hainaut when he marries Richilde, so how do you think Uncle Henry will respond?'

'Not well I suppose, but nothing changes. We are always having skirmishes along that border.' Mother joins in. 'We also have a new English visitor staying in our court, Earl Godwin, who has been expelled by King Edward.'

Father speaks quickly and perhaps defensively. 'We are his natural refuge as Tostig Godwinson and Judith are still with us, having been expelled as well. I don't approve of my sister being expelled, but of course, she *is* one of the Godwins now!'

'She certainly is and how is Aunt Judith? I have always been fond of her.'

'She is well and we hear she is expecting a baby in the late spring.'

'Good news, but I don't suppose hosting the Godwins makes our family any more popular with King Edward!'

'You are right, King Edward won't like it, but if the Godwins are with us in Bruges, at least he knows where they are. Tostig has always identified himself as a Norseman, loyal to his mother's Swedish family and no friend of the English. At least he is not in Norway with his fellow Norsemen who remain a threat to any of our shores. If and when they do plan an invasion, Tostig is bound to be involved, if not leading it.'

Now Mother, fidgeting, looking fed up with this subject, declares she is off to spend more time with Robert before they leave on Friday. Three more days of trying to be welcoming and interested in their affairs is going to be so hard while I am desperate to know what is happening at Domfront and Alençon. I can't think about anything else and really do not want them here when William returns. I'd rather be on my own when he gets back. As if reading my mind, Father asks me about the present campaign, and I say I obviously can't tell him anything much and that I do not know how it is going let alone the outcome. Father says he has great sympathy for William with so many enemies particularly from his father's family. I tell him I was consulted about strategy and he says he is not surprised having been taught by the expert! He then looks at me in intently and adds that if William does turn up unexpectedly, they will leave immediately. I give him a hug. What a relief!

I make sure I spend equal time with Mother who says she can tell I am in the early stages of pregnancy. I tell her she's right and she is supportive and kind. I hold my breath, praying that for once she won't say it, but of course, she does.

'Does William know?'

'Not yet.'

'He will be delighted that a second son is on the way.' Mother has no idea that this is an annoying remark. Of course, William would prefer a son! I bite my tongue and remind myself she does mean well. The days pass, my parents leave and on the Saturday a message arrives, saying 'Successful campaign, back tomorrow.'

Sleep is elusive and I go to Mass knowing I should be feeling relieved and thankful to Mother Mary for the reported outcome of our campaign. Yet, there is a heaviness in my heart which I try to ignore. What has happened?

I hear the horses arrive and go out to greet William. There he is, but then his three friends appear, Count William FitzOsbern and the two Count Rogers. What is going on? Why are they here when they should be going home? The men retire to the washrooms, but it's Count William who comes straight to greet me.

'Your plans worked well, Your Grace. We've pushed Martel back to Maine!'

'All the plans?'

'Pretty well, but there were unexpected outcomes.'

'Is William all right?'

'No, he's not all right which is why we've come back with him. We generals needed to make sure you were here.' Before he can continue, William appears and the Count rushes off, presumably to the washroom. William picks me up to kiss me, face-face, holding me as if not wanting to let go. He puts me down when the Counts join us and we go into the Hall for refreshment.

'This is most welcome Your Grace, just what we need to keep us going on our onward journey to Rouen.' Count William makes it clear they are not staying, thus leaving us on our own. Good, please go now! After the minimally decent time for refreshments, Count William glances at me.

'Come, my friends, time to go.' Each of these foremost generals of William's forces and our closest friends lightly embrace me while thanking me gruffly for my part in their latest campaign. They embrace William strongly, giving him the typical male bang on the back. Their accompanying guards and horses, all fed and watered, are ready too. We see them off and return to the palace, straight to our quarters. Oh, what am I going to be told? Mother Mary, keep me strong and bless my beloved husband.

He says he is desperate for me and I tell him I feel the same and we couple immediately with great passion. He kisses and strokes me, combining his male domination with tenderness. He never causes me any pain which is quite a feat considering his immense size in all parts, nor does he force himself on me or rush me which might be expected from someone in his position. He is a wonderful lover and fortunately, I am most enamoured of coupling too. We lay there, the unknown problem to be sorted out in time, but until we have to do that, we cuddle together and soon start to couple again. And again. Eventually, as we lie together, I realise something has changed. He is crying, deep body-shuddering sobs. I hold him, stroking him and wait. He will tell me when he's ready. Gradually, he calms down and is still. He seems to be asleep, but then he starts to talk.

The campaign went almost exactly as planned. Martel and his border force were driven back to Maine leaving whoever was still inside Domfront Castle to be dealt with later. In the middle of the campaign, his Uncle William of Talou and Arques left our ranks and joined Martel. William and his army marched on to Alençon where Martel's men and the local people had not surrendered, but stood on the walls jeering as William approached. They had hung animal skins along the route to taunt William about his humble origins, his grandfather being a tanner. Worse than this, they shouted 'Pelterer' at him inferring that his grandfather had also been an embalmer dealing with human skins. Even worse was the disrespect to his mother as they shouted her name with rude allusion to her involvement in her father's business. Worse again were the taunts that the displayed human skins were those of William's men recently killed in the present campaign.

'Matilda, I saw red and did something I think I may regret.'

'Go on.'

'I had the people responsible brought before me and I gave orders to blind them and cut off their hands and feet and throw them away.'

'Only after they schemed to give you the most offence they could imagine! They knew you would be goaded into extreme action.'

'Are you shocked?'

'Yes, by the depths of their personal cruelty to you rather than by your strong reaction. Their actions were carefully and maliciously planned and, understandably, your immediate need was to inflict pain on the perpetrators. You did that and you are bound to be disturbed by your extreme punishment, but your response was entirely human. We cannot all be perfect like Mother Mary without sin. You must go to Abbot John tomorrow, confess what you did and make due penance. Naturally, it's going to be on your mind, but confession will make a start to getting it into perspective.'

'Why do the people of Alençon hate and despise me so much?'

'Of course, they don't, not in their right minds. How could these simple townspeople plan such detailed personal insults if not put up to it? It's most likely the scheme of those snakes Geoffrey Martel and Guy de Brionne. The local people had no detailed knowledge of your family background and were forced to take these actions. They had no choice in the matter. Did any of them seem drunk?'

'Now you mention it, they behaved like madmen shouting abuse.'

'Out of their senses. If they had thought about what they were ordered to do, they would have known it meant certain death, however delivered.'

'You are right! I don't deserve you.'

'Of course you do, and you've also got your top generals, your friends, on your side.'

'They are affected by the incident.'

'I expect they are, but as soldiers they understand these things are part of war. One thing is certain: no-one is going to goad you like that again!'

'True! When we got back to Domfront, the news must have got through to the castle because it was empty. We must go down to secure it in the next few days.'

'Well, that's off your chest and I want to hear about the rest of the campaign later. Meanwhile I have some news for you.'

'Really?'

‘Real enough. Our next baby is on the way, but it is early days.’ He seems to recover for the moment, laying his cheek against my stomach and whispering to its occupant. He tells the tiny being in there that he’s going to build a new palace as our family is already outgrowing Fécamp. Good, that means he’s moving on. We pull ourselves together and go to see Robert before he goes to bed. Our son is lively as ever and roars with laughter as his father tosses him in the air, swirling him round. Will he ever settle after such excitement? He’s a bundle of energy and has a most engaging smile. He still seems small, but he’s bound to be since he takes after me. We have a simple supper and retire. William falls asleep instantly and I lie there thinking about the Alençon business. Yes, William’s response was definitely cruel and better to have shot the culprits, but in his red rage, fired by the heat of the moment, that was too good for them. After Mass the next morning, I leave him with Abbot John and pray for his absolution.

CHAPTER 13

INVASION OF ENGLAND ON THE HORIZON

1052-3

It's nearly Christmas and we welcome Count Herluin who brings his three daughters and two nannies. Poor children, it must be so hard losing their mother. Robert comes up from Falaise and, of course, the pompous Bishop of Bayeux is here anyway. I must get over my misgivings about Odo and acknowledge his exalted position by asking him to say Grace before all meals. Let's pray he doesn't let the food get cold. On Christmas Eve, William bounds in and says some more visitors have turned up, a surprise for me. In comes Adeliza, full of joy. How wonderful and as we hug each other, I say, 'You are, aren't you?' She laughs,

'And you are too!' This is so exciting and just what we need. Two more babies on the way. She is followed by Count William and little William who looks exactly like his proud father.

Apart from the deep religious significance of Christmas, its celebration is a joyous time with the family, relations and friends, but underneath it all, I am dissatisfied. I know it's ungrateful, but I yearn for more military planning and taking part in the governance of Normandy with the responsibilities and respect these positions engender. Instead, I envisage being permanently pregnant with a baby every year until I am past having them by which time, I shall be old and exhausted. Part of the problem is that as this pregnancy progresses into the spring, I know it is completely different from my first one. This baby is going to be much bigger than Robert. I feel uncomfortable and as I balloon up and the kicking starts, I feel bruised and half-expect a limb to burst through my skin. I am tired and impatient. Nor is coupling easy, although William is thrilled because he says his next son will be just like him. I fear he's right and Dame Mabel's spiteful words come back to haunt me, 'wait until you have a huge baby with shoulders like Duke William. Most women would not survive that.'

And so, we go on and see in a new year. Adeliza's daughter, called Emma, is born in June. The image of her mother, she echoes the FitzOsbern pattern of likeness following father and son. She is a pretty child and I am proud to be her godmother. I'd love to have a daughter after producing a male heir, but it won't be this time with this big William baby inside me. In early July, I go into that wretched birthing-chamber and pray that the birth is soon and quick. This time, my midwife is Colette's mother, a dear soul, unlike the hateful Maria for which deliverance I thank Mother Mary. Colette comes too, telling me she is going to be a midwife one day. The birthing-chamber itself is not as suffocating as last time as the people around me are so much nicer, although the pregnancy is increasingly difficult. I hear the women whispering that my petite bone structure may prevent me having this baby naturally and he may have to be cut out. I pray Dame Mabel has not cursed me. Adeliza says that if he is as determined as his father, he will come out properly and not give me trouble. We laugh and I feel better. The labour starts and it is a great effort to push him out, but my pain is helped by a concoction of hemlock, henbane and opium poppy, mild I'm assured. At last, he arrives, but the midwife says 'Your Grace, You have a beautiful daughter!' *A daughter?,* Can't be - I don't believe it! Not a William-like baby? No, our daughter looks at me, big-boned like her father, almost the size of Robert who, brought in to see his sister, shows utter disdain. I would not call her exactly pretty, but she is, well, 'striking' is the best word, with strong features. William is surprisingly enthusiastic about 'ma petite femina bellator', as he calls her. I suggest we call her Cecilia, but William declares her name is Adeliza, repeating it loudly as I protest that the name is over-used at present. I tell Abbot John her name is Cecilia.

Next to give birth is Megina whose second son, Bernhard, looks exactly like Stefan. The timing is perfect because she will be my wet nurse again, this time for Adeliza, my choice of name discarded by William without further consultation. Stefan is now walking although rather ponderously and he is so serious. Megina says he looked at Bernhard for a long time as if examining every part of him, his expression never changing. He hardly ever smiles, has not yet laughed, but did give his baby brother a little poke when he eventually had to leave this fascinating being.

Once churched, I have visits from Abbot John, William of Jumièges and even Prior Lanfranc and as ever, I am much stimulated by their conversation and realise my daily life is looking less restricted than I'd feared. Abbot John asks after my new baby Adeliza and after some discussion, he tells me she was so christened so that's that! I do not mention the matter to William which I think is admirable self-control! Naturally, he doesn't mention it either. William comes and goes, but is often away trying to anticipate trouble from his enemies. Geoffrey de Martel and Guy de Brionne are quiet at present, but that won't last long. It's time to deal with his other hostile relatives. I make a family tree to remind myself exactly where they fit in. My three clerical visitors supply much of the information.

I note that William's Uncle Mauger, Archbishop of Rouen, is a generation older than his brother William of Talou and his nephew Guy of Brionne, who are both around William's age. Apparently, Mauger has always opposed William's right to be Duke of Normandy denying the fact his father officially made him heir before leaving on his fateful pilgrimage. If he ever entertained the idea of being Duke himself, he's now given that up to promote the cause of his younger brother William of Talou. William told me that William of Talou has always treated him with open contempt as a bastard, but to keep him on side, he ignored this offence by giving him the lordship of Arques with its magnificent castle, Arques-la-Bataille, as well as the County of Talou. His generosity was repudiated by William of Talou's continued if covert hostility, his true position confirmed when he deserted to Martel's side in the recent campaign.

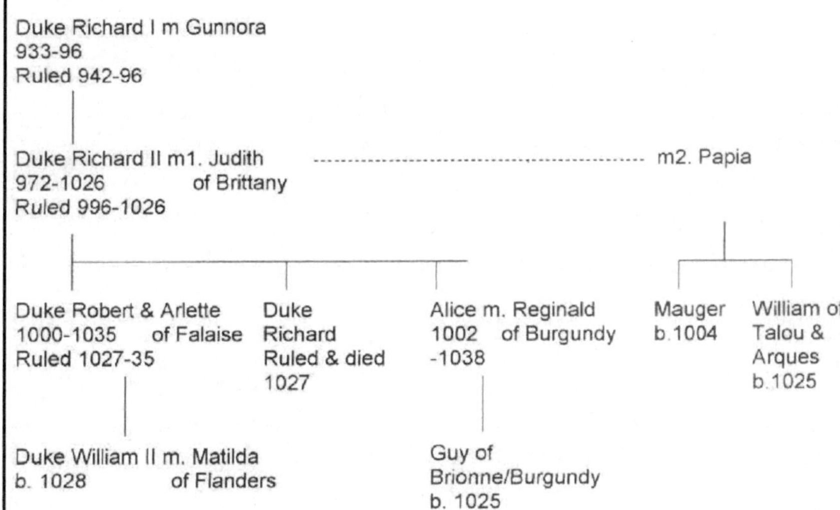

Duke Williams Hostile Relations

Regarding the Campaign, William secured Domfront Castle with more difficulty than anticipated. No sign of Martel or Brionne who had put in a sizeable force of men to defend to the death. Our men smoked them out in the end and left them to flee back over the border to face certain punishment. He now sets to sort out his Uncle William of Talou and Arques. He sends envoys commanding him to swear allegiance, but he replies with insults about William's low-class relations and bastard status. He goes further and gains the support of William's ex-brother-in-law Count Enguerrand of Ponthieu and worse, my Uncle Henry, King of the Franks. Just as well that traitor Enguerrand is now divorced from my sister-in-law Adelaide. As for Uncle Henry, I can't say I'm surprised that he's changed sides as he begins to realise the scale of William's ambitions. Nor will he be overjoyed about Father having designs on his lands through arranging my brother's betrothal to Richilde of Mons and Hainult. Well, we know where we are with William's real enemies buzzing out of the night's shadows like biting insects.

William lays siege to Arques-la-Bataille Castle, but finds William of Talou well-ensconced, no doubt expecting attack. William's knights are sent to stop supplies to the castle with an element of surprise, but this tactic has no effect. Talou remains in his castle and continues to be as offensive as possible to his nephew. William takes this unusually calmly, but I know that each poisonous remark makes him more determined to wipe out his verminous cousin. I watch him carefully, ready to praise his resilience and ability to rise above such mean conduct.

William summons his three generals and invites me to the campaign meeting. He proposes an immediate large-scale attack with all available forces. He is supported by Count William, but opposed by the two Count Rogers who assess the risk as too great against the combined military force of William of Talou and Count Enguerrand, backed by King Henry's Frankish forces. Stalemate. They look at me, expecting a response.

'Duke William is right. Our men are battle-ready. This campaign is as important as Domfront. If we let this enemy get away with treason, the rest will cause us more trouble.' William gives me one of his glances, Count William nods and the two Count Rogers are resigned, looking away. William takes charge, 'Muster our armies from Falaise and Rouen for immediate attack.'

The counts depart to put the plan into action. William gives me a hug and off he goes. He is back in less than a week and reports that the forces of Talou and his allies, while formidable, were less than anticipated due to the speed of our attack. A fierce battle took place about a mile from the castle and the first significant event was the death of Count Enguerrand which routed his men in disarray. William praised the bravery and skill of the Count, which was generous considering his former treachery. Using our advantage, we defeated them surprisingly quickly and took the castle. William of Talou was banished and warned that any attempt to return to his estates would be punished by death. At the same time, William banished Mauger for his disloyalty, so these two traitors are dealt with, for the moment. Presumably, the procedure for unseating an archbishop will follow.

William is pleased with the events, and especially appreciates the praise of the Count Rogers who say his instinct was right. They should have had faith in him. No-one mentions my input.

Easter is nearly here and William and I are going to Bonneville to resume our delayed honeymoon. We are to have the week before the festival on our own and then be joined by Ralf and Megina and the four children on Holy Wednesday. I want Megina to have a comparative rest too so in addition to our personal servants, plenty of nurse maids and kitchen staff will be engaged. We did discuss asking some of our close friends, but decided not to because of inevitable embarrassment of the required social intercourse between the different classes. Anyway, William said he'd have Ralf as a companion to go hunting in Saint-Gatien Forest. Seeing my expression, he gave me one of his quizzical looks.

'Do you know a monk called Maurilius, here at Fécamp Abbey?'

'Only to pass the time of day. He is reputed to be that rare soul who properly observes the Rule of Benedict.'

'Indeed, he is and when he was Abbot of St Mary's Florence, the monks revolted against his austerity and he returned here to Fécamp.'

'I approve of him and also I know from Abbot John and William of Jumièges that he is "a renowned scholar". Why do you ask if I know him?'

'I thought we might invite him to accompany us to Bonneville. It will be Easter and as an ordained priest he can take Mass and give the Holy

Eucharist while we are in residence. He would also be stimulating company for you when Ralf and I are at the Chase.'

'What a good idea! Yes, please ask him.' I sense there is something more to this suggestion, but I won't enquire just now as his presence would make my second week much more interesting than I had thought. Of course, Maurilius will accept.

Our first week is relaxed with plenty of coupling, laughing and going on gentle rides. William's order that Galathea should be brought is inspired for as soon as I mount, my doubts about riding again are dispersed. During this precious time together, William talks about his ambition to be King. Have I guessed which country he is planning to rule? Of course, it's England! William seems disappointed that I guessed correctly, but it has been obvious to me for some time.

'What do you think about this?'

'Wonderful! Naturally, you should be King of England!'

'I didn't know you felt so strongly?'

'Well, you do now and I want to be your queen, Queen of England!' He looks less than enthusiastic.

'It's not usual wanting that title, ladies are known as 'The King's Queen'.

'Well, this one won't and after all I am descended from King Alfred the Great of England and have every right to be Queen of England when you are King.'

He looks only slightly more convinced and takes a safer course. 'My father, Duke Robert, set off to invade England in an attempt to reinstate his cousins Edward and Alfred who had fled to Normandy with their mother, his Aunt Emma, when King Cnut took the English throne. However, the venture was a failure as adverse winds took the fleet off-course sinking many ships. I remember Edward who I met as young boy before his father died and then saw him from time to time over the next eight years or so before he returned to England to become King in 1043.'

'Do you think my father's recent brushes with King Edward had any effect on your long-term relationship with him?' William laughs, 'King

Edward knows it's nothing to do with me and we have been good friends for many years. I'm sure King Edward would prefer me to be King of England rather than a Dane or member of the Godwin family most of whom who he expelled from his shores to land up in the Flanders court.'

'So, are you planning an invasion?'

'Before I make any plans including invasion, I shall go to England to see my uncle, King Edward, who, as I said, I first met when I was that young boy left at Falaise Castle. I expect him to confirm me as his heir.'

'So, when are you leaving?'

'As soon as the weather improves, so probably next month.'

'Does that mean that you will not invade if King Edward promises he will name you to follow him?'

'It depends on whether I feel it's solid. Any doubt and we will make plans to invade.'

'Will that be soon?'

'No, because my first task is to take complete control of Normandy by sorting out my enemies. Also, we need to wait until Robert is old enough to take my place when I'm away.'

'He's only three so perhaps in fifteen years or so?'

'If he's anything like me, he will ready sooner than that. I had to take control at the age of twelve!'

'Your position was unique and you have done a great job ever since.' He's pleased with this praise and things are good between us.

The rest of our party arrives, the irrepressible Robert rushing in first and hurling himself at William, shrieking with delight. He is followed by Stefan, solemn as ever and walking at his particularly studied slow pace. And here come dear Megina and Ralf and our two babies with their nurse maids. After a few minutes, Maurilius arrives and greets us warmly, saying he is privileged to join our family at this special time. Can this be the austere monk I've observed at Fécamp? He is so warm and friendly and asks if the boys would like to play football in the yard. Of course, they would and Stefan is placed between the makeshift posts as he's never been known to run anywhere. Maurilius is going to be a great asset on this holiday as priest, child minder and scholar.

Our routine changes completely and I realise how unsuited I am to the minutiae of daily family life. I would not tell a soul how boring and exhausting I find it. Easter is the well-trodden emotional journey from infinite sadness to great joy and celebration. The children are too young to understand, but know it is special with more sweetmeats than usual. William and Ralf go off to St Gatien and now that Megina and I are together more often, it's obvious to both of us that our relationship has changed. Her focus is now on the children and management of her nurseries whereas I was always her main concern. We don't say this, of course. Always intuitive, she says Brother Maurilius is in the Hall and would I care to join him? Down I go and he stands to greet me.

'Did you know I was asked to leave St Mary's Abbey in Florence because I was too strict?' Straight to the point; I like that.

'I did know that and ask if you expected more of your monks than keeping to the Rule of Benedict?'

'I did not, but they were so far from this standard that as their Abbot it was my duty to take steps to remedy this.'

'Well, I respect you for that, but I'm afraid this laxness runs through the Mother Church.'

'Indeed, which is why I am relieved to be back here because Abbot John runs the sort of abbey where any departure from The Rule is noticed and dealt with immediately. That is not to say that long-established behaviours can be sorted out quickly. At least Pope Leo is seeking to improve standards among the clerics.'

'Have you met Pope Leo?'

'Yes, because when he received complaints about my austere rule at St Mary's he sent for me. He was disappointed to hear about the monks' poor standards.'

'Did he try and persuade you to continue as Abbot?'

'No, he didn't because he agreed with some of the criticism of me. He said he thought it would take a long time to change the customs of

St Mary's Abbey, and in his words, I had "tried to set new rules too quickly".'

'Do you agree with his judgement?'

'I think it's fair. Pope Leo became Head of the Universal Church a mere three years ago with no experience of religious life and from a background of wealth and business. When he now meets monks who have been living in religious houses for most of their lives, he is respectful of their views, but in saying I had "set new rules" it is obvious that he knows little of The Rule of Benedict. We should not expect too much of him and anyway his present focus is not so much on procedural reform of the abbeys, but the maintenance of celibacy among the clerics and the promotion of marriage in the nobility.'

'Did you know that as a young cleric St Benedict himself fell deeply in love with a lady and would have suffered pain through his vow of celibacy?'

'I did not know that.'

'He also had the reputation of being gentle and understanding at the same time as he sought to lead his erring monks out of temptation.'

'You have great knowledge which could inform Pope Leo.'

'I doubt if I'm the right person to talk to the Pope since there is the issue of his views on my marriage!'

'I was waiting for you to bring up the subject. The Pope asked after you and the Duke. He knows you married despite his Ban and it's obvious that he feels he has not treated you fairly and will soon lift it.'

'That's good to hear. Now, how you think Odo, Bishop of Bayeux, my young brother-in-law, is progressing in the religious life?'

'Your Grace, my respect, but it is not my place to discuss Bishop Odo. Abbot John is the person to ask.'

'I'm sorry, I should not have expected you to answer that. Quite right, but I do have two more questions to ask. Do you agree that Duke William is the legitimate hereditary Ruler of Normandy and do you support his right to confront his enemies to establish peace and unity in his domain?'

'My answer is "yes" to both questions.'

'Thank you. I appreciate your frankness and most of all, your support. And now if you will excuse me, I must attend to household matters. I have so much enjoyed our conversation.'

'As have I; I look forward to further discussions.' So, do I really want to engage in further discussions with Maurilius? It seems ungrateful for while I find Maurilius a good man and sincere cleric, his ability or desire to discuss the wider implications of church reform is restricted by his single-minded focus on the Rule of Benedict. Or is it because he does not gossip! Probably, but that does not reflect well on me! Whatever reason, I must not appear unenthusiastic about talking to him if he seeks to visit me at Fécamp. William appears.

'How are you getting on with Maurilius?' I make a suitable reply and he continues, 'My idea of inviting him here was not just to provide you with a theological companion, but also to see if you would bring out a warmer side of this apparently austere cleric.'

'So, have I succeeded?'

'Of course! Just look at how he enjoyed playing with the children!'

'Children are not the same challenge as recalcitrant monks!'

'Indeed, but I am pleased with him.' Off he goes on men's business again and there I am, on my own again. Oh no, I take it back - here he is again.

'The weather looks fair, so I am going to England as soon as possible. We've sent a pigeon to King Edward and he'll send a guard to escort me to the palace.' We embrace.

'I'll be back in a few weeks and we'll celebrate with a holiday. My beloved wife!' We kiss passionately and he leaves as my body throbs with desire, my womb contracting in spasms, although I don't really want another child just yet. The next few days are tedious, especially as I realise that while he is still in Normandy, he could be with me in a short time. While he is so far away, the time passes slowly. Now he's back! Already? 'Did you go to England, did you see the King? What did he say?'

'Woah! I didn't go, I…'

'*Didn't go*, why not?'

'When I got to the dock, I saw Eustace de Boulogne about to board the same ship...'

'That toad!'

'He may be a toad, but he knows what's in his best interests just now and he's sworn allegiance to me. I've ordered him to go instead of me to better plead my cause to King Edward. He is the perfect advocate, his first wife Goda being King Edward's sister and, of course, the daughter of King Ethelred. He and Edward already have a close relationship as well as sharing political views.'

'Can you trust him?'

'I think I can and he knows what will happen if he deceives me. After all, he is far more familiar with the English royal family than me.'

'Why would the King support you over his blood heir Edgar Atheling?'

'Edgar is young, he speaks no English and worse, no French and he's a "puny lily-livered little boy" who would have no idea of how to lead the English army against any invaders, especially the Vikings.'

'Poor Edgar! Not many young men are like you leading Normandy and fighting battles at his age! What about the Godwin family? They are said to have ambitions for the throne?'

'Edward has been quarrelling with them throughout his reign and more so recently when the Godwins put it about that his wife, their family member Edith Godwinson, is barren because he refuses to couple with her.'

'Beautiful Edith, poor thing!'

'Poor thing, just like you!'

Just like that, we're off to the joy and excitement of our coupling. I keep thinking about Edith and ask Mother Mary to bless her and send a sign to King Edward to do what he should. William says he took a vow of celibacy and would rather be a monk than King. He added that Edward's court was always full of his male 'favourites' so plenty of gossip about that too. We lie there, sated and peaceful, but I still have questions.

'Why should Edward swear you his heir?'

'We are related and through you, my veins of my heirs course with English royal blood. I am also a firm Christian. Edward knew me as a child and youth in Normandy. He knows my strength in consolidating the Dukedom of Normandy. He knows I shall never relinquish Normandy, but on my death, it will pass to Robert, linking England and Normandy as a powerful world force. Perhaps the most important thing - we always got on well in the past.'

'So, he has never resented you marrying the daughter of his adversary Baldwin of Flanders?'

'With no disrespect to you or your father, I don't think so.' And this magic spell of intimacy is over until he deigns to come back and see me.

Here I am moaning again and you have every right to be unsympathetic. You have probably spotted that I am bored with my life. I should do penance for feeling like this when my blessings are so great. I have nothing to complain about. How dare I be bored with every comfort, good health, a faithful loving husband, no problem with childbirth or producing a first -born, son and heir? The truth is I know I have so much more to give. Why can't I be a man and experience the excitement of the Chase, go to battle, conquer lands and build up a kingdom? I have the same burning ambition as William, but cannot be more than his help-meet, counsellor and patient loving wife and child-bearer. Oh, and his lover of course! This reminds me, our third child is on the way. This is how it will be until I am past child-bearing age. I am thirty-two and child-bearing goes on until about the age of forty. I could have eight more children! I shall always be pregnant. Get a grip Matilda. All right, but I am only going to give the bare facts until I feel more like writing in my usual detail.

I have news from Flanders about the continuation of Father's battles with King Henry of Germany and his building of heavy fortifications of his domain. Mother is active in attending a ceremony elevating new relics of Saint Bertin and donating gifts to honour the saint. My brother Baldwin, having married Richilde, heiress of the rich lands of Hainult, is now titled 'Count of Flanders and Hainult'. Richilde's son Roger, from her first marriage, is apparently deemed unfit to be heir to his mother's fortune so she and Baldwin have excluded him by making him the Bishop of Chalons. I see this as a crafty move to clear the way for Baldwin's son, nephew Arnulf. Knowing my brother's consummate ambition, I doubt if Richilde had much say in the matter. My brother Robert is still single.

I ask William if he has news of Eustace of Boulogne's visit to England to talk to King Edward about naming William as his heir. He has and apparently Eustace was received with honour at the royal court where he found an immediate ally in Edward the Confessor against the powerful Godwin family. When Eustace told him that Godwin's son Sweyn Godwinson had been feuding with his stepson, Ralf the Timid, the political alliance of these former brothers-in-law was further strengthened. Unfortunately, Eustace was vague about his assigned task beyond saying King Edward has sent William his greetings. Pushed further, Eustace reported that when he mentioned William as Edward's heir, the King had said he certainly had a valid claim to the throne and worthy of consideration. We agree that Eustace probably made that up to please William. It seems unlikely he persevered as his visit was embroiled with a brawl between him and his servants and the citizens of Dover. As fortune would have it, these men were under the jurisdiction of Earl Godwin who refused to punish them. King Edward took this as an insult to his authority and outlawed Earl Godwin and all his family. Where do they spend their exile? In Flanders with my parents, of course! William reminds me that we did think that Eustace took William of Talou's side when he rebelled against him, but that was not established and he is certainly on William's side now.

Father builds a new castle at Lille, replacing our old home. Henry IV of Germany succeeds his father and immediately invades Flanders, but is defeated by Father's forces. Our third child is born, a boy we name

Richard, a mixture of William and me, bigger than Robert, but not with William's large Viking stature. He is a dear little baby, but I'm more interested in Robert who is now coming up to five years old and can hold an interesting conversation. Before we get monks and teachers in, I am teaching him to read and instructing him in simple Latin and Theology. He is a keen and able student even at this young age, naturally following in my footsteps.

Now, there is news. The Pope's Council has tried and found Archbishop Mauger guilty of treason against William. His punishment is permanent banishment to our furthermost land, an island in the Narrow Sea called Guernsey. He is accompanied by his common-law wife and his many children. So, that's got rid him at last, that traitor and hypocrite who dared to preach clerical celibacy! Who's the new Archbishop of Rouen? Maurilius! William says he thought I'd realise why he'd asked him to join us at Bonneville and why he needed my opinion of him. Surprisingly, it did not cross my mind being somewhat pre-occupied with confinement and birthing, but I am not going to admit it. William can be exasperating at times. Just as I am feeling quite annoyed, William reappears, his large body blocking out the light through the doorway.

'You need a change. We'll go to Bonneville tomorrow morning, on our own.'

'I'd love to!'

He gives me one of his looks. What's he planning? He is obviously pleased about something. This is exciting and my mood changes. Off we go and I'm on tenterhooks to see what's going to happen. Bonneville is particularly beautiful in the May sunshine. We have a gentle ride through the woods and when we return, William asks me to wear his favourite dress this evening, the cream silk which clings to my body like a second skin and a little more tightly than it used to. We have Supper, which is a delicious game pie followed by Rijstpap, my favourite Flemish pudding of course and a full burgundy on offer. As usual William drinks little, but I have my vessel refilled defiantly often which causes him to make only a small change in expression. I raise my glass to him and he does manage a smile. We sit in a rather tense silence as he continues to look at me intently. As we rise to leave the Hall, he turns to me.

'For a considerable time, I've been waiting to observe something I've seen in the past.' He picks me up and slings me over his shoulder, quite roughly, like a soldier's kit bag.

'What are you doing?'

'You'll see!' I am aware that one of his hands is clutching my buttocks together firmly and when we get to our chamber, he lies me face down on to our bed, suspended over a pile of cushions. My bottom is sticking up in a most undignified way.

'So, you're bored.' Flick! Mon Dieu, it's that riding crop again!

'Bored with me, are you?' Flick!

'So, you'd rather be soldier than a wife and mother, would you?'

'Fed up with the nursery, are you?' And it's not a flick this time; it's his huge hand gently smacking my bottom. He rests his hand on me and then there's another smack and then more of a squeeze, then a caress, his hands cupping my buttocks. He is kneading them in a rhythm and I give in to the tremors that build up and go through and through me. I hear him laugh and he turns me over to watch my face, my eyes screwed up in ecstasy. He laughs and lies with me and we couple in a frenzy of passion.

'I do understand, you know.'

''I'm sorry I'm not like other ladies, who are content at home all the time.'

'Of course, you're not, praise God! I would never have wanted to marry a pious worthy woman who prays all the time and only puts up with coupling as marital duty. I love the way you enjoy it as you do and how I can discuss military strategy and plans with you. I love you as you are, and I have plans for you in the future.'

'What plans?'

'I'm going to be heavily involved with planning the England campaign over the next few years and would like you to join us in making them. Then, during the Campaign, I shall be away from Normandy along with my generals and armies which will leave us vulnerable to land-grabbing on the Frankish borders, though not from Flanders of course. Robert will not be old or mature enough to take over at that point.'

'How do I come into it?'

'I shall want you to take control of Normandy, probably with Roger de Montgomery who has said he will give every support to the England campaign, but would prefer to stay in Normandy to keep an eye on the French border of his domain and I suspect also to keep a close watch on Dame Mabel.'

'Do you really mean it or is it just a possibility?'

'Of course, I mean it.'

'That would be just what I'd love to do.'

'And you'd be good at it, safe hands. And on another matter, we are swiftly outgrowing our Fécamp palace and I think we should set about building a new one.'

'In Caen as you once said when we visited the old city?'

'Yes Caen, strategically positioned in the centre of Normandy.'

'When do we start?'

'Now!'

CHAPTER 14

PLANS FOR OUR NEW HOME AND MILITARY STRATEGY

Late 1050s

What can one say about building a huge new château which is to be not only our palace and our home, but a fortress, a meeting place, a business centre and a dominant landmark in the whole of Normandy, if not France? Quite a long business, but it's exciting seeing it taking shape. I'll be grateful when our new palace is finished as we are so crowded here. And, I'm about to have our fourth child. What with the pregnancy and this huge project it is a weary wait. Our last child, Richard, is a lively baby, a mixture of us, probably going to be fair-haired, and like his sister, much bigger than Robert at birth. He is no trouble and the wet nurse arrangements follow smoothly as ever. During the next two years, the crowding here gets worse, especially as we have prolonged visits from Adeliza and her household. All our available accommodation is used and while our new home seems to take for ever, my time here is made much easier with Adeliza's company. I have a friend, someone of my own age and status with much in common. We play music together and go on trips which have cemented our friendship. My past opinion that her lack of interest in politics and theology made her my intellectual inferior shames me now. How ungenerous I was and how unappreciative of her other qualities like having a sense of fun and readiness to go out and always be an agreeable companion. In my defence however, I do have to say that my interest in government and military strategy has overtaken other more esoteric subjects and William is really the only person who can fulfil this need.

The weeks and months go by, each day in the same routine and I cannot believe two years have passed. Now Adeliza and I are both about to give birth again, for each of us a fourth child. Doing the preparations in tandem has made it all so much easier than in the past. I have a second daughter, Cecilia, and she has a son, Roger.

I tell Count William that his son Roger looks like his father, a fine figure of a man and the said person cheers up at this uncustomary eulogy. Cecilia is a strong baby, smaller at birth than Adeliza, but strikingly like her with quite a lot of golden hair. There's much rejoicing yet again, although William appears to be sulking! However, his scant acknowledgement of Cecilia's birth is nothing to do with her being female, instead caused by his disappointment that the building of Caen Palace is going to take the best part of ten years. William is not here all the time, but we do manage a few trips to Bonneville, a welcome a break from the domesticity of my existence. The months go on and I give birth to a third son. As soon as I see our new baby my first reaction is mirth because he is making exactly the same sort of face as his father when a bit disgruntled. When his father does see him and I make this somewhat tactless remark, William says huffily that he does not see that himself, but agrees he should be called William. He does deign to look at his new son, actually smiles, remarking he will be a soldier. William is a heavy baby, the one I thought I was having who turned to be Adeliza and, praise Mother Mary, Dame Mabel's predictions were nothing but rat-droppings. Megina finds me a noble lady to be a wet nurse to baby William as she and Ralf move in to one of our guest rooms for a few months. I am not expecting a change to this predictable and uneventful lifestyle until one day William rushes in and tells Adeliza that she and her party must go home immediately under guard and I am not to leave our domain until further notice. He is strengthening our defences and will explain later.

All at once, the Caen building work and everything else is put on hold because of the hostile invasion by my Uncle, King Henry of France and our old enemy Count Geoffrey Martel of Anjou. Their troops are coming from the South bypassing Falaise to raid, burn and pillage around Bayeux and Caen, provoking William not only in his territory, but also in his proposed new stronghold. This is serious, yet despite his urgent instructions to us, it would appear elsewhere that William is choosing to ignore this onslaught. Appearances are deceptive.

William musters his forces at Falaise Castle, apparently occupied with the customary military training of troops in peacetime. The men are seen and heard to be enjoying noisy tournaments, seemingly relaxed, drinking ale and certainly not in battle-ready mode. Does Uncle Henry really think that William owes his avowed Liege Lord such loyalty that he can accept without rebuff this hostile intrusion into his now personal domain? He must know that Williams' spies are about? Does he not realise that William knows Normandy like the back of his hand, every nook and gully? I know William will be keeping a close eye on the situation, no doubt planning when to make his move and I'm desperate to know what is happening. I should not be left out of this important decision-making which affects our future.

Ah, I have a visitor. It's Count Roger de Montgomery who comes to discuss the campaign. William wants my opinion! I am told that when the enemy makes for Caen and Bayeux, they can only cross the River Dives at low tide at a ford near Varaville. William is watching their pattern of raids and the ebb and flow of tides to and from the Narrow Sea, carefully calculating his attack. Just before the full high tide is due, his army will march to the ford and hope to cut off ranks of the enemy on the East bank as the tide comes in.

'Do you have any suggestions about managing this strategy, Duchess Matilda?'

'I do, because whenever we went to Bonneville, the men would go to the Chase in St Gatien Forest while we ladies would tour the countryside in a carriage with escort. If on my own I would ride Galathea, with escort of course. I know the countryside bordering both the River Touques and River Dives in some detail.'

'That knowledge could be key to our plans.'

‘Thank you. So, the enemy has been coming without challenge through your domain of Hiemes avoiding Falaise and then over the River Dives to Caen and Bayeux?’

‘Correct.’

‘Tell the troops at Falaise, castle servants and as many local people as possible that the army will soon be setting off to Rouen for further military practice. Put it about that Duke William is expecting invasion from the North by Frankish forces sailing along the coast of the Narrow Sea. The enemy will hear this information and not expect immediate defence of Caen and Bayeux from the South and East. Yet, our army will not march the seventy or so miles to Rouen, but half that distance to Touques, which can be done with suitable halts in under two days. There is room to muster troops in the privacy of our estate. From Bonneville, it is thirteen miles to the River Dives by first crossing the River Touques which is no problem as it is reasonably shallow and covered in board walks. Planned accordingly, it should be possible to trap the rear guard of the enemy forces waiting to cross because the tides are fast and the narrow ford only accessible for a short period. With heavy attack on the rear guard, the advance army will be marooned without back-up.’

‘Duke William said you’d know and we agreed, but we could not have known in such detail without your help.’ I bid Count Roger farewell and feel satisfied with my input.

And now I am going to have to wait, enduring endless days and nights with the campaign always on my mind as I attempt to carry out my duties as Duchess, wife, parent, and military strategist. I repeat the title of ‘Military Strategist’ to myself with decreasing satisfaction because it doesn’t make up for being ignorant of the action at each stage.

Now, another baby is on the way. He or she will be our sixth child. I spend a miserable night tossing and turning, but find comfort at morning Mass with Abbot John. He seems to sense what is happening without prying. He tells me he prays for William and me every day and especially at this time. He is sympathetic about my worries that our partly built palace may be a target for the raiding armies. I tell him that it is on high ground giving advantage to our guards who are well equipped to see off any marauders. Robert asks me if Papa is fighting a battle today and I tell him the truth which is that I think he may be, but I don't know for sure. Abbot John comes in to teach him Theology, but he is not nearly as interested in this worthy subject as he is in hearing about battles fought by his father and grandfather. Abbot John can talk about this too, but the best teacher of all subjects is Prior Lanfranc although he cannot spare us as much time as we'd like. I continue to be pleased with six-year-old Robert's progress. Oh, and I realise that with my concentration on military matters, I have not mentioned we have had another daughter, dear little Alison and of course, there's another baby on the way. I feel guilty over such small mention of these new babies and Alison, the easiest birth I've had, must be exactly like me at birth, small and fair-haired. Will she be another 'Poupette'? We'll see and if she is, she will not be allowed to behave as I did as a child!

Mother sends a message to tell me she has founded the Abbey of Messines, her fourth such establishment which is an action to be celebrated, revered and followed. Surely, she is inviting me to follow her example of founding abbeys which I will do, however not just at the moment with so much on my mind.

I am surprised and delighted to see William is back from the Campaign within two days, accompanied by Count William FitzOsbern. Mission accomplished and the rear army, left struggling as the tide surged down the River Dives, was comprehensively defeated. William also reports that the forward ranks, terrified by the massacre going on behind them, scattered fearing further attack from the North West. Instead of sending defence forces to halt any further raids of Caen or Bayeux, William placed men along all their escape routes back to Maine. The fugitives were challenged, deprived of their weaponry, and probably taught some sort of horrible lesson, but allowed to go on their way. Their reports would have much more impact on their leaders than their silent corpses. What about Uncle Henry and Geoffrey Martel? William let them escape on purpose, pretending they were not seen, because slaying the King of France, however justified in defence of his territory, would have serious repercussions throughout the Holy Roman Empire. He now asks his servant to run a bath. Off he goes and Count

William looks in to congratulate me on the part I played in the planning. I am really furious with Uncle Henry. I ask Count William.

'What does Uncle Henry think he is achieving by this hostility to us both?'

'I am convinced he sees Duke William as the most serious threat to his kingdom and to himself. I much doubt he shares our knowledge that Duke William's real goal is not to conquer West Frankia.'

'You must be right, but you'd think Uncle Henry had better things to do than persist in provoking William so sorely. Now, I want to know exactly what action was taken in defeating the enemy left behind on the bank of the River Dives. Was there any repeat of the sort of trouble we had at Domfront?' Count William pauses and looks at me as if weighing up what he is going to say.

'I will tell you the truth because you know exactly what happened at Domfront and

you coped with what Duke William did. He told me that you discussed the details of what happened after such severe provocation by the inhabitants of Alençon. He says you understood and you are concerned that it could happen again. Well, it did happen again, but not to the extent of cutting off limbs and blinding live people, but it was a massacre and every man in that river and on the East bank was killed. Some tried to surrender, but William was in battle fury and ignoring their pleas, vented his frustrations over the recent raids with merciless slaughter.'

'This is unwelcome news, Count William. Thank you for being honest with me. Battles and death are part of a ruler's lot and William was certainly not provoked as he was last time. However, with such treacherous enemies within his own family, he had personal scores to settle. I am also angry with Uncle Henry for threatening our future domain and as for Geoffrey Martel; he's a thug, justly called "the hammer". I doubt if either will return to raid our domain after what has just happened to their trapped army.' As the Count is agreeing, William returns and we three have a good supper, the men eating quickly and heartily. Count William will leave at sunrise and regrets not joining us for Mass to give thanks for our successful campaign. There is a silence after we finish eating and inevitably the conversation turns to the future and that means preparation for the English campaign. None of us can manage a meaningful conversation at this point or offer anything to buck us up because we are all completely exhausted. My suggestion that we all retire and get a good night's sleep is greeted thankfully by the men. Unusually, William is asleep before I even get to the bed and as I look at him, I pray fervently that his actions are more moderate in the inevitable battles to come.

We pray during Mass the next morning, giving thanks for our victory and for the souls of all who have perished in battle. I hear William mutter 'my men' instead of 'all.' I take a sideways look at him and while relieved that he looks calm, I am nevertheless concerned that he shows no signs of penitence for his harsh killing of the enemy who were surrendering to him. Abbot John gives me a sympathetic look as we leave, then tells us we can expect some good news shortly. He does not say what, but it can only be one thing. I don't discuss the subject with William until at last we hear that our marriage has papal dispensation by the grace of Pope Nicholas II. I give thanks to Mother Mary as I know our children have been considered bastards by those who chose to ignore our marriage or believed that we share blood. These people are spurred on by William's hostile relations who have neither the intelligence, diligence nor the will to examine the facts behind the original verdict. Thinking all this over, I realise I do feel different and much relieved about the reversal of the Ban which has haunted our lives for so long. It's obvious that William is relieved too and released from this burden we can now concentrate fully on our new home and the England Campaign. And we have another two daughters in quick succession, Agatha and Adela. Like them all, they are dear babies, but when I think of the excitement over our firstborn Robert, I fear their welcome was rather muted. I thank Mother Mary for having seven healthy children, the eldest being Robert, a small, but robust boy of ten years. Adeliza has a daughter, Emma, and our eighth child is probably on the way. We need to move NOW!

As ever, I need a project to engage me while enduring the challenges of building our large castle in Caen. For some time, I have wanted a little chapel away from the bustle of Fécamp so that I can pray with my ladies in peace. There's the perfect place on the banks of the Seine, not too far from here and although a full day's journey from Caen, it would be a place of refuge and sanctity when I need to pray and rest without interruption. William is in favour and Abbot John agrees to oversee the plans with his experience of building holy places of worship. It takes a surprisingly short time to complete this very simple dwelling which I name "Nôtre Dame du Pré".

Chateau-des-Contes-de-Flandres

Fécamp, 1698

Ruins of Fécamp Castle, built in the 10th Century for the Dukes of Normandy

Falaise Castle today.

89 BONNEVILLE-SUR-TOUQUES — Le Château de Guillaume-le-Conquérant

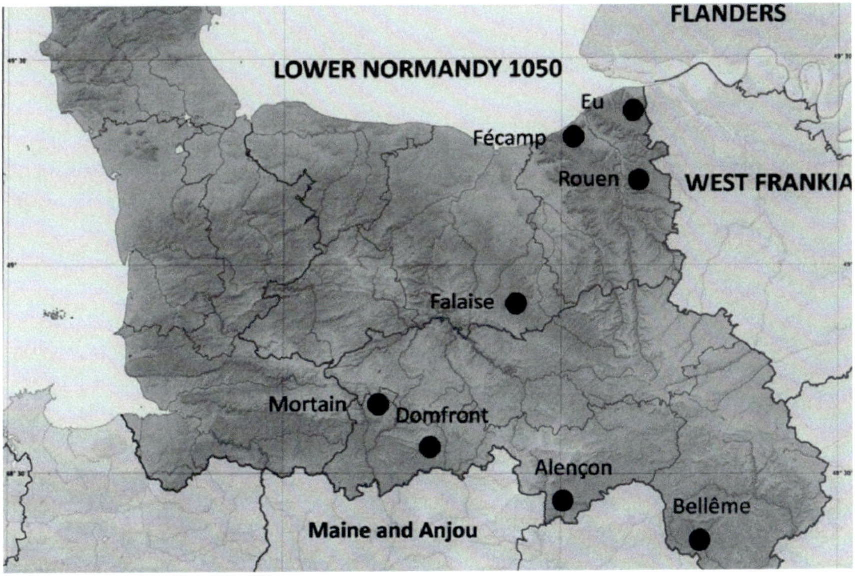
FLANDERS
LOWER NORMANDY 1050
Eu
Fécamp
Rouen
WEST FRANKIA
Falaise
Mortain
Domfront
Alençon
Bellême
Maine and Anjou

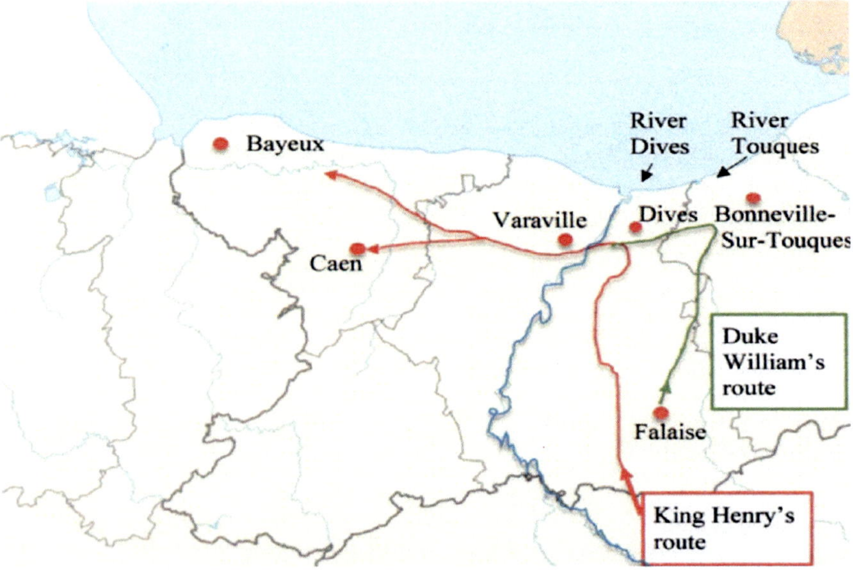

Sketch map of Varaville Campaign 1057

Caen.Palace today.

CHAPTER 15

OUR NEW HOME

Caen Palace, 1060-66

Well, it's all quite different at Caen and I'm surprised at how sad it is to leave Fécamp despite the difficulties of having outgrown it for some years. Megina, Ralf and their family have come with us which makes our lives easier as they know how we like things done. I have arranged for Megina to have plenty of help with the care and education of her children so that she can give me the personal attention I value. We are going to miss our daily Mass with Abbot John, but William says he has ordered two chapels in the castle's domain which will continue our present system of ensuring Mass is a daily service for everyone. There is also an old church in the town called St Étienne le Vieux on the site of a former Benedictine monastery. I look forward to visiting it. Built on a hillock with commanding views of Caen, the scale of this castle and its grounds is awesome. Its strong fortifications include the keep which has a large square section with round towers at each corner. All the buildings are also protected by a moat. It's going to take some time for us all to find our way around. Although the whole place is somewhat daunting, it will be wonderful to have so much accommodation for our growing family, increasing number of servants and for visitors.

During this time, we have been wondering what my Uncle King Henry is up to, his absence from our lives is an uncertain relief after his previous aggression, but now we know, as Mother writes to tell us of his death. The guardianship of his heir, seven-year-old Philip is to be in the hands of his mother, Anne of Kiev, and Father. For many years, Mother has co-signed Flemish Charters, adding "Sister to the King of France". Now the Frankish Charters have to be signed as well, to which she will impose the word "late" before "King". I am beginning to realise I am far more like her than I've allowed myself to admit. Like her, I enjoyed playing a part in Father's leadership of Flanders and now I am working hard to have the same role in Normandy. I also see Mother's lack of warmth to me increasingly apparent in myself with the arrival of so many babies, one after the other.

Our daily life goes on much as it did at Fécamp. I realise I won't see so much of Robert as he participates in the sports suitable for a young gentleman and now accompanies William to military training. He seems young to be doing this, but when I think about what William had to do at the same age, it reminds me of how difficult and lonely that must have been for him whereas Robert has both parents and siblings with more on the way, no doubt. Although William and his eldest son could not be more different in stature and strength, their shared hunger for winning all contests, sporting or military, pushes them to become battle-ready soldiers. I went to watch the training the other day and wish I had not. Robert was finding some of the exercises difficult and his father was shouting at him and in frustration no doubt, addressed him as 'Brevis-ocrea', meaning 'short boot', so mocking his short stature. I couldn't watch my son being so humiliated and when we returned, I took up the issue with William who told me to mind my own business. How could he be so cruel? Well Matilda, you ought to know by now! Yes, but when it's my beloved child, it's different from the cruelty of battle. Yet, or is it? I don't see a happy end to this. As if in remorse and to please me, William has now confirmed Robert as his successor to the Dukedom of Normandy, but surely he should be supporting him not degrading him in front of his future subjects. William also dislikes the lessons I have arranged for all our children to receive, and whereas he does not mind the girls being educated, he scoffs at boys needing it and often arranges military practice when the tutors are due. Although the reason behind this is obvious, it is nevertheless annoying and, in my opinion, not in our sons' best interests h

Unlike Robert and little Richard, Adeliza, aged nine is much taken with Theology which the tutor introduces suitably for her stage of life. She tells us she wants to be a nun. William's reply is to forget that nonsense as she will be betrothed any time soon to a suitable nobleman of his choice. I ask her why and she says she longs for the peace of a convent and time to study the scriptures. I listen to her, but dare not make any promises for fear of serious reprisals from my dear beloved.

Plans turn into real ships and the exact name of each leading officer in preparation for our Invasion of England. William seeks to persuade everyone that he is King Edward's chosen heir. Hassume he went to England, in person, and no-one dissuades them of this important knowledge. Nor would I dare to tell anyone it is not true. William refers to his young child's memory of a meeting and subsequent occasional attendances in Edward's Norman court during his exile. These encounters were no doubt cordial, but hardly an influence on the King today compared to the competing claims of the Godwins, the Vikings and probably others. The only reason why King Edward might favour William is that they are blood relations, first cousins, William's father being Duke Robert of Normandy and his Aunt, Emma of Normandy, being Edward's mother.

Talking of the Godwins, William has just heard that Harold Godwinson, Earl of Wessex, has been shipwrecked off our shores and captured by Count Guy de Ponthieu who is holding him by force in Beaurain Castle. Count Guy inherited the castle after his brother Enguerrand was killed in our recent successful battle against William de Talou and King Henry's Frankish forces. William is leaving instantly to demand his release. He's had a disappointing relationship with the Counts of Ponthieu after his sister Adelaide was divorced and abandoned by Count Enguerrand, the Pope having annulled their marriage. However, Guy de Ponthieu has now switched sides and is a vassal of William. When William eventually returns, he reports that he has secured Harold's release by requiring him to swear on Holy Relics that he will be Duke William's vassal and support his bid to be King of England. It may help I suppose, but the Throne of England is neither hereditary nor in the will of any of the presently known claimants. It is, of course, customary that a King's son is his successor and if still looking for a bloodline, childless King Edward has two claimants with his bloodline, Edgar his fourteen-year-old great-nephew and William, his first cousin. In addition to these two are Hadrada, King of Norway, and Harold Godwinson of Wessex. Each has his supporters who will press his claim, but the decision is made by the King's Council, the Witan. There may be others by the time the old King dies.

Now we are settled here, we are to found two abbeys in Caen, outwardly signifying our gratitude to the Pope for removing the Ban on our marriage. However unreasonable it was at the time, it was a great relief to hear the Vatican proclamation, the stigma of bastardy hanging over our children being removed. William's foundation is the Abbaye d'Étienne aux Hommes (the Abbey of Saint Stephen, 'the Men's Abbey') to the West of Caen Palace. My foundation is the Abbaye de Sainte-Trinité aux Dames (Holy Trinity, 'the Women's Abbey'), to the East of Caen Palace. The Abbess is my namesake, Matilda. To our great delight, the first Abbot of Saint Stephen is none other than our old friend, Prior Lanfranc, who played the crucial role in persuading the Pope to reverse the Ban on our marriage. Prior Lanfranc is to oversee the works and all that goes with preparing the buildings for the religious life of the brothers and sisters. He is William's personal Chaplain and will be such a great support too us both, especially in the coming months. Having our abbeys so close to our castle removes the need to bring in visiting tutors for our children. Our daughters love Holy Trinity because the nuns spoil them with sweetmeats and keep little birds in cages for everyone's delight. The reason why our children get this attention is that our abbeys are not obliged to offer education to rich nobles' children because William and I keep them generously endowed and others follow our example to keep in our favour. When I say 'our children', the pupils are invariably our daughters as our sons seem to be permanently engaged in military and sporting activity. Our eighth child, a daughter Constance, is first of our children to be born at Caen Palace.

With congratulations from my family, we hear that my younger brother Robert has married Gertrude of Saxony, dowager Countess of Holland, and is now known as "Robert the Frisian". On its heels comes the announcement of the birth of Robert and Gertrude's son, called Robert. Within a few months, he is followed by Baldwin. Almost all the men in Flanders and Hainult seem to be called 'Baldwin' or 'Robert' which is nearly as confusing as when these sons actually appeared!

Also, and very significant in our family life, is that William has responded to Adeliza's desire to lead a religious life. William asks her to wait six months while all Norman churches are tasked to include prayers for the Duke's eldest daughter to make a considered choice. Adeliza will be placed under the guardianship of Count Roger de Beaumont and enter the Noviciate the Abbey of Saint-Léger de Préaux, founded by Count Roger's father. I am surprised and pleased that William has abandoned his past insistence that she should marry, as is the custom of daughters of our class. However, I don't think that his action considers Adeliza's wishes at all, but is influenced by his relief that the Ban has been lifted by Pope Nicholas who looks on him favourably. A rather unpleasant thought is that he is further bolstering his justification for Invasion of England by the gift of his eldest daughter to the Church to add to his claim that Harold Godwinson has sworn to support him.

CHAPTER 16

THE BATTLE OF HASTINGS

Normandy and England, 1066

January

We get news that King Edward of England died yesterday morning, God rest his soul. He was buried in Westminster Abbey in the afternoon, closely followed by a meeting of the Witan, the King's council. A full house, due to the noble lords being at Westminster for Epiphany, has chosen Harold Godwinson to be King and already crowned him. We are not surprised as the Witan's membership includes a large number of Wessex lords, sworn to support Earl Godwin. So, we know where we are. William leaves immediately to hurry the progress of building our fleet at Dives-sur-Mer which is reached from here in under a day. What I have not yet told William is that I am planning a surprise for him by building a very special ship, much larger than any in his fleet. The site is at Barfleur, well away from Dives, but I doubt if the secret will be kept as there will soon be rumours about it between the gangs of shipbuilders. I am thinking hard about what to call her and it's important to get it right. William's lords had been initially hesitant to join the Invasion force due to the inevitable risks of such a venture and concerned that if it failed, their Norman lands and property would be lost. Now they have been told that the Church is blessing the venture because of Harold Godwinson's oath, sworn on Holy Relics, to support William, they are won over to our cause.

May

Within a few weeks, another pigeon arrives with news that Tostig Godwinson has led a fleet of sixty ships to attack our furthest territory in the Narrow Sea, the Isle of Wight. He occupied Sandwich and leaving a force in command, sailed up the East Coast of England to the mouth of the River Humber, no doubt to take his revenge on the earls of Mercia who forced his expulsion by King Harold. The earls saw him off and he's taken refuge with King Malcolm of Scotland. So, where is he now and what are his plans?

Count Roger de Montgomery and I discuss this unexpected development. Is Tostig hoping to depose his brother King Harold? Where is his ally King Harald Hadrada or is this a pact between them to divide and conquer separately? Or is this an internal Viking battle? Is Tostig trying to provoke us into defending our territory and interfere with William's ship building programme? Whose side is he on or is he a loner? Count Roger reminds me that Tostig was the much hated Earl of Northumbria until last year when his brother Harold forced him out. We agree that Tostig's siting of a military base on the Isle of Wight is probably in support of our cause; nevertheless, it's a hostile invasion of our territory, which is disrespectful to William and me, leaving us in doubt about his motive.

When Count Roger leaves, I ponder the character of Tostig Godwinson, son of Earl Godwin of Wessex and Gytha Thorkelsdóttir of Denmark. Tostig and his brother Harold notoriously failed to get on from early childhood, Tostig aligning with the Viking side of his family and Harold choosing the Saxon side. King Edward, God rest his soul, married their sister Edith, an unhappy event for both of them from all accounts. It seems that King Edward had little regard for his wife's family, resenting them for blaming him for the childless state of the marriage through his refusal to couple with Edith. Tostig was among the Godwins who when expelled from his court, turned up in Flanders with us. The court gossip said Tostig was one of King Edward's 'favourites' so was the expulsion personal on yet another level? Who knows what's going on and this also pinpoints how often noble family members are often related or connected. Tostig has entered my family too in marrying my Aunt Judith; my father's much younger half-sister. So much connection! Thinking of that, I expect Judith and their teenage sons are also with my parents. So much for loyalty to William and me!

June

The building works at our two foundation abbeys are finished with customary skill and uncustomary speed to our combined satisfaction. During this time of celebration, William has another unexpected change of heart and declares that our second daughter Cecilia should enter the Noviciate of my Abbey of Sainte-Trinité at its Dedication Service on the eighteenth of June. He announces to all that presenting a child to the Church is an act of great significance. I do know this and find myself irritated by his new ownership of piety. I pray to get over this unworthy feeling and vow to give generous support despite my misgivings and sadness at losing yet another of our dear young pious and highly intelligent daughters. William tells me he wants to show his gratitude not just to the Pope, but also to the whole Church for blessing his approaching Invasion of England. He's been swayed by Cecilia's continually expressed wishes, especially at her young age. He would not have agreed to this without her fervent desire to go. Cecilia is clearly delighted and deals with this profound change in her life in a calm and mature manner, surely unusual in such a young person. The Service is moving, and I feel both grief and joy as I watch my child taking her vows of chastity, renouncing worldly goods and devoting herself to prayer, religious studies and caring for the poor. William is clearly as affected as I am, but we only have to look at Cecilia to feel she has chosen what is right for her. We are relieved that one of William's cousins, Abbess Matilda of Holy Trinity, will take particular care of Cecilia's well-being and education. Mother Mary, please keep our beloved daughter safe and happy in your service.

July

As the weeks pass and the supply of ships grows, I am thankful to have some part in the preparations for the Invasion by regular visits to Barfleur to check on the progress of my gift ship to William, the 'Mora'. I hope he will enjoy the rearrangement of the letters to sound like 'Amour.' It's going to be perfect. Meanwhile, Robert comes to see me; he is not confident he is doing as well as William expects in commanding the older soldiers as they train for war. I tell him that it was never going to be easy following in the footsteps of his father. He thinks if he had William's size and strength as well as his very loud voice, he would be more successful. He's right, but I am not going say so. I tell him that he has a good brain and can speak English which will be an asset in the future and that military strategy is just as important as force in battle.

'Why can't I fight in the Battle with Father and my friends?'

'You are fifteen and that is too young to go this time and you are needed here to rule Normandy when your father is absent.'

'Father ruled Normandy by himself from a much younger age,' same old question and same old answer.

'He had no choice, and you know very well there is no-one quite like your father.'

'I know I shall inherit Normandy one day, but at the moment you and Count Montgomery are in charge and will continue to be if Father wins the Battle or not.'

'Don't worry; we'll be in charge together, in a team.' He seems somewhat mollified, but I don't hold out much hope for him getting an army of argumentative and rebellious Normans under the same tight leash as held by William.

Oh no, the worst has happened! William reports that Tostig has sent a message to say he has a big fleet provided by my father! I'm furious! 'How could Father?' William puts up his hand. 'Stop Matilda, you must get over your grudge about Tostig; this is war, and it was I who suggested to Tostig he asks your father to help our Campaign and that is exactly what he's done.' Well, he could have told me this before! William continues, 'We need to forget grudges and muster all the forces we can, and I've sent messages to the lords of Poitou, Brittany and Burgundy to send as many men as possible.'

'So, by invading the Isle of Wight was not an insult to us?'

'Far from it; he would hardly give notice of attacking us. No time for histrionics, just listen to what I'm telling you. Tostig and his fleet are on their way to Norway to persuade King Harald Hadrada to join him in the invasion of England. He asks us to invade at the same time to provide a simultaneous attack. The plan is to send me a message when they arrive in Northumbria, a beacon lit to signal to set sail.'

'Is that it?'

'Just about'.

'What about the wind?'

'Something we can't control so I will act accordingly.'

'Where are the Saxons at present?'

'Mostly at the Isle of Wight, but the farmers and field workers will be going to the Harvest as soon as it starts. I am sure that's why Harold wants to delay the date of Battle until Harvest is brought in.'

'We've got men in The Fyrd too, haven't we?'

'We have, but not as many as the Saxons and I forbid our farmers to leave the army for the Harvest; they must make other plans if a battle is to take place. As our Harvest is usually finished before the English Harvest, this could be to our advantage. Yet, abattle of the scale of this one will not be won by the Fyrd, however strong and willing, as their hay rakes and sticks make little impression on armoured housecarls. Like us, King Harold has a large force of housecarls so we can't be complacent; it will be the Battle of all battles.' Off goes William again and we all wait for news.

I feel left out of things and worried about the impending Battle, so I send a message to Adeliza, inviting her and her children and servants to stay here at Caen. She is in the same position me, Count William being one of William's chief generals and right-hand man. She sends a message to say that her elder son William has already gone to the Abbey of Bretueil where he is about to be Abbot. She will be delighted to come with Emma and Roger aged twelve and ten, respectively. I do wonder about this small flurry of births and then none for the past ten years. I'm torn between envy and pity in Adeliza's life. Perhaps she'll confide in me. Through all this, I am excited about the forthcoming Battle. I want to become Queen of England.

August/September

William has come to say he couldn't believe his eyes when he saw the 'Mora' sailing down to Dives to join his fleet. He cannot understand how I have managed to keep this secret from him! He is in awe of her Drakkar design and clinker construction, her multi-coloured sails and, most of all, the Papal Banner at the top of the mainmast, consecrated and sent from Rome with the blessing of Pope Alexander II. He is not surprised that the "Mora" is so perfect because I planned it all. Well, it was worth it seeing his pleasure. Did he see that the letters mean 'love'? He looks perplexed and I realise that was a stupid question. Of course, he says hurriedly, adding, she's perfect for leading out his fleet of seven hundred ships as soon as the signal comes from Tostig. Then he's gone.

We get news from Dives that they left when the first beacon was lit on the Northumbrian Coast and onwards, agreed in the pact with the Vikings. Tostig Godwinson and King Harald of Norway are presumably landing and starting to invade the North Eastern shores of Northumberland. At the same time, false news was leaked to King Harold that William's fleet would only set sail across the Narrow Sea in a favourable wind. The truth was that William's huge fleet would sail whatever the weather and is now on its way to invade the Sussex coast. Before William left, we knew King Harold's men were waiting for us on the Sussex coast, but I do not know where they are now. I won't hear if our plan worked or indeed get any news just yet as sending pigeons in any weather along with managing the fleet is not a priority. Anyway, if the news is bad, what could we do? All our resources have gone into this Invasion and all I can do is delight in the fact that the 'Mora', is the best vessel ever. I also celebrate the Pope's blessing of William's Battle Banner and that the Clergy of the Continent deemed our Invasion of England a Holy War. All is set and William has left. I'm consumed with sudden grief as I must accept that I may never see him again. No

Matilda, you've got to be strong for him, for our children and for Normandy. Mother Mary, keep him safe. Megina comes in as I go to bed and seeing I am upset, she is very understanding. Now I feel guilty because Ralf has gone with William and she must be feeling exactly the same. She brings another message, just arrived from the pigeon house, that the Vikings have slain the lords of Northumbria, overcome their forces and are now on the way to take York. I find this surprising because the plan was to march south and take on Harold's army in a pincer movement with us.

Through all this tedious waiting and not daring to go beyond the castle grounds for fear of missing a vital message, I am highly diverted by Adeliza's accounts of the wicked actions by Dame Mabel, obviously relayed out of the hearing by Count Roger. Her long-standing feud with the Giroie family has caused her to poison at least two of its members to death, further confirming her nickname, 'Mabel the Poisoner'. However, she got a dose of her own medicine after a disagreement with Theodric, Abbot of the Saint-*Evroul.* Her dislike of all priests and religious orders made her jealous of Count Roger's patronage of the *abbey. She always has a large army for her personal protection, so she billeted numbers of them on the poor monks until they became destitute.* Pushed to the limit of his endurance, the Abbot told her she would suffer great pain if she failed to remove them. That night, she was seized with violent stomach pains from which she did recover only to carry on with her evil ways.

We are called by the servant. A pigeon has arrived from Count William to say that William's fleet is stalled off the Isle of Wight, not sheltering from strong winds and rain as you might presume, but because the 'Mora' is so much faster than the rest of the fleet. Good news that she is so fast, but not good news that we are delayed. At least I can discuss this information with Count Roger and Adeliza. It's such a joy to have her here, another adult who understands exactly what I am going through. After Supper one evening, she tells me that over the last few years Count William has not coped well with the stress of continual battles among the lords of Normandy who are trying to take the Dukedom from William. He has found the last few months especially trying with the planning of the Invasion of England. He is the most brave and loyal of William's lords and would lay down his life for him, but his character is more of diplomacy than warlike. Hearing this, I think that Adeliza may not know how shocked he was by some of William's cruel actions after provocation. We skirt round this and I'm certainly not going to tell her any details, but say how much we sympathise with those who find warfare more stressful than others. She does not venture any confidences about her married life, but if someone's depressed like Count William, this could be affecting his energy in all parts of his life. She herself is a bit subdued and it's not surprising as she is on her own more than me and still has to cope with her household and see to the children. We used to enjoy walking together and I'm sorry that this time she says she is grateful to have a rest and just talk.

I decide to go to the Chapel of Nôtre-Dame-du-Pré with a party of my ladies to pray for our success in the Invasion. The travel takes half a day, followed by prayer all the afternoon and through the night before returning in the early morning. It is peaceful and calming.

At last, we get news that the Viking invasion did reach King Harold, prompting him to lead his Saxon army north, marching day and night, to take on the enemy, already occupying York. However, no news of this manoeuvre reached the Vikings leaving them confident that King Harold was still in the South, waiting for us. Mostly asleep in their tents and unarmed, they were caught unaware and their forces annihilated in a ferocious battle at a place called Stamford Bridge, with only twenty-four of their mighty fleet of three hundred Dragon Boats returning home. This was not our plan. Harald Hadrada and Tostig Godwinson are dead, sad news for my father and Aunt Judith. More news is now coming in fast; we have landed on the Sussex coast and occupy Hastings. Presumably, King Harold is now informed of this and marching back to Sussex to face us. Battle will take place. We have lost all Viking support, but the Saxons have also lost some of their force and will be battle-weary which is in our favour. On the other hand, King Harold will have called up the Fyrd who will have completed harvest by now, although these farmers and countrymen do not have the weaponry and certainly not the horses of his regular army. HarI pray to Mother Mary for William's life and for our victory, such a significant changing point in our lives. More news arrives of no Submission and a stand-off between the two armies. The Battle of Hastings will take place on the fourteenth of October. We wait, trying to fill our days with activities and get but rare spells of sleep. The management of the children, meal times and attending chapel pass some of the time. Count Roger is increasingly restless with all this going on without him, so with my blessing he makes an unscheduled journey across the Narrow Sea to help command the troops.

My ladies and I join the sisters at Abbaye aux Dames for some of their daily Offices to fill this time of waiting with prayer. I long to return to my little chapel on the banks of the Seine, but eighty miles is too far to travel and too far from any of our pigeon message sites.

14th October

It is an agonising wait, but news is beginning to filter in not from our fleet, but from our stalwart Norman allies, already resident in England. We've won! I can't believe it! We defeated the Saxons! William has declared himself King of England and he will go to London to be crowned. I give thanks to Mother Mary and pray that William is no longer in danger. The Battle was close-fought, fierce and bloody with great loss on both sides. The Saxons wielded their terrible two-handed axes, and to start with, had the advantage of the uphill site called Senlac. Three of William's horses were killed beneath him and rumours of his death abounded. To show his troops he was still alive, William raised his helmet and perhaps it was this show of strength that gave his men that extra push to victory. It seems that two matters were in our favour. One was the different orders given by the leaders on the eve of battle. King Harold and his men had no sleep, and were drinking and singing rousing battle songs all night whereas William assembled our men in prayer for an hour, reminding them this was a Holy War. He sent them back to camp to get some rest. Our second advantage was our army having more men on horseback than our adversaries. Rumour has it that King Harold died of an arrow through the eye slit in his helmet piercing his brain and William, ever generous in favourable military outcomes, pronounced the King had fought most honourably.

The ladies and I return to Holy Trinity and, with joy and thanks, we name its chapel 'Nôtre Dame de Bonnes Nouvelles', Chapel of Good News indeed! We prayed for that!

Now William and his men will march north to London and the scant returning news is that the Saxons are not going to give in easily; he must be vigilant as it only takes one arrow from a hidden adversary to take him down, the prime target down. We now hear William did not march straight to London, but went to take Canterbury first, only to find that Archbishop Stigand had fled to London, protesting he will never submit to Norman rule.

On they go, but there's the problem of crossing the deep and swift flowing River Thames with all our horses and supply carts. It is solved by the Sheriff of Wallingford, the place name explaining why it is the best place to cross in safety. This Sheriff is called Wigod, a strong supporter of our cause and may well be a relative, a name of Bigod and Wigod interchangeable in some families and of course, the Sire name of William's ancestor, Rollo the Viking. Eventually, we hear that William has left the generous hospitality of Wallingford and is on his way to London, overcoming bands of rebellious Saxons in skirmishes on the way. The evenings are really drawing in and Christmas approaches. Here we are on Christmas Day without William because today is his Coronation. He is being crowned King of England in Westminster Abbey by Ealdred, Archbishop of York. We had expected it would be by the reluctant Archbishop Stigand, but he is currently excommunicated for the holding of the See of Winchester as well as of Canterbury, forbidden by the Pope. I am interested to hear that Ealdred asked the assembled crowd, in English, if it was their wish that William be crowned King. The Bishop of Coutances then did the same, but in Norman French. Well done Ealdred, I am looking forward to meeting him.

So, that's that and we move into a new life. I suppose I shall be crowned Queen of England one day. Count Roger returns and tells me all the news. I'm pleased to see him back, but it's not the same as having William here. He always has news and tells me that Count Herluin died just after he got the news that we had won the Battle, as though his weak heart was holding on to let him die a happy man.

What I find particularly hard is that no message from William can come to me privately, nor can I send him a private message because he cannot read or write. Up to now, I have been strongly, and I hope secretly, disapproving of his illiteracy, but have managed to cope with it because I see him so regularly. Now he's far away which is frustrating, and I am lonely and left out of the important decisions being made. All I'm good for is to continually bear children and manage the monotonous daily routine of this vast Caen household. I am, of course, with child yet again. I do have a great ally in Count Roger de Montgomery who is highly literate and extremely well informed on many topics, especially religion. He's been left here too, although he did have the satisfaction of commanding the right flank of our army with great distinction in the Battle. Now he's returned, we can manage Normandy together, which is hardly a topic of concern to us at present with the focus entirely on the successful Invasion. Pull yourself together Matilda! Think how much worse it would be if we had been defeated! Nor should I feel entirely left out as William has detailed Count William FitzOsbern to keep me regularly informed. Following the Coronation, William's first deed was to place an eight o'clock curfew throughout, the only exception of nine o'clock being given to Wallingford. That's not going to make this foreign interloper popular with his new subjects, but that's William all over, strongly marking the fact he is now in charge. Count William has been appointed William's Steward and made Earl of Hereford and my brother-in-law, Bishop Odo of Bayeux, is made Earl of Kent. These two join William in a triumvirate to set about the task of naming which Saxon lordships and lands are to be the rewards for the men who had contributed to winning the Battle of Hastings. No doubt, these promotions are a great honour, but I don't envy them the grim task of outing the Saxon lords and replacing them with Normans.

William now has the South East of England under his control and the remaining English nobles have submitted to him including the previously most opposed: the northern earls, Edwin and Morcar. I send him a message via Earl William to suggest inviting these nobles to

Normandy to join him hunting in St-Gatien Forest and visit Falaise to indulge in the jousting which the men enjoy so much. William's reply comes with a 'yes', and he is returning now with these men. Wonderful, I can't wait to see him again! Count Roger will escort them to Falaise on arrival while he comes here for a few days to see us. While I'm pleased William took notice of my advice, I'm not too happy with the family and me being given so little of his time.

CHAPTER 17

AFTER THE BATTLE

1067

I begin to wonder what my life is going to be like when I'm Queen of England. Will we continue to live here or in an English palace? What will our friends do? Simple answer: they will do what Williams decides. His right-hand men are bound to be given English Earldoms, so in which country will they and their families live? Adeliza is bound to go to England and I shall miss her so much. Who is a friend to me like Adeliza? No-one! Meanwhile, it's now March 1067 and William is on his way home. Or is it his home anymore? Adeliza and her family leave feeling disappointed that they won't see the new Earl of Hereford who's been left in charge in England. He won't be here to tell his family about the successful Invasion and his second Earldom of Wessex, but at least he and Adeliza can exchange private messages without having to have someone to read them out. I am quite envious of that. Never mind, William will be here soon.

In he comes, obviously very tired, but jubilant and all the children from babies to Robert are summoned to attend Supper to witness the return of the conquering hero. He tells us stories of the battles, suitable for all ages, but it's a lot to take in and we begin to tire, the youngest children quickly sound asleep. We retire and I am so pleased to see him. We couple in a rather awkward perfunctory manner that night. I don't know why, but something has changed. He is sound asleep immediately, nothing new there. I lie beside him thanking Mother Mary for answering my prayers and reflecting that while I may complain about him sometimes, I do miss him when he's not here.

Now settled down to some sort of family routine, although short, it is obvious that things will never be the same again because England is always there, in the background, behind every decision and in every conversation. William expresses his displeasure about the increased activity of the predatory lords of Normandy who, as soon as he left, decided the Dukedom was ripe for the picking from the inexperienced young Robert and his men. They did not expect William to be back so soon. I expected William to return to his new Kingdom after a short period of rest and respite, but so far there's no sign of it. He is enjoying being host to his new English nobles too much and Normandy is calm as while he is here, the predators back off, knowing what will happen if they push him too far. I counsel Robert, telling him that his father realises how brave he is and how much he is trying to fill his shoes. I asked if his father had called him 'Brevis-ocrea' again as I'd reproved William about this. Roberts says 'no', but the other boys call him 'Curt-hose' or 'short pants' which he can cope with that. They are not being mean saying that and if he ignores it, they will probably give up. I praise him for this mature attitude, but tell him he must listen to his father's advice and gradually he will gain the same sort of power. I'm not sure Robert is convinced by my words and my spies tell me he has taken to frequenting places of ill repute. This reminds me of my brother-in-law, Bishop Odo, now Earl of Kent. I pray Robert conducts himself with more decorum in his new appointment than in his teenage years. He's such a lovely boy, beautiful manners and intelligent conversation. William made him Count of Maine in 1063 because he had been betrothed to Margaret of Maine since he was a young child, but sadly she died within a year, resulting in Maine becoming one of our enemies' most obvious targets. I really don't believe the rumours about Robert and must discuss with William the importance of getting Robert betrothed again to a young lady of noble class.

I think about William's other close friend, Roger de Beaumont, and reflect he was too old to fight in the Battle, but took part in the military planning and contributed sixty ships to the Fleet. son and heir Robert was made Earl of Leicester for his part in the Battle. The other close ally was William's brother-in-law, Robert of Eu, who, with his wife Beatrice, made us so welcome in the early days of our marriage. He was deemed to be the most effective general in the Battle and awarded the Earldom of Hastings for his contribution. Count Roger de Montgomery is also sure to have rewards waiting for him.

After Supper tonight, William frowns, looking at me.

'Are you ailing Matilda? You don't seem your usual self.'

'I am not ailing thank you, but as I have only recently had our ninth child, dear little Adela, no, I am not quite my usual self and there's something else.'

'I'm sorry you couldn't be crowned at the same time as me, I knew you would be upset, but it had to go ahead, at a very difficult and inconvenient time.'

'It's not that.'

'Then tell me!'

'I feel left out of everything going on and miss our exchanges of information. I would be pleased if you would discuss at least some of your future plans with me. Is it safe to leave Earl William and Earl Odo to run England without you?'

'It is, but they do have a heavy task of sorting out the Saxon lords. This was never going to be easy, and I've left them a big army to keep order if needed.'

'Do the two of them get on well together?'

'I doubt it, but that is not important as each has sole authority in his own territory, making it unlikely they will fall out over decisions and manner of rule. Odo is strong and ruthless, but is respected as a bishop by the Church whereas William is a much more appeasing character who gets things done in a different way. It also helps that he speaks enough English to communicate with the Saxons. His willpower is just as strong as Odo's and shouldn't be underestimated. Some Saxons are being allowed to stay in post, mainly the sheriffs, because their local knowledge is valuable to us as are the taxes they collect. Of course, they have to swear allegiance to me before they can stay on. Some nobles are also staying in position having sworn to me and we shall keep watch to make sure they don't backslide. And talking of Saxon nobles, what do you want me to do with the Duke of Gloucester?'

'I've been thinking about Tewkesbury where I would treasure its historic monastery with its seventh Century Christian foundation and I am told the surrounding lands are beautiful.'

'Leave it with me!'

'So, going back to the other nobles, what sort of reception did you get from the English after the Coronation?'

He looks away and mutters, 'They hate me!'

'Naturally, they do!'

'What do you mean? I'm their King; they can't hate me!'

'They would hate anyone who has just conquered them and taken their country, someone they can't understand and someone they are frightened of.'

'How long will this go on? I don't want to see them.'

'Put yourself in their place and think how angry and frustrated you would be if this man before you had taken your Dukedom, your position, home and land. You'll have to give them time. Meanwhile, build some castles, give them some work.' 'I'll do that, good idea, but the most important thing is they obey me as their King.'

Oh dear, this does not bode well. Now he starts on Normandy.

'I can't go back with the local lords trying to take Normandy from us.'

'You've already put your trust in Count Roger and me to rule Normandy while you, King of England, should be establishing yourself with your subjects.'

'You two can make the laws and see they are kept, but you yourselves cannot be out there leading our army in the inevitable battles that will take place as soon as I've gone. And Robert's just not up to the job.'

'No-one can be up to the job compared to you, but our enemies will be aware of the threat of you returning to sort them out with an extra force of Saxons if they step out of line. By staying here, the English will think you're hiding away, and they will not respect you, nor will they obey your orders unless you are there in charge.'

'You are right as usual. I'll stay for now and see how it goes. Oh, and it was very good idea of yours to invite these lords to Normandy. I think we shall get on better from now on. It was all quite jolly on the voyage; they were going on holiday!'

In a better mood, our coupling is particularly satisfactory, especially when he tells me that one reason for his reluctance to go back to England is not just coping with his hostile subjects, but the fact he misses me. Yes, he misses our frequent enjoyable coupling, but also my support and conversation. On that happy note, he returns to Falaise and we are quiet for a few weeks.

More news comes from Earl William who has ordered the construction of castles at Chepstow, Monmouth and Berkley. At the same time, he and Earl Odo have put down a rebellion by Saxon Lord Eadric the Wild, trying to reclaim his previous lands in Shropshire and Hereford. It sounds as if the newly appointed dukes are having plenty to do. As I ponder over all this, a servant comes with two messages. One is from Earl William who is coming back to Normandy to see us urgently about a serious matter. How mysterious! What can it be? The second message is from William who is riding back here now. When he arrives, I ask if he has any idea what all this is about and he is just as mystified. We wait impatiently, but the voyage is always uncertain with the wind and the tides, although favourable conditions usually prevail in summer as we are at present.

Earl William arrives, looking exhausted and miserable. I think he's been crying. He brings the terrible news that Adeliza has died suddenly. I am crying now and can scarcely compose myself to write it down. The poor man is distraught saying he thought she was not well and he should have been with her, not far away in England. He says she died of 'ladies' problems.' We don't know what to say or do.

'I should have realised when she didn't want to go for walks. I should have tried to get her to talk to me.' Earl William shakes his head.

'Don't blame yourself, Duchess Matilda. She wouldn't talk to me either and it was all very private with her. I did feel something was wrong; she was not like she used to be with me if you know what I mean and she was touchy, quite unlike her usual self. I couldn't talk to her about it and now it's too late. I couldn't even say "good-bye" to her.' The poor dear man. William shifts about.

'I'm sure William will be well cared for by the monks of Breteuil Abbey. What about sending Robert to come and do some hunting and jousting with our boys? He enjoyed that the last time he came.'

'That's a very kind offer, but I was going ask…' I know what he wants to ask. 'Earl William, you don't need to ask, we'd be delighted to have Roger and Emma with us for as long as you like.' William speaks up.

'Of course, we will and they will be safe here until you settle a home for them in England. I shall return myself before long and catch up with you over there. Matilda will see to them now.'

'Thank you, both, that's such a relief, I know they'll be in excellent hands.' William takes the shaking Earl to his quarters, no doubt for a strong drink.

Oh dear, I couldn't feel more miserable, but I must pull myself together for everyone's sake, especially those poor children. The next day, William escorts his old friend to the port and off he goes, back to his new country of England where his task is demanding and demoralising, leaving his Normandy home empty of his family as his servants keep a lonely routine in his absence. The children arrive, bereft. Robert takes William and Roger for a game of kick ball with Richard, our William and himself, the coach. Emma joins Adeliza who has planned to do some painting. As I pass the door, I hear her telling Emma about Cecilia becoming a nun, saying she's going to be a nun too. I would not want all our daughters to be nuns, but as we presently have six, it's unlikely. I wonder if the next generation is more or less likely to live in England or stay in Normandy. William's younger brother Robert, Count if not Duke of Cornwall, is quickly settled in England with his family. I am reminded that his wife is Matilda, daughter of Earl Roger and Mabel de Montgomery and Robert's teenage friend. Thinking of Dame Mabel, I note that Earl Roger never refers to the gossip about his wife's notorious goings-on, but he is happy to gossip about William's brother Odo's scandalous behaviour. While a bishop, a trusted royal minister and the second most powerful man in England under the King, the new Earl of Kent is ruthless, ambitious and immoral. Apparently, he has a son called John, but no-one seems to know much about him or his mother. Whoever she is, she is not married to Odo who remains single.

At Supper, without William for some reason, the young girls talk enthusiastically about the pets kept by the Sisters at Holy Trinity. There are lots of stories about these pets not only from our abbey, but also from others across Normandy. We are told that Sister Belin said that no squawking birds are allowed because they disturb the nuns in prayer or sleep. Another bird came to a nearby abbey and came out with very bad words, the sort you are not allowed to say. They giggled a lot at this point, and I had to ask them to refrain from all bird stories at the table and also in the time spent on their own. Young ladies do not discuss such things I told them disapprovingly. They promised not to, but I expect they will! Of much the same age, they are getting on well together, especially important for Emma who is missing her mother and for Adeliza who has been missing Cecilia. Emma closely resembles her mother in looks and disposition whereas Adeliza has William's bigger build and darker countenance. She is intelligent like our dear Cecilia, but unlike her, rather too confident in giving her opinions. Her betrothal to Harold Wessex was wiped out when he died at Hastings and no other arrangement has followed. I think she will certainly become a nun although she would struggle with the vow of obedience Now I see her blossoming into womanhood and a princess of great beauty. Why had I not noticed this before? I know the answer perfectly well: I have committed the sin of vanity by connecting female beauty with small dainty girls like me and ignoring the striking countenance of our eldest daughter. I shall do penance for such a sin of pride and unkind perception of my child.

I consider the boys, our sixteen-year-old Robert and William at fourteen and the two ten-year-olds, Richard and Roger, and see the FitzOsberns and ourselves looking back at me. What is immediately obvious and a shock to me is Robert's lack of height and stature. The other younger boys are as tall if not taller than him already. Soon the difference will be even more marked as they are at the growing age. It's not just height; in Robert I see the male version of the tiny, small-boned and rather fragile stature of Mother and me. I remember the trouble that caused my similarly boned elder brother Baldwin being overtaken by his stalwart younger brother Robert. I'm going to have to work hard to help Robert find a path in life that does not depend entirely on male strength and dominance. I consider my other two sons: Richard is good-looking, personable, fanatic about country sports and ambitious, just the son his father wanted. William is determined to take him with him when he next goes to England. Although I have to respect his wishes, I shall miss Richard whereas I despair of his brother William whose only virtue is his desire to be the best soldier in the world, but otherwise can only be described as a coarse peasant. There I've said it, forgive me Mother Mary. I pray that he gains some manners, pays attention to body cleanliness, learns to speak in a language that people understand rather than grunting and controls his ferocious temper. Oh dear!

William comes in and beckons me to sit with him. He is pouring Perry for me.

What now? He sits beside me and holds my hand. This must be serious.

'Matilda I'm so sorry, your father, Count Baldwin, has died.'

'He *can't* die, I haven't said "good-bye", No, not Father, NO!'

'Oh Matilda', he puts his arms round me and tries to comfort me in his big bear-like hug, patting me and saying 'There, there'. I hug him too like I used to. He's holding me!

'I'm relieved I sent your father the message thanking him for supporting us with sixty ships for Tostig to command and commiserated about the death of his brother-in-law and the defeat of his Viking comrades.' I hug him tighter, ''And I'm thankful I did that too, especially after I had misunderstood Tostig's intentions and implicated Father in what I thought was hostile invasion of our territory. Oh, but poor Mother, William. She'll be grieving and I am not able to go to her. What will she do? It couldn't have come at a worse time.'

'Your mother has a strong character and her pride in her royal heritage will not allow her to give way to a show of grief. She is so proud of you becoming Queen of England and imagine how proud your father would have been too.'

'You're right and we must be strong too as we look forward to our English Kingdom and a bright future.' William looks at me with 'that face'.

'Talking of England, Tewkesbury and Gloucestershire are yours.'

'That makes me very happy.' I give him a questioning look.

'And the Earl of Gloucester is in a dungeon for the rest of his days.'

'Good riddance! Now, on the subject of my coming to England, I am going to need a castle to live in with as many servants as we have here. Where do you suggest?' William looks evasive, 'You must not expect the same standard in England as you are used to here. The Royal Palace at Winchester is the grandest, but it is occupied by King Edward's widow Edith and it is not in our interest to turn her out. Westminster Palace is acceptable, although not on the scale or manner of our castle here at Caen. Another we can use is the Palace of Kingsholm at Gloucester and at least these are built of stone with glazing and decorations. King Edward built a number of stone castles on the Welsh border, but in most of the Saxon nobles dwell in small castles built of wood, some fortified with stone and some with a moat. They resemble your home before your father built the new palace at Lille or our home at Fécamp before we built here. There should have been a big castle at Rouen, but that never happened partly because I liked to get away from the business at Rouen. I see myself as the master castle builder and as one of my first tasks as King will be an extensive building programme.' This doesn't seem very promising, but I will manage as I always do.

'After the voyage across the Narrow Sea, Westminster will be convenient. I have about eighty servants here for all the things I have to do, and I shall need a good number when I am in England, especially with a new baby on the way.'

'I shall do my best in the short time we have and set up Westminster for you to start with.'

'Thank you and please include midwives.' 'I will, oh and Matilda, I nearly forgot: There was a message for you too, from your mother. I think we know what it's about.'

Mother has written to tell me Father has died after a short illness which sounds as if his heart gave out. He is buried at Lille. Mother writes sadly, but calmly, her firm faith sustaining her. She is to take up Holy Orders and join the nuns at her foundation, the Abbey de Messines. I am not surprised by this news and feel quite envious. How lovely to be free to follow a familiar routine of prayer and work, with no vital decisions to make or people dependent on you to encourage and nurture. I might do the same at her stage of life. Thinking back to Father, it was he who established the union of Flanders and Anglo-Saxon Britain which was effectively run by the Godwin family rather than King Edward. Our Victory has broken that union which would have caused him regret and may have contributed to his illness and death. I look back with affection on those days when we made decisions together about Flemish military and political matters. How my life changes every day! I thank Mother Mary that my faith is strong like Mother's, enough to sustain me, through all these demands, responsibilities and passions of my life.

At the same time as being sad about Father's death, I also feel joyful because Adeliza, our eldest daughter, under the guardianship of Earl Roger de Beaumont, is about to enter the Noviciate at the Abbey of Saint-Léger de Préaux, founded by his father. Poor Adeliza suffered greatly when her much loved Betrothed, the newly appointed King Harold of England died in the Battle of Hastings. She was then besieged by new betrothal plans suited to William's political agenda and deeply unhappy about the prospect of Marriage to King Alphonso of Spain of cruel reputation. Now the Earl Roger de Beaumont has removed these possibilities while William is still occupied with the affairs of his new kingdom. It's a relief to know that even he would not remove her from her avowed religious calling.

I am called 'La Royane', 'The Queen', in Normandy, but what the English call me I would not wish to contemplate. William has to return to England as the Northern lords are getting together and making trouble. He takes Ralf with him and will meet up with Earl William, his brothers and other Normans, now lords in England. I am delighted that Beatrice is going to accompany me as well as Megina who is leaving her children in the safe care of our Caen nursery and servants.

CHAPTER 18

MY CORONATION

England, 1068

I am on my way to England to be crowned Queen and determined to make it an occasion to be remembered. I am pregnant yet again, probably from our coupling just before William departed for the Invasion which means a summer birth. We are to have a gathering of all our nobles at Winchester to celebrate Easter followed by my Coronation at Westminster Abbey at Whitsun. I send my requests for everything I am going to need at Westminster Palace. My first voyage to England is across a choppy Narrow Sea and seems to take a long time. Fortunately, I have a cabin where I can lie down and rest and try to quell the horrible feelings of sickness. Eventually, we get to Westminster and it is a modest palace compared to home, but I am pleased with what William and I have managed to order at such short notice. My apartments are surprisingly luxurious with everything I could want. William says he is going to extend this castle and build a keep in the form of a large round tower. I find he has arranged some excellent servants, especially Humphrey the Chamberlain, who is delighted I can speak some English and I am delighted he can speak a little French. He was Chamberlain to Queen Edith and experienced in all royal duties, being most discrete. He makes me welcome and introduces me to Albold the cook. We have a short conversation about food and meals which was just right leaving me confident that the household will be run just as I like. I am also introduced to Wulfweard, who is the First Rider when I travel, in charge of the journey and our bodyguards. These are wealthy well-connected Saxons whose submission to William has ensured they continue to own land and keep their status of trusted royal servants. I manage to have a good rest here, relief after that awful voyage.

It's Easter and we travel to Winchester for our first formal outing as King and Queen Elect. As I walk into the Cathedral on William's arm, it's like a wedding with hushed gasps as we pass down the aisle, probably because of the very marked difference in our height and stature. The Easter Service is a joyous celebration of the light of the Resurrection after the darkness of the Crucifixion, the music played on the famous organ installed by Bishop Æthelwold in the last century. After the service, we walk back to our carriage, noble lords bowing and noble ladies curtseying as we pass. Then I pause, distinctly hearing the words:

'*Who* does the little pudding think she is?' I turn and there is, one of the court ladies, hand over her part-open mouth, her horrified face in rictus. I look her straight in the eye.

'*She* is the Queen Elect of England. And you are?' She stutters something.

'Guard, remove this person from my sight. She may not attend my Coronation.' When I tell William about it, he roars with laughter. 'I'll have a whining lord in front of me in no time!'

'I'm not changing my mind. Word will get about; it's a warning!'

'Quite right, I wouldn't expect anything less.'

The English have never had a Queen who is equal ruler with her husband, so I anticipate further opposition to my future role. My spies tell me that the Anglo-Saxon Chronicles, reporting news of my arrival, refer to me as 'The Lady Matilda', so diminishing my status to that of my stature. Some call me 'The Strange Woman' and so I am at present. I shall make it my business to meet as many people as possible and show them that their Queen is not only pious and reasonably bilingual, but also approachable and understanding of their lives. I shall follow the example of William's aunt, Queen Emma, who in my childhood was the stranger in our Court who became much loved by the Flemish people.

Today is the eleventh of May, my Coronation Day. The Service is formal, ceremonial and unique to this rare occasion. William and I wear gold apparel as we did at our wedding in Eu. We are delighted with 'The Laudes Regiae', a new hymn commending a ruler, which has been composed for the occasion by Ealdred, Archbishop of York. William and I think very highly of Ealdred, William telling me he is the only Northern Lord to support him. The Lords show due obedience to the King and Queen of England on this occasion, but beneath their apparent fealty, we cannot be sure of trusting former supporters of rival claimants to the Throne. As I survey the guests, I am shocked to see someone I did not expect, older certainly, but I definitely know who it is.

Back at Westminster, Albold has done us proud, producing a sumptuous feast served on gold and silver platters. It is a grand occasion with no expense spared and everyone seems to be having an uproariously good time. I am addressed as 'Your Majesty' which is pleasing.

Afterwards, as we reflect on its success, I am still stunned by seeing someone who has tarnished my enjoyment of the feast. William, occasionally sensitive to my feelings, asks me if anything is wrong.

'Who invited the Duke of Gloucester?'

'Oh no, I forgot to do what I promised. I am so sorry, but all the dukes were invited.'

'Don't worry, as long as the necessary actions are taken soon.'

Our general satisfaction with my Coronation is swiftly replaced by news that the Northern Lords are causing increasingly serious trouble. Fearing a major rebellion, William has to return to York immediately to establish his stronghold and make plans for countering any attacks. I was supposed to accompany him around the country to show my face, but he goes without me, his speed of travel inevitably faster than mine. I leave later in a luxurious carriage shared by my dear Beatrice. Megina and Agnês, Lady of the Bedchamber to Beatrice, occupy the second carriage. We have a strong military escort of mostly unfamiliar faces, but at least I know and trust Wulfweard out there in front. The distance is two hundred miles and the tracks are rutted and narrow, a most uncomfortable journey, especially as I am nearing the birth of my child.

I don't know which is worse, crossing the Narrow Sea or traveling from Westminster to York. Both are to be avoided. Beatrice is such a friend and comfort.

Not only has she has brought Agnês with her, but also two of her own midwives who will work with Megina. We stop at inns on the way and it seems to take forever. As we travel, Bridget relates an extraordinary story, which Robert told her, about Benedict, a monk from St Germaine's abbey who was visited by the Saint in a dream. He was told to go to Selby in Yorkshire to build the new abbey in his name. He has to take a precious relic from the Abbey hidden about his person. He is said to have stolen a finger bone from Saint Germaine's tomb. When he got to Selby, everyone would hear about this and search for a suitable site. When three swans were seen flying past, that would be the place to build the new abbey. Benedict turned up in Sarisberie, mistaking the name for Selebie, and impressed the Sheriff so much that he not only gave him a golden casket in which to place the holy relic, but also arranged a boat to take him up the coast to Yorkshire. Benedict is now in York waiting for an audience with King William, hoping his Majesty will complete this mission. It is a great story and diverting from our arduous journey. Bridget regales me with all sorts of other stories and we get there eventually. I hear that her son William fought in the Battle of Hastings and was given lordships in the West Country not so much for his small part in the Battle, but because of his father Robert's major contribution to victory. I'm the 'Duchess of Hastings', she tells me with great pride.

I felt exhausted travelling yesterday, so we rested at an inn. I don't feel much better today, but we set off again with the same old dreary motion of the wheels bumping along. After a few miles, I feel a strong jolt of another sort, the one I know only too well and nothing to do with the carriage. Agnês lays me down to have a look.

'You are opening up well', she says, it won't be long. I ask Megina to get Wulfweard, Officer in charge. He is prepared for this circumstance and says that while our carriage is an acceptable place to give birth, we will not go to York, but divert to Selby which is quite close and set up for our arrival. Well done Wulfweard, good planning! A rider is sent ahead to Selby and another to York to tell William the baby is on its way. Agnês is very experienced and says the birth should be straightforward, but it will take some pushing because this is a big baby on the way. Between contractions, I tell her that one of my daughters is called Agnês which pleases her. We arrive at Selby and I am moved on a pallet carried by four strong women and laid on a bed in what looks like a well-equipped birthing-chamber. The birth is relatively easy and our fourth son is born, a big-boned baby with black hair who is like William, but not nearly as similar as his elder brother, his namesake. William returns and is delighted with the baby, no doubt relieved to have another son after a run of daughters. Back at the lodging we discuss his name.

'I've decided,' states William.

'And I've decided, let's say it together after the count of three.'

'All right, one, two, three.'

'Henry!' We shout in unison.

'King Henry the First, fourth heir to the throne of England!' booms William proudly.

'He's named after my late Uncle Henry, King of the Francs!' William ignores this comment and I decide not to repeat it.

The next day, we go to York and are made comfortable in William's castle. There is a good nursery and plenty of help. Megina, Bridget, Agnês and I have time to rest. I found the journey far more challenging than giving birth and never want to do that again, although I expect I shall have to.

With William, talk about the baby soon returns to discussion of the present troubles. When he was last in Normandy, William did not tell me he had marched with an army to take York and found it seething with discontent and the whole of the North in rebellion. The Viking influence is striking in speech, customs and control, and the Anglo-Saxons as much despised as we Normans. Apart from Ealdred, the Northern lords are grimly determined to unseat William and put the late King Edward's great-nephew Edgar Aethling in his place. Edgar, described after King Edward's death as too puny and foreign to be King of England, is now a sixteen-year-old soldier of a mature man's stature and strength. The

Northern Lords clamour their support for him, disregarding the fact that Edgar has sworn allegiance to William. Perhaps they don't know about this oath. I believe William in this because he always remembers loyalty in great detail and circumstance. If there is a serious battle in the North, Edgar is not someone he will seek to punish, unless he turns traitor of course.

William has started to build a new castle here to be followed by a second and plans to make York a large and prosperous hub of his Kingdom. He is here to hold court, listening to his subjects' requests and complaints. He left a garrison of five hundred men to protect York while he was in Normandy, but matters have got steadily worse. Beatrice asks William what he thought of Benedict the Monk and he says he believes his story and was impressed by the golden casket given to him by the Sheriff of Salisbury. William asked the name of this generous sheriff. When told it was 'Edward the Rich', he invited Edward to Selby to join him in investigating the site for the new abbey to be dedicated to Saint Germaine. The plan is to go to Selby tomorrow and he's sorry I won't be able to join the party. I tell him I shall be waiting to hear all about it and see if the prophesy comes true.

He leaves us in safe hands and gallops off to Selby to see what the monk's dream brings forth. Of course, three swans appear and William, in celebratory mood after the birth of Henry and this welcome change from dealing with rebellious subjects, chooses the perfect site, promising a very grand abbey indeed. Benedict is to be the first Abbot, so everything is lovely.

Earl William had hoped to escort me home to Caen and stay for a while to catch up with his children, but has had to go to Exeter to support William in an uprising organised by Gytha, mother of the late King Harold. Our forces put Exeter under siege and dug tunnels under the city walls to collapse them and take control. This was accomplished, although Gytha managed to escape. Earl William eventually arrives here and is very pleased with his children's progress and happiness considering they must be missing their mother so much. I note he is far more interested in his son's budding military prowess than his daughter's artistic and linguistic skills. He is good company and we are able to discuss all sorts of matters relating to both England and Normandy. When telling me about the Exeter uprising, I am furious to hear that Brihtric, Earl of Gloucester, was among the rebels. I explain that we want this man arrested and locked up immediately. I am not going to give the reason, but he can check with William if he chooses. Earl William looks puzzled, but agrees hurriedly, which reassures me the punishment will be done. All too soon, the call comes to him to return to England as new troubles are brewing. I shall miss him as he's an old friend and I don't have many of these.

Almost as soon as I return to Caen and introduce my children to their new brother, I am summoned back to England as the situation is deteriorating to the point of real threat to our Kingdom and our thrones. William wants me with him, flattering, but highly inconvenient as our hold on the Dukedom of Normandy is tenuous to say the least. Also, I really do not feel up to repeating that arduous journey so soon. I am still getting over the last one as well as the recent birth of the most exceptional baby, Henry. I admit only to myself that his arrival has been as exhilarating as the birth of Robert, both stirring in me a passionate love, sadly not felt when my other children were born. I am not proud of saying this, but I always want to honest and pray that I may be a kind and loving mother to them all.

I have to go to England. No real choice. William has sent a posse to meet me and I am escorted to Winchester where Odo, Earl of Kent, is waiting. Relieved to meet a more mature and modest man than I had expected, the Earl explains the situation. The opposition to our rule is far more serious and widespread than the immediate problems in the North. Frequent attacks are coming from all sides. Eadric has joined forces with the Welsh kings and the men of Chester. In the South-West, the men of Devon and Cornwall are in revolt. The ever-recalcitrant Northumbrians are now led by turncoat Edgar Aethling and joined by a huge Danish army, a fleet of two to three hundred dragon boats off-shore. This combined force is occupying York. Alerted to the advance of this vast army, William thought his men would have no chance, so he moved to the South and gathered all his forces together for a longer-term strategy.Leaving the South West with one army under two trusted generals, he led the rest to take on the Welsh and allies, defeating them at Stafford. He then marched to York and the threat of his advancing troops sent the Danes back to their ships and the Northumbrians into hiding. William bribed Danes to leave with a very large pot of gold, so they have gone. Now he is here in Gloucester and the day after tomorrow I am to join the Triumvirate of himself and the other two leaders, the earls Odo and William FitzOsbern, to discuss our next plans.

Following this rather exhausting and depressing narrative, Earl Odo tells me that to celebrate our Victory at Hastings, he has requisitioned a long tapestry showing the Battle and William's Coronation and it is to be stitched by the noble ladies of Kent and the surrounds. I tell him I think this is a wonderful idea and praise him for his imagination and enterprise in planning this. When I ask if it is to be kept in England or Normandy, he replies it will be in Normandy, in his Diocese of Bayeux. He says it is a tribute to his brother's successful Campaign and while I appreciate this, it would have been tactful to have consulted us about the content and eventual home of the tapestry. I know why he didn't! Odo would not want us to have any say in the content of the tapestry, leaving him free to ensure his unique contribution to the Victory and important position are properly chronicled.

Kingsholm Palace is not to the standard of Westminster, but most acceptable. William is very pleased to see me, and we enjoy a good Supper together and very satisfying coupling. Now after Mass, he puts his plan past me before tomorrow's meeting.

'I have no option but to 'Harry' Northumbria to bring out the rebels in hiding. My men will starve them out by destroying their crops, animals and food stores. My policy of scorched earth is to fire the land, and if necessary, spread salt to prevent anything being able to grow. If they do not submit, their homes will be burnt down and there will be mass killings, first the adult men and then the rest. I will not be beaten. I will be in control and I will do all that is needed to wipe out all opposition and make it clear that any other regions who will not submit to me will suffer the same consequences. What do you think?'

'Well, thank you for including me at last. We are joint rulers are we not? He looks both annoyed and rather sheepish.

‘You weren’t here, I had to decide myself.’

‘Yes, just as I am making decisions without you in Normandy.’

‘So, it’s the same for both of us.’

‘No William, it is not the same. These actions you call ‘Harrying’ take warfare to an uncomfortable level for me. I concede you need strong action to put down the Northumbrian rebels, but this scale of merciless destruction and mass killings of everyone will confirm our reputation for brutality among some of our subjects.’

‘So, you don’t support me.’

‘I do to a point because these men have been thorns in our flesh since we took over. I support the first moves and formal notice given to the Northumbrians of what will follow if they do not appear and submit. Where I draw the line is killing everyone else, women and children.’

‘Are you prepared to give them this formal notice?’

‘No, I think it’s unsafe and too late for me to go to Northumbria, but I could start in other places by taking some of the work of holding courts from you.’ Is he going to shout at me? No, he changes like the wind; he gets up and gives me one of his big bear hugs.

‘That’s what we’ll do. What would I do without my wonderful wife?’

‘Can’t imagine and whatever I say, I am very proud of you. I am also proud that you are prepared to take a bit of female advice on taking a softer more conciliatory approach to our subjects.’ Let’s hope he means it.

Today we meet: the Triumvirate and me. William gives the same speech as yesterday and both men agreed wholeheartedly. Seeing my probable expression, he launches into praise of my desire to take part in the southern courts to hear peoples’ requests and preside in legal proceedings where appropriate. Earl Odo and Earl William are fulsome in their support of my intervention, no doubt relieved that they can devote more of their time to their preferred option of warfare. This whole business of ‘Harrying’ fills me with foreboding, but I have taken vows to be a dutiful wife and Queen and must support William in whatever he has to do to take control of England.

After starting in Northumbria, these measures are also taken into Yorkshire and beyond. Nowhere is safe. The campaign is effective. I see no effort to spare anyone, men, women or children. William's armies spread out over more than a hundred miles of territory. No-one lives up there now, there's salt on the land so nothing can be grown, no-one survives and whatever judgement it put on these actions, they are resulting in William at last having control of England as its King.

I go to and from England and Normandy. In Normandy, I carry out the political, legal and economic duties as joint-Regent with Count Roger de Montgomery. In our meetings, I have always called him 'Roger' or 'Count Roger', but he gently reminds me he is now Earl of Shropshire, so 'Earl Roger' will do very nicely thank you! I apologise and he says he has always called me 'Lady Matilda', but realises he should be addressing me as 'Your Majesty'! We laugh and agree that we will greet each other formally and then revert to our old ways. He is such a friend. Of course, I always ask after his family, but he never says anything revealing about his wife, 'Mabel, the Poisoner'. He is now looking at me as if to assess if I'm able to take bad news.

'Come on, Earl Roger, out with it!'

'You will hear about this eventually, so I want you to you prepare yourself.'

'Go on.'

'I'm sorry to say that there was a rebellion in the Marcher Counties, on the Welsh border last year, which was led by William of Eu, the King's nephew. He plotted with Earls Lacy and Northumberland to overthrow the Crown, but before any real action, they were found out and reported.'

'What happened then?'

'They were summoned before Earl William FitzOsbern who, with the King's permission, dismissed the earls with a severe warning and William was sent to explain himself to His Majesty. The King decided not to take the usual steps when a traitor is before him because of his loyalty and regard for his brother-in-law Earl Robert of Hastings and his sister Bridget.

William of Eu was told he would not become an Earl and he would not tell his parents about this until after your Coronation so that your passage to York would be peaceful. Because Earl William is not here now, he asked me to tell you the regrettable news.' I thank him for carrying out this unpleasant task and wonder how many more restless offspring of the earls will rebel again in the future.

In order to become better acquainted with the contents of documents that arrive on my desk, I have hired an English tutor. Although I can understand English quite easily and speak in simple words, I need to learn more about conversation, idiom, grammar and the declension of verbs. I need to know the language of the law courts, the military and business. I find being a pupil at this stage of my life is most satisfying and fortunately learning comes easily to me.

I ask Roger if he thinks Earl William has changed in any way. I tell him I can understand Odo being right behind William in the 'Harrying', but doesn't Earl William find it too brutal? He says that Earl William has changed into an ambitious man who admires William's strength and envies his status and is now trying to emulate his methods of gaining power. We agree that this change in the Earl's behaviour started after Adeliza's death suggesting she was the one to temper him down just as I try to do with William. Roger also gives me a warning, saying that although William is proud of all my efforts and grateful for my management of English affairs, he is also envious of the adulation I'm getting. People are beginning to worship me, and William will increasingly resent this. I tell Roger that I am well aware of William's feelings about this and have tried to persuade him to take a more conciliatory way of dealing with his new subjects. The problem is that he doesn't appear to heed this advice resulting in the people being unable to love their King. William hates being hated, but really, he only has himself to blame.

I am now returning to Normandy with a heavy heart, aware that my beloved husband is struggling with the challenges of being King of England. This was his life's desire and should now be his life's satisfaction, even delight. The truth is, it is anything but and while he is one of the most powerful men on this earth, he is also one of the most disappointed. All I can do is pray for him and for all of us as I contemplate my lonely and weary passage across the Narrow Sea to my home.

CHAPTER 19

FAMILY TROUBLES

Caen Palace, 1069

As we move into the next year, Abbot Lanfranc comes to see me. Looking forward to one of our usual theological debates, I am taken aback when he tells me that he is leaving us immediately to become Archbishop of Canterbury. I congratulate him on this honour. The Pope has approved his acceptance of the Almighty's call to head the Church in England.

'Thank you for taking the trouble of telling me in person. We shall miss you very much and assure you I shall pray for you every day.' He smiles ruefully.

'I assure you I will need much prayer because I take on this post with many misgivings. I am not optimistic about leading the English Church because from what I observe and hear, the English are far from being a God-fearing people. Nor can I dismiss my opinion of our own leaders, indeed the "Harrying of the North" is action that puts a heavy burden on God's forgiveness.'

'Believe me, I have done my best.'

'I know you have; William told me and be assured that I shall pray for you every day, your Majesty. Before I leave though, I want you to know that your example of piety, support to our abbeys, your investment in the education of your children, your theological scholarship, your Regency of Normandy and support to King William all form a beacon of light and hope to us all.' I am stunned and embarrassed by such fulsome praise and mutter my appreciation.

He nods. 'If helpful I would like to make a few comments about your own children and wards, but not if unacceptable? 'I'd be very grateful for your opinion as they reach their maturity.' Oh dear!

'So, first we have Robert who comes to maturity quite soon. In my view, he has chosen a sorry course which is too ingrained to expect him to change his habits. It is disappointing that his ability and classic education is being wasted. Here is a clever, charming and sociable young man who thinks he has the right to be crowned Duke of Normandy very soon and the licence to do whatever he likes, however unsuitable for a Prince. We both know the King's position on this and must respect his duty to see that both Normandy and England are governed properly. So, while sympathising with Robert's frustration, if he can't see that his present conduct is compromising the achievement of his target, it will not end well. One good thing is that Earl Roger de Beaumont is going to try and improve matters. I shall pray for Robert.' My goodness, is there anything he does not know?

'I am so sorry to hear that the Lady Adeliza did not take the veil at the Abbey of Saint-Léger de Préaux. The prayers of the Abbess of Préaux and Abbess Matilda have not been answered. I hear she is on her way as we speak to meet her betrothed, King Alfonso of Spain.'

'What did you just say? Adeliza? No!'

'My dear lady, did you not know?'

'I did not know! How dare William send his terrified teenage daughter away to a man with a cruel reputation? He's ignored her calling to the religious life she has chosen. Oh, my poor child! And he didn't tell me or give me the chance to say "good-bye". I'll *kill* William for this.'

'Come, calm yourself, we will pray together. Mother Mary, hear our prayer for the life and soul of the Lady Adeliza as she makes her way to a new life. Soften the heart of King Alfonso of Spain and guide him to be a kind husband to her. We pray for Queen Matilda who suffers the loss of her daughter's company and unfulfilled wish that she take the veil. Mother Mary, hear our prayer. Amen.' Wait until I see William and Earl Roger de Beaumont. I will never get over this.

'Would you like me to leave, your Majesty?'

'Oh, sorry, just composing myself; I would like you to stay because I need to otherwise occupy my mind from my poor Adeliza.' He turns to Richard.

'Richard excels in sport, particularly horsemanship and archery. He is popular with everyone including me and is the most dedicated of all my pupils in completing educational assignments. He seems to be making his permanent home in England where I hope he continues his studies and religious observance with the same enthusiasm he gives to hunting in the New Forest. I'm sure you are very proud of him.' Now, here we go.

'William is a rough and ready soldier, a skilled military leader, very like his father, but without his charm. You may not want to hear this, but since we are being honest, he does not join in parties with young women present because he prefers the ale house with his male friends. Do you take my meaning?'

'Oh, well, I think I understand; it does explain quite a lot. Has William mentioned this to you?'

'No, nor do I intend to bring up the subject with him and suggest you don't either.'

'I understand. What about young Roger FitzOsbern?'

'Roger is keen to follow in his father's footsteps and is serious in pursuing a similar path to be a top general near the Crown. I have insisted he spends more time in my class than he would choose, but I promised Earl William I would keep him to his studies and explained that battles need strategists as well as soldiers. I hope his ambition does not lead him astray.'

'I hope not too, and I think we can be happy about the progress of the young princesses, especially now Alison and Agatha have joined Emma in Abbess Matilda's lessons. Thank you so much, Abbot.' He looks at me, weighing up if he should say more.

'Tell me immediately if I am stepping out of line, but I'd like to say something you may not want to hear.' I gesture him to proceed.

'I think you are over concerned about what you call "the goings-on" at Falaise. This behaviour is normal for groups of young men, especially soldiers, because it binds them in comradeship and gives welcome respite from ever practising and exercising warfare. The likelihood of dying young is always on their minds. King William himself enjoys bawdy raucous evenings with his men and, as you know, he and most of his men do not share the appreciation of the finer arts of music and poetry as you ladies. In insisting Prince Robert stops all this, you infer criticism of King William as well. The important difference between the King and Prince Robert is that King William would never take the risk of fathering a bastard child whereas Prince Robert is already named as the father of at least one child. Such behaviour is regrettably true of many noblemen and also disgracefully, senior clergy. As King William's chaplain, I will continue to suggest he includes Prince Robert in a more participatory role in the Regency of Normandy, although I do not think this will happen. His mind is firmly set against it, being determined to remain the hands-on Duke of Normandy. I'm so sorry.'

I thank him and bid him good-bye with a heavy heart. I am devastated to lose his wise counsel, religious scholarship and just knowing he is present in our domain. He has been such a friend and example to us all. When William is in England, he will still have Lanfranc as his personal Chaplain, but we shall miss his presence here in our abbeys and the Palace. I won't have any more debates with him or the chance to seek his advice although I suppose I could organise a meeting with him when I'm in England. No Matilda, you are selfish; worse than your disappointment will be our children's loss of their exemplary teacher and role-model. What other person would ever speak to me so honestly, but kindly? Who else could have told me about the fate of my poor Adeliza?

William returns unexpectedly and brings Richard with him which is good timing as Bishop Lanfranc's observation that he seems to have chosen to be in England permanently did upset me. Talking of Lanfranc, William has entrusted him with the governance of England in his absence. When we are on our own, having struggled not to take up the burning issue immediately, William looks at me.

'What's on your mind?'

'Can't you guess? It's your removal of Adeliza from Abbey of Saint-Léger de Préaux, with no compassion for her fear of the Spanish King with such a cruel reputation? How could you? And I am angry and feel betrayed because you did not consult me about this.'

'You would have chosen to stop it!'

'Of course, I would! Have you no pity or love for her? The Almighty called her to take the veil and you ignored it. I've a good mind to travel to Spain and rescue her.'

'Matilda, stop and hear me for just a little. As Duke and King, I have to not only preserve our territories, but also look to take control of borders which are a threat which is the case with the land of the Spanish King. Adeliza's marriage to Alfonso will be most advantageous to us. You know the rules and customs concerning our noble families if anyone does. I am sorry to lose Adeliza and particularly sorry for you, but this is life. That's how it goes.' He's right of course, but I hate it all sometimes.

There's a knock at the door and William calls to come in. A message, marked 'Urgent', is delivered. William reads it and starts to cry. Whatever can it be? Through choking sobs, he hands it over, 'Read it. I can't believe it.' Adeliza has died on the way to Spain 'of a very sudden wasting disease' when she refused to eat or drink and cried all the time. Her carriage has turned back and taken her body to Bayeux. William puts me on his knee and we sob our hearts out. He's not so bad, I suppose. At least he can cry with me.

Then there's more bad news: the unexpected death of my brother Baldwin at the age of about forty. I know he was not my favourite person, but I am really shocked. Poor, *poor* Mother; she's now lost her son as well as her husband. I feel so sorry for her, but thankfully she has her strong faith to sustain her in her grief. The joint Regents of Flanders and Hainult are Baldwin's widow Richilde and his fifteen-year-old son Arnulf. I will pray for them as they look a vulnerable pair, unlikely to summon enough force to see off the growing number of claimants to these desirable lands. William, who has stayed here to support me after two bereavements, gives me the latest news; my brother Robert, known as 'The Frisian', is claiming the throne.

'We, of course, will be supporting Richilde and Arnulf.' He could have asked my opinion before making this declaration! I agree with him, deciding not to go into a contest over which of us has the greater authority and connection to those involved. He can be so irritating in his assumptions and my equality in making decisions escapes his consciousness far too often. Seeing my expression, he puts on his supplicant tone.

'Sorry, I rushed ahead, you do agree, don't you?'

'I do, Arnulf is the heir.' Thus encouraged he carries on. 'I think we should send FitzO to Flanders to support Richilde and Arnulf. I'll send him a message.' Off he goes. I agree that Earl William, our oldest friend, is the perfect ambassador to relay our support. Now a widower himself, he will understand the position of my recently widowed sister-in-law. We decide not to tell his children about this journey as the boys are bound to hear their young military friends talk excitedly about the likelihood of battle. My father's Will left Flanders and Hainult to his elder son Baldwin and with his death, his son Arnulf is the heir. Our younger brother, Robert, made a solemn oath to protect his nephew, young Arnulf, until his Majority should anything happen to Baldwin and now he's broken that promise by claiming the throne himself. How could he?

I am so fed up with them all that I think I'll go riding this afternoon. My dear Galathea died a few weeks ago and I have a new mare called 'Ganache' because of her dark colouring. Kind Ralf comes with me today as his services are not required by William. We have a gentle trot and canter in our beautiful parkland. I always feel better after an outing like this, needing calm and strength to cope with everything happening around us. William is waiting for me and I see it's not going to be good news.

'I've ordered some pastries; we'll be in our small hall for privacy.' Oh, what now?

'Your nephew, Philip, King of The Franks, is furious with your brother and is amassing an army to assist the cause of Richilde and Arnulf.'

'That's good news, isn't it?'

'It would be in other circumstances, but the army is to be led by FitzO!'

'FitzO? *Earl William*?' I can't take it all in, questions buzzing around in my head.

'So, you're going to lose your right-hand man and top General in England?'

'Exactly; I am and that's not all. Richilde has proposed marriage to FitzO which he has accepted, no doubt planning to be Count of Flanders and Hainult, as well as Earl of all the swathes of England I've given him.

'He must have gone out of his mind!'

'I didn't think he would desert me like this. He's far more ambitious than I thought.'

'I'm just so sorry it's my family that's caused this upset.'

'We can't choose our family and I think we'd better keep out of this now.'

'Agreed, nothing we can do. Shall we tell the children?'

'Not our job to do that. Let's see how things turn out, but no good will come of it. As if we hadn't got enough worries.'

'All we can do is count our blessings and keep up to date with what's happening.'

'One thing we can rely on about FitzO is that he will always keep in touch.'

Thinking about Philip, I remember him being crowned King of the Franks when he was seven years old, the same age as William when he became Prince of Normandy. Philip is my first cousin, making us a generation apart, just as our new baby Henry is a generation apart from our firstborn, Robert. I am left wondering if I shall go on having children now I am nearly forty years old. I hope I don't, but it's hard to tell as the usual sign, 'the flow', every month has rarely happened to me as I have been pregnant for most of my life. I start thinking about my ten babies, especially the perfect baby, Henry, most likely our last child. I have to put the girls out my mind because I'm still so upset about Adeliza. I go to Robert, and remember the excitement over his birth. Oh Robert, I wish you would behave more like a Duke with responsibilities so that William hands over Normandy rather than interfering with what you do and struggling to reign over two domains. This reminds me that William is looking his age and is increasingly corpulent making everything he does more difficult. I suppose I do too, wrinkled and shrinking which is equally unattractive.

Talking of difficult, Robert came to see me about William's recent visit down to Falaise to oversee the military training of our young men where he greeted the sons of our noble families whose fathers are in England in their newly acquired domains. Robert was in charge of the military exercises put on for the King's visit which were going well until his father stopped them in full flow, suggesting that his younger brothers, Richard and William, should also be given the chance to direct the exercise. When they did, William was loud in praise, his obvious high regard for their activity in strong contrast to his hardly concealed disappointment in Robert's efforts.

'Father is King of England so why can't he be content with that and not come back here and make me look a fool?' I sympathise with my dearest boy, but I must be loyal to William too.

'You owe respect to your father and must earn his respect.'

'How can I earn his respect when he compares me to everyone else and I fail every time?'

'You must stop feeling sorry for yourself. You are a rich young prince, heir to the Dukedom of Normandy with the status and privilege it provides.'

'Tell me what to do, Mother. Please help me'.

'You won't like it!'

'Fire ahead.'

'You are Prince of Normandy and you must act like a prince. These young men, who gather at Falaise, are lavish in praise of you in too obsequious a manner. Discourage it. Moreover, they treat you, their Prince, as their equal, their friend, a good fellow for a drink and a laugh. Prince Robert, you are not equal to them; you are superior, you are their

Lord. You allow young women to come to the castle for entertainment and diversion and you join in with it all. This is unacceptable in your position. The servants talk; you must behave like a noble gentleman to gain their respect. They and local people see who comes in and out of Falaise Palace and there's gossip; stories about your goings-on are abroad. The local religious community prays regularly for your soul. I am thankful that so far, your father does not know the extent of it all. Prince Robert, distance yourself from such goings-on. The rules you must make will not make you your men's best friend, but will earn you respect. You have a choice. Leading military activities does not come naturally to you, so why not establish your authority in different ways? Delegate the military training to William or Richard when he's here and anyone else you choose and make sure you oversee them from time to time, not as their co-leader, but as their General, Prince of Normandy. I want you to be successful and start by taking a bigger part in the rule of Normandy with me. I hardly ever see you and should anything happen to me; you would have little idea of what being Regent entails.' Robert stands in front of me and bows, 'Your Majesty, thank you for your helpful advice. I fear I disappoint you.'

'Prince Robert, thank for your gracious response. Now as your mother, you must know I really want to help you. You can ask for my advice and help at any time. Please take some positive action and make some changes. Don't go back on what you have ruled. If anyone complains or is disrespectful, remind him he is free to leave Falaise at any time.' We hug each other and again I am reminded of his size and find myself missing William's hugs even if I am annoyed with him at present. Interesting that now I don't think I can have babies any more, my hunger for coupling is as strong as it ever was in my youth.

Earl William, having abandoned us to protect Richilde of Hainult, is replaced by his brother-in-Law, Earl Robert of Hastings, as messenger to us from William. Robert describes the huge English building programme, castle after castle. One site is Ely near Cambridge which has provoked a rebellion by an infamous brigand from Lincoln, called Hereward 'The Wake', meaning "watchful".' Exiled from England at the age of eighteen for disobedience to his father, he was declared an outlaw by King Edward. His passion for warfare led him to become a mercenary and he turned up in Flanders about ten years ago to join Father in his many battles. This is astonishing because I remember him so well! He appeared in Father's Court after being made to buy suitable clean clothes to befit a nobleman. He made his appearance at the time I was receiving attention from the one who caused my disgrace. I remember wishing this snake looked more like this big bronzed beautiful man! Of course, it was no good me lusting after him as he was not of my social status. Oh well, back to Hereward, as he is now, having returned to England after the Battle of Hastings to discover his family's lands had been confiscated and given to the Norman Ivo de Taillebuis. His father and brother had been killed and his brother's decapitated head placed on a spike at the entrance to his house. His revenge was the killing of fourteen Normans and putting their heads on his gate because he heard them talking disrespectfully about the Saxons. He then went to Peterborough Abbey where he was knighted by his uncle, Abbot Brand, who is obviously not on our side either. Hereward was next alerted to news that the Danish King had sent a small army to try to establish a camp on the Isle of Ely, so Hereward rushed off to join them.

On arrival, he found Abbot Brand had been replaced at Peterborough Abbey by a Norman abbot called Turold, whose bellicose, unpriestly behaviour had banished him first from Fécamp Abbey and last, from Malmesbury Abbey in England. With the aid of the Danes, Hereward stormed and sacked Peterborough Abbey, claiming that he wished to save the abbey's treasures from us, the rapacious Normans. Our troops have been foiled three times by Hereward's local knowledge of the marshy fens. We lost a number of men on a bridge which looked deceptively solid, but collapsed under our army's weight, drowning our men. Hereward, disguising himself as a travelling potter, managed to enter William's camp and hear his plans. Accepting that the Isle of Ely was virtually impenetrable, William decreed that surrounding lands owned by the church would be guarded round the perimeter and the resistant inhabitants starved out. The monks found out about this plan and fled with the treasures of the church. After William took back control, they sought a peace treaty with him and he, in return, allowed them to keep their lands and possessions. Earl Robert reports that William said he had to admire Hereward's skills of resistance, and I have to say he is not the only one to admire this man!

After the Battle of Ely, William is back to have a rest from his turbulent rebels. Richard has remained in England. We decide it's time to consider betrothal or even marriage for our younger daughters, Alison (fourteen), Adela (eight), Agatha (six) and Constance (four). We would have done this earlier if we had not been in such turmoil. Before we start, we remind ourselves never to divulge the distressing circumstances of Adeliza's demise to her sisters who continue to mourn her daily. We agree that Alison is one of the most beautiful young girls we have ever seen; she has my blond hair and unlike me, a tall slender figure with a very sweet smile. Unfortunately, she has the condition we call 'The King's Evil', an unkind and horrible name for shortness of breath and weakness requiring bed rest more often than we like to think. We decide it's unfair all round to go ahead with any present arrangements for Alison's future. We have some concerns about Agatha too, so we leave her out as well. The betrothals of out two remaining daughters have been made by William for political and economic advantage. Adela, a pious child and strong in will and body, unlike her poor sister, is to be betrothed to Count Stephen of Blois. Constance, who has inherited my physique and appearance, is to be betrothed to Alan IV Fergent, Duke of Brittany. So, that's that and since I don't know the ins and outs of these arrangements, I have no reason to disagree, so William is pleased.

CHAPTER 20

BATTLES HERE AND BATTLES THERE

1071

We hear that Richilde has placed a heavy tax on the Flemish people, causing unrest and more persistence by my brother, Robert the Frisian, in furthering his claim to the Flemish throne. His army is now joined by King Henry of Germany making it a greater threat. We who support my nephew Arnulf's claim should take this very seriously. Our army, encouraged by my sister-in-law Richilde, is led by her new husband, our old friend, Earl William FitzOsbern, and now young King Philip of France who has been persuaded by my mother to intervene. Apparently, Mother says she must support her grandson who is the rightful heir to the throne rather than her son Robert. I agree with that, but surely it's not her business to use family connections to risk the life of the teenage heir to the Frankish throne as well as that of young Arnulf. William says it's going to end badly and he's right. All seems eerily still until we hear that one of Robert's army, one Gerbod, Earl of Chester, known as 'the Fleming', led a surprise attack on our forces at Cassel and won. We learn of the deaths of sixteen-year-old Arnulf and also Earl William. We are both shocked. William has lost his oldest friend and trusted general and still feels hurt by his desertion to Flanders. I shall miss him too, but this sad situation has left me chastened. Robert is now Count of Flanders, stealing that venerable throne that was occupied all our childhood years by Father. Mother should have stayed out of it all and Robert has behaved disgracefully. I feel deep shame about my family's behaviour and rather surprisingly, it's William who becomes my rock once again; calm, comforting and practical. We have the awful job of telling Roger and Emma that their father has died, but at least they have us and a stable home where they have lived long enough to be able to cope with becoming orphans than under different circumstances. At least this has taken the problems of Robert and his ménage out of my immediate thoughts. I am concerned about William's loss of the Earl's personal support.

As if reading my mind, our visitor today is dear old Roger de Beaumont who bounds in, although he's getting on for sixty. I must remember he is now Earl of Leicester so when I refer to 'Earl Roger', I must be clear if it's Beaumont or Montgomery. I leave them to it, but I catch a word or two and I think I hear them discuss Robert. The bell rings for the servant to bring refreshments so I move out of hearing. No doubt, I shall be told unwelcome news when he's left. The door opens and William asks me to come in to have refreshments and join in their conversation. We first discuss the recent scene in Flanders and Roger is sympathetic with us over the loss of Arnulf and of course, of Earl William, also one of his closest friends. There's a pause and Roger says he regrets to tell us that Robert and his comrades are getting a bad reputation for unseemly behaviour, especially regarding young girls invited into his Palace. They are not the daughters of any of his servants which those in charge would disallow, but from the surrounding areas and are paid which is an attractive inducement for poor families. One young woman claims that Robert has sired both her bastard sons. William's face starts to flush and I see a rage beginning.

'I am opposed to this with all that I hold precious. No son of mine will sire a bastard. I won't have it!'

Roger looks to me,' Perhaps you could have a word with him?'

William intervenes, 'I shall have more than a word. I shall thrash him!' Roger is obviously worried.

'I'm not sure that is going to help matters; it might be best if his mother speaks to him.' William is furious, staring at me.

'You'll give in to him as you always do. He's always been spoilt and your favourite child and look what he's like now!'

‘I gave him a serious warning quite recently, telling him how to conduct himself as a Prince, delegate the daily military command to his brothers and take a proper part in his Co-Regency of Normandy with me.’

‘I’m not having him in charge of Normandy. I’m back now and he can stay out of it.’ Roger, witnessing our disagreement accelerating, becomes the tactful, objective counsellor.

‘I’d like to offer to go to Falaise Palace to support Robert and make sure the situation improves. However, when it comes down to discussing what should be marital behaviour, I will leave that to you.’ What a relief, but I’ve got a difficult task ahead!

‘An excellent solution, Earl Roger, we are in your debt.’

I ask Robert to come and see me. He’s his usual charming self and says he has been trying to quell the excesses of Falaise and thanks me for my previous advice. I praise him and then say his father knows about the woman who says he fathered her child. Robert is full of denial. I ask him straight if he has coupled with young women at these parties. He says he can’t possibly discuss such matters with his mother.

‘Well, who else could you talk to?’

‘No, Maman, I can’t.’

‘You must be married for the sake of Normandy; it’s your duty to have a child to be the Duke.’

‘I am looking for someone to marry.’

‘But you prefer common girls to ladies of your class, don’t you?’

‘Yes, exactly.’

‘You may be surprised to find that young ladies of your status are just as fond of coupling as you are.’ He looks unconvinced. ‘You need to meet more of them rather than spending all your time at Falaise with the military and local girls.’ He nods.

‘And I can give advice because I have had ten children and there’s not much I don’t know about coupling and babies and that’s not only from my own experience, but also from what I am told by the young village girls we’ve had in our castles. Your father still suffers greatly from being called “William the Bastard” and until the Pope removed his ban on our marriage, some called you a bastard too.' He looks really worried now.

'If you have to couple, which is what we want to do to carry on our race, be careful. Do you practise "coït interrompu"?' He looks dazed,' The men talk about it, but I'm not quite sure what it is.' I explain and he looks even more dazed, scarlet in the face and then rushes off, 'Got to go now; thank you, Maman', kisses my hand and departs. Poor Robert, what a horrible session with his mother! He's so lovely and I know any noble young lady would be happy to marry him.

William is back again, with Richard, declaring England is more peaceful at last and he will leave the earls in charge and spend his time making sure Normandy is being well run. His last major task was to deal with King Malcolm of Scotland who, during his fifteen-year reign, had been giving asylum to Anglo-Saxon rebels like Edgar Aethling and Gospatrick, Earl of Bamburg, as well as making frequent raids on our Northern borders. Overcoming the Scottish army, William forced Malcolm to sign the Treaty of Abernethy. In return for swearing allegiance to William, Malcolm was given estates in Cumbria. When William tells me this, I remind him he is following in the venerable steps of his ancestor, the Viking Rollo, which is clearly the right thing to say. Where did the Aethling and Gospatrick find asylum? With my brother Robert in Flanders, of course! I have to be careful about what I say now as William is touchy about everything. He says he is pleased to be back in Normandy, his home.

He plans a visit to Falaise without giving notice to see if rumours about Robert's lifestyle are true. This does not look promising and much as I would like to warn Robert, I will keep out of it because it would make things worse. I have invited all the children here for Supper tomorrow to welcome William home and I am not going to make any excuse to speak to Robert on his own. Yes, you do have to attend; I've had to tell them. Robert is at his most charming asking his father details of the Scottish Treaty about which he is well –informed. I see William melting a bit. Richard wants to know more detail about using falcons and hawks for hunting and William tells them about this and also mentions dogs. All is going well at the moment.

'I have dogs trained for hunting', says our son William in a loud gruff tone, but actually comprehensible, 'Two greyhounds and a Boar Hound, some call a "Mastiff". He's a great big fellow, called 'Rolf; knocks a man down if he jumps up.' This sets off the children who love animals, but we see it's all getting rather bloodthirsty and frightening for the younger ones. William invites Roger FitzOsbern to tell us which horse is his favourite. He describes his horse which is all going well until he starts talking about hunting with falcons in Herefordshire where the numbers of deer and boar have been increasing. He pauses, looking defiant.

'Of course, now I am Earl of Hereford; I shall go there very soon and see for myself.' I see William going puce in the face. 'Steady on young man, your father has just been put in his grave.'

'My respects, your Majesty, but if you hadn't sent him to Hainult, he would still be here.' William takes a threatening stance and I stand between them. Everyone stands.

'Robert, please accompany Roger from the room and help him to calm down.'

'Of course, Mother' and off they go. I think nineteen-year-old Roger is crying. William sits and we all sit, most uncomfortably.

Lovely Emma starts to talk about her horse which is much bigger than her last one.

'Your Majesty chose her for me didn't you Sire?' Oh that girl should be a diplomat as everyone wants to know the details of each other's horses. William is returning to relatively normal as they eagerly ask for his advice. Afterwards, we discuss what Roger must be going though and agree he should be told the real truth of the matter. It should come from us as we are in loco-parentis and he will hear the details anyway. I offer to do that and William nods his gratitude. Otherwise we decide we are rather pleased with the evening.

The next morning I tell Roger of Montgomery what has been going on and hear he is now the Earl of Shrewsbury making him probably the wealthiest man in England as well as Normandy. He has approaching eight hundred lordships in England alone. He is obviously proud of all this, but at the same time rather ill at ease and I ask him if everything's all right. He says that now William is usually back here, he would like to be relieved of his duty of Co-Regent in Normandy and go to England to make himself known to his local lords and tenants. The King has agreed to this, but says my agreement is paramount as this change will affect me most. I have no choice but to wish him all the best in his new territories and thank him warmly for his support since the Battle. I shall miss him, but no doubt will see him when I am in England.

William says he is planning to spend the next year in Normandy, feeling that he can now leave England for longer spells.

1073

We discuss our Kingdom and the least settled areas which continue to be in the North East. Earl Gospatrick of Bamburgh has been replaced by Earl Waltheof, closely related to many of the East Midlands lords and is one of the few Anglo-Saxons still in favour. He did take part in a rebellion, but his vast family connections make him such a useful contact that William has overlooked this single transgression and even married him to his niece Judith, daughter of his sister Adelaide. Being so well connected, Waltheof holds multiple lordships. His other influence, especially with the clergy, covers a large area and the only contentious issue we had with him was land at Ely, bequeathed to the Church by his mother. William managed that in his inimitable way and that is where he excels. Apparently Waltheof's underlying ambition is to succeed to the Earldom of Northumbria, following his father, but William says that's a step too far considering his record. He tells me that we still need to keep an eye on the situation, noting that alongside the advantages of Waltheof's close-knit family, there are also long-standing feuds which cause unrest within an already belligerent region.

Robert is back again having made sure his father is safely away. It's obvious why he's here and he asks me again for money, pleading real hardship.

'I am considering it still, but first of all, we should talk about the fact you lied to me about the young woman who claimed you are the father of her two sons.'

'I didn't lie!'

'Nothing stays a secret in this court. You continued to deny it and in the usual way, the woman was forced to hold a red-hot iron in her bare hands and continue to make her claim. She managed this and so, you are guilty as charged.' He looks at me, weighing up what he should say to defend himself and soften me up.

'I am sorry; it's true the boys are mine and called Richard and Robert.'

'Sorry I found you out or sorry to have two sons?'

'I'm very sorry I lied to you, but not sorry to have the boys, they are very promising little chaps.'

'And what if your lady friend had been unable to hold the irons, would you have had her suffer terribly and her children abandoned?'

'None of that, because I bribed a clerk to allow her to quickly say 'yes' to her claim that I fathered her children and bribed the blacksmith to drop the irons as soon as they touched her. I am actually fond of her, but I can't marry her for obvious reasons. I will make sure she and the boys are all right, but , as you know, I have very little to give them.'

'A bit risky wasn't it?'

'I know, but I can't go all my life without coupling so I'll do what you advised in the future. I suppose this means you won't help me now?'

'I am tempted not to, being disappointed in you lying to me. You will just have to wait and see and do not ask me again.' When he's left, I cry with frustration and shame that the son so close to my heart appears to be fulfilling his father's worse fears. Can he really be so lacking in human kindness and pride in himself and his position? Mother Mary, I pray my beloved son walks the way of righteousness.**1074**

Although William is officially in Normandy, he is not necessarily here with me to hold Court for Norman citizens who come to ask for permissions about land, tenancy issues and legal matters. Without Earl Roger of Montgomery at my side to hold court or at the Palace for less formal consultation, I am often on my own and without him, the recipient of stories of the wicked actions of his wife Mabel. Everyone seems to know someone involved. She has continued to misappropriate the lands of many Norman lords, leaving them destitute. It's no good reporting this to William who says this is Earl Roger's responsibility not his. His surly response makes me sure he feels abandoned by Earl Roger, yet another of his closest circle, following Earl William FitzOsbern's departure and demise. I invite Robert to join me when his father is otherwise engaged, but he doesn't come saying he's so busy with all his duties as Prince of Normandy.

William keeps saying he will now be here as long as possible, but we have heard that before so I'm not counting on it. One of the first issues is that Roger de Breteuil, the new Earl of Hereford, has sent a message to ask for William's sanction of the marriage of his sister Emma to Ralf de Guader, Earl of Norfolk. William has refused. He says he will probably allow it, but at present he is finding the new Earl of Hereford both arrogant and unsupportive. At least, I didn't "give him Wessex", he says with some humour. He has discussed the young man with Archbishop Lanfranc who has taken Earl Roger to task, but he does not think he got very far.

1075

William must have been psychic when he said we should watch The East Midlands. Dear Emma, our previous ward, has married Ralph de Guader, and we had to assume that this was managed by her brother, Roger, Earl of Hereford. This union was eventually agreed by William, but no acknowledgement was received; we were not informed or invited to the wedding which is not the protocol expected of our noble families. In fact, it is a snub which puts up a definite marker of trouble ahead.

Trouble does follow with The Revolt of The Earls against the Crown. Roger of Hereford, Ralf of Norfolk and Waltheof of Bamburg who have amassed an army against us. Each of the earl's resentment is that he has not been given the same power and privileges enjoyed by his predecessor. Supporters include Ralph de Bernay, Sheriff to Earl Roger's father William, who feels less important than he thinks he should be. Archbishop Lanfranc's assessment of the situation is that Earl Roger was led astray by evil men. William and I do not share his opinion and think he was probably the ring leader.

Our superior forces, the main defence splendidly led by Earl Odo, have overcome the traitors. William has dealt with them and they are all excommunicated by Archbishop Lanfranc. Emma's brother, Roger of Hereford, is deprived of all his lands and imprisoned for life. Her husband Ralph has escaped; we don't know where, but no doubt he will turn up again sometime. Emma is left to defend Norwich Castle and despite the odds against her, she has refused to give in to our men. William is leaving her alone for the time being. Waltheof is imprisoned, waiting trial as a traitor which will result in his death.

News of Ralph comes eventually; he had sailed to Denmark to get forces to join him in another attack on our shores, but this quest failed and he returned to Brittany. When things die down a bit, William and I discuss Emma of whom we have always been very fond. None of this was her doing; she was a puppet, her strings pulled by her nearest and dearest. We admire the way she has organised the defence of the town and William eventually compromises with her to restore peace. Ralph's lands are restored to the Crown and in return, she is given safe passage for her entourage and herself to leave England and join her husband in Brittany. I can imagine what sort of meeting up there will be when she does re-join Ralph. I will pray that they love each other enough to give her happiness in the coming years.

Today we hear that Queen Edith, widow of Edward, King of England, has died. Since the Battle, William has treated her kindly and with a little prompting, I might say, allowed her to remain at Winchester Palace for the rest of her life. He has ordered that she is carried in state to Westminster Abbey where she will be buried beside her husband after the Funeral Service which is conducted as if she were a reigning monarch. No expense has been spared on her magnificent send-off. This action should help William's reputation by showing his deference to the Anglo-Saxon Queen who was much loved, the trouble he has taken with her Funeral and the reminder that William has high regard for the sanctity of marriage.

While I spend most of my time in Normandy, I visit England on a regular basis, about every two months. Over there I sign treaties, witness benefactions to our monasteries and abbeys and hold court as I do in

Normandy. I am treated with the utmost respect and generosity and as everywhere else, there are good and bad people. On my last visit, I sought an audience with Archbishop Lanfranc who, true to the sound of his name, can always be relied on for frankness about sensitive issues. I ask for news of William's younger brother Robert who holds nearly eight hundred lordships, but has not been made an earl although people call him 'Earl of Cornwall.' Lanfranc deems him a most reliable and effective general who always leads his men from the front, winning many battles. His granting of the monastery of St Michael's Mount to the Normandy monastery of Mont Saint-Michel brought him universal respect and grudging acceptance as a Cornishman.

As a person, he lacks the scholarship of his brother Odo and the ambition of the King. He is a dullard without conversation. Lanfranc enquires if anything prompted my enquiry, to which I said 'no.' Giving me one of his uniquely penetrating looks, he tells me that William had asked the same question so as we are Co-Regents, he will tell me of a regrettable situation. Robert is a religious man and when his chaplain, Vital, received news of Robert beating his wife Maud, Vital intervened, threatening to end the marriage if Robert did not repent. He then left Robert's service, but returned when Robert begged for Vital's pardon for his actions. I tell Lanfranc how fond we were of Robert as a young man often in our household at Fécamp and while at Falaise he lived in the Montgomery household and would talk about young Maud Montgomery, his best friend. The Archbishop will include them in his prayers and I will make it my mission to see Maud for myself. I almost wish I had not enquired.

An invitation arrives to attend Abbaye de-Sainte-Trinité to witness Cecilia's vows to become a full nun. This will be joyous occasion after so much sadness in our family.

1076

No rest here with continuing battles throughout our Kingdom and Dukedom and now Brittany is the focus. Our two main adversaries are King Philip of France and none other than Ralph de Guader, Emma's husband. King Philip seeks to take both Normandy and Brittany into his Kingdom and Ralph also seeks to control all of Brittany, having lost his English Earldom in the Revolt. He remains Baron of Gaël and Montfort in Brittany and has had taken control of Dol Castle from Duke *Hoël* of Brittany. William advanced to support the Duke and laid siege to the castle. King Philip of France later relieved the siege and defeated William at the Battle of Dol, forcing him to retreat back to Normandy. Although this was William's first defeat in battle, he persevered to quell another attack, this time on Maine. Soon after, we had another setback when Simon de Crépy, one of our old friends, retired to a monastery giving his County of Vexin to King Philip. This State is a strategic buffer between Normandy and the lands of the French King, which is not only a blow to William's ambitions, but also damages his tenuous relationship with my nephew King Philip.

I can hear William coming in. From the heaviness of his tread and the hoarse puffing, which is partly due to his corpulence, but increasingly to bad temper, I am not looking forward to his arrival. In he puffs and throws himself into the largest chair in the Hall.

'That Ralph Guader turned up again, bane of my life. We lost Dol and I am fed up with all this rebellion in my ancestral lands. There seems no prospect of peace and there won't be until Robert is fully behind me. I will not be here forever and it's about time he conducts himself in a properly ducal manner. He is useless and his brother William is a surly youth, although he is a very good leader of any battle force. He is not respectful to me and questions my decisions on military strategy. What does he know? As for being King of England, I might as well leave you to reign by yourself. Over there, people are respectful but there is no light in their eyes or smile on their faces when they see me. They are frightened of me and the only enthusiasm they ever show is when they ask when you are going to return. Queen Matilda this and Queen Matilda that; I'm sick of it. It's not fair: you do all the nice things like deal with them in court, ask after their families and make bequests to the religious houses and, in order to get where we are, I had to do all the dirty work and look where it's got me. They know you can understand them when they speak, even the Scots and the Danes, and they know you can read and write in their language too. They despise my lack of learning and blame me for all the troubles in the North. They knew what would happen if they did not submit so it was their choice and not my fault.' He goes off in quite a temper, but we still have commitments including going to Bayeux tomorrow for the Dedication of Bishop Odo's reconstructed abbey.

As we approach, we see the magnificence of the new Bayeux Abbey and anticipate viewing the promised embroidery people are calling, 'La Telle du Conquest.' The abbey is a divine creation and its spiritual atmosphere extraordinary. We see Bishop Odo himself at the height of his achievements. He has ordered the abbey in the sort of detail that could only be planned by a theological scholar of devout persuasion and comprehension. I begin to see Odo in new light, not ostentatiously pious as he used to be, but quietly and convincingly sincere. Mother Mary, I pray to quell other considerations of his character that come to mind. The Embroidery is breath-taking and William is really enjoying this tribute to his achievements. It is exactly what he needs just now. I could hug Odo, but I won't. Each scene shows people we know, those who were involved with the Battle of Hastings. It would take many visits to look at them all and understand who everyone is and exactly what action they depict. We shall be returning many times, I'm sure. Despite returning home in better spirits than for some time, my suggestion we go on holiday meets with ill-tempered derision.

'What holiday? Where to? I haven't got time or the inclination to go on a holiday. I've got battles to fight.'

'Well, I suggest you make time and renew your energy. I shall be going to Bonneville anyway and taking young Henry.'

'Bonneville? Henry is only nine or ten years old. What would you do with him all day?'

'We are going to Bonneville because he's already a good rider and keeps asking when he can go hunting; I thought you could arrange to take him to St-Gatien. He would be delighted.'

'Ah, well then perhaps I could fit that in and if the boy is so keen, it could work quite well. Is anyone else invited a well as our servants?'

‘I thought we could ask Earl Roger de Montgomery’s son Arnulph as he’s about Henry’s age and they made friends at Falaise in the group of younger boys doing their military exercises. Perhaps Earl Roger would come too.’

‘That’s all good as long as Dame Mabel doesn’t come too!’

‘Don’t worry, I’m sure she wouldn’t want to spend any time with us and she’s probably well occupied raiding some lord’s property or poisoning someone as we speak!’

‘Ralf and Megina?’

‘Of course, they must come and Megina tells me that Ralf is training Stefan and another young lad to be grooms to the ducal family and what good experience it would be for us all.’

And, so it is for all of us, especially William. He cannot believe he’s got another son like Richard who has the same talent in horsemanship, is interested in military matters and respectful to his father. Henry bombards him with questions and actually listens to his advice. William is changed from that bitter man to the husband I love and that is a great help in making our coupling enjoyable and, especially for me as I now know there will be no more children. We have quite a good party here, but I’m afraid we didn’t invite Robert and Beatrice because of the awkward situation concerning their eldest son. William just brushed it off when I mention it to him, but I know he feels very let down by yet another member of his family. Talking of family and I have time here to do some thinking, I am really pleased with Constance who is now sixteen and certainly the most academic of our children. She shares my interest in Theology and the governance of both Normandy and England and we discuss detailed matters of law, politics and music. I haven’t given thought to music for so long that this new enthusiast kindles a wish to take it up again. She is very like me in character and interests and is taller, but has a slightly fuller figure than I did at her age.

CHAPTER 21

THE FATHER AND THE SON

Normandy, 1070s

I see the relationship between William and Robert getting worse day by day. William still insists Robert has no part in the governance of Normandy and nothing I do or say improves matters. Another problem between them is the control of Maine. Robert was assumed to have control while betrothed to Margaret of Maine, but after her death in 1069, William returned the lordship and territory to her father, Hugh of Maine. Robert claims to be is the rightful owner and resents William for taking it away from him and is increasingly frustrated by being so powerless. His next humiliation was 'a jest' by his brothers William and Henry who emptied a chamber pot full of urine over his head in front of his men at Falaise. To add insult to injury, his father treated it as a joke and did nothing about it, so undermining him yet again. When William eventually returns home, he is furious about the incident and it's not about his sons' prank, which he dismisses as nothing, but about the chaotic brawl that followed, reportedly heard throughout Falaise. He says Robert was useless and did nothing to stop it and my mild comment that he was probably having a wash, incensed him further, saying I always take Robert's side against him. He stomps off to his chamber and we sleep apart. After Mass which, unusually, he fails to attend, I find he's left, and to where I don't know.

Now, Robert is here with the same determination to be Duke of Normandy I saw in his father wanting to become King of England. It is highly unfortunate that the main obstacle to him achieving his object is his father. Despite William's more numerous obstacles to kingship, like bad weather and resistance from every quarter, Robert's one obstacle is no doubt more troubling. He tells me that although he has the tacit support of many of his followers' parents, some of whom are our close friends, no-one dares to give him the financial support he badly needs for his mission. He tells me that his men ask him why they have to live in poor accommodation and eat unpalatable food when his father is King of England and the richest man in the world. His sole income is his army pay just like all his men. He envies Henry de Beaumont whose father, Earl Roger, has given him the modest lordship of Le Neubourg, in central Normandy, which is not much but something, and a token of his support. This is a real shock; I had no idea and always thought that William was generous to our sons. How is Robert supposed to manage? Robert has been to his Uncle Odo who supports his cause, but cannot be seen to give him money. Now here he is asking all around, no doubt, and now he's asking me. I say I will consider it. I am very well off and could easily make a great difference to his life, but that will seriously undermine William and flag up his miserly treatment of his son and heir. Meanwhile, Robert seeks refuge in the Flanders Court. Through my spies, I learn that he and his supporters behave disgracefully in my brother's court and Robert has had to reprimand them. My spies tell me some of Robert's companions include prostitutes of both sexes.

My spies also report that Dame Mabel has taken entire possession of the territory and home of Hugh Brunel de la Roche. They now have nothing, and I wonder how long this can go on without doing something about her. William continues to leave it to Earl Roger to sort.

Now here is Robert's army back in Normandy attempting to take Rouen Castle by siege. Treason! William orders their arrest, so Robert leaves Normandy accompanied by his band of young men, many of them the sons of William's present earls. They include Robert of Belleme, son of Earl Roger de Montgomery, and William de Breteuil, son of the late Earl William FitzOsbern, who has either relinquished or ignored his previous Bishopric. Here's another unwelcome name: Roger, son of William's elder brother Richard FitzGilbert, First Lord of Clare in

Suffolk. They take the castle at Remalard, from where they proceed to raid into Normandy, supported by many of William's continental enemies. William immediately attacks the rebels and drives them from Remalard, but King Philip gives them the castle at Gerberoi, where they are joined by new supporters. Who are these new supporters, you

ask? No real surprise, I suppose, it's my brother, Count Robert of Flanders and although King Philip of the Franks has so far not given military support, Philip claims to be backing Robert. However, his history of switching sides to his advantage means he will oppose whichever army threatens his kingdom. This generation is seeking to take over from their elders and I have sympathy for them, in fact so much that I send Robert gold with a servant I can trust. William is back and, judging by his approaching footsteps, in a rather better mood, 'I am not going to discuss the situation with Robert.'

'Good!'

'You *will* enjoy my other news.' I nod enthusiastically.' The four Brunel brothers crept into the castle of Saint-Germaine-de-Montgomery, entered Dame Mabel's chambers, found her in the bath, chopped her head off and left! They have escaped and I'm certainly not going after them!'

'About time too; she was awful to them like everyone else. What a shock for poor Roger; he must have loved her despite everything!'

'Don't worry about Roger; I've already betrothed him to Adelaide du Puiset, daughter of Éverard de Breteuil, Vicomte de Chartres.'

'Seems rather soon; is Roger happy with this?'

'In his words, he's "in ecstasy"!' We laugh at this reply and pray for their happiness.

As I'm taking in the news of the murder of Dame Mabel and remembering her eventful visit when we were first married, another message arrives from Flanders, with news that Mother has died at her abbey. My thoughts turn to her and I know I haven't been as in touch with her as I should, but I'm pleased that we've been closer over the last few years than during my childhood and teenage years. I owe her much for giving me such a good education and encouragement to be a scholar as well as a noble gentlewoman. Mother Mary, may she rest in peace.

William lays siege to Gerberoi and after three weeks, Robert's besieged forces emerge from the castle and take the besiegers by surprise. William is unhorsed three times, the last by Robert and only saved from death by Toki, son of the Englishman, Wigod. After this, Toki is killed on his way to fetch another horse for the King and Wigod, the Lord who enabled William's army to cross the River Thames at Wallingford, loses his only son and heir. William's army is forced to abandon the siege and he is now in Rouen, presumably on his way home. I anticipate a difficult home-coming with my husband deeply humiliated by being unhorsed by his eldest son, the one he despises and ridicules. William is subdued and irritable and bursts out with blame directed at me, accusing me of encouraging Robert's arrogance and ignoring his debauched life-style. I respond saying I have tried to persuade Robert to act like a duke-in-waiting and forgo his misdemeanours. William snorts.

'And don't imagine I know nothing about the trial of the woman who claims Robert is her sons' father. I don't know what he told you, but the clerk and blacksmith came to me, their rightful Lord, to ask what they should do about Robert's plan. I told them to accept his bribes and that I fully support the idea. While I wish my grandsons were not bastards, I have to accept that they are. Their lives will be blighted enough without the added probability of their mother's incapacity or even death after such a trial. They will join my court shortly.'

'I am proud of you. That is the generous action of a true leader.'

'Matilda, do *you* think I should relinquish Normandy to Robert?'

'I do: you are overburdened with the responsibilities of both Normandy and England. It's a heavy load for anyone, but while you remain extraordinarily fit and strong, you are not a young man.'

'I know that, but I can't give up Normandy. It's been my life-blood since I was seven years old. In fact, I don't think I could give it up to anyone and perhaps I use Robert's faults as an excuse to refuse. I was almost persuaded to hand over until he showed disrespect for my well-known views about bastardy and now he has done the worst thing he could possibly have done to me: he defeated me in battle.'

'You could look on it differently: the first defeat of the most feared warrior in the world is by his son which is a symbol of Robert's inheritance of your skill in battle!' William looks thoughtful, but he doesn't shout at me this time and for the first time for a while, we couple peacefully that night. The situation is not resolved, an impasse and Robert remains in Flanders.

CHAPTER 22

THE SECOND DISGRACE

Caen 1079

I am in disgrace. William storms in, his red hair flying and his face inflamed with anger. He's found out about the gold I sent to Robert. He is livid, deeply distressed that I could be so disloyal. I have forfeited my rights as Queen of England and Regent of Normandy, a statement I ignore as pursuing this line is untenable. He rants, claiming treason, betrayal, disrespect to our marriage, ruin of the trust he had in me, a bad example to our children. On and on he goes, stomping round the room. I listen and then stand.

'Please sit down and hear me out. It's my turn now and I have much to say on the subject. I could not stand by and see our son and heir unable to house, feed, supply and train his men on the pittance he receives from you. His men are the next generation of noblemen, many the sons of your old comrades. They see your refusal to provide proper financial backing for their job, the defence of Normandy in your name as an indication that you have little regard or respect for them. If properly supported, Robert and his men would be fighting on your side, not rebelling against you. Nor can we expect our son to live the lifestyle and keep the household expected of a Prince without more financial help. His shabby castle holds nothing of artistic merit, comfort or style. The questionable character of many of Robert's servants and hangers-on prevent him associating with his equals, especially young ladies of high-class and virtue. He lacks the means to employ the right servants and host the right guests. Before coming to me, he's approached nearly all our relations for help and, he failed because it's in no-one's interest to risk offending you. People are frightened, if not terrified, of you. Since I am wealthy in my own right and as the Queen of England, I felt there was no option but to help him. I was torn between my duty to you and my sympathy for Robert's miserable circumstances. In the end, my undying affection for our eldest son drove me to take this unwelcome step. At the same time, I thought our strong bond and mutual affection would be enough for you to see I was acting in everyone's interest including yours, my beloved husband. I am sorry you feel let down and realise how much I have hurt you.' He stomps off without a word and I have no idea where he's going.

The rumours are rife. The much-recounted story of how William dragged me along the ground all those years ago have prompted new accounts of how I have been shamed for giving my son money. I've been dragged naked along the streets, flung from my horse and worse. Other stories hint at William seeking out young women for his pleasure, being a hot-blooded man. It's not pleasant hearing, but what I do know for certain is that William's pious nature and acute fear of siring a bastard makes licentious behaviour unlikely. It's stalemate.

Well, I'm not giving up on Robert and provide more gold, silver and valuables, which he collects himself. When he heard that my servant who brought the last lot had been found out, he somehow managed to find him and get him escorted to a safe abbey. He had a narrow escape for William had forecast details of his punishment if apprehended, the details too gruesome to relate. I reflect I nearly caused the death of an innocent man. It seems that nothing can escape William's spies, but when it came to it, William did not mete out the usual punishment of a traitor to me. It's obvious that I shall be found out a second time which will end my life on the gallows. I do not regret my action, so I wait in anticipation of the storm to break.

I have been found guilty of the same traitorous act. William summons me to his court which is crammed to its full capacity, each one avid to witness the proceedings. He is the actor, the prosecutor pacing the court to proclaim his betrayal by a faithless wife. I am the guilty party who stands before him.

'You see before you my beloved wife who has born my children and my heirs. You see the Queen of England who I sought to rule by my side with equal authority. Here is the one I could always trust, who has heard all my confidences, but has broken her sacred marriage vows. Here is she who has sinned before Almighty God and the Holy Catholic Church. You see the traitor who has plotted against me with those who rebel against their King.' There is a pause at last, so I walk towards him and kneel.

'O my lord, do not wonder that I love my first-born child with tender affection. By the power of the Most High, if my son Robert were dead and buried seven feet deep in the earth, hid from the eyes of the living, and I could bring him back to life with my own blood, I would shed my life-blood for him and suffer more anguish for his sake then, a weak woman as I am, I dare to promise. How do you imagine I can find any joy in possessing great wealth if I allow my son to be burdened by dire poverty? May I never be guilty of such hardness of heart; all your power gives you no right to demand this of me.'

I played my role, guilty as charged, kneeling in humble supplication to confirm my respect to His Majesty. At the same time, I had to show that I am not to be bullied into pathetic weakness. I had to stand up to him, justifying my actions. From the accused, I became the accuser, our roles reversed. When I stopped speaking, I stood up and William departed abruptly. Everyone was silent as I left the court to be escorted home by Earl Roger de Montgomery.

For some weeks there is no sign of William and I miss him. Roger de Beaumont looks in and I believe him to be an emissary from William. The King is at Rouen and although he professes to remain angry about my betrayal, he does admit he had no idea of the depth of my feelings for Robert. We agree that this must be William's start of creeping back to some sort of truce, because in truth, he has been reliant on me to do the work he couldn't or wouldn't do, particularly in England. Apparently, I am never to return to England and my regency in Normandy is to be taken over by others. Dear Roger understands not only William's character, but also some of the strengths and weaknesses of our relationship. I explained to Roger that William confessed that he resented my popularity among the English a while ago. Now Roger tells me William is jealous of my love for Robert, saying Robert comes first in my affections, with himself following behind. At present, that is certainly true, but a love for a child can never be the same as love for a husband and I know William well enough to say he will be missing coupling, laughing together, pride in our family and the support and counsel I have given him over the past decades.

William and Robert announce a truce, with William once more affirming that Robert would receive Normandy when he died, but this doesn't last long. Within a few weeks, there's another attempt by William to fully regain his Dukedom. Unexpectedly and unusually, the Church, backed by the most senior nobles, intervenes; its elders concerned about the outcomes of yet another battle. It may be peaceful for Normandy, but there's no sign of William and Robert becoming reconciled. All I do know is that Robert is at last well-financed by his father.

CHAPTER 23

BATTLES AND RECONCILIATION

Normandy and England, 1080-1

William's first serious defeat at Gerberoi is the likely cause of fresh unrest in England including raids into the Northern counties by King Malcolm of Scotland and rebellion in Northumbria. The reported feeble response of the Anglo-Norman lords, results in not only an unstable situation in England, but also here in Normandy with the stand-off between William and Robert. William obstinately refuses to hand Normandy over to Robert and chooses not to return to England to sort out the rebels himself. Now the Northumbrian situation escalates with the death in battle of its lord, the Bishop of Durham. At last, William comes to ask my opinion on his next action. We agree that his brother Odo, almost as fierce a warrior as his elder brother, is the man to sort them out. We now discuss the Scottish Raids which have been frequent and aggravating ever since the Battle.

'How about you and Robert lead a campaign to fend off the Scots for good? Robert has inherited your persistence and bravery in battle and could learn from your experience in leadership.' William is silent, this bold suggestion being quite a challenge, no doubt.

'I'll think about it. Meanwhile, I wish you farewell, your Majesty.' Pretty formal, but perhaps this is a small step forward? The next news reports their departure to England. Yes! Soon I hear of the success of the Campaign with an agreement by the Scots to stop raiding. We back up our position with the immediate building of a defence fortress at

Newcastle-on-Tyne. On return, it seems that Robert has a new perspective, professing to live more conventionally, although the dubious delights of the Falaise courts are probably the last thing he will change.

So, we go on in a rather depressing routine, and then everything changes for the better. In July, our daughter Adela is betrothed to Count Stephen of Blois, a highly desirable match. The family and guests stay with us in Caen Palace and the celebrations are enjoyable. During this visit, a Charter records our gifts of manors in Essex, Gloucestershire and Dorset to my Abbey of Holy Trinity, Caen. Family witnesses are William and me, our sons, Robert, William and Henry, and William's brother Robert of Mortain, Earl of Cornwall. Earl Roger de Montgomery attends as does Earl Roger Bigot of Norfolk. Archbishop Lanfranc and other clergy are also witnesses. All this contributes to family unity and at last, things are peaceful.

Heartened by the improvement of family matters here and the success of last year's Scottish Campaign with Robert at his side, William decides to visit England after a four-year absence. I am delighted that Robert and I are invited to join him to spend Christmas at Gloucester and Whitsun at Winchester. We are to wear our crowns and full regalia when the occasion demands. At some point on our tour, when Robert and I have time together without William, we agree that while we are pleased to be included, we think that William's motive was to keep his eye on us, rather than leave us to rule Normandy without him. Robert adds that in our absence, the Regency has probably been given to his brother William which could encourage him to challenge Robert's position. William would be emboldened in such an attempt by the little effort the King makes to disguise the fact that he is his preferred son.

During our visit, William and I are invited to be godparents to Edith, the baby daughter of King Malcolm and Queen Margaret of Scotland. William is very pleased about this as he thinks the connection will help cement the relationship between our two countries. Queen Margaret and I share the ancestry of the ancient Saxon House of Wessex and I reflect on how that would have pleased my dear late mother. I chuckle to myself remembering how Mother always signed her documents 'Sister to the

King of France' and imagine she rather looked down on the Flemish aristocracy. William goes to Wales to see how things are being run since the constant battles on the border are now under our control, although future troubles can never be ruled out. He has been to St David's to pay homage to the Saint and see the new cathedral which was built last year by the Norman bishop Peter de Leia. This visit has been a success, partly because I have had no choice but to keep a low profile. William doesn't want to be outshone and there is definitely more noticeable support for him, with the years passing since the infamous 'Harrying of The North'.

We return to Normandy in the autumn with William and Robert. I go home to Caen. I think about our marriage and sadly conclude that while civil and reasonably friendly, our previous close relationship and coupling are over for good. I am sorry for my part in what has happened to us and while I don't think I will ever change William's mind, I bestow, in penitence, most of my worldly wealth to abbeys and churches. Roger de Beaumont calls and says the records show I have made over a hundred of these gifts.

I am happy about my daughters: Cecilia now Abbess of Holy Trinity and dear Constance, happily betrothed, but still at my side. I visit the Abbey of Saint-*Evroul, so generously endowed by Earl Roger de Montgomery. The monks make me welcome and I ask them to pray, especially for Constance. I also ask them to pray for me* to be delivered of a pain that has become more noticeable just lately. I thought it must be the tension I'm feeling about everything that has happened to us, but underneath I fear it's more serious. I am not afraid of death. I shall welcome it as I shall be with Mother Mary in Heaven.

CHAPTER 24

COMING TO AN END

Normandy, 1082-3

William comes to see me at the palace and confides his concern that his brother Odo, who despite his immense wealth and power, now seeks to be Pope. William, always fiercely opposed to bastardy, especially in the royal family, knows Odo has sired children thus breaking his vows of celibacy as Bishop of Bayeux and Archbishop of Canterbury. His ambition to be Pope is not only disrespectful to the Papacy, but also to our family's reputation. William suggests we invite Odo to meet us at Grestain with the aim of building a new abbey in honour of their mother Countess Arlette who is buried there. She and her husband Herluin de Conteville founded the present abbey in 1050 when Herluin, who suffered from Leprosy, said he'd seen a vision of the Blessed Virgin Mary who told him to take the spa waters of the stream in Grestain. At first, Odo is very pleased to see us and full of enthusiasm about the idea, but once I am out of the way, looking into the stream, William confronts him, saying his job is to rule England in his absence and keep his vows to the Crown. He will strongly oppose Odo's claim to be Pope. I hear shouting and uncouth swearing from both men before Odo departs abruptly, rushing past me in an unholy rage.

Back at the Palace, William orders his pigeon keeper to send a message to all his main lookouts on the coast and soon enough we get a message that Odo is preparing to embark for Rome. Odo is captured as he is about to set sail and imprisoned in the Tower of Rouen, with no prospect of release in William's lifetime. We have Supper together and then sit for a while in the Hall. William is subdued.

'Have I been unkind to you, Matilda?'

'You have never put your hand on me except in love, William. You have been generous to me in many ways, but I don't think you can ever forgive me for helping Robert. Some may call that unkind, but I've said my piece and I know you try to do your best for your Kingdom and for Normandy, dear to your heart. I want you to know I have loved you from the first moment you threw me in the dirt, through our marriage and the challenges of joint regency. I shall love you to the day I die.' He looks up, aghast.

'What do you mean? You can't die! You won't leave me by myself, will you?'

'We are all going to die sometime. I'm not the woman I was, and all this recent trouble has taken its toll on my health.' He gets up and walks over to me.

'Will you just sit on my knee with my arm round you? Like we always did? Please Matilda?'

'Of course, but you'll have to pick me up; I can't get up there on my own!' And there we sit, his arm round me as usual and unusually, just cheek to cheek, no kisses and nothing after that.

And thinking of that, I'm not sure I could couple at the moment because the pain in my belly is much increased. I try to think of lovely times in the past. How I wish I could sit here for ever, happy that my beloved husband and son could be reconciled.

Sadly, life changes very little and the mutual disrespect of William and Robert is escalating again. I feel tired and lonely and really don't feel strong enough to cope any more. I say my prayers and sleep.

AUTHOR'S NOTES

The Author - Jane Cox

Fact or fiction?

This is an historical novel. The dates are as correct as I have been able to research. While some are agreed by historians, others remain the subject of conjecture and debate, for example, the birth year of Robert, the eldest son of William and Matilda. The secret marriage of William and Matilda is imagined, but I believe it makes sense. This is but one of the different versions of William's 'rough wooing' of Matilda. There is no definite record of the exact birth years of some of the royal daughters.

All speech is imagined, except Matilda's response to William when accused of Treason for the second time, starting, 'O my Lord…'

The names of members of noble families are well documented, but only very few of everyone else in their lives, exceptions being the English attendants, Wulfweard and the cook, Albold. Regarding Clergy, the only imagined people are Father Henryk and Father Paulus.

What happened next?

Queen Matilda's death was felt deeply throughout Flanders, Normandy and England. She was loved and missed by everyone who had met her. Her piety and generosity were much cherished by all the religious institutions she endowed throughout her life and in her will. Her funeral was attended by clergy from far and wide and she was buried at her beloved Holy Trinity at Caen, where her daughter Cecilia was becoming increasingly respected as the Abbess. King William was at Matilda's bedside in the days before she died. He was beside himself, weeping with grief and probably guilt. He mourned throughout the four years he survived Matilda and made numerous bequests in her name. He gave up all pleasures, including the Chase, becoming morose, with the tyrannical side of his character taking over the softer side, encouraged by his wife. In order to fill his already bursting coffers, he launched his Great Land Survey in 1085, later called 'The Domesday Book'. Despite its real intent, it offers, along with Magna Carta, our one most valuable sources of information about the people, places and economy of Norman Britain.

After Matilda's death, William made it clear to Robert that he would never consider him heir to the English throne, instead favouring and preparing his younger brothers, William and Henry. He also went back on his word by not accepting Robert as heir to the dukedom of Normandy. Matters reached a head when he sent Robert into permanent exile. This only lasted a short time, because when William launched an attack on the Vexin, Robert returned to support King Philip of the Franks in defence of his realm. At the advanced age of sixty, William fought in this battle with the ferocity of his youth, but when his horse took an unexpected turn, he sustained a mortal injury as the pommel of his saddle pierced his bloated abdomen. In the few days before his death, he repented, particularly for his 'Harrying of the North'. On his deathbed, William decreed his son William should go to England immediately to take the Crown. He railed against Robert becoming Duke of Normandy, but persuaded by the clergy present, he forgave Robert for his sins and willed him the Dukedom.

Queen Matilda's grave is at Abbaye-de -Sainte-Trinité aux Dames, Caen, France

King William's grave is at L'Abbaye-aux-Hommes, Caen, France

I owe a debt of gratitude to Tracy Borman, author of 'Matilda, Queen of the Conqueror', 2011, which is the account of Matilda's life by a 'proper' historian. Other sources are my large collection of Norman history books and online sites, especially 'Calendar of Documents, preserved in France'.

Post script to my last book

In my book, 'The Norman Conquest of Box, Wiltshire', 2016, I said the bearded guest at Archbishop Odo's feast, in the Bayeux Tapestry, is Humphrey de Bohun the elder, known as 'Humphrey with the Beard' or 'Humphrey the Old'. A cousin of Duke William, he was Baron of St André-de-Bohun and St Georges-de-Bohon in Lower Normandy. He always sent troops to support Duke William in local uprisings which resulted in his sons Richard and Humphrey being invited to take part in military training at Falaise. These boys, the same ages as William Rufus and Henry, formed a bond which resulted in the young Humphrey De Bohun becoming Steward to both King William Rufus and King Henry. Humphrey married the daughter of Edward of Salisbury, the richest man in the Kingdom, and later became the Earl of Hereford and later, Trowbridge. Old Humphrey fought in the Battle of Hastings and his miserly reward of a single lordship, Tatterford in Norfolk, suggests he may not have contributed enough to be depicted as a guest at this celebratory feast.

Now, I see that Earl Roger de Montgomery is also a contender for the bearded guest at the Banquet. He remained in Normandy at the start of the Conquest in his role as Co-Regent with Duchess Matilda, but did go to England to direct strategy in the last hours of the Battle. He was also a generous supplier of ships for the Invasion. The Bayeux Tapestry was commissioned by Archbishop Odo who is, of course, the central figure in the group above with King William on his right looking up at him with adulation and their younger brother Robert of Mortain on his left. The bearded man is looking away, engaged in eating, his left elbow thrust rudely in front of His Majesty. It's possible that the Archbishop in his usual habit of self-aggrandisement, directed the designers of the Tapestry to portray Earl Roger unsympathetically. Or is it dear old Humphrey de Bohun who was hardly a threat to anyone? I'd like him to be the guest as his descendant became the overlord of Box, my home village, but who knows?

JMC